HOUSE INSIDE THE WAVES

Fiction by Richard Taylor

Tender Only to One
Cartoon Woods

HOUSE INSIDE THE WAVES

domesticity, art, and the surfing life

RICHARD TAYLOR

an imprint of Beach Holme Publishing

PROSPECT BOOKS
VANCOUVER, BC

This book is published by Beach Holme Publishing, 226–2040 West 12th Avenue, Vancouver, B.C. V6J 2G2. *www.beachholme.bc.ca* This is a Prospect Book.

The publisher gratefully acknowledges the financial support of the Canada Council for the Arts and of the British Columbia Arts Council. The publisher also acknowledges the financial assistance received from the Government of Canada through the Book Publishing Industry Development Program (BPIDP) for its publishing activities.

The Canada Council | Le Conseil des Arts
for the Arts | du Canada

BRITISH
COLUMBIA
ARTS COUNCIL
Supported by the Province of British Columbia

Editor: Michael Carroll
Design and Production: Jen Hamilton
Cover Art: Dale Taylor
Author Photograph: Dale Taylor

Printed and bound in Canada by Houghton Boston, Saskatoon

This book is printed on Eco Book stock from New Leaf Paper using vegetable based inks. The stock is 100% ancient-forest-free paper and 100% post-consumer recycled.

National Library of Canada Cataloguing in Publication Data

Taylor, Richard, 1953-
  House inside the waves

"A Prospect book."
ISBN 0-88878-428-7

1. Taylor, Richard, 1953- —Journeys—Australia. 2. Australia—Description and travel. 3. Novelists, Canadian (English)—20th century—Journeys—Australia.* 4. Surfing—Australia. I. Title.
PS8589.A94Z53 2002   919.404'7   C2002-910164-6
PR9199.3.T37Z47 2002

For my girls, Dale, Sky, and Quinn

CONTENTS

It might be said that a great unstated reason for travel is to find places that exemplify where one has been happiest: looking for idealized versions of home—indeed, looking for the perfect memory.
—Paul Theroux, *Fresh-Air Fiend: Travel Writings 1985–2000*

All good writing is swimming underwater and holding your breath.
—F. Scott Fitzgerald, Letter to His Daughter, Scottie

PROLOGUE
Reflections of a Crazed Househusband

A pod of dolphins escorts me out, undulating through the rolling swells of the Coral Sea. Usually I get my best waves in the first half hour of a soul surf. That's when I'm fluid and strong. I'm hungry for it, all my pent-up energy is there, ready to be transformed into elegant sweeps up and down a big wave. After the emotional pistol-whipping my two daughters administered to me this morning while I refereed them up through venomous snakes and poisonous spiders to their school bus, I was happy to be paddling alone into the glorious surf, immortal, oblivious to the notion that *sharks happen*, just paddling out to sea with an overwhelming feeling of rapture, staring ahead at the enormous waves breaking on the outer reef of Lennox Point.

It's funny the things you don't forget. In the dead calm of early 1960s suburbia, just after the first Kennedy was shot, about the same time the Beatles arrived to save us from ourselves for a while, I remember my sister and I helping my mom while she tried to make homemade apple pie. One of her hand-rolled cigarettes was smouldering in an ashtray of butts. The counter was dusted in an alarming amount of flour, the rolling pin splotched with a Rorschach's of damp flour, the entire crust cruelly adhering to the counter so that even three spatulas couldn't tempt a corner free as she was gradually overwhelmed by the pie-making, uttering such profane words as *fudge, son of a gun,* and *ah, shoot the cat!* I was right under her elbows, licking spatulas, baton-twirling wooden spoons, and snatching pieces of dough out from under the lumpy rolling pin to play with in my own dirty hands. Gobbling as much raw dough as I could swallow while my little sister, Jan, waited patiently for her share, I was far too close to my mom's personal space in the days before self-help books even defined what that was and how much each of us needs.

Sometimes when my mom got so wound up doing one of these apparently simple jobs, I couldn't figure out what her problem was. Years later, at home with my own snarling kids, a strangling mortgage, and the slow rain of time, I got an inkling of what it was all about.

Not long before heading out into the Coral Sea, I felt pretty close to my mom and sister as I stood at my kitchen counter above the Pacific Ocean in Australia, enduring my own epic culinary fiasco. I had been forcing my two daughters, an eleven-year-old and a six-year-old, to listen to the Beatles' *Anthology*, trying to make clear the profound impact the Beatles had on nearly everything we did back then. Trying to point out, no doubt overexplaining, the simple, heartfelt lyrics of songs like "I Saw Her Standing There," "Roll over Beethoven," and "You've Really Got a Hold on Me." I was listening to these haunting, rough drafts of early Beatles songs, singing at the top of my lungs with my two girls and our imaginary guitars—lump-in-the-throat stuff as we harmonized with the primitive, grainy music. I glanced down at the ocean and tried not to think about my dead sister. Instead I recalled falling in love every time we stepped out the door in the early 1960s, all the intense, sappy Beatle shit that still made me swoon. The memories were always there: old Beatle 45s on a small scratchy record player, my nine-year-old sister teaching her skinny eleven-year-old brother how to slow-dance to "This Boy" so he could impress other girls, all the dreamy possibilities of life still ahead, stretching forever.

After the brief euphoria of vocalizing with my girls, we began cleaning the house. Of course, after our singing frenzy, the girls refused to pick up their things, start their homework, or behave at all. My energy was sapped, so I suggested the great pacifier—making chocolate-chip cookies. The girls would help their househusband dad in what should have been a bonding, even poignant moment but instead unravelled into a fifteen-minute interlude in hell. You see, my bickering daughters were starting to drive me crazy—the cute little one, Quintana, up on a wobbly stool with her face too close to mine, while her pretty sister, Sky, fished broken eggshells out of the yolky batter in a bowl, the same stuff she was licking from the front of her shirt and trowelling off her sister's bare leg with a knife. The two were viciously name-calling and swatting each other, the knife flashing, their red nail-polished, dirty, after-school fingers darting into the bowl to gobble raw dough as I yelled at them to settle down, worrying about money, our mortgage back in Canada, the stress of my wife Dale's teacher exchange, the throbbing, surfing-induced ledge of a cold sore on my bottom lip I could set a bar of soap on while I showered. Even the thought of our inevitable plane trip home to the grim reality of a Canadian winter, eleven months away, weighed on me. Because, to be quite honest, I didn't really want to go back to Canada at all.

As I continued pouring and mixing the wet ingredients into the dry and, like a fool, trying not to mess up the counter or floor, seeing and hearing my girls eat the moist dough faster than I/we could blend and spoon it onto the cookie sheet, dollops schlopping to the floor, wondering if they had stepped in it, their hands, their arms, their legs, even their warm angels' breath insanely irritating against my skin until all I wanted to do was leap out of my flesh and sweep everything off the counter, having to muster all my inner strength so I wouldn't implode, then thinking about my mother almost losing it while making pie in 1964, or her horror thirty-three years later when my sister died in the fire, and here I was going to pieces baking chocolate-chip cookies, standing outside myself and saying calmly, "Hey, what's the big problem? You're only making cookies for God's sake." And possibly answering one of the mysteries why so many people spend their evenings caved into big, soft chairs, giving into television, booze, drugs, salt, or sugar, sharking their way through whole containers of cookies, steadily and relentlessly breaking off small pieces of tombstone-size chocolate bars or tucking into a bag of corn chips as big as a pillowcase because sometimes it's all a bit too much.

Although for more than a decade I occasionally suffered the self-esteem of an aardvark and barely managed to survive my roles as househusband, queen bee, house spouse, primary caregiver, housebitch, Mr. Mom, SNAG (sensitive new-age guy), and doormat to my lovely wife and two beloved daughters from the time my girls were four months old, I did learn to honour and appreciate the world from the perspective of children, women, and mothers. Some people might consider it risky to stay at home to look after kids, especially for a man. For any parent it can be a real gamble to step out of line to take care of children and try to endure financially and psychologically, and then years later attempt to plug into the game again intact. So, to be on the safe side and to keep my manly soul afloat, I also nurtured other roles like woodcarver, beachcomber, teacher, expatriate, writer, outcast of the islands, and surfer.

I was born a rabid Pisces and have been more than enamoured by water all my life. For years I swam and surfed the planet until the reality of our second child and our first mortgage encouraged me to trade the exotic locales and solo excursions of open-water swimming and surfing in the ocean for a house in mid-continent suburbia and a chlorinated, crowded lane at the Nepean Masters Swim Club. Still, in the past decade, without a lot of money, and our kids in tow, Dale and I managed a year-long aquatic trip around the globe, another year teaching on an island near Hong Kong, and then, inadvertently, because of a teacher exchange hit the jackpot and got parachuted into a beach house along one of the last unspoiled classic surfbreaks on earth.

Banking on the notion that passion was contagious in this twenty-second year of our marriage, our so-called mid-life crisis, we came all the way down here with our girls to Byron Bay and Lennox Head, two small coastal towns of twenty-five-hundred Australian souls each on the Queensland–New South Wales border. We wanted to see if it was possible to have one last blazing adventure before who knew what domestic surprises swamped us in the future. For too many years we'd been based in the heart of suburbia with only the smell of Bounce fabric softener in the air, row upon row of beige vinyl-sided houses, very few trees, and our grinding routine of schedules.

We craved to get away from the noise of the late twentieth century. Also we needed to escape the recent death of my sister and nephew in a tragic house fire. And, like everyone, we sought to heal the psychic scars from other personal nightmares. Which was to say we committed the sin of wanting to unplug for a while and find a little paradise. My family didn't come to Australia to save the planet, or to discover a cure for AIDS, or to rescue the whales or the Aborigines, though perhaps one day we might return for more noble pursuits. We clawed our way out of our former lives to go on a twelve-month South Seas walkabout in pursuit of *mana*, the sacred, magical power of the primitive with its inherent hope, freedom, and escape. And to many people, especially since I had a wife and two daughters to help support, I might have seemed like a crazed, burnt-out, middle-aged Huck Finn with a surfboard tucked under one arm and a long, wistful surfer's gaze. But I saw it as a romantic desire to give my family a safe, temporary harbour from the modern world, a kind of Dreamtime versus Machinetime in the South Seas.

And yes, ever since I first started travelling and seriously reading other writers and thinking, maybe a little too deeply, about *life*, I had always wanted to sit by a window overlooking the sea and write a book about the Big Mystery. So a week after we arrived from the death grip of an Ottawa winter to live in this wonderful house by the sea, I dragged an old oak desk from another room, positioned it in front of an open bay window with the best drop-dead view of the ocean, the hills, and the sky I'd ever seen, and started to write.

Now, through a long channel, a passage where fewer waves break, I casually stroke out farther and farther from shore. Finally, when I stop paddling, I turn and sit up, straddling my board. I survey the small town that will be my fate, nestled into the sensuous contours of the coastline. Salt water runs into my lips, sunlight warms my back. There is no other sound but the distant crash of waves on the beach. Alone with a contented heart in the middle of the ocean, rising with the swells rolling in from the horizon, I wonder what I've gotten myself into. It isn't just going to be about bravado, the search for the perfect wave. It's something much more elusive that will have me reach out to touch the glory. I'm already bewitched.

I
Anatomy of Restlessness

Even before we left Canada for Australia, I had quickly jotted on a scrap of paper these questions posed on the jacket copy of Bruce Chatwin's Australian odyssey, *The Songlines*: "Why is man the most restless, dissatisfied of animals? Why do wandering people conceive the world as perfect whereas sedentary ones always try to change it? Why have the great teachers—Christ or the Buddha—recommended the Road as the way to salvation?"

Because Dale had already gone out and Quinn was sick and still in bed, Sky sat eating breakfast alone with me. Down in the bay, huge swells of the Coral Sea were rolling in, and the morning air outside our verandah was filled with the melodious warbling of swooping magpies, lorikeets, galahs, and parrots. On the breakfast table beside the messy pile of my notes were two books I'd been reading for pleasure and plunder: Gretel Ehrlich's *The Solace of Open Spaces* and Susannah Clapp's *With Chatwin: Portrait of a Writer*.

Clapp had been the editor of Bruce Chatwin's first classic travel book,

In Patagonia, and in the process had become a close friend. Her memoir is an intimate look at a remarkable, contradictory man. On the front cover of the British edition Chatwin sits bolt upright on a paint-spattered wooden chair, hands resting tentatively on his knees. A startled, pretty-boy face with the penetrating, horizon-crazed eyes of a nineteenth-century explorer stares straight at you with absolute eye contact. Wearing old jeans, well-worn moccasins, and a rugged travelling shirt, he's by himself in a bare, pine-floored corner of a room that recalls Vincent van Gogh's famous painting of his lonely, empty bedroom.

Between heaping spoonfuls of her cereal, oblivious to the vast glory of the sea view outside our window, Sky looked at Chatwin's picture and asked, "Why would anyone want to read a book about him?"

I told her Chatwin was one of the world's most famous travellers who, in a short career of ten years, produced a handful of beautifully crafted works, and that I was writing about him in my book.

Sky dropped her spoon in her cereal. "Dad, you're putting *him* into your book, but you won't put Narmeen in?"

I assured Sky I'd mention Narmeen, her best friend in Canada, in my book somewhere. What I didn't tell my daughter, because it was too complicated and would have upset her too much, was that the restless odyssey of a dead travel writer was one of the reasons we were living here. How, for example, could I have explained to a homesick kid the malaise suffered by romantic wanderers who feel most at home with themselves when they're away from home? How could I explain that all travellers want to get away from the routine of their lives to reinvent themselves for a time and perhaps find a little paradise?

Ever since Dale and I were married in 1975 we'd been living a life of travel that can only be described as fabulous, even without money. In all those years as I struggled to become a writer and Dale became a teacher, and later when I stayed at home to take care of our girls, we never had two full incomes. We scrimped, we budgeted, and we sold coin and stamp collections, family heirlooms, paintings, and first editions of books. In short, we garage-saled everything the second it outgrew its usefulness. We did without big-screen televisions, CD players, dining-room sets, and a big house with new cars in the driveway, things a couple who have been married for more than two decades usually aspire to, material things that family and friends have constantly urged us to acquire. Long ago, though, like Chatwin, we decided to use our money, time, and energy for travel. We never stay still for long. Every few years, as romantic nomads, we've managed to rid ourselves of our material possessions so that we can explore the most amazing places on earth. Even with kids.

We've been very lucky. And certainly we've been charmed. Our bank account is always overdrawn, but our soul account is perpetually brimming.

Over the years as I read Chatwin's books I actually felt, much as anyone does who gets a writer into his metabolism, that I knew Bruce personally. Each book was a message from a long-lost friend. I soon discovered that what I liked best about him was his jaunty, wistful quality, his endlessly curious intellect and comic angle of vision. And although he could be neurotic, his profound optimism in the face of nearly everything revealed a brave heart. Still, for someone who appeared in print to be so upbeat and on the move, there was also something doomed and static about him, tendencies that were confirmed the day I heard he had been struck down so young.

Chatwin died in 1989 at forty-eight, supposedly from a rare bone fungus after eating a so-called thousand-year-old black egg somewhere in China. Actually he died unglamorously of AIDS in Nice, France, and was buried in an unmarked grave next to a tenth-century Byzantine chapel on Greece's Peloponnese Peninsula. If Chatwin and his wife, Elizabeth, had managed to have the kids they had claimed they wanted, and Bruce had stayed at home to look after them and travel the world the way I do, maybe he'd be alive today. And perhaps he'd have written a book similar to this one.

Instead, Chatwin's unconventional marriage had probably allowed him too much leash. He was childless and unencumbered by an all-consuming domestic life. Besides being an obsessive traveller and insatiable romantic, he was a promiscuous bisexual, a connoisseur of the extraordinary, and a brilliant amateur photographer. For better or worse, he was the quintessential Peter Pan. He could be annoyingly pretentious, chauvinistic, metaphysically suspect, and downright flighty, but his boyish Robert Louis Stevenson charm, his rampant enthusiasm, and his talent as a writer usually won the day.

When his first book, *In Patagonia*, turned the world of travel writing on its ass in 1979 and became an instant classic, Chatwin was able to become a full-time writer and a wanderer with a mission. What no one could have predicted was that he would inspire a generation of travellers to break loose and roam the world with their pens.

As early as 1970, even before Chatwin considered himself a writer, he had dug up evidence to validate the itch to wander. In an early *Vogue* article, "It's a Nomad Nomad NOMAD World," he said that brain specialists who took encephalographs of travellers found that changes of scenery and awareness of the passage of seasons throughout the year stimulated the rhythms of the brain, contributing to a sense of well-being and an active purpose in life. Monotonous surroundings and tedious, regular activities wove patterns that produced fatigue, nervous disorders, apathy, self-disgust, and violence. So, Chatwin argued, it wasn't surprising that people protected from the cold by central heating, from the heat by air-conditioning, should feel the need for journeys of mind or body, for drugs, sex, and music. After all, he wrote in the *Vogue* piece, "We spend far too much time in shuttered rooms."

Being an incurable nomad himself, Chatwin struggled for a couple of decades to breathe life into a "big" book about nomads that he wanted to call *The Nomadic Alternative*. After he gave up his cushy job as one of the youngest-ever directors of the great art auction house, Sotheby's of London, after he terminated his intensive research and field studies in archaeology, he decided to write and travel as much as he could. When he left Sotheby's, Chatwin wanted to get rid of his horror of expensive art objects that had to be assessed, sent for, put up, possessed, and sold, so he set out to study nomads. Two sweeping statements he came up with were that the Bible was about the conflict between nomads and settlers, and that religion was the travel guide for settlers. Instead of hunting objects, he decided to pursue stories. As he once put it, "To have your fingers twitch for a notebook is better than having them twitch for a checkbook anyday."

Leaving only a cryptic telegram that said "Gone to Patagonia for six months," Chatwin embarked on the first of many journeys that led to a half-dozen extraordinary books. *In Patagonia* was an attempt to limn a Cubist picture of that remote part of southern Argentina that is peopled by expatriates and exiles. Although the book avoids introspection, it is full of deeply personal material—a blend of fiction and the oddest facts imaginable, a collage of impressions, memories, histories, and stories that take into account Elizabethan sea voyages, Butch Cassidy, the revolutionary uprisings of Native Indians, the lonely farms of Welsh Patagonians, and a possible source of Samuel Taylor Coleridge's *Rime of the Ancient Mariner*.

After he published the exquisitely bizarre *The Viceroy of Ouidah* and a haunting novel, *On the Black Hill*, Chatwin felt driven once more to write the nomad book. It was to be a wildly ambitious work that would enlarge on Blaise Pascal's famous dictum about people being unable to sit quietly in a room. The contention in *The Songlines* would be that man had acquired, together with his straight legs and striding walk, "a migratory drive or instinct to walk long distances through the seasons." Chatwin wanted to trace the longings of civilized people for the natural life of nomads and other primitive peoples. He had a nostalgia for paradise, a belief that all those who resist or remain unaffected by civilization had a secret happiness the civilized had lost. Such notions were bound up in the idea of the Fall of Man, utopias, and the Myth of the Noble Savage.

Chatwin insisted that we were travellers from birth, that our mad obsession with technological progress was a response to barriers impeding our geographical progress. Movement, he felt, was the best cure for melancholy, and all our activities were linked to the idea of journeys. According to Chatwin, our brains had an information system that gave us our orders for the road, and that this was the mainspring of our restlessness. Early on people discovered they could release this information all at once by tampering with the chemistry of the brain. They could fly off on an illusory journey or an imaginary ascent. Consequently, Chatwin asserted, "Settlers naively identified God with the vine, hashish or a hallucinatory mushroom, but true wanderers rarely fell prey to this illusion. Drugs are vehicles for people who have forgotten how to walk."

So, in December 1982, he packed up his old nomad notebooks, which he had kept after he burned an earlier unpublishable manuscript. Like most writers, Chatwin's notebooks contained a mishmash of nearly indecipherable jottings, thoughts, quotations, brief encounters, travel sketches, and notes for stories. He brought all this material to Australia because he planned to wander the desert, away from libraries and other writers' works, and wanted to take a fresh look at what was in his journals.

After arriving in Sydney, Chatwin succumbed to total hedonism at a beach house in Bondi Beach. Then, from Adelaide, he journeyed to the Outback and on to the Aborigines' Red Centre where he visited Alice Springs and Uluru (Ayers Rock) in Northern Territory, searching for proof to validate his nomad theories. A couple of years later, while he attended the Adelaide Writers' Festival with Salman Rushdie, he made a second important trip to Alice and Uluru. In a four-wheel-drive Toyota he and Rushdie toured the Outback, talked about life and literature, and climbed the great "sacred" rock. All told, Chatwin's time in the heart of Australia totalled a mere nine weeks.

A few years after that, however, he produced *The Songlines*, which became a literary bestseller. In the book Chatwin and his eccentric friend, Arkady, set out to discover the paradoxical meanings of the invisible pathways that meander all over Australia, trails known to Europeans as dreaming tracks or songlines (the latter term popularized by Chatwin) and to the Aborigines as the Footprints of the Ancestors or the Way of the Law.

Two-thirds of *The Songlines* deals with this Don Quixote/Sancho Panza quest of two holy fools—Chatwin and Arkady—as they roam the desert to investigate nomadic Aboriginal culture that had been operating for nearly fifty thousand years. On this journey they speak a profound and silly dialogue concerning both sides of Chatwin's own inner conversation about restlessness. Arkady—a name that deliberately suggests poetry and an ideal, rustic paradise—is actually an invented character inspired in part by the Outback dialogues Chatwin had with Rushdie. But more important, Arkady is modelled on Anatoly Sawenko, an Australian-born son of a Ukrainian immigrant. Sawenko worked as a consultant to the Central Australian Land Council. It was his job to make sure the proposed railway line from Alice Springs to Darwin didn't interfere with sacred Aboriginal sites. Hooking up with Sawenko gave Chatwin an inside access to indigenous desert culture.

The remaining third of *The Songlines* consists of Chatwin's loosely connected scribblings and quotations about the book of nomads he always wanted to write. It isn't until the middle of his Australian book that Chatwin confesses he had a presentiment that the travelling phase of his life might be over and that before the malaise of settlement crept over him, he wanted to shed light on what was for him the question of questions: *the nature of human restlessness.*

"Why," he asks by way of Pascal, "must a man with sufficient to live on feel drawn to divert himself on long sea voyages? To dwell in another town? To go off in search of a peppercorn. Or go off to war and break skulls."

As is the case with all unencumbered male writers, Chatwin would probably have been severely cramped by a nagging mortgage and a couple of snarling kids. Even attempting to be a stay-at-home dad would likely have killed Bruce much earlier. Nevertheless, *The Songlines* drew me into a walkabout with Chatwin and, along the way, I had the opportunity to experience wild Australia and the wounded Aborigines' collision with the white man's burden. Chatwin, via arresting images and a perfect ear for dialogue, speaks of the Aborigines' seasonal return to sacred places to make contact with their ancestral roots, established in the Dreamtime. And, as usual, he slipped out of the back door of his own unfinished story—neither settler nor true nomad.

Some Australians feel Chatwin exploited Aboriginal culture in what they contend amounts to a literary hoax, while others believe he articulated something profound. Australian writer Thomas Kenneally, who penned the novel *Schindler's Ark*—the basis of the film *Schindler's List*—claimed in an interview that *The Songlines* was a truly cosmic book. Kenneally added: "Australians were raised to think that at the heart of Australia there was a dead heart. Australia is not European-sensibility friendly and it took a mad desert freak like Chatwin, a sort of literary T. E. Lawrence, to go to places like that. To realize that far from Australia having a dead heart, there was a map, there had always been a map."

While gathering material for *The Songlines*, Chatwin actually stayed in the hills above Byron Bay pretty close to where we live. Unable to get his nomad book moving and utterly depressed by his ceaseless quest for heightened reality, he only found solace windsurfing in the ocean. Even though he spent most of his time reading books, surfing, swimming, and experimenting with health food and magic mushrooms, Bruce managed to piss off almost everyone he met.

Many of the travellers I've encountered so far out in the surf and on the beaches and hiking trails around Lennox and Byron who aren't reading Robert Hughes's *The Fatal Shore* or Marlo Morgan's *Mutant Message Down Under* are devouring *The Songlines*. The Chatwin nomadic itch has inspired many to take off, despite the fierce umbilical pull of "shuttered rooms" in houses filled with stressful belongings that tie people down. Although I suspect Bruce's whirling personality, his chiselled, eloquent prose, and his wanderlust are things people either love or hate, his attempts to escape, if not physically, then by the invention of mystical paradises, were heroic.

Wandering may have quelled some of Chatwin's natural curiosity and restlessness, but he was always tugged back by a longing for a real home he never found. He had a strong compulsion to explore and perhaps an equally insistent need to return, a homing instinct like that of a migratory bird. An unfortunate irony, given Bruce's death shortly after *The Songlines* was published, is illustrated on the last page of the book when he says the mystics believe the ideal man will walk himself to a "right death" because he who has arrived "goes back."

Chatwin wasn't of this earth even when he was alive. Yet, like all good writers, he isn't really dead. Each of his books is still an invitation to a higher plane of romance and travel. Since 1989 a river of posthumous words has been published by and about Chatwin. Like all wanderers caught in the necessary delusions of any number of fools' paradises, Chatwin, a little doomed by yearnings that could never be truly satisfied, is perhaps best summed up by something Robert Louis Stevenson once wrote: "You must remember that I will be a nomad, more or less, until my days are done."

Bruce was interested in everything. He was always trying to figure out the hidden links between things. Like myself, now brooding in Byron Bay far away from the rest of the world, Chatwin dealt with the anxieties of modern life by writing and travelling. His books infused nonfiction with glamour and mystery. He claimed that the borderline between fiction and nonfiction was extremely arbitrary and invented by publishers. One writer commented that Chatwin opened horizons: "He'd wander carelessly in and out of someone's life in an afternoon and they'd be dazzled for the rest of their lives." Another writer who often hiked with Chatwin, the historian James Lee-Milne, noted: "For one so comparatively young and only recently acknowledged the obituaries are amazingly long and eulogistic. You would suppose Lord Byron had died."

What I'll always take from Bruce is his passion for making connections, his reach, and his enthusiasm for the journey. What I'll never forget are two lines from his unpublished notebooks: "never sit your life out at a desk" and "life is empty without children."

Somewhere I hope Bruce is enjoying a well-deserved *swimgloat* with the dolphins.

2
Heaven and Hell

No camera could ever duplicate what is in front of me. The view from my window is the north end of Seven Mile Beach. I'm alone at this desk, looking out at heat and stillness. I can see an entire new world. White-maned surf rolls on a blue sea into an empty golden beach. Delicious salt air blows the spicy rustle of eucalyptus gum trees into my face. Already the hot morning is filled with so many butterflies I could get knocked over by them on our verandah. Occasionally I hear the sudden, screeching metallic clatter of squadrons of insane parrots. The coastal rainforest of Broken Head, humped in the distance, drops right to the sea. And in the foreground I stare out at a green cliff studded with grazing horses etched against the ocean and sky.

Although we still haven't really met anyone, and our kids are doing their damnedest to make us feel guilty for bringing them to the other side of the world, we've managed to shake off Canadian winter. Also we procured a 1985 Mitsubishi rust bucket for wheels, whipped this moody old house into order, and signed our kids up for school, so that now we can finally slow time down a little and give into the seductive dream of this tropical landscape.

Mid-January is the glorious beginning of a long, lazy summer at the bottom of the world. Each night in this house on the hill in Lennox Head I've been reading Robert Hughes's phantasmagoric tome about crime and punishment and the founding of Australia. It recounts the fate of the convicts transported from England to Botany Bay (Sydney) on the First Fleet from May 1787 to the last convict ship in 1868. Reading *The Fatal Shore* has left me more sleepless than the thought of all the sharks I will surf and swim with in the ocean. His early chapters with their vivid descriptions of the strange isolation of this primeval continent and its enigmatic Aborigines held me breathless, listening for "white" demons outside our window.

A little more than two hundred years ago there was no such thing as white Australia. All there was "down under" was this big prehistoric island with eternal waves washing against a tree-fringed coastline of extraordinary beauty and mystery, a lost realm where nomadic tribes of Aborigines roamed, hunted, and gathered, minding their own business and living off the sacred land. Think of the first group of beachcombing Aborigines who beheld the first "white" men anchored in their tall ship, staring at one another across so much water. But the Aborigines simply turned and kept walking, retreating into the sanctuary of the bush because they couldn't have cared less; they were that well adjusted, that satisfied, lost in the Dreamtime of their profound life on this island.

The talented navigator and explorer Captain James Cook of the British Royal Navy sailed along this coast, right past my view, with his shipload of botanical specimens; horny, stir-crazy sailors, artists, and scientists; and purloined sacred artifacts. From time to time Cook's men would row into shore at some secluded cove to leave the usual beads and nails as gifts on the beach. But the trinkets were ignored. Each night, alone and perplexed in his ship's cabin, Cook wrote in his journal that they were unable to make contact with Aborigines. Apparently the natives weren't curious about the white men and had no sense of material possessions. "All they seem'd to want was for us to be gone," the captain tartly observed.

But Cook shouldn't be blamed for what followed in the terrible wake of his mapmaking journey of discovery to the Great Southern Land. Although his romantic quest had real vision, integrity, and desire, from the moment he dropped anchor it was pretty much downhill for Aborigines and most of the indigenous people of the South Seas. Luck ran out for Cook in 1779 on the Big Island of Hawaii in Kealakekua Bay where he was killed and probably eaten by Hawaiians who had worshipped him as their reincarnated god, Lono.

From other books I tracked down on the dusty shelves of the library in this old house, I discovered a few other eye-openers. Even though Aborigines are among the world's most primitive cultures, they possess one of the oldest continuous artistic traditions. They are the living representatives of the ancestors of mankind. Their mythical Dreamtime relates to a period from the genesis of the universe to a time beyond living memory. Dreamtime describes a spiritual and moral order of the cosmos. And, as Cook learned, status for an Aborigine isn't determined by material goods but by the acquisition of knowledge.

During the Australian Bicentenary in 1988 when we lived for four months down here with Sky on our second trip around the world, a fleet of tall ships left England to re-create the First Fleet's founding of the colony that became Australia. While the armada sailed triumphantly into Sydney's harbour in front of the world's cameras, escorted by thousands of pleasure craft, fireworks, and hysterical fanfare, a small vessel filled with Aborigines quietly left Australia for Britain to plant its own flag on English soil.

Until quite recently Aborigines have been better known and respected by the rest of the world than by white Australians. Ever since the early Europeans declared Australia *terra nullius*—the empty land—thus sidestepping any claims of indigenous sovereignty, Aborigines have struggled to maintain their identity and move forward in time from the once-proud nomads of a haunted, ancient land to the poorly urbanized and often marginalized people who have suffered in the murky depths of a sometimes hateful immigrant population.

In Plato's *Republic*, settlers in a new country were advised to find and reconsecrate the shrines and sacred places of the local deities. That is what white Australia seems to be attempting with its reconciliation with Aborigines. Despite the fact that it has been suggested the indigenous people of Australia might have knowledge pertinent to the survival of the planet, they are at the bottom of the socioeconomic scale, plagued by unemployment, alcoholism, and a high suicide rate.

At the time of the white invasion there were more than five hundred tribes, each one linked by its own religion, language, and family relationships. Aborigines had no writing but relied on a complex structure of spoken and sung myths passed on by elders. They were incredibly proficient nomads who flourished on a seemingly empty, inhospitable continent without money, property, "work," houses, clothes, kings, priests, or slaves, something that pissed off the white man since he first offered baubles in exchange for what little Aborigines appeared to possess. And that something was a spiritual oneness with themselves and the land that was Australia. Aborigines were totally in tune with their environment and the cosmos long before aromatherapy, secondhand religions, dynamic protected mutual funds, facelifts, silicone implants, expensive chocolate-chip cookies, big-screened TVs, and the World Wide Web.

Our bedroom here has a big window that takes in the top acre of the grassy knoll and sky that constitute our yard. The front of our house, facing the dead end of a road that overlooks the rolling hills of the hinterland, is a wild garden shaded by a hundred-yard-long Aussie-style verandah roof tangled with flowered vines and garlands of sweeping spiderwebs. It is inhabited by evil, warty cane toads, green tree frogs, rodent-size spiders, and some pretty serious snakes. Lurking in the rafters of the verandah roof is at least one three-yard-long strangling python. For some peculiar reason our Aussie exchangees decided to close off a third of their house, which included the master bedroom, living room, sauna, and fireplace. Instead of a sumptuous bedroom with lots of space, Dale and I are crammed into what we have begun to call our "grim little boudoir." By day, from the back of the house, we have glorious sunlit views down to the dazzling sea. But each hot night in our cramped front bedroom we lie with damp sheets pulled to our chins, gazing at a huge print of a monstrous Brueghel oil nailed to the wall across from our tiny bed. The black-framed painting is in Brueghel's typical red-and-ochre slaughterhouse style and depicts a claustrophobic village scene of human torment, suffering, chaos, and depravity. It's certainly not the kind of art you want to cozy up with after you've travelled with your family from the other side of the world to attempt a little spirit mending.

Each evening we're alone with this painting, our sizable window left open to encourage what little breeze might be loitering under the snaky roof of the verandah. But, as already mentioned, our bedroom is on the wrong side of the house for comfort. The back of the house, which faces the sea, is buffeted by tremendous sea winds we can always hear and taste but never feel in our bed. Still, our airless bedroom does have a stunning view of the night sky, more stars than I've seen anywhere else in the world—the Southern Cross and every other constellation perfectly etched white on black, and so close to the earth. Our neighbours on each side of us on their own two-acre blocks of land have left for Sydney for their summer school holidays with kids we'd hoped would be our daughters' playmates. So we're marooned with our companionless children with more than enough time for bonding on a darkened ridge on the back ten acres of Stoneyhurst bluff.

Everyone here has told us that one of the first useless things Canadian exchangees try to do in Australia is attempt to make their new home bug-proof. Like fools, we spray everything, set out traps and poison, seal windows and doors, fill cracks and plug holes. We sweep away cobwebs, hack through creeping foliage, and hose down all outside walls. But each night a million armoured cockroaches, black, red, and green armies of biting, stinging, poisonous, people-eating ants and bloodthirsty mosquitoes (some carrying the dreaded Ross River fever) begin to mobilize. They incite venomous snakes, poisonous spiders, sneaky rats, lizards, crazed rabbits, echidnas, night birds, and a thunderous reverberation of cicadas, cane toads, and lovely green suction-cupped tree frogs. This ungodly cacophony of wildlife seems to descend only on Dale and me and our two girls reading alone in our three darkened bedrooms. For our whole married life Dale and I have always read ourselves to sleep, and we have encouraged our girls to deal with all bumps in the night the same way. Needless to say, there has been a great deal of strained reading going on up at Stoneyhurst Manor. Although we love this place dearly, the house can be quite dark and sombre inside. Covered outside and in with gossamers of sticky cobwebs and furnished in crumbling, oxblood-stained antique furniture, and portraits of severe, questionable-looking ancestors, our kids have affectionately begun to call Stoneyhurst Manor, the Addams

Family House.

Still, while lying in bed and trying not to look up at the death-saturated Brueghel painting, I read on about Hughes's doomed convicts who were shipped seventeen thousand miles to the South Seas, transported to the bottom of the world to a lost continent that had only been "discovered" by Cook eighteen years earlier, realizing, of course, that *The Fatal Shore* wasn't exactly the best choice of reading material for new arrivals like ourselves. To cheer me up I should have been rereading Quinn's *Santa Visits Australia*, or even one of Sky's macabre Roald Dahl novels. But here we are, Dale and I, with the tugging burden of guilt from our terrified little girls, both of us wondering if we've done the right thing hauling the girls out of school in the middle of their school year to go around the world on this teacher exchange, this creative mid-life crisis. Leaving our poor collie, Ruby Doo, to fend for herself at the breeders, leaving our families, our friends and neighbours, and our house at the mercy of our Australian exhangees, whom we are gradually becoming more and more concerned about, who at this very moment themselves are being sucked dry by our hot, efficient furnace, lying under our blankets shivering in *our* bed, reading their own books, listening to an eerie snowstorm howling outside our hermetically sealed, sensory-deprivation style, bug-free house. I'm sure they're also tossing and turning, tormented by their own deep soul-searching, thinking, *Why in God's name did we ever agree to leave heavenly Byron Bay's endless summer to live for a year in the bland suburban hell of Barrhaven in the merciless heart of a Canadian winter, shovelling our way through snow to a frozen car?*

Anxiously I wonder if my nerves will hold out tomorrow while I push the ancient lawn mower through the deep, snake-infested grass of our tree-shrouded, two-acre property fringed by jungle. Will I overcome a towering wall of writer's block? Attain authenticity? Will my shaky karma hold out while surfing over reefs, trying to avoid two-thousand-pound predators with razor teeth? Will Dale be able to teach in an English department made up of a tight coterie of good old fair dinkum Aussie mates? Will my girls find friends and do well in a school without French immersion, a school where they have to wear slightly fascist grey school uniforms every day, situated less than a block away from and within earshot of a seven-mile beach? Will shedding our Nordic angst in the tropics leave us with enough willpower to concentrate and get down to work with all of this lovely ocean so close at hand?

To solve England's perceived social evils, most of the hardened criminals and even the loaf-of-bread-stealing innocents were shipped to Australia for the rest of their lives. One hundred sixty thousand of them "clanking their fetters in the penumbral darkness," as Hughes lovingly puts it. The convicts were kept in the worst possible conditions in the bowels of rotting ships; many died en route without seeing the light of day. On arrival the fun really began. To prepare the foundations for a new colony, they were put to work, whipped, tortured, beaten, starved, and thrown into leg irons and isolation cells. Many were transported to Tasmania or Norfolk Island to even crueller and more desolate hells. Hughes's salivating, pitch-perfect descriptions of these jails and their demented jailers and the early struggles of the first settlers who managed to get a foothold by scraping back the red earth, planting crops, and building homes and towns were so heartbreaking and visceral that I couldn't sleep at night. Nor could I stop reading this brilliant redneck Australian who had left Australia thirty years earlier to live as an expatriate art critic and celebrated writer in America. The admiration and fear Hughes instills with the visionary sweep of his epic prose had me at its mercy. The brutality of the beatings, the crack of the lash, the blood, depravity, and gore, the loneliness of so many misspent lives exploited by the colonial government went on so long I couldn't help feel I had not only endured it myself, but that I somehow deserved a little of the harsh punishment.

In nightmares some evenings I dreamed I was locked inside one of the hells he describes so well. Once I even tried to read a surfing magazine to unchain the lock of *The Fatal Shore*'s grip, but I always snuck back into it like some shameless, masochistic thief. To be honest, reading about how the disinherited Aborigines and the unhappy convicts jump-started Australia's traumatic birth as a country was a tour of an inferno that had singed me. But then aren't heaven and hell related?

As a kid growing up in the late 1950s and early 1960s before I ever surfed on a real wave, I thought heaven was a place where you could sit back for eternity and watch whatever movie you wanted as many times as you wanted. What I had in mind was sitting in a kind of heavenly cinema, taking in my favourite movies, say, *Swiss Family Robinson*,

Kidnapped, *Treasure Island*, or the 1949 version of *The Blue Lagoon*, viewing them repeatedly for all time. In my naive youth I actually thought this would be bliss. These days a lot of people have big-screen televisions—booming entertainment centres with surround-sound and split-screen capabilities. They can pull in hundreds of channels and endless movies. On VCRs people can see films as many times as they desire, whenever they like, while exercising on treadmills, huffing and puffing toward some meaning, higher purpose, or authenticity, each person a kind of wired George Jetson crossed with the Steve McQueen who paced a jail cell in *Papillon*.

At a time when surfing has been appropriated by big business and has become the sexy, fashionable metaphor for every kind of sedentary activity—channel surfing, couch surfing, surfing the Net—I'm actually *surfing in the ocean*. I'm attempting to live unplugged at the bottom of the world. Less than a hundred years ago much of the world was still a profound mystery, and the concept of the armchair traveller was at its peak. The South Seas, the Dark Continent, the Orient, and the Antipodes were barely visited by Westerners and loomed large in the imagination. Even for me as a kid the world still seemed fantastic, infinite with possibilities. Now the romance of travel and human imagination itself has been altered because of the threat of an escalating virtual reality. Greedy cameras probe the interior of the *Titanic*, or focus in on the most enigmatic ancient cave drawings in the Aboriginal Outback. Artificially CD-ROMs try to reproduce the music, the life and times, the private words, the very soul of Beethoven. Without our asses leaving chairs, or our faces ungluing from screens, we think we can go anywhere we like. In the whole world almost no place is remote enough or untouched. Thank God the human heart and mind are still holding out.

Lying in the dark in bed these nights in Lennox, unable to sleep, incapable of not dwelling on all the wildlife trying to get at us, I suddenly realize there has been an unnerving shift in reality. More and more humans on this planet don't seem to be bothered by the fact that instead of really living, they're mesmerized by televisions or computers. In the smallest steaming village in Bali, far-flung backwater of China, or frigid shack in the Arctic, people are transfixed by their screens. Already the Internet has hundreds of millions of users. A totally wired generation has emerged, with instantaneous communications and entertainment and an arrogant belief that it will be happier and freer than all the generations that preceded it. A generation of wired imperialists is pushing the notion of the unlimited possibilities of life acquired at a TV screen or keyboard. Given their firsthand experience with interpersonal McCarthyism, abuse, AIDS, and the world's emotional and economic depressions, e-mail is a lot less intimidating, and not even remotely as messy as real personal contact. Virtual reality is in and old-fashioned reality is out. It's the digital kids, my kids, versus us, the doomed romantic boomers.

Last night while the kids were flipping through TV channels, Bruce Springsteen's "57 Channels and Nothin' On" was heard and, for a moment, I was tempted to trash our set until I remembered it didn't belong to us. Instead, I thought about the guy I met surfing the other day who was celebrating his fiftieth birthday. He'd ducked out of his job for the day, doing the long, hot drive from the small inland town of Kyogle to prove something to himself. "How ya goin', mate?" he announced, a happy-go-lucky bloke truant from what he'd described as a semi-buggered life of trading his soul for money. Tall and bearded, he had receding hair and a potbelly and was straddling a brand-new thousand-dollar Heart & Soul longboard he'd received for his birthday. The warm sea was heaving around us, and the sheltering sky was a gorgeous, penetrating blue—a sight to inspire any tuckered-out fifty-year-old. During a long lull between sets of waves, I casually mentioned I was just getting back into surfing, that I was here with my family from Canada on my wife's teacher exchange and writing a book about looking after my two daughters for the past decade. For once I didn't receive the usual suspicious sidelong glance a writer and househusband or a Canadian inspires here. He was probably trying to wrap his brain around the idea of my being a kept man, but thankfully he didn't mention it. Without a care in the world we were both riding our surfboards out in the Pacific in the middle of a workday, a couple of middle-aged, unencumbered family men taking in nature's gift.

The only company we had were dolphins. He was obviously used to them, but I still got excited whenever they appeared. They were cruising and flipping through the waves, skewering the water right under our boards, their grey bodies flashing by, almost touching our feet. "Oy reckon these dolphins are even bigger bludgers than the pair of us," he said wryly. "Look at 'em swimmin' around with no worries. Lucky bloody bastards!" Then, just for my benefit, he pointed out to sea. "Humpbacks'll pass in June on their way north from Antarctica to warmer waters. On their return leg in September, they'll beat it back down south."

We both stared out to the mile-long rolling swells approaching from the horizon. "Mate, you'll be able to sit here on your board with your laptop computer watching the whales breach." When I told him I was trying to escape from the late twentieth century, he suddenly exploded, "Hey, Oy hear ya, mate. Just last week Oy unplugged the telly and locked it up in our humpy in the backyard. It's been bloody tyrannizing us oll! Yeah, well, Oy reckon my family'll just have to learn how to talk to one another again."

And I thought, *Good on ya, mate.*

After an hour of arthritic, casual surfing, we struggled out of the water and walked until we came upon a man and a beautiful woman. The young man wore a straw hat, loud surf shorts, and no shirt. He stood up to his powerful thighs in the foam of spent waves, fishing, gazing intently at the tip of his rod in the air. The woman sported a black string bikini that barely managed to hold all her ample curves together. The couple must have been tourists from Sydney. No local would ever fish with his wife or girlfriend. When she bent over an up-turned surfboard to bait the hook of her line, I thought the eyes and the molars of my new friend would spring out of his head. With water still dripping from his beard, he turned to me and said, "Oy, it's a good loif, mate."

There's way too much processed information, too much artificial experience and not enough real life. Because high technology instantly transmits data back and forth, it guarantees our isolation from one another and provides very little authentic experience. Hence all the seductions of lonely people caught in the Net. Hence the quote by English novelist John Fowles taped at the top of my computer screen: "Random personal creativity is offensive to all machines."

While we've been enjoying this unplugged Gauguin-esque exile in the South Seas, our friends from the Northern Hemisphere have become pretty antsy. They're demanding to know why we're not plugged in. So

I joyously banged off a hand-illustrated ten-page newsletter to say we enjoyed being unplugged. Friends mentioned they were surfing the Net and miraculously found Lennox Head and Byron Bay. Some downloaded enough information to claim they had almost experienced being here themselves. A few spoke about the sublime glories of travelling in virtual reality. But how could I tell them we have no intention of hooking up our computer with e-mail? How could I gently tell them I could care less about the bumper-to-bumper, warp-speed, McDonald's-strewn, porno-bloated, diarrhea-running information highway, because we had reached a saturation point where we needed to disconnect for a while? We were too busy with old-fashioned reality: walking along the beach, diving through waves, sniffing the sensual odour of frangipani, taking in the salty night breeze rustling in our cocas palms. Or just giving in to small-town chitchat while watching dear old Mavis behind the counter of her little general store looking over the tops of her glasses as she sizes up a mango for ripeness in her gnarly old hands. Traditional stuff that can't be experienced on the World Wide Web. Besides, weren't webs something you got trapped in and might never escape?

Like a prisoner who has bided his time with good behaviour and sheer ball-breaking endurance, I'm finally in paradise, living above the ocean. I'm trying not to feel too guilty about anything in my former life. I'm striving not to feel bad about all the sad, unfinished business with the Aborigines. For the moment, as the Aussies say, "Oy nevah felt betta."

And as I look up from the grip of my computer screen to verify the Pacific is still rolling in, for the first time since we arrived here I notice how butterflies out past our verandah flit in the wind. In a looping figure eight they seem to go nowhere, but also manage to get exactly where they want to go. And like the early Aborigines who first drank in this same sweet view, this same vast ocean, I'm filled with absolute hope, awe, and peace. Then, for some strange reason, I think about what a Russian prisoner in Alexander Solzhenitsyn's *First Circle* said: "It's better to drown in the ocean than in a puddle."

3
Melancholy Lawn Mowers

In the morning, after everyone has left for school, I am the king of my domain. A lucky bastard. This big old house to myself, the sweeping ocean view, the real possibility I might get it all down now that I have the time. But according to my hazy recollection of Greek tragedies, first came Hubris, then came the thunderbolts. So, in the back of my mind, I'm thinking, *You don't want to piss off the gods. Don't let it get around you're having a good time, or someone, or something, will clobber you down a few notches.* Like Brian Wilson who wrote all the Beach Boys feel-good surfer hits in the early 1960s and created a California dream still pursued by big business and, by extension now, almost every fashion-conscious person on the planet. After reaching for the glory, Wilson succumbed to a depression so all-consuming that he hid in bed for three years. He tried to live the wet dream he helped to invent, but couldn't even get his feet wet, although the poor guy has made a Herculean effort to fight his demons. He once commented that living close to the sea was good for your head. When you're living at the foot of eternity, it gives you perspective when you're overly fixated on survival.

The tall, rustling cocas palms are losing the sheaths that cover their heavy clusters of dates. The peach, orange, and lemon trees bend with fruit. All the frangipani, hibiscus, and orchids are in ferocious bloom. I hold one yellow-centred white frangipani, the same kind of flower they string together to make Hawaiian leis and drape around the necks of newcomers to the islands as a symbol of the aloha spirit. I put my nose into the sweet ear of its vortex and inhale the Pacific.

Later, I stoop to fill huge chlorine buckets with pineapple-size pinecones that have blown off the two rows of towering pine trees that run down both sides of our property. A moist salt breeze lifting off the ocean washes its damp blanket of heat over the ridge and takes my breath away, suffocates me with the weight of its closeness. From time to time cicadas start up their grinding resonance, like the beginning of an apocalypse, letting me know I might be all alone at the bottom of the world, after all.

I stop to gaze across the hill overlooking Seven Mile Beach because I've noticed a frisky colt rocking back and forth on his back, hooves kicking madly in the air. And then he's up and prancing around for joy, with no worries, stiff-leggedly romping until he's down again, rolling about in the mouth-cropped grass of the cliff. The older horses gaze meditatively, perhaps recalling their own playful youth, nose to tail with one another beneath the shade of a lone tree at the top of the hill.

So far I've filled ten chlorine buckets with pinecones, and I'm almost ready to cut the lawn. The pinecones are going to my next-door neighbour, Steve, for his fireplace. It's about forty degrees Celsius, early morning, and I'm already dripping in sweat, worried about the razor fierceness of the sun, even with a goofy brimmed hat, oversize shirt, shorts, and my trusty Wellies, wondering how the weather in a few months will change enough to require a fireplace.

The lawn takes me five hours to cut without a break, except to drink water and pick up, kick, or toss into the bush any of the smaller grenade-size pinecones I missed with my buckets. Also I must dodge lurking snakes and poisonous spiders the size of rodents. Among the trees I'm lacerated by long, cruel thorns, low-hanging branches, and aggressive magpies that have already swooped to skewer me once. As always, I'm wary of the ever-dangerous anvil of the antipodean sun.

I fire up the old Briggs and Stratton Blue Thunder lawn mower. It's a heavy iron beast held together with too many pop rivets and chicken wire. The throttle is forced wide open with a tightly knotted pair of someone's panty hose. I bitterly resented my Australian exchangee the first time I had to cut his lawn with this oil-belching relic. But taking so much time to cut the grass did offer me the chance to get intimate with the property and its wild inhabitants. In Ottawa we have a wimpy orange electric mower and one of the city's smallest lawns, which suits me fine. After a decade of taking care of my girls in their pink Barbie world, I've found that physically working outside old Stoneyhurst Manor has done wonders for my readjustment into manhood. My muscles are pumped, and I glow with hard-earned perspiration. Most of the time on this big, lonely property I feel like a strolling naturalist on a casual jaunt through a nineteenth-century novel.

The upper acre of the lawn allows me to stare down at the ocean as I walk, shearing back and forth along its football-field length. In many places the lawn tilts steeply, which tests my scrawny legs. And I have the added pleasure of sudden rocks that ricochet off the blade like gunfire, scaring the hell out of me and jolting my arms all the way to the spurs of my heels. The bumpy bottom half of the lawn below the swimming pool is choked with an impenetrable jungle of eucalyptus and tangled creepers, and if I were a deadly snake or spider, this is definitely where I'd thrive. The scary grass there is so thick and long that the mower invariably sputters and sometimes stalls. The last time it died I nipped through the pines over to our "mystery" neighbour's place and pulled down a few papayas and mangoes for the next day's breakfast.

With this crushing heat I can still smell Steve's snake. The other day he accidentally sliced one with his ride-on mower and rushed over to beg me to put it out of its misery. I guess you could say I've become the local serpent charmer here. The six-foot snake was partially slashed by Steve's blade. It flailed and whipped in the grass, its accusing eyes penetrating us both. Steve couldn't bear to see the poor creature suffer, but he's terrified of snakes. So reluctantly I raised a shovel and, with several strokes to the head, ended the slitherer's quicksilver life. I wasn't very happy to be the one to take out the snake in this Eden, but I scooped him up and flung him deep into the jungle for the bush to consume. Now it's not only the smell that haunts me.

As I cut grass hour after hour, it's not surprising that I sing and get a bit introspective. One of the biggest fantasies of my generation coming of age in the 1960s was to become a rock star. At some point I must have decided that being a writer would be much the same thing. Fame, fortune, and freedom. I have about as much of the first as the character John Candy played in the movie *Home Alone*, who says his polka record sold really well in Boise, Idaho. As for fortune, my last royalty cheque was $13.13, about the same as F. Scott Fitzgerald's final royalty cheque when he was on his fabulous alcoholic decline in Hollywood, writing screenplays that were never made into films. Luckily, though, I've learned to appreciate my share of naked liberty. And second acts.

Nothing evokes the pangs of memory like a good song. Even the death rattle of a gonad-vibrating mower can do the trick. As I clip the grass, I belt out tunes from The Who's 1969 rock opera *Tommy*. The beauty and intensity of that album still makes me shiver. While listening to myself warble The Who as I push my melancholy mower above the sea and enjoy the feel of my working muscles, I surrender to nostalgia and think about my childhood mate, Jamie, who died a few years back. He was only forty-two, and for a time at our cottage in Norway Bay, Quebec, in the early 1960s he was one of my best friends. By the time he died, we weren't friends at all. I didn't hear about his death until months later from another old friend who I never see much anymore.

In 1969, when I lived on the side of Grouse Mountain in North Vancouver, Jamie flew out from Ottawa to stay with me and my family. Heroically we cruised the Lower Mainland in my orange 1960 Volkswagen whose windshield I eventually went through when I wrapped it around a telephone pole driving drunk. Singing along to Steppenwolf's "Born to Be Wild" and Creedence Clearwater Revival's "Who'll Stop the Rain" while checking out the babes, we roared around in that deathmobile with lousy brakes and no windshield wipers, hitting all the hotels to drink underage. One evening Jamie sat on my parents' verandah and watched me cut our huge lawn, which was fringed with pink and white carnations whose heady cinnamon scent used to drive me crazy with a desire that had no tangible outlet.

A year later I spent a week at Jamie's parents' cottage at Norway Bay, then a lost week at their home in Manordale, a suburb of Ottawa. I can still see Jamie comatose in a chair, eyeing me as I cut his parents' never-ending grass.

Sliding away on the amazing journey of *Tommy*, I revisit the first time I glimpsed Jamie in the summer of 1966. He was shuffling along the oiled road at our cottage in Norway Bay. I was sitting on the fence that ran down to our beach. With me were a bunch of ten- to twelve-year-old kids I'd grown up with most of my life. They were sort of my gang—my sister, Jan; my best friend, Brent Storey; his nephew, Ronny Rowat; Johnnie Schultz; Mike Couillard; Keith Wilson; and my sister's best friends, Sandra Landsburg and Bonnie Beams, who for years were my on-again, off-again girlfriends.

Jamie was bopping along in a fabulously loud Hawaiian shirt, a transistor radio tucked in the crook of one arm. He was stuffing his mouth full of Pink Elephant popcorn and singing to Tommy James and the Shondells' "Hanky Panky." On his little finger was a flamboyant plastic ring he'd won as the prize inside the box of popcorn. Jamie was short and had a longish nose and a faintly dopey grin. But he radiated definite cool. I had seen him around, but not up close. Even before Jamie got to my gang sitting on the fence I could hear him confidently squawking out, "Ma baby does the Hanky Panky."

Back then we all lived charmed lives each summer at Norway Bay. Every June, on the last day of school, our mothers would pick us up in family cars loaded with belongings, and we'd head to Quebec for the entire summer. When we finally returned to the city, our closed-up, empty houses seemed much bigger and a little ominous. They smelled damp and exotic, the trees and shrubs having outgrown their yards. And in our dark bedrooms our neatest stuff held potent new magic.

Our fathers commuted. The poor buggers drove down to the hot city on Sunday night or early Monday morning, listening to Tony Bennett, Mel Tormé, or the early Barbra Streisand, then sped like hell back up on Wednesday for a quick, cathartic dip in the river before suppertime. Like war heroes, they were temporarily pampered because they had to leave in the wee hours before dawn for the city and wouldn't return until Friday night, panting like abused dogs with their loosened ties and sweat-drenched clothes. Sometimes, if we were lucky, they'd arrive with treats from the city: greasy little bags of expensive mixed nuts, a damp box of assorted doughnuts, an accessory for a bike, or maybe a new snorkel and mask. All summer we lived with our mothers and hardly ever saw our fathers. It was an Oedipal dream and a discipline nightmare. Back then most of our mothers stayed at home with their kids. Each day they oiled up and lay on the beach, reading paperback novels, watching us play in the water, feeding us incredible snacks, and not giving a hoot about careers, time passing by, skin cancer, or half-forgotten lives in the city.

All day we ran around in bare feet, cutoffs, or bathing suits, in and out of the water, in and out of the fridge, in and out of trouble. We only went inside to sleep. Unsupervised and free, we lived like wild Indians, because in those days you could say that and everyone knew exactly what it meant.

Jamie's mother and father were older than everyone else's parents. They were more like grandparents—soft touches compared with our young, stressed-out parents who were still looking for fun themselves, but had too much responsibility. Jamie's mom was too old to hang around oiled up on the beach, and besides, she had her elderly mother living with her. Jamie's dad had been a Cameron Highlander during World War II, and often drank while singing dirty, rousing songs with a few other red-nosed Highlanders up at the bay. Whenever the regiment went on one of its frequent, good-natured benders, one of the old vets played a haunting screed on the bagpipes.

Because Jamie was an only child, he was accused of being a little spoiled. After his parents bought their cottage, they built Jamie his own cabin, which boosted his status with us one hundred percent.

When Jamie became part of our gang, we almost lived in his cabin. His parents never intruded and hardly ever said no. There were raucous sleepovers, and we kept a stray dog named Tippy, who wandered down from a farm on the hill. She hung out with us for most of the summer and then ambled home in September. Tippy slept with us in the cabin. In the river she furiously dog-paddled to keep up with us as we dived for clams at the drop or even while we water-skied. The dog followed us into the bush as we explored old logging roads to abandoned pioneers' cabins or waded to the source of creeks and waterfalls upcountry. Tippy was our gang's dog. A loyal stray. A free spirit. A black-and-white-and-tan flame that still blazes through a lot of our summertime memories.

We even had a rock-and-roll band. Jamie and Brent played electric guitar, while Ronnie had a set of drums. I had to get by on an intense desire to sing because I had absolutely no music in me. Besides singing badly, I could only remember three or four lines of even my favourite songs. But crooning my best-loved tunes at the top of my lungs made my heart soar. And still does.

Shamelessly we attempted to play maudlin renditions of the Beach Boys' "Barbara Ann," Jimi Hendrix's "Foxy Lady," Cream's "Sunshine of Your Love," Wilson Pickett's "Midnight Hour," The Who's "My Generation," and the Rolling Stones' "19th Nervous Breakdown." Jamie could do flawless impersonations of Mick Jagger's pucker-lipping songs, or Pete Townshend's coy hip wiggle and manic guitar gyrations. Sometimes in the same song he'd do such intense Mick and Pete contortions that we thought he might injure himself. With his long, curly black hair, sad, puppy-dog eyes, and tragic aura, he captured the hearts of girls and boys alike. Wired into a lethal black guitar, Jamie was transformed into an electric warrior.

It was Jamie who could introduce and explain radical albums like The Who's *Tommy* or an obscure bubble-gum album by Dino, Desi, and Billy and make you believe the words in the lyrics might change your life if you listened to them hard and long enough. And loud enough.

Back then we all had scurfboards instead of skateboards. It was market-ed as "surfing on wheels." As deprived mid-continent kids with a hankering for uninhibited beach culture, we were swept away, consumed by our manic energy and a "don't give a fuck" attitude. Scurfboards were short, extremely rigid wooden planks with steel roller skates nailed to the bottoms. We used to pull each other on hairy ropes behind our bikes.

One day Jamie surfed down Jim's hill. Although at first he executed perfect form, right away we all realized he'd been launched too fast by someone's bike. The scurfboard and its wheels weren't flexible enough to withstand high speeds or sudden cracks in the pavement. Jamie roared down the hill, Tippy barking and nipping at his ankles. Soon he was going too rapidly even for the dog. Jamie's long, curly hair blew straight back in the wind. From the bottom we saw his scurfboard shimmy uncontrollably. But, stoically, poor Jamie just stared ahead with all the stunned inertia of the doomed until the wobbling board finally catapult-ed him off in a spectacular somersault. After bouncing off the pavement, skinning his forehead, arms, legs, knees, elbows, nose, and one ear, he sprang up and then tottered a little dazed and off-kilter. By the time we rushed over to him, he was chanting, "It's cool, man. I'm all right. It's cool."

So we sat at Jimmy Lucas's store and drank RC Colas, checking under the bottle caps to see if we won anything, and inhaled Coffee Crisp and Oh Henry! chocolate bars while Jamie sat with his cut-up legs crossed, meditatively munching on a big box of Pink Elephant popcorn.

For a couple of halcyon summers before we started to drink and get into real trouble with life, our gang was inseparable and immortal, even though we got toes caught in bicycle chains, sliced our feet open on clams, broke eyeglasses, and lost brand-new graduation watches. We took fish hooks in all the wrong places and endured poison ivy even on our private parts. All our money was spent on ant-covered penny candy at Jimmy's. We drank too much pop, smoked licorice pipes and cigars, and occasionally inhaled pine needles stuffed into the tubes of empty Pixie Sticks. Passionately we collected and traded Beatles and then Monkees cards. We broke a few bones and got stitches. Half-naked, we strutted around with ghastly scabs of draining impetigo or poison ivy and half-eaten food all over our faces. Like Huck Finn, we were allowed to go almost anywhere alone, unencumbered by the adult world.

People gently teased Jamie about being in his own world. In his usual trancelike fashion he'd slowly respond to any person's statement with questions like "Did he?" or "Would you?" or "Is it?" His passions were typical: rock and roll, bikes, and later, fast cars and a string of girlfriends. In the late 1960s when Jamie announced he was going to Highland Park High, some kids said it was a technical school for dummies. But lots of dummies went there and got jobs and a head start making money while many more dummies in university squandered a great deal of cash and long, meaningless years pursuing box-canyon degrees in geography, political science, or psychology that, in some cases, paved the way to absolutely nowhere. I should know—for a time I was one of them.

At a New Year's Eve party the weekend before I quit drinking in 1973

I had a falling-out with Jamie over something I can't recall because I was so drunk. We were in the groping teenage wasteland of a low-ceiling rec room with the thunderous riffs of Jethro Tull's *Aqualung* reverberating. Most of my friends would simply drink all night, get louder and dopier, and then run out of steam and quietly collapse. But I was one of those unfortunate drinkers who felt the need to bring a whole room full of people wherever I wanted to go. Which was somewhere fantastic, if I was up for it, or I could haul everything down to the darkest levels of teenage angst. That night, because of a big, ugly, drunken mouth, my friendship with Jamie was irreparably damaged and I lost one of my best friends. The next weekend I quit drinking forever.

Our lives took divergent paths, and we saw less and less of each other. I went to university, then began travelling the globe. Jamie married his high-school sweetheart, who really was a sweetheart, and they had a child before the rest of us did. He changed jobs a few times, split up with his sweetheart, then married someone else we didn't know and never got to know. And finally he settled into real life and a secure, uncomplicated job in the government for what he probably figured would be the long haul.

Up at the bay one summer in the early 1980s, after I returned from my first trip around the world, I spied a five-year-old kid running down to jump in the water. I was thunderstruck at how much he looked like Jamie in the early 1960s. Instead of having curly black hair, this kid was blond, but the resemblance was uncanny. It was a hot summer day, and everyone was in the water or sitting on the beach in bathing suits. As soon as I came in from the water, I spotted Jamie alone in the shade. He was dressed in a plain dark shirt, long pants, and running shoes, watching his son play in the water. We tried to chat about the present, but there wasn't much to talk about. As usual I was in a hurry, impatient. Not yet being a parent like Jamie, I couldn't understand why he seemed so tired and spent, a mere shadow of his former self. So I tried to rev him up with a little nostalgia. We used to water-ski together on two ropes behind his dad's enormous 50-Evinrude. In the back of the boat we hooked up an eight-track stereo to listen to Led Zeppelin. Cranking up the volume, we blasted off to the opening lines of "Black Dog" and "Rock & Roll," slitting the glassy waters from Norway Bay to Sand Bay on the Ontario side. Jamie would cut under my tow rope so we could insanely crisscross the big wake, the pair of us belting our lungs out with the tunes of Jimmy Page and Robert Plant. By the time we headed back across the wide river, our legs were cooked. But we were happy to ski stiff-legged as we let the heart-searing words of "Stairway to Heaven" take us back to shore.

After his dad died of cancer, Jamie's mother had to sell her son's cabin and the family cottage to a Portuguese couple. Many years passed and there was no news until I heard that Jamie had also died of cancer. One night, in the spring of 1996, I phoned his mom. She sounded very old because, after all, she was. And I realized I was getting up there myself. She was sad but seemed pleased to hear from me now that she was alone in that big suburban house of ghosts. I was a direct link to her only son who was now dead, as was her husband and her dear mother. While we talked I thought about the summer of 1969 when I flew back from Vancouver to spend an epic summer with friends in Norway Bay. The late 1960s were exciting times with the psychedelic swirl of Woodstock's earthy rebellion, the Beatles' last albums, hippies marching against the Vietnam War, the moon landing. Falling in love every other day, I was bursting with life's possibilities and ideas I had gleaned from living in Canada's California.

Because Jamie's father was working and had rented the family cottage to some lucky people, Jamie and I ended up marooned in the suburbs. That week is still bathed in a harsh white light of inertia and emptiness. I learned to fear and dislike the suburbs that hot August week, bitterly resenting the fact that I wasn't up at the cottage swimming in the river and running free. I remember the first morning Jamie's grandmother asked me how I liked my bacon and I replied, "Crisp." And so for the rest of my stay that was what she called me. The streets had that forlorn desolation they have when everyone is on holidays, at camps and cottages, or who knows where. I vowed I'd never live in the suburbs when I was an adult, but I've since learned that a lot of promises can't be totally honoured. That tired old joke: if you really want God to have a good laugh, just tell him your plans.

Every day I was there Jamie refused to cut the lawn for his mother because he rarely helped out around the house. To be a hero, I volunteered to mow the grass for something to do outside and to work off some of my pent-up energy and frustration. And so, from inside Jamie's father's immaculately organized garage, I rolled the mower out onto the driveway and filled it with gas. After I pulled the cord, the contraption exploded to life, and for an hour I cut that endless, boring, rectangular suburban lawn, edging around picnic tables, plastic bird baths, and a weedy, bumpy ditch. Under the unforgiving sun in Manordale with that ancient, wheezing mower, not unlike the chugging, stinky two-stroke I now use to clip Stoneyhurst Manor, I thought I'd never escape. I was doomed to a Sahara of the soul in suburbia forever.

Jamie's mother, Grace, would tell me years later on the phone that she loved it when I came to stay with "Poor Jamie" because I used to eat so well and "Poor Jamie" had always been a fussy eater. She didn't have to remind me; I could still remember him, even at eighteen and twenty, listening to Deep Purple's "Smoke on the Water" or Grand Funk Railroad's "Closer to Home," eating countless bowls of Cap'n Crunch instead of the great country food his mother offered.

His mom kept referring to Poor Jamie and his last words—"Well, I guess this is it, Mom"—which he said one evening in a hospital bed after the cancer returned to consume him with an even more fatal ferocity. As she spoke sadly and tenderly about her sweet, lost boy, I recalled a day in the late 1960s when Jamie sat me down to explain the incredible narrative complexity and wonder of the Beatles' *Sgt. Pepper's Lonely Hearts Club Band.* I heard Jamie singing "Baby You're a Rich Man" at the cottage on the beach: "How does it feoh to be one of the beautifo peopo?"

I guess you could say Jamie had a neat childhood, but later on I'm pretty sure he didn't get his fair share of the sweetness of life.

In the wind at the moment, our big ghost gums and palms are thrashing, and the ridge above the ocean is covered with restless horses. The cocky little pony is up now and romping about unrestrained. All I can smell is freshly cut grass. The old mower rests under the jungle of the verandah roof. The truth is, although Jamie and I were like brothers for a short time in our glorious youth, even then there was a hint of mortality. My sister, Jan, and Jamie are both gone. Time passes. Along the way we all fall into traps, living faster and faster until time runs out. In the end, there is only memory and the solace of a little wisdom: pay more attention to your loved ones, and your friends.

When I snap out of my funk, I get rid of Poor Jamie and remember the maniac on the electric guitar wildly strumming the chords of his uptempo rendition of The Who's "I'm Free" from *Tommy*. He keeps the beat with his bobbing head and wolfish ear-to-ear grin and squawks "I'm fwee, I'm fweee!" so intensely it makes a ropy vein along his throat stand out. And I think, *Yeah, and freedom tastes of reality. I'm free, and I'm waiting for you to follow me.*

4
Confessions of an Unrepentant Beach Bum

Years ago, before I knew the whole story, I used to think the most uncompromised life belonged to free-spirited beach bum Paul Gauguin, who had quit his dull job as a respectable stockbroker in Paris to escape to the South Seas and devote himself to painting. Even now above my desk wherever I write I keep an old black-and-white framed photograph of Gauguin when he was an unknown Sunday painter. The photo shows the artist standing alone in front of a shimmering wall of foliage, poised and noble, dabbing a brush into his palette as though he had all the confidence in the world that a passion for one's art was enough to define and defend a life.

Like many people, I almost got derailed by Gauguin's restless, overwhelming personality. Because I had already been somewhat of a surfer, despite living in the middle of the continent, and had managed to surf and taste a bit of the primitive beauty of the Hawaiian Islands in the 1970s, I bought into the Gauguin myth completely. Eventually I was seduced by an idea that I might find creative inspiration and spiritual awakening somewhere even farther down in the South Seas. In my youthful yearnings, before I had children, I saw heroism in Gauguin's famous mid-life crisis, his escape from domesticity and civilization, and his attempts to return to nature on an exotic island. So I searched for some of the things I thought Gauguin was looking for, though I didn't realize it would take nearly twenty years to find the place he sought.

Gauguin was tranquil and tender, vicious and cruel, a civilized savage. When he abandoned his wife and children to paint in the South Seas, he became one of the world's most notorious deadbeat dads, though for years he continued to write personal letters to his wife, Mette, and suffered ferociously because of the absence of his children, especially after the tragic early death of his daughter, Aline, whom he adored. In their time the Gauguins' scandalous marriage breakup was a rarity, but today marital troubles like the French couple's are played out by restless millions around the world, including most of my friends and family.

My first book, *Tender Only to One*, which seemed to sail right off the edge of a flat world after it was published, was inspired by the final years of Gauguin's life in the French Marquesas. After the creative explosion of his first stay in Tahiti in 1893, a short, triumphant return to Paris for the history-making exhibition of his works in the Durand-Ruel Gallery, a wild Bohemian stint on the coast of Brittany, and the memory of a productive but dangerous three-month interlude living with Vincent van Gogh in the Yellow House in 1895, Gauguin left France for good and sailed for the South Pacific.

But already at the end of the nineteenth century Gauguin believed Tahiti had been ruined by European civilization and tried to find another untainted Eden. So, in 1901, he ended up marooned in the French Marquesas. A thousand miles above Tahiti in the middle of the Pacific, these lush, volcanic Polynesian islands are considered the most remote paradise on earth. Gauguin couldn't have desired a more lonely exile. Even today the Marquesas are hard to get to and expensive to visit. Unfortunately the painter was too late; the Catholic and Protestant missionaries, businessmen, and the local French government had already spoiled the Marquesas for Gauguin's impossible kind of South Seas fantasy. Still, in his House of Pleasure the artist managed to produce beautiful paintings, watercolours, woodcuts, drawings, and wood sculptures.

Through his revolutionary use of uninhibited colour, he helped to bring representational art to the brink of abstraction. What is less well-known is that Gauguin was also an impassioned author who published several books and wrote many journals, articles, and letters. With this combination of painting and writing, he created a compelling body of work and an unshakable legend—the archetypal romantic who at all costs must go off to paradise to find himself.

Today Gauguin's paradise is still offered in the pages of glossy magazines and travel brochures. I was tickled to discover that a cruise-ship line runs an ad in *The New Yorker* for the MS *Paul Gauguin*, which sails from Los Angeles to Tahiti. Ironically it was launched the same week of December 1997 that we flew to Australia to live in our beach house. Year-round this immaculate white, 320-guest vessel cruises for seven days to Tahiti and other legendary islands in French Polynesia. For an arm and a leg (about $4,000 to $10,000 U.S.), now even mere mortals can experience a paradise that is "closer than you imagined, more than you dreamed." In the ad the *Paul Gauguin* floats before two stylized images that promise something of the Gauguin myth. One is a remote, cloud-wreathed volcanic island surrounded by a luminous turquoise sea. The other is a raven-haired Tahitian beauty who undulates before the lush texture of tropical leaves. In a low-cut flowered pareau, her long, sensuous neck deliciously exposed, eyes closed, she is about to take a full-lipped bite out of a ripe, forbidden fruit.

Even though the Gauguin myth has been perpetuated and appropriated for a hundred years by soul-searchers larking around the globe in search of tropical paradises, and affluent tourists on comfortable, safe, packaged holidays, the real story isn't that pretty. Apparently going native in French Polynesia was no picnic for Gauguin and cost him dearly. He suffered, and made an unholy mess of his family life. But like a precocious child, he didn't have an uncreative bone in his body. And so, for a while, painting and living in a hut next to the mountains and ocean in Tahiti must have been like discovering heaven. After the grey pallor of tight-assed Europe, Gauguin drank in Tahiti's enchanting landscape, tropical colours, and mysterious light. All day and most evenings he wrote and painted, enjoying an unencumbered freedom to turn his life into art. He sketched young women bathing in streams or floating bare-breasted with wet black hair and seductive stares. In letters back to Europe the artist spoke of late afternoons swimming in the warm sea, then the mocking laughter of beautiful girls following him into bed at dusk for long, dark nights. For a short time, while succumbing to a debauchery of the senses, Gauguin indulged himself in a sanctuary of vermilion, emerald, tangerine, lilac, lemon, and violet.

Although everything he ever touched is now priceless and his work hangs all over the world, the painter found no healing waters in the Marquesas. Despite giving the finger to European civilization, he was no trouble-free beach bum. Nevertheless, people love to fantasize that Gauguin ducked out and escaped the grind in a South Seas Shangri-la. But while he lived in the South Seas he pined for another paradise—a simple home in Paris where he could enjoy the cultural stimulation of his place on the cutting edge of the art world he had helped to change. In the Marquesas each day he walked the sand, reciting lines of poetry like prayers or mantras to assuage his enormous loneliness and the guilt over the family he had abandoned in Europe.

After researching Gauguin through his paintings, letters, and journals, and by visiting Paris and London and art galleries in Honolulu, New York City, Boston, and Toronto, I thought how wonderful it would be to visit his island nemesis. Late one cold snowy Ottawa night in early 1981 while doing research upstairs at a cubicle in the Carleton University library, I suddenly heard ocean surf slapping against a shore, then looked at the sky, half expecting to glimpse the painter's island. At that moment a lonely, elegiac voice came into my head and I wrote: "Nightcloud horses are galloping the sky outside my window. Yellow fires like sequins in the dark. Clouds moving across the moon like white horses in a carousel. Imagine if I could open this tropical night to a village in snow. Cold against my naked belly, clutching my balls with its icy grip. Tree branches cracking and jumping with the breeze. By God, cold clean French air with a faint whiff of chimney smoke. The wind outside my hut could be the winter wind of Paris. Here the wind is the sea, the sea the wind. Tonight, as I wander the House of Pleasure, occupying myself with simple things, I need more than a little soothing poetry. I stand in my doorway and watch purple clouds drape along the mountains. Church bells ring from both the Protestant and Catholic churches, and God is everywhere down here in the islands. I wind up my music box, remove the lid. The sea is a woman's body I have lost."

Instead of being thankful for getting in touch with the voice I needed to write my Gauguin book, like a fool I mistook this sound of waves to be a sign that I must go to Tahiti and then somehow get up to the isolated village of Atuona on Gauguin's Hiva Oa in the Marquesas. From that moment on the Marquesas became an obsession, my Unholy Grail. And although getting to Gauguin's island proved to be one of the biggest fiascoes and ego-shaking crises to haunt my life, in many ways it inspired me.

Later in 1981, right after Dale and I spent a long summer in Hawaii where I wrote more of my Gauguin book and we surfed in the south swells breaking over coral reefs, living the sexy freedom of beach culture to the hilt, Dale flew home to Ottawa while I jetted to Tahiti. There, alone in Papeete, in a stifling hot, dingy hotel room in front of a cracked mirror, I was so possessed by Gauguin that I breathed his very soul, inhabited the mercurial corridors of his troubled mind. But I couldn't write.

Many people know about Gauguin's failure and conceit, the primitive religious iconography of his paintings, his love of red dogs, gardenias, frangipani, nipples, fruit, jagged mountain peaks, and tattooed faces, but do they understand that in the last year of his life, at the age of fifty-five, he discovered the eternal mystery—death, loneliness, isolation, the void in the human condition—at night alone in his hut with only a sliver of courage left, his back against the thin wall as he listened to the tropical rain?

Not surprisingly, inside that cheap, sordid Papeete hotel room where I couldn't write, I was overwhelmed by a fear of personal disintegration. I became convinced that if I took a rusty freighter to the Marquesas to write about Gauguin's final years, I'd never return home alive. Rather than follow Gauguin to his island, I decided I'd had enough. So, at great financial loss and psychological risk, I flew back to Canada, a coward. And up in our garret apartment, in an inspired bout of shame, guilt, and desire, I feverishly hammered out the first draft of *Tender Only to One* on an ancient Underwood portable typewriter. Instead of being a book about Gauguin's escape to the South Seas, it became a collection of linked stories, miniature "paintings," about doomed romantics, a fugue on the theme of isolation dealing with Gauguin, van Gogh, Claude Monet, Edgar Degas, Pierre Bonnard, Emil Nolde, and Robert Louis Stevenson.

Now, sixteen years later, I'm once again in the South Seas—a semi-lapsed househusband, wood sculptor, and born-again surfer. An unrepentant beach bum, happily cast up on the shores of Byron Bay, obsessed with the same old themes of my fallen hero. Except I'm in paradise with my wife and two girls. And I'm alive.

Gauguin oiled the evolutionary cycle of unconventional white bohemian eccentricity, utopianism, and back-to-the-earth hippiedom. As a former blue-collar whaling town complete with a talc mine and a nasty abattoir, Byron Bay is only a recent paradise. In the late 1960s the town was reinvented by star-crossed, stoned Aquarians, surf mystics, and urban dropouts who flocked here for a no-holds-barred Aquarius Festival, and stayed. Today Byron Bay thrives on a palpable magic and its unmistakable physical beauty. There's a rag-and-bone tribe of New Age beach bums, writers, artists, dancers, surfers, unorthodox yoga instructors, massage therapists, chiropractors, mediums, osteopaths, marriage counsellors, tarot-card readers, drifters, musicians, dreamers, jugglers, ferals, actors, swimmers, losers, and winners all trying to play out the dramas of their rampant egos, reenacting the ancient Gauguin myth of finding themselves in heaven on earth.

Byron Bay is located on the most easterly point of Australia at about three o'clock. It's only a fifteen-minute drive from the more conventional, family-oriented town of Lennox Head where we live and I try to write. I've told friends in Canada that Byron Bay is as uncomplicated and undeveloped as Hawaii or California in the 1960s. With a population of three thousand and a couple of thousand transients at any given time, it's touted as having the alternative lifestyle—the unplugged, wild, dreamy, beautiful, inspired, sweet, rank, deluded, sublime, magic centre of the continent nation. Which is saying a hell of a lot.

Along eighteen miles of natural beaches there are no high-rises, commercial buildings, or even houses on the beach. Club Med, Pizza Hut, and Kentucky Fried Chicken have all been aggressively banned. So far Byron and Lennox have been uncompromising in their desire to remain unplastic. They don't want to be chained to the conformity of mega-malls and the Disney/McDonald's conglomerates of America. You can drive two hours up to the Gold Coast in Queensland below Brisbane to a place called Surfer's Paradise for the false glamour of ugly beachfront high-rises that actually shade the beach, glitzy casinos, over-the-top-whore-house-style restaurants, and embarrassingly priced tourist traps that cater mainly to the relentless swarms of Japanese tourists. Surfer's Paradise is a place where travel writer Pico Iyer once observed that nothing was missing except surfers and paradise.

Almost as soon as we arrived in Lennox Head I nipped into Byron Bay to visit the Byron Bay Community Centre Literary Institute, established in 1906. I figured I'd get a literary foothold in Australia by tacking up posters for a creative-writing workshop. My posters show a bare-chested, barefoot writer who could be me or Gauguin, sitting inspired at a type-writer under the shade of a lone palm tree on a tiny desert island. Unfortunately I discovered that the Literary Institute was only a com-munity centre, and that Byron Bay was the workshop capital of the world. Behind a desk, a long-haired, greasy waif smirked and said, "Go ahead, mate, put your little poster up if you can foind a spyce in that dog's breakfast on the walls."

Poor old Gauguin would be appalled by the number of people these days who are trying to find themselves. Could there really be this many messed-up people in paradise? Without a trace of irony, all of the walls were feathered with hundreds of solemn notices for workshops that offered spiritual growth and unorthodox solutions for and permission to wallow in every personal problem in the cosmos. On one uneven wall posters announced Arnold's Ballroom Dance Centre; Bali Mountain Retreat; Celestial Clairvoyant; Moonlight Tarot; Live Genuine Telephone Readings; A Cappella Singing Workshop for All Levels; Heart to Harp; Jive, Latin, and Irish Dancing; Deepak Chopra: Body, Mind, Soul, and Quantum Healing; Women's Drumming Group and Sacred Drum-Making Workshop; Direct from the U.S.A., Bodhi Avinasha, Author of *Jewel in the Lotus*; Samadhi Float Centre; Accelerated Learning Techniques Incorporating Juggling-Brain Gym and EK;The Gift, a Woman's Right to Herself, a Profound Three-Day Journey of Initiation into the Core of Feminine Being; Arise and Shine, the Clean Me Out Detoxification Program; Vibrational Healing Centre; Luxurious Aromatherapy, Facials, and Reflexology; Sandplay Therapy and

Support; Craniosacral Balancing with Svarup; Integrated Healing with Reiki Master Hiske Tas; Prenatal Yoga, Soma Yoga, Hatha Yoga; Kinesiology and Deep-Tissue Massage; Zen Shiatsu, Watsu Water Shiatsu; Hawaiian Lomi Lomi Massage, Thai Massage, Sensitive Massage; and Liquid Bodywork, Float, and Massage Two Hours, $40.

Then there were a few renegade posters advertising tree lopping, fencing, sewer choking, house painting, carpentry, mobile hairdressing, slashing and lawn mowing, and quick and easy rubbish removal. And finally one big hand-painted poster: QUIT YOUR JOB AND FOLLOW JESUS, LUKE 14:33.

Among all the other come-ons affixed to the walls I tacked up my equally improbable CREATIVE-WRITING WORKSHOP WITH CANADIAN NOVELIST AND SHORT-STORY WRITER RICHARD TAYLOR, then left to find the ocean at the end of the street so I could wash away a little of my burgeoning disenchantment. On the sidewalk on the way to the water I elbowed past wannabe hippies, slippery beachcombers, mystics, and sweaty ferals down from the hills surrounding Byron, dressed or undressed accordingly, some in animal-skin vests, billowing pantaloons, and Indian headdresses that sprouted feathers, bones, and fur. I came face-to-face with the glistening breasts of Amazons, and many of the other scantily clad females were stapled with nose, ear, navel, tongue, lip, eyebrow, and nipple rings and jewelled studs, some with silver chains connecting the various appendages. Humourless, blank-faced jocks and budget backpackers jostled with down-and-out druggies, evil skinheads, and creatures who looked like escaped extras from *The Road Warrior* or *Mad Max*. My head swivelled in dizzying wonder and disbelief at the flamboyant facsimiles of Long John Silver; the reject aliens from *Star Wars* and *Star Trek*; the clones of Scott and Zelda Fitzgerald, Gauguin, van Gogh, Henri Toulouse-Lautrec, Lord Byron, Percy Shelley, and John Keats; the extreme incarnations of Madonna; and the odd furtive slumming family sheepishly sipping herbal concoctions, wide-eyed and uncertain as to their status in the ebb and flow of so many wild characters.

As usual the mere sight of the endless turquoise sea and open sky overwhelmed me. Eagerly I tossed my clothes and backpack onto the sand and in my Speedo speared into the water. Breast-stroking out and ducking under the incoming waves, I swam into the swells until I got spooked by the idea of marauding sharks. Reluctantly I turned and por-poised back through the clean, six-foot shorebreak that could easily have ended my vertical existence. Trying to avoid a chiropractor's special, I bodysurfed more of the big waves until I was nearly whole again.

Once ashore, I retrieved my clothes and backpack, then ambled off barefoot, a carefree beach bum. Greedily I savoured the warm sunlight on my body as I half inspected topless women while looking at foot-prints in the sand. From time to time I picked up seashells, pocketing a few and carrying others, then tossing each one into the water for good luck. Eventually I found myself on a grassy outcropping above Main Beach at Byron. There, among other soul-searchers, I lay down and drank in the unbroken vista across an open bay of rolling waves. My eyes traced the sensual, womanly contours of the pristine coastline all the way to the distant outline of Mount Warning, which Captain Cook had christened while sailing past these treacherous reefs two hundred years earlier.

As I sat anonymously on my towel, marvelling at the miracle of such an unspoiled twelve-mile curve of beach in this day and age, a young man and woman, their hair still spiky with salt from the ocean, materi-alized on the edge of my vision. The pair gazed out at the azure waves, a surfboard upside down on the grass beside them. As the man reached over and gently took the woman's face in his hands, she closed her eyes and parted her lips, waiting for the kiss. He moved away, hesitated, then slowly returned, tenderly kissing each eyelid. His hands slid down her bare back, pulling her body a little closer, his lips exploring the inside nape of her lovely neck, where he found a soft down. She shivered at the touch of his hot breath against her skin, breathing herself through him for a moment before she returned the kiss. Now she was kissing him, as well, and ever so slightly began to caress the small of his back, the white tan line of bare skin just above his board shorts. And as they kissed, both lovers drifted to the grass, entwining their legs, attuned to each other's gathering desire.

I tore my eyes away for a quick look at the other people mesmerized by this epic kiss, the famous Byron view now forgotten, and thought about how, like paradise, these kisses were so rare, so potent, and needed the right time and place, the right frame of mind, and a certain personal freedom. Now the lovers were locked into a new version of the kiss that was much less tender, more urgent, as they rocked back and forth, erotic now, carried away in broad daylight on the open grass above Byron Bay before the majesty of the sea. All this was happening amid the gathering music of a ragged group of intense, quite possessed Aborigines beneath windblown trees, playing a dark, visceral rhythm of blood-and-bone-driven didgeridoos and drums akin to the increasing tempo of the kiss.

The lovers' accelerated rhythmic breathing paced them beautifully. They continued to kiss each other's face, neck, and shoulders, their hands working other geographies, the two soaring, eyes closed, within the confines of their own bursting Eden until, suddenly, they unclasped, toppled, and lay prone, arms and legs spread open to the sky, their mouths gulping fresh air. This was a kiss with the meaning and weight of a miracle, a kiss that rated with the best along the quays of Paris or the inner sanctums of a villa courtyard in Florence.

Finally, after the spectacle was over, I got to my feet, a little wasted myself, and stretched. Feeling pretty damn lyrical about everything, I looked out over the ocean and thought about Gauguin and the poetry of an ancient Aboriginal proverb: "Those who lose 'the dreaming' are lost." Even after witnessing such a kiss, I shuddered at the prospect of this natural coastline one day becoming a shimmering wall of Surfer's Paradise high-rises. And as I turned from the water, one of the Aborigines who had been playing music under the trees during the kiss began walking toward me slowly, carrying his long, primitive wooden didgeridoo. I was on a collision course with my very first Aborigine—a big, rust-bearded fellow with thick, coil-sprung, sun-bleached hair, a punched-in-the-face squint, and a wide, blunt nose chiselled from Ayers Rock. Noticing that my casual scrutiny had lasted too long, he grunted, "Did you fackin' lose somethin', white man?"

5
North-Coast Perfection

Today is Valentine's Day and in a week I'll turn forty-four, the same day George Harrison turns fifty-four. That used to seem pretty damn old to me, but lately my definition of old age has relaxed and undergone a few radical changes. I hope old George got lucky the way I did: two hand-made valentines from my sweet girls, and the promise of a long, slow Byron kiss tonight from Dale.

After school our nice-looking American friend, Denise, arrives with her daughter, Rhea, who is the first little friend Quinn made here. I met Denise and her Aussie husband, Bernie, at the end of January: we three adults stood delinquent outside the tiny school office like punished kids waiting to register our daughters in grade two. Shy and dying of loneliness, Quinn and Rhea hit it off right away. Bernie and Denise had just moved north up the coast from a hectic life in Sydney. After selling their house and getting out of the rat race of the real-estate game where they had worked as a team, they'd escaped up here for fun in the sun, empty beaches, and the promise of a laid-back country lifestyle. Every three weeks Bernie worked on an offshore oil rig in the Timor Sea. When he came home, he was free to play. Rhea was now in school all day, and Denise was taking some time off to find herself. Seemed like the perfect plan.

Early the next morning after we registered our girls, Bernie showed up at Stoneyhurst Manor with his surfboard and his Toyota pickup or "ute," for utility. He'd generously offered to take me under his wing and help me get back into surfing. I was relieved, given how much of a beating I'd already endured on my own on the reef.

Like me, Denise is at the desperate end of a long sabbatical. Now that our girls are in school our roles as caregivers have more or less dried up. For both of us and our nervous spouses, money and the employment issue are always there. Because I appear to be hanging out a lot myself, while Bernie is away Denise has started dropping by and hanging out with me. We swap recipes, supervise our quarrelsome, at times semi-vicious children, and talk books and writers because Denise has confessed that she's a closet writer and intends to take one of my writing workshops in Byron. But I have had to make it clear that if I don't spend the better part of my day writing, I'll never come up with another book. And I don't want people to get the wrong idea about Denise and me.

At the moment Bernie is out on a lonely oil rig on the Timor Sea with eighty other men. Poor Bernie has a tough time getting his head around the idea of my being a househusband. I'm sure the loose concept scares the hell out of a lot of chauvinistic Aussie men who still live under the illusion they'll rule their roosts with iron fists forever. A lot of week-ends I've stood beside them around their precious smoking barbies. They swill beer with their mates, overcook the expensive arse end of a cow until it resembles old leather upholstery, and think their lucky wives are liberated.

Still, there's something about driving like crazy along the bumpy coastal road to Byron with Bernie in his ute—our surfboards strapped on top, our bare arms resting on the rolled-down windows as we set out to do a little surfing. Sunlight dances before us on the open road, our old backs and butts bounce on the forgiving seats of his 4WD, the radio blares the classic Lynyrd Skynyrd song "Free Bird." Bernie drives way over the speed limit so we can catch the tide change and beat the wind that always blows out the surf at Wategos before 10:00 a.m. As the slow beginning of "Free Bird" gives way to the progressive, manic buildup of wailing guitars and out-of-control vocals, we calmly talk about why our daughters, who have been best friends outside school, are mortal enemies in school and have divided the girls in the school yard along the lines of their bitter feud.

But mostly Bernie is relieved to be home, on terra firma, and not way out on the lonely oil rig he manages three weeks on, three weeks off. Bernie grins and says in his rather thick Queenslander accent, "Oh, mate, it's hard to beloyve thet in two dies Oy'll be out on the rig agyn." From here he'll take a small plane up to Darwin then helicopter to his oil rig in the Timor Sea, where he'll work twelve to fourteen hours each day. And from my perspective, after spending the past decade almost exclusively with women and small children, I'm nearly out of my mind with gratitude to be able to surf with Bernie and take a break from laundry, weepy little girls, and my computer.

After a flat stretch through sugarcane fields and then low, rolling hills, we drive the winding, shaded road that cuts under the same rainforest arbour of Broken Head that I can see from my window at Stoneyhurst Manor. There's no traffic because it's the middle of a workday. Every time we go surfing, it feels as if we're the only two people not plugged into the system—two old fart surfer dudes at the bottom of the world. Absolutely free.

One of seven brothers, Bernie hails from a small town up in Queensland where he learned to nurture a sense of humour while doing hard work. He's what they call in Australia a good bloke—tough and efficient on the job managing nearly a hundred ocker and yobbo pirates, but a puppy dog with his mates and an unemployed househusband like me. Out in the surf he's a helpful, patient teacher who relishes watching me take nasty drops and loves to see me pull out before I get taken over the falls, shouting, "Whoa!" But he always goads me into bigger and better waves, yelling "Rick, get into that one!" as he flashes me his trademark white-toothed, wolf grin.

When Bernie turns onto the road between The Pass and Wategos, I'm already going nuts with anticipation; even through the trees I can feel the presence of the sea and sky. In the ten or fifteen seconds it takes to round the last corner above steep, treacherous cliffs, we suddenly take in all of that ocean, all that muscle of swell pushing up from the Antarctic, wrapping around the point at Little Wategos in a sweeping white wall that continues to break over Wategos Reef, then breaks again and again on the inside reefs. Tubular lines without a soul riding them. "Jesus, look at that, Bernie," I whisper as the smell of the sea floods into the open windows to meet our childlike gratitude. And for an instant suspended in time, as Bernie wheels the Toyota around the last sharp curve, we both gawk over the edge of the cliff at all that open water and surf peeling off in north-coast perfection.

With the flash of a conspiratorial grin, the beautiful, inevitable bastard I've come to know and appreciate says, "Looks like that outside break's working, old son."

"Our *Hawaii Five-O* wave."

"A rock-and-roll wave, mate."

"Just for us, lad."

We park the ute, unload, strip down, saddle up, then paddle out to where the biggest, hungriest predators like to cruise the deep edge of the Australian continent. But we don't care. We paddle out insanely far, up and down through lovely mile-long swells that lift us a couple of stories and haul us down until we disappear. Finally we take off on the biggest bloody wave you can imagine. And as we do our vertical drops, like the breaking wave in *Hawaii Five-O*, our hoots of joy can be heard all the way to Canada.

Even though Bernie lives half his life on rigs in the open sea, he always goes straight back into the water on a surfboard when he returns. Lately he's been accused of surfing too much with me when he gets off the rig instead of spending time with Denise, who whiles away a lot of hours with me when he's on the job. But so far no one's nose is really out of joint, except maybe the local gossips. Denise is tickled by the fact that I'm a househusband. I know Bernie thinks that staying at home for a decade to look after my kids was just a dodge, a slack bludger's trick. Denise, though, has pointed out to other women in Lennox that I can simultaneously speak about a ball-breaking surf session or the brief, tragic life of an obscure short-story writer, rave on about an easy Greek recipe for chicken cooked in brandy and cream, then comment on what colour of frilly top will suit what pair of pants for my girls.

At the moment Denise is reading things like *The Tibetan Book of the Living and the Dead*. Sixteen years ago Denise fled America to come to Australia for adventure and to begin a new life. Like many of the people we meet here, ourselves included, she journeyed to the bottom of the world to reinvent herself from who knows what dark former self. She married a true-blue Aussie and never expects to go back to America.

Out on our 100-yard verandah Dale talks with Denise and takes in our astonishing view of paradise while I get drinks and our girls and Rhea put on their swim togs. From the kitchen window I hear the kids leap into the pool, shouting and splashing. Our thirty-foot pool is surrounded by tall palms, frangipani, hibiscus, oleander, and explosions of flowers that cascade to the water's edge. Parrots swoop by and I can hear the sea.

Dale, Denise, and I sit on the verandah in front of this window where I write every day. In harsh sunlight we squint at our wild acreage with its towering pines and sea view. Dale explains to Denise that years earlier our exchangees planted two rows of one hundred small pine trees to mark and protect the boundaries of his turf. "Actually," I say, "the two hundred pines thrived so well, I'm sure they've helped out with the hole in the ozone. You can probably see them from orbiting satellites." Farther down the hillside at the foot of our property, the pines enclose a jungle of eucalyptus gums, wild lemon and lime trees, Norfolk pines, scrub, creepers, and a thousand lurking snakes.

Back inside the house I start to make a quick tray of killer nachos for everyone. Squeals of delight from Quinn, Sky, and Rhea pierce the air as their frisky bodies paddle through gurgling water. From out on the verandah I catch the womanly murmur of Dale and Denise above the constant sigh of the sea breeze. Nibbling on some Monterey Jack, I glance out over the trees to the ocean and shake my head at my sweet luck, happier than a kid at the beginning of summer.

As I dice green jalapeños for our side of the nachos, all of a sudden the air is filled with bloodcurdling screams. Then Dale and Denise begin shouting, so I rush out with my knife. To my horror, I see the girls being pursued in our swimming pool by a black snake. From the verandah we adults watch our girls barely manage to scramble out of the water before the snake reaches them. Half crying, half laughing, terrified and exhilarated, they run up the steep steps of the verandah to the safety of their mothers' arms. Then we all lean over the vine-tangled railing to gaze at the snake. My daughters, Rhea, Dale, and Denise are quite hysterical—arms and hands out of control, making choking sounds as though the snake that sizzles around the perimeter of the pool might actually end up down their throats.

While the snake whips and lashes through the water, Dale begs me to go over to Steve's place for help. So I stash my knife for the time being and in bare feet hotfoot through the snaky grass to Steve's. After we moved in next door and I announced my uncertain profession, Steve didn't miss a beat. Right away he claimed he, too, was a househusband. A professional sign maker who had left Sydney with his nest egg for the quality of a more simple, authentic life on the north coast, Steve works at home, and his wife is also a teacher. So far he's one of the most sensitive, hardworking, soulful guys I've met here. He's still one of the mates, though, but not at all macho and crude. Although he's a sort of stay-at-home dad and has school-age kids, I found out that twice a month he hires a pair of girls to clean his house. And he's reluctant to do laundry and says he wouldn't be caught dead hanging clothes on the line in case one of his mates pulls up in a ute.

Now, in response to our serpent emergency, Steve grabs his *Selected Snakes of South East Queensland* and we hurry back to the girls who are even more hysterical about our pretty black snake still slicing around the pool. According to the book, our boy is venomous and fairly deadly. For a split second in my mind I dive into the water to outrace the terrible viper, wrestle him like Johnny Weissmuller, Tarzaning the serpent with deep, plunging dagger thrusts before the awestruck eyes of the girls. At the last minute I decide against diving into the pool with a knife between my teeth. And, to make matters worse, I know from previous experience that Steve is more petrified of snakes than anyone on the verandah. The smell of Steve's slashed snake that I had to finish off and heave into the jungle still lingers at the bottom of our properties. Last year when Steve's poor wife, Sherry, opened their linen closet and came snout-to-snout with a large carpet snake, he had to call in a professional. But feeling the desire to save face, and being a cheap bastard, I'm not

54

about to pay a professional. So I decide there's no other choice: it's up to me to go *mano a mano* with the snake.

For protection Steve begs me to at least put on the pair of Wellingtons I've been wearing each day I work on this property. The rubber boots are part of the country squire uniform I've taken on at Stoneyhurst Manor. They make me look a little like Ian Anderson of Jethro Tull, marooned on a ridiculously ostentatious estate with an ambiguous new role, a nagging disenchantment, and absolutely nothing to do for the rest of my life. Shaking off this image, I pick up the long scoop I use to clean deadly spiders, hairy centipedes, and forefinger-size millipedes out of the pool and walk to the shimmering water. Part of me wants to run; another part recognizes that this is my moment of truth. In one efficient swish of the scoop I capture my puny adversary. Then, casually, I escort my friend to the bottom of the property and, in a gesture of fair play, flip him out of the net over the fence and into his jungle. From the verandah there is silence, no movement. Then I'm assaulted by a crescendo of loud applause from the girls—their hero for the moment.

Today I'm my daughters' only valentine. But down the road in a few years when Sky and Quinn are both ripe, wanton teenage girls, and then young women chased by other kinds of snakes, I'll be a spindly, balding bugger with all the status and respect of a broken rake. I'll be puttering around the garage, fussing with my old MGB, trying to be oblivious to the cocky young vipers who'll be ringing on the phone and arriving full of ulterior motives to sniff around my daughters.

6
Mr. Mom

Near the end of the summer of 1990 in the birthing room where Quinn was born, after I cut her umbilical cord with my bloody hands, I babbled in front of the doctors and nurses about how I'd be surrounded by beautiful women for the rest of my life. Hopelessly deluded, I thought, *Looking after a wife and two girls will be easy. No problem.*

All I could think was: no male threats. No conflict with a psychotic, ungrateful son, the son I was to my poor, forgiving dad who did a marvellous job coping with my bed-wetting in the 1950s when he dubbed me Wild Ricky Wet Bed Rides Again. He slogged it out as the manager of a finance company, calling people in the evenings to lean on them for loan payments. He endured my exploding puberty and long hair during the wide-open 1960s. More than thirty years later I can still recall his words when the Rolling Stones appeared on *The Ed Sullivan Show* one Sunday night like a dangerous nest of strange birds, "Don't they look like a nice bunch of girls," he said, smirking. "They won't last!" And in the unhinging 1970s, when many of my father and mother's friends' marriages seemed to be unravelling, I was drinking and going vegetarian, moody as Rasputin, listening to rock and roll, and pumping iron to bulk up into a suburban Tarzan who was unwilling to help out around our home because "housework" was my mother's job and would interfere with my workouts. Then, finally, I got zapped by love, was engaged to be married to my soulmate, and flew the coop so that my dad and I seemed to be through the worst of it together.

But nothing could have prepared me for what lay ahead: surrounded by beautiful women or, more accurately, overwhelmed by the opposite sex—a life of tens of thousands of man-hours doing the job of mother, social convener, maid, nurse, psychiatrist, short- and long-order cook, harried waiter, and mildly abused lad about the house within the confines of kitchens and laundry rooms, wading ankle-deep among Barbies, My Little Ponies, garish plastic toys, and so much bloody pink.

Among the carnage of Barbies littering our rec-room floor was poor Ken, his only companions a wonky-necked Aladdin and one other bland, naked son of a bitch. Barbie had the flashy pink convertible, a stable of horses, drawers of clothing and cupboards of accessories, a pink multifloored mansion with a pink-canopied bed, the fully loaded barbecue, sumptuous pink hot tub, thirty pairs of shoes, a windsurfer, a camper van, a sleek cabin cruiser, her own mountain bike, and a stately pink Edwardian place in the country.

I should have taken heed of the omen when I first noticed that poor Ken, who also had the self-esteem of an aardvark, was always lying around dejected and abandoned, with no accessories, no car, no house, no horse, no crowd of good-looking friends in the pink-doll-infested world of our rec room.

For our two girls Dale and I had built an enormous Barbie house the size of a kitchen counter. It was Mediterranean pink, with sky-blue windows and chalk-white walls—a villa painted like a seaside house we once lived in and loved on the Greek island of Samos. Except Barbie's house had wall-to-wall carpet, closets stuffed with frilly clothes, and jewellery. Four rooms were divided into two floors you entered via a pair of elegant French doors. All the rooms were filled with aggressively perky Barbies and their materialistic paraphernalia. Dale and I had constructed the house by hand, using all the talent and creativity a thwarted writer and artist could muster in the suburbs.

In the early years many of our girls' little friends would come in and work out their demons with their own Barbies, using the dollhouse as a kind of theatre of possibilities. Catholic girls would solemnly hold impromptu Communions; girls with Oriental or black Barbies or buck-skinned Pocahontases would conduct politically correct powwows before the open doors of our daughters' house. To no avail, boys would try to storm the walls with their secretly imported, politically incorrect, renegade GI Joes, Ninja Turtles, Mighty Morphin Power Rangers, wired spacemen, and demented aliens armed to the teeth with an assortment of impressive weapons. Quiet kids, like quiet kids in most situations, would simply sit like furniture in front of the TV rather than take on the Barbie house. And as our girls got older, Barbie and her uncontrollable brood were joined by Spice Girl hooker Barbies who would hold wild parties so that from time to time I'd steal downstairs, tentatively wade across the pink-strewn rec room, and discover poor naked Ken facedown on the floor beneath the tall pink closed doors of the Barbie house.

I don't want to fool anyone. Days at Stoneyhurst Manor above the Coral Sea aren't much different than those at home in suburban Canada. They aren't all hugs and kisses. Today is just another typical early-morning pink apocalypse. Right after I feed Dale toast and a fresh-off-the-tree papaya/banana shake and carefully kiss her off to work with her brief-case in hand, both my girls begin squeezing the life out of each other as though they're in a barroom brawl. Sky has on a pair of pink socks that Quinn claims are hers. And for the life of me I don't know who owns the damn socks because the blue and pink dots we labelled them with have been worn off by the too-diligent work of the sleepy laundry guy.

It's 8:25 a.m., and I have to leave the house by 8:30 to walk uphill with my daughters to catch their school bus. I'm in no mood for a quandary about a pair of pink socks that constitute the only possible swerve in the fascist grey Australian school uniform my Canadian girls can't totally conform to. My first mistake is to yell at Quinn to be reason-able. "Please just get another pair *now!*" I roar, and she starts to cry even louder, which has the opposite effect on me but usually works miracles for Quinn. She only wants the pink ones Sky has on—because they're Sky's, of course. And Sky knows her little sister desires them more than anything on the planet. She's all but trembling at the thought of being empowered over her little sister. But Sky is also so full of teary-eyed, accumulated, jealous bitterness from other imagined atrocities and poorly negotiated squabbles I may or may not have resolved in the past that nothing short of a hefty cash settlement will ever get those pink socks of Sky's anywhere near the pink-nail-polished feet of her darling younger sister.

So I dash into Quinn's bedroom closet because, in most of the older Australian bedrooms, there are no drawers, only open shelves in the closets that aren't the best organizers for little girls who are scatterly disorganized. My second, fatal mistake is when I pull out another pair of slightly less pink socks and, for good measure, green and white ones, then lay them out on Quinn's bed in a tantalizing display for her to select.

With only a minute to go and absolutely no idea what to do to speed Quinn along, I've reached the critical mark of the morning. Aside from choosing a pair of socks, Quinn still has to brush her teeth, slap on sunscreen, and lace her shoes. If I don't hurry my girls to their bus stop in time, I won't be able to go for an early surf before it gets blown out, then return to write in unencumbered bliss for the rest of the day. If I'm unable to move them out the door, I may face the unthinkable: the possibility they'll think they can stay home to write and frolic in the ocean all day "just like Dad."

Wearing the pink socks, Sky finally leaves to walk ahead along Stoneyhurst Lane, with its staggering view down to the sea. From experience I know Sky will lean over a fence to feed handfuls of long, sweet grass to the gentle horses standing beneath the palm trees. But she's only loitering, waiting for me to accompany her the rest of the way down a road patrolled by crocodile lizards and covered in dead, flattened cane toads the size of huge, ragged leather gloves. She'd never go alone up the steep hill under the Sherwood Forest canopy of trees no doubt filled with poisonous spiders and too many venomous snakes. Ever since a good neighbour told us about the ten-foot-long diamond python crossing this very lane, my girls have refused to walk to or from the bus stop without their fearless dad. But even before Quinn refuses *any* of the socks I've set before her, I've lost it. In fact, I'm caught up in the all-consuming fury of a full-on adult tantrum, sitting on the edge of her bed among the fine selection of tiny socks, doing my version of the Elephant Man's weeping and gnashing of teeth.

So, later you can imagine what a revelation it is to have the laundry washed and flapping brightly on the line, with everyone hugged and kissed, well loved, and bundled off to school, each lunch bag carefully tucked into the correct little backpack, while I paddle into a glassy swell a quarter mile out on a reef with the dazzling sun and so much holy ocean to myself.

Where I estimate my first wave will break, I turn until it sucks me back and I glide down its steep face. I arch myself, snap to my feet, half crouching, and cut left, riding high on the shoulder of the peeling wave, enjoying the sublime view along its glassy wall. And as the wave gets ready to close out, I shift all my weight and swerve hard over the lip until my board and I are airborne and free.

By the time I catch a number of glorious waves and sustain a severe beating on several others, I'm no longer alone. After my last hold-down, I feel as though I've lost a terrible fight in a washing machine. Tenderly I return to the outside of the lineup where the waves aren't breaking. I ease my aging carcass off my surfboard and flop backward in the water. With the heels of both feet resting on my board, arms outstretched, I float and look heavenward. Then I push my hands into the small of my back to give it a little chiropractic hyperextension, soothing the fourth and fifth vertebrae, which have been compressed by the drawbridging surf and too many years chasing, hoisting, piggybacking, and play-fighting with my girls. After executing this rather unorthodox but necessary aquatic self-adjustment, I spot a couple of unfriendly local surfers. They appear more like unshaven biker dudes rather than the mellow surfers, dreamers, and mystics I usually encounter here. They've been laughing, and now they're sneaking filthy glances in my direction after the Satanic one once again mouths, "Go fack yourself, mate."

On their way out they've no doubt scrutinized my lanky surfing style and have obviously enjoyed my spectacular wipeouts. Don't ask me why, but I decide to paddle over for a few words, wishing I had Big Bernie with me. "You know," I say, trying not to sound too sarcastic, "back where I come from in Canada, in the winter, we have a six-mile canal that's the longest skating rink in the world. Can you imagine what it would be like if you guys tried to skate six miles?" The stubby, potbellied one who, up close, I recognize as a tough brickie—bricklayer—in town actually seems to ponder the implications of what I've said. But the Satanic one remains unimpressed. He's beyond communicating with because, to him, I'm simply a foreigner who doesn't belong in *his* country enjoying *his* waves at one of *his* breaks. Years earlier his unfriendly, Anglo, sun-buggered ancestors may well have been among the whites who herded Aborigines to their deaths off cliffs into the sea. Even his surfboard with its wicked slashes, black iron cross, and grinning shark suits him perfectly. His flame-burnt, dried-out wrinkled face attests to a raw life in heat. He has one of those heads you want to push into a jar of cold cream. Of course, I don't mention any of this to him.

As I scan the lines of approaching swells on the horizon for my last wave, I decide Stubby and Satan's macho sensibilities will implode if I attempt any further Canadian geography lessons, comment on the merits of yoga classes, postpartum or postkindergarten depression support groups, or discuss what I plan to surprise my brood with for tonight's dinner. They'll have a fit if I try to sway their entrenched Aussie chauvinism anywhere near my domesticated, feminized worldview. But don't worry, I have something else in mind for these boys, something that will help bolster my newfound manhood.

In 1985 when I first began pushing a tiny-wheeled, squeaky stroller with Sky downtown in Ottawa's Glebe, I was pretty much on my own. Back then few men stayed at home to look after babies. Women friends, mothers from that time who are still my closest friends, tell me that when I arrived at the Tot Lot with Sky, I looked pretty damn unhinged, starved for sanity and adult conversation. Tall, blond, and frazzled, wearing a leather bomber jacket whose torn grenade pockets were armed with nippled bottles of leaky milk, disposable diapers, a slim blue plastic container of Wet Ones, a packed lunch for the day, and an extra soother, the popular joke was that the second soother was really for me.

Beneath an intense, hooded demeanour I was painfully enthusiastic, totally wired into the househusband trip. Women claimed I made the job seem fun, even glamorous. It was as though I was the first and only man on earth caring for a baby. Like a crazed junkie, I hung out on downtown street corners with my cuddly Sky and other bawling Winston Churchill–faced newborns and psycho toddlers shepherded by their severely overwrought mothers. Barefoot and shamelessly basking in the sun for hours shirtless, I chatted on the rim of sand-filled parks with saintly, breast-feeding women. Occasionally I sat in trendy cafés with Sky, who sometimes dozed in her stroller so I could neurotically leaf through a slick magazine, even if it was usually upside down. With Sky bundled Russian-style in a sled, only her furtive eyes exposed, I skated, pulling her six miles up and down the Rideau Canal. In summer I propped her up, helmeted in her bicycle seat, and jauntily explored the city, cruising along the canal and bike paths, park-hopping all over Ottawa.

I was so happy in my domestic bliss that I stopped writing, reading and, to a certain extent, thinking. With hands permanently strengthened from so many anxious hours squeezing homemade Play-Doh, I became what every caregiver must become for a time: selfless, an empty vessel at the beck and call of snarling emotional tyrants with runny noses and more energy than any mortal adult can ever hope to match.

The role demands absolute devotion if it is to be carried out properly. On one level it appears to give airtight security. You spend so much time with cute little human beings who break into laughter or song at the drop of a hat. You read hundreds of sugarcoated children's books, watch too much morally appropriate kids' TV and Disney movies, and hang around parks with ripe, nurturing women and small children who are all buying into cozy, safe, magical cocoons spun to ward off the hard, cruel world. I can attest that staying at home with kids helps one avoid the real world for a while. But facing that outside world again when caregiving is finished is quite another matter.

In suburbia when you're a man or a woman and you decide to remain home with a baby, you have two choices: keep to yourself, hide in the house, and slip out for a quick roll with your stroller, then scoot home and hide again; or do the social scene, hit the parks and sidewalks, stay there most of the day, meet the other mothers, and get right into it. Because the confines of a new town house in suburbia had become maddening at best, I opted for the latter. Although looking after Quinn changed me from a strong, silent, arrogant type into a veritable, loosey-goosey chatterbox, it was character-building.

Unfortunately most women are a little suspicious of a man who takes care of his kids. Is he out of work? Is he a loser? Is he a single parent? Did the real mother die, or just leave him? Does he have serious manhood issues? Is he a child molester? Most women nowadays don't remain home to look after their own kids, and their husbands certainly wouldn't survive full-time duty in the house. Women either embrace househusbands wholeheartedly or give them the cold shoulder, as if they're invisible or the scum of the earth for muscling in on their sacred turf. Even hired nannies and paid, listless caregivers who can be cruelly aloof and cliquish whenever a stressed-out father and his stroller arrive in their midst searching for a little adult solace, might mumble under their breath, "Here comes one of *them*."

Some women try to use you to make their husbands jealous, employing you as an exemplary man to rub in their husbands' noses, hoping to get them to toe the line around the house. A few come on to you. While living in Hong Kong in 1992, I noticed most of the spoiled Western women had Filipina amahs hired for $500 a month to look after their kids six days a week, twenty-four hours a day. One neglected pilot's wife came up to me and purred, "I've heard you do plumbing. Why don't you drop by sometime?"

In the bland Canadian suburbs of the early 1990s before the big food stores started pushing a gourmet's delight of specialty foods onto the masses, I began making innovative chocolate-chip cookies, orange-zest date squares, and cauliflower-size muffins of various textures and ingredients that women claimed were to die for. From scratch I also made hummus, babaghanoush, tzatziki, tabouli, and lots of pita bread with spicy Kalamata olives. Dale would arrive home from work and one of the women would yell from across the street, "Hey, Dale, you should have tasted the yummy cookies Rick baked today." Poor Dale would rush into the kitchen and visibly sag when she discovered all the cookies had been ravaged.

Often I'd be invited to one of the ladies' houses. Because I was a man at home spending inordinate amounts of time with so many women, things could get a little awkward. Over the years some men got a little nervous when they returned worn out from their offices to see a house-husband grazing their properties, crawling over their living-room floors to chase toddlers, or lounging on their children's plastic furniture drinking Kool-Aid out of their favourite beer mugs. But the worst situation a husband had to endure was coming home to find his wife eating the cookies I had baked. For some peculiar reason that caused more trouble than seeing a spouse's panties draped over my head or a bra strap hanging out of the corner of my mouth.

Even though I'm still happily, eternally married to an intelligent, beautiful woman who is the mother of my girls, mean-spirited gossip mongers from Australia to Honolulu, Ottawa, Auckland, and Hong Kong have always gotten sick pleasure spreading dirt about my bonking housewives. This idle chatter used to infuriate me—blame it on a *Bridges of Madison County* plague—but the reality of any married woman taking up with a sorry-assed, unsalaried househusband is downright absurd.

Women get together to let their kids play but mainly they meet to socialize, download worries, share knowledge about parenting, and subtly or not so subtly badmouth their missing husbands. Because I'm a man and a writer and have travelled a bit, back in those earlier days of house-husbanding I was often invited along as a semi-exotic guest, a mild diversion, something vaguely interesting to speculate about with other women at the end of the day. I moved a little furniture, watched the odd kid, was handed broken appliances to inspect until the ladies realized I wasn't what you'd call handy. But to tell the truth, I was so bloody lonely and isolated as a househusband in the suburbs that I hungered for the simple company of other adults.

Restless and desperate for a larger world, I used to spend more time on the streets than a bottom-feeding alcoholic. In every season, as the convoy of deadened commuters rolled out to work in the mornings and roared home late in the afternoons, I was out on the pavement with kids. I played hockey with yellow-and-red plastic sticks that were only three feet long. I instigated tag, Simple Simon, hide-and-seek. I organized catch with children who stood with their arms at their sides as the ball bounced off their foreheads or chests. I encouraged enough abstract expressionist paintings from kids to fill New York City's Museum of

Modern Art with completely new artwork. I chased Sky and then Quinn over people's lawns and inside garages, trampling through flower beds and backyard hedges, and up onto sundecks, apologizing to the startled residents as I dragged my wayward offspring back to my own turf. All over our front lawn I coordinated extravagant teddy bear and Barbie picnics on lacy blankets, complete with miniature plastic tea sets and severely over-handled food and tired drinks. I helped my children construct shameless ramshackle forts in our driveway, using cardboard boxes, contraband milk containers, old sheets, frayed blankets, wonky chairs, brooms, rakes—anything that would hold up a roof. In winter my daughters and I proudly executed monumental snow sculptures that somehow always ended up as phallic abominations that resembled a mélange of Loch Ness Monster, lop-eared llama, and Henry Moore creations.

In these social forays outside the house, and sometimes inside, as well, I'd pull my children off other kids, wince at teeth marks, fingernail impressions, stick welts, ball marks, rug burns, tricycle tread tracks, then deal with psychological wounds inflicted on neighbours' offspring incurred in the heat of sandbox or rec-room battles. In the perilous vacuum of suburbia I tried to interact with a few individuals who I'd have to describe as suffering from profoundly incurable cases of charisma bypass. Each day I waylaid the plump, cheerful postmistress, hoping to glean deeper levels about life, the weather, or even the mail. Purposefully I crossed paths with slippery door-to-door salesmen, inviting their insincere, breathless spiels. I even went as far as to strike up a conversation about God with a carload of stiff-suited Jehovah's Witnesses who arrived one day like the FBI, letting them have their way with me.

Before Sky was born I thought the ideal place to write was alone on an island. Not long after my first daughter's birth I realized the only place I'd be writing from was the exotic locale of our kitchen table with the unmistakable whiff of curry-filled diapers, my pockets stuffed with damp Kleenex, and my feet ankle-deep in plastic toys. With Sky either attached to my body or extremely close by, I was completely swallowed by an all-consuming, ferocious love. And for a long time who wouldn't be happy with that?

Because of our fear of home and children, men have been excluded from what many women call the most satisfying aspect of life. Like many foolish men, I once believed my life would end with children. I procrastinated through ten years of marriage before finding the courage to become a father. The deal was that if we had kids I'd stay at home, look after them, and write while Dale worked. In theory, if I became a househusband and jumped in up to my eyeballs, I'd be more connected to the process of parenthood and avoid the dilemma of changing into an unhappy, alienated breadwinner like so many of the tight-collared, doomed men of my dad's generation. And like many men, as soon as my own child was born, I was transformed by a deeper love than I had ever imagined. My secret longing to have a child was satisfied, and I redis-covered a strong need for play, spontaneous laughter, and pure joy. Suddenly the male image I had of myself was unbound, and I was free to be a person.

Due to the increasing demands of modern women, even men who work are obliged to help out much more with children than their own fathers were. Most fathers feel a similar release from maleness, but househusbands experience an even more dramatic change. John Lennon and John Irving romanticized the role of men at home with kids. Over the years many of the male caregivers I've met were shipwrecked at home because it solved an unemployment problem rather than a burning desire to nurture children. A lot of men threaten to stay at home because of a warped notion that looking after kids will be a cakewalk. But less than five percent actually follow through to be full-time caregivers. After only a hint of the realities of child rearing, almost all men actively seek employment to escape the home.

The few househusbands who do survive the initial shock of the long, brutal hours and never-ending work learn to appreciate the opportunity of spending more time with their children. Even though there is now a growing, albeit sheepish army of men pushing strollers, changing swollen diapers, and feeding babies in public, they exist in an uncertain limbo. They're caught between the acute insecurity of having no societal support, power, salary, or status, and discovering the life connectedness with others and the potent joy caregiving can bring. What begins as a last-ditch option often turns out to be something precious and extraordinary.

On a good day I own up to a lot of this. On a bad day I'm unavailable for polite comment. Basically, in our confused, accelerated society where women still shoulder the weight of almost every household, it's a rare and sacred privilege to be able to stay at home with your kids. With more than a decade under my belt, I've been taught by firsthand experience how to navigate tricky interpersonal waters, throw together an edible meal from the meanest scraps of leftovers, and get any stain out of the most viciously soiled laundry. And although at times being a househusband has put an awful rift between myself and other men, I can say with absolute conviction that I've been lucky. Who cares if I dangle one foot in the men's camp and the other in the women's? After all, I've had the chance to care for and love my children intensely. And they've loved and cared for me the same way. More important, though, I've discovered the heart of what women have always known and men have been afraid to find out. For better or worse, it's never over, because I now realize this is only the beginning of the eternal mystery that leads to and from the heart.

Already a southerly is getting into the swell. Soon the surf will be completely blown out. I haven't exactly made househusbands or ice skaters out of Stubby and Satan, but my spiel has shut them up and I feel a little better. Hell, we're straddling our boards in the middle of the ocean on a great day with waves tumbling in and not a shark fin in sight. What more can a surfer ask for? Apparently a lot more! So, to get back a little dignity, I decide to take the next swell, which proves to be the "wave of the day," and hope I don't piss off my new "friends" too much.

Silently rolling in from the horizon, the wave arrives big and clean, a half-mile long. When its upper lip begins to feather in the offshore wind, it finally breaks as large as a drive-in movie screen, and I paddle like mad to be in the right spot and do a vertical drop down its face. I carve back up along its shimmering wall, then find a sweet line, trimming the glassy inside tube with a fluid poetry of grace that is nothing less than sexual.

As the initial wave starts to close out, the whole tonnage of the Pacific sucks off the inside reef bottom and I execute another drop, riding again on a new, steep section of the same wave, looking down at a dark shoal of schooling fish silvering the water beneath my board, ghosting through, pursued by dolphins and phantom sharks. I surf, crouching low until the wave begins to run out of juice, then drop to my knees and stretch over my board and paddle like crazy, keeping in front of rushing water, belly riding in fast, holding on to the nose of my board like a kid as I enjoy a free ride all the way into the beach.

Finally, as I stand on the hard-packed sand with my board tucked under one arm, I scan the horizon until I spot Satan and Stubby hulking in the blown-out drop zone of the outer reef. They would have torn me to pieces like sharks if they knew I'm a candy-assed Ironing John who stays at home to look after two little girls. Those weather-toughened surf cowboys also wouldn't have coped well with the notion of my being a pansy writer who hasn't had a drink since 1973 and who's been married to the same woman for more than two decades. But there they are, childless and unloved, miserably hunched over their surfboards, waiting for the big one I've already stolen from under their noses.

7
God Save the Queen

All the horses are forlornly huddled against the sky beneath a single tree. Through shifting islands of clouds I watch a wall of rain arrive off the ocean that is barely visible in a creeping mist. The rain hammers on our tin roof with such ferocity that I think the house will lift off the ground.

I don't know if this is a good or bad sign. This morning after reading a Canadian publisher's rejection of my novel *Blue Mornings*, I simply slid the manuscript and the letter into the bottom drawer of my desk and decided to bake a cake.

I emptied all the cupboards to get rid of the latest wave of ants, wiped down the shelves, and put everything back inside. Then I did the dishes and cleaned up after making a luscious chocolate cake that, hopefully, doesn't have too many hidden ants. The cake is only slightly lopsided, with chocolate icing waves like the swells rolling into Wategos. Because of the intense, damp heat it has a pretty serious list to one side, so I've placed it in the fridge to surprise my girls when they return from school.

More and more we're feeling that this house we're in, which we love and cherish as though it were our own, is haunted by the Australian exchange couple. We now believe it might have been better if we hadn't met the couple here that one night at the end of December. The very first sour remarks about "all of our luggage" at the tiny Ballina airport when we arrived set the tone for that unfortunate encounter. And when we got into their house, the husband took me aside to say, "Oy neveh wanted to go on the exchynge in the fest playce. As of a week ago, Oy wasn't even bloody goin'." Then he turned and disappeared into the part of the house we were told we couldn't use.

In Ottawa we left our place spotlessly clean. Beside a bottle of red wine was a five-page letter describing all the quirks our house and appliances have and where to get help or information on just about anything in town. In retrospect we might have left the place too tidy and pared down, especially since our nearly new house in suburbia in the dead of winter is so different than this idyllic setup in Australia. Still, we left food in the fridge, a Canadian calendar on the wall, an unopened package of queen-size sheets, and a new set of towels for the master bedroom. Our friends and relatives were at the exchangees' disposal.

It's true our Aussie counterparts left this tropical paradise and landed in a howling twenty-five-below-zero snowstorm. They had no car, and the wife had to start teaching a couple of days later. The husband has no intention of working, and unless he fancies chopping a hole in three feet of ice in a frozen river or lake to fish, he won't have anything to do for another four months. We arrived in the zenith of summer, and Dale didn't have to begin teaching for a month. I'm the first to admit our modest town house in bland Barrhaven is a far cry from this rambling hillside retreat overlooking the Coral Sea, complete with swimming pool and rolling hills dotted with horses. Presumably our exchangees journeyed to the Northern Hemisphere to experience something of the other side of the world. They didn't attend a party our neighbours threw for them. They've shunned our friends and relatives, people I've avoided now and again myself over the years, but hopefully for different reasons.

I'm getting quite concerned, especially after the letter that arrived yesterday from our exchangees in Ottawa. They don't like our house, our neighbourhood, the students in Dale's grade five enriched class, the other teachers, the principal, winter, or Canadians. The letter states flat out they plan to break the agreement and return home early, which for us means the unthinkable: this paradise could be taken away from us.

In our minds questions begin to rise like spooked birds. Why, when it was such a complicated bureaucratic ordeal, did they apply for an exchange in the first place? Why, after so many years living here, do their neighbours not know them? Why is it that we hear nothing positive about their exchange?

After uprooting our two girls halfway through their school years, after paying for airline tickets to fly to the other side of the planet, after all this dreaming and planning for our year in Australia, it's impossible to visualize packing up and flying home with our tails between our legs. The letter arrogantly says they'll move back into their house and we'll have to stay in a caravan park until it's time to fly home early—in July instead of the end of December. We've since found out the housing agreement isn't binding, but the yearlong teaching contract is. Rather than tell them what they can do with their proposal, we merely write a diplomatic missive suggesting they try to enjoy the wonderful opportunities a teacher exchange in a foreign country offers. *Because we're staying.* We're not going to be railroaded out of paradise just yet.

So a certain amount of anxiety is building toward what I imagine, if I know human nature, will be an uncomfortable showdown. It wasn't the nasty curl of a lip, a lack of social graces, or even the algae-rimmed pool that cost me hundreds of dollars and a week's worth of elbow grease *African Queen*ing it to make it usable, but the fact they closed off a third of their house and said we had to stay out.

As I sit at this desk, if I turn my head to the right, I can look through the windows of two French doors and stare into the part of the house we're not supposed to use. The French doors are so close to me now that I can reach over and touch the glass. Beyond the glass is a big living room with a fireplace, a book-lined study, a sumptuous master bedroom, a bathroom, and a sauna.

From where I am I can either close my eyes and take in the roiling cinema of memories, or gaze straight ahead at my view of the ocean. Or I can turn and peer into the out-of-bounds section of the house. Not surprisingly, it bugs the hell out of me. Right now I'm studying a large handmade wooden rocking horse flanked by a tall wooden jockey whose startled painted eyes gawk back at me. Behind them a cabinet with a mirror reflects me looking at the sinister jockey and horse. Even when I'm in the kitchen, thirty yards across the length of this house, I see them through the glass. On the off-limits sofa there's a faded khaki explorer's hat, the kind from the days of Stanley and Livingstone's pompous British Empiring. A stern grandfather clock stands across from two bookcases filled with books that are taboo for us. The clock doesn't tell time because its pendulum is stationary, as though everything froze the day our exchangees left.

Naturally we go into the other part of the house whenever we get the chance. We were "instructed" to keep an eye on it, whatever that means, and so we use it to store some of the more objectionable artwork, personal memorabilia, and clunky antiques we can't live with. Several Aussie friends suggested that all the people our exchangees don't like should be assembled and bent over buck naked in the sauna we're not permitted to use. Then a group photograph should be taken and sent to our exchangees in Canada. But I declined, because although the sauna is roomy, it's not big enough to accommodate that many bodies. Also, to be fair, Dale and I would hate to receive a similar photo of our enemies in Ottawa.

In the part of the house we're "allowed" to live in there is an impressive, dusty library. The extensive literature section is alphabetical, categorized into general fiction, children's literature, poetry, and drama. Your basic Beowulf to Barbie collection. In nonfiction there is a wide range of practical subjects such as cabinet-making, sheep shearing, spear fishing, the seashore, surfing, scuba diving, judo, squash, geography, and enough history to give a pretty good overview of humanity's ardent struggle to move forward. In short, there are enough books for any eccentric to hole up for years in splendid isolation, which used to be the Australian way.

According to local mythology, our male exchangee buggered his back working on a building site, so he retired early to be a simple fisherman. He also makes impressive hand-carved rocking horses with real horsehair tails. His wife is a bookish teacher with a penchant for antiques and classical studies. They raised three fine daughters who have flown the coop. I'm guessing the exchange was an attempt to find some new pizzazz as they begin the long decline toward their sunset years.

It doesn't take much to imagine what complicated things raising three daughters will do to a couple. We only have two daughters, and we still have about twenty years before they're both on their own. Because we had kids ten years into our marriage, there will be no empty-nest syndrome for Dale and me. By the time Quinn and Sky leave, they'll simply walk out the door over our worn-out, dead bodies. If *our* kids were off on their own and we needed a year away from the family abode to reestablish the former glory of our relationship, a beige vinyl-sided town house in wintry Canada wouldn't likely be the ticket. Still, in their pre-exchange letter our Aussie counterparts mentioned they were keen campers with an interest in cultural pursuits. They have two months off in the summer to travel Europe. Toronto, Montreal, and New York City are nearby with all their cultural hoopla; they can ski in nearby mountains, skate on the longest rink in the world, and camp to their hearts' content in the lush primeval Canadian wilderness. Let's hope they/we will be able to work everything out. Let's hope it doesn't get too ugly. But I've got a bad feeling about this.

Besides, we can't be booted out of the country just yet, because now we've become pipsqueak foreign celebrities. A local surfer and editor of *The Northern Star* arrived with a humourless photographer dressed in black to do an interview and write an upbeat article about our teacher exchange: "Canadian Novelist Swaps Snow for Sunshine." The article also promoted my creative-writing workshops in Byron. My posters had disappeared in the flurry of hundreds of other workshops being hyped all over Byron, but the article's Canadian connection enticed a fair number of nostalgic North American expatriates.

As usual my writing workshop boasts a fascinating group of aspiring writers. I'm still licking my wounds after the rejection of *Blue Mornings* and feel like an utter charlatan in the midst of all these hopeful authors. You wouldn't know that, though, as I pontificate at the head of three wobbly card tables in a small Country Women's Auxiliary Hall in Byron under a large framed photograph of Queen Elizabeth II. A severe handwritten reprimand below Her Majesty's dour photograph says: DO NOT

REMOVE. Apparently, in the past, other people renting this hall have tried to remove the queen or turn her face to the wall. And some cheeky buggers even had the gall to take her down and fling her behind the building. But damn, she persists.

The motto of the CWA is: "honour queen, country, and other women," outdated sentiments for the hip, irreverent, wide-open alternative lifestyles of Byron Bay. The CWA was set up in the 1920s to support women in the days when they couldn't vote. In male chauvinistic Australia the only power women had was in the solidarity of their own downtrodden sex. These sturdy little brick halls still exist all over rural Australia, even at this so-called sophisticated end of the millennium in our obsessively computerized I-me-my-mine liberated society. Tonight I'm speaking passionately about writing, and I'm getting my old, burning confidence back simply by talking to these enthusiastic would-be scribes about the mysterious process of writing. One student, who is accompanied by her huge, panting black lab, has penned a serious exposé on Hare Krishna. Another, a smouldering, ponytailed surfer, intimates he really wants to get published, but only sort of wants to write. A tall, intensely antisocial man arrives in a sputtering dune buggy, climbs out half-dressed, opens a can of beans, and begins eating the contents with a bent spoon while he slouches on the side of his buggy and reads a newspaper. Still another neophyte is writing about his five-year exile as an English teacher in Japan and the recent freefall from an airplane he undertook to soar beyond fear all the way to euphoria. That man is also anxious to relate the complicated relationship with his new Japanese girlfriend and the terrible pain of sharing his beloved daughter with a psychotic ex-wife who lives twelve hours away in Sydney. A beautiful American who married an Aussie urgently desires feedback and encouragement on the manuscripts of children's books, short stories, and poetry that have been piling up so high around her over the years she can't see a way out. Deb, another American who's living here for a year with her husband, Dick, and their two kids, has written part of a self-help book on healing through imagery. Already she's intimated that Dick wants to get together with me for a little dawn patrol in the surf. Then there's the ageless sixty-year-old sweetheart I recruited when she was the foreperson on the crew that put in Steve's new swimming pool next door. She wants to write about her life working with men in Australia, then claims she loved every man she's ever toiled with, all the while gazing at the panting lab and wishing human males could be as easygoing, content, and docile as the dog that slumbers spread out on the floor. She also announces she had the honour decades earlier to attend university in Sydney with the famous Aussie expat Robert Hughes, whose *The Fatal Shore* spooked me those first nights at Stoneyhurst Manor.

After the writers give their biographical spiels, I jumpstart everyone with a surefire writing exercise. I tell them good writing is made up of memories, experience, and imagination and that writers should be aware of their senses. Then I ask them to stand, and we go outside for a silent stroll around the building's perimeter. As we walk, I urge them to think about this place and imagine the next five minutes will be the last in their lives. Look, listen, smell, touch, I say. Take everything in, savour these last moments. Back inside, after we sit for a few minutes bathed in our separate sensual reveries, I instruct them to write short pieces that occur in this setting from the point of view of a man or woman who has just fallen in love, or from the perspective of a person who has witnessed a murder or lost someone close, without mentioning the loved one or the murdered or lost people. Although this exercise can elicit savage, purple prose, it can also extract an unusual intensity of language, perception, and feeling.

In the stifling heat, as we write on the wobbly card tables in the darkened CWA hall, we can feel the Byronic night outside the open windows, smell the musty odour of young Queen Elizabeth's 1950s, which still seems to permeate this old place. Amid the reassuring chuffing of the dog asleep on the floor and the scratching of our pens and pencils on paper in our quest to retrieve the magic from our lost memories and wild imaginations, we can faintly hear the Mardi Gras night sounds of anarchist revellers in Byron.

While I sit with them, I let myself wander down another tangent away from the exercise and think about the hundreds of other aspiring writers I've taught since Hong Kong in 1992, and all the authors I look forward to coaching in the future. Then I scribble "hear us O Lord from heaven thy dwelling place," a prayer for every one of us, with our broken-backed novels, bittersweet confessional poems, thinly veiled family disclosures, wonky short stories, limp genre fiction, leaden trilogies, lost haikus, panting romances, titillating soft porn, hectoring nonfiction rants and raves against contemporary life, bright grocery lists, and dark epitaphs.

At the end of class a few handwritten lines from two Byron poems— "She Walks in Beauty" and *Childe Harold's Pilgrimage*—are given to me by the beautiful American with all the manuscripts. She tells me I won't be able to write my book without a nod of recognition to Lord Byron.

> She walks in beauty, like the night
>   Of cloudless climes and starry skies;
> And all that's best of dark and bright
>   Meet in her aspect and her eyes…
>
> And I have loved thee, Ocean! and my joy
> Of youthful sports was on thy breast to be
> Borne, like thy bubbles, onward: from a boy
> I wanton'd with thy breakers—they to me
> Were a delight; and if the freshening sea
> Made them a terror—'twas a pleasing fear,
> For I was as it were a child of thee,
> And trusted to thy billows far and near,
> And laid my hand upon thy mane—as I do here.

After the workshop, I drive from Byron Bay to Lennox in a fresh, biblical rain along the winding coastal road flooded with water. My car window is open as I listen to "Burning Beds" by the Aussie band Midnight Oil. Because most writing workshops aren't necessarily about getting published but about people communicating their private ideas with like-minded souls, I'm feeling an epic grandeur as I ponder the writing life, surfing, and the freedom of my time away from home at the bottom of the world.

I pick up Sky at the house of her Fleetwood Mac–inspired friend, Rhiannon, who also lives on Stoneyhurst. Dale has flown to Sydney for a conference, and Quinn has gone for a sleepover to the house of her best friend, Lahni. So it's just Sky and me. Sky has had her dad at home with her every moment since she was born, yet because we're father and daughter and belong to opposite sexes, already there's a widening barrier between us. I'm conscious of it more and more, especially when we hug or if I kiss her in public. The only time she's unguarded is when I sit on the edge of her bed at night to talk. Ever since she was a baby this sacred time has forged us into the best of friends because we can both speak freely and openly. For years, just before she fell asleep, I'd repeat magic words of reassurance like a prayer or mantra. I still say them to her on nights when she's nervous about something or too excited to sleep, whispering them before I kiss her good-night.

As I park the car above our house at the end of the road and turn off the headlights, it is absolutely black with only one light above the door. We rush down the creature-infested lawn, then scuttle along the scary brick walkway of the verandah and slip in through the front door. Stepping into this mysterious, spooky house, we flick on a lot more lights than we have to. I open the sliding glass doors to check if the swimming pool is overflowing with rainwater yet. Singing frogs, a million insects, and the booming sea fill the entire night as in some furious lighthouse tale by Robert Louis Stevenson. Sky is scared and misses her mother and sister. She wants to stay up for a midnight snack, watch TV, read a storybook out loud, talk about stuff, play cards, listen to loud rock and roll, walk around the house, and spend a lot more time with me. But it's already way past her bedtime.

Sky directs me to the counter to look at an ant in a bowl of water. She claims it reminds her of a lonely man swimming. What lonely man? I wonder. What body of water? Even though I've been waging a neurotic, mortal battle with tens of thousands of ants since we arrived in Australia, for some reason I let Sky talk me into rescuing this one. I lift the ant on my finger, gently enclose him in my hand, and release him into the black universe of the verandah.

Sky and I are both uneasy and excited about being in this house together because the house isn't ours and is located on a dead-end street on a dark hillside above the Pacific. The wind blows and rain thunders on the tin roof forcing us to shout comically at each other. We brush our teeth together in the mirror, and then Sky runs and dives into the bed where I sleep with Dale. Cuddled beneath the duvet with her trusty teddy bear, Puffy, she asks if she can sleep with me.

"No, honey, it's...no," I say, taking her by the hand to her own room.

I sit on the edge of her bed to give her a pep talk about her swim meet the next day—a fifty-metre freestyle race. "Stand on the platform. Visualize swimming down to touch the wall, do your flip turn, and swim back as fast as you can. If your goggles fall off, keep swimming and kick as hard as you can, because it'll be all over in less than forty seconds. Remember, take in one big breath, then exhale. Shake your arms and hands and legs to loosen up. Look straight down to the far end, and when the gun goes off, dive in and do exactly what you visualized. Only faster."

Then I kiss Sky's sweet, smooth forehead. "Night, honey." *Sleep safe forever*, I pray to myself.

"Daddy?"

"What?"

"Remember the words?" she prompts.

"Sometimes the coziest place in the whole world is your own little bed," I assure her. Then she rolls onto her tummy and I rub her back and sing "Four Strong Winds" and "Yellow Submarine" until she finally falls asleep.

Sky is only eleven and already I feel as if I'm losing the little elf I rediscovered the world with for so many years. Now, whenever I show up at school holding Quinn's hand, Sky is embarrassed and self-conscious. One morning at the outdoor assembly they have each day she turned and registered horror, then repugnance at the sight of her father stand-ing there with her little sister. It was as though I were some mooning loser at a school dance about to make the fatal mistake of walking across the room to ask her to dance. All of this transpired in a split second, after all my years of love and care and tenderness. I was hurt to the quick, knew I had lost something with her.

Even after eleven years of taking care of Sky like a mother, I'm being phased out of her life the same way Santa Claus, the Easter Bunny, and dolls were abandoned. Luckily Quinn is still keen to hold my hand any-where, anytime, but I guess I have no choice other than to accept this rift with Sky as a natural progression. I should probably use the extra slack on my leash to get on with my own life the way mothers have done since the beginning of time. Just let go and look back with fondness on the good old days of being everything for Sky.

Together in the morning we peel and break apart a banana, dropping the pieces into the blender, slash open a papaya we yanked off one of the trees in the jungle next door, scoop out the black seeds, and then dig out the soapy-smelling flesh. We dollop in thick Greek yogurt and a spoonful of wild honey and pour in milk. Sky insists we add liquid custard to make it a touch less healthy. I agree.

While she pops in two pieces of whole wheat into the toaster and I peanut-butter mine, she tells me about her dream of falling. We talk about how real it seems, how strange, when you have a dream like that: the freefall of flight and occasionally the sudden, surprising jolt of landing. Lying in bed half asleep, you wait in the aftermath of a terrible plunge that never really happens. I want to tell Sky that losing her is like dreaming about falling.

This morning I'm not as stressed as I usually am. I have the car, there's no school, no evil little sister for Sky to compete or bicker with, no nerve-frazzled mother getting ready for work. So we talk like old friends, which we are. I actually have time to listen to my daughter. She's a great kid and fun to be with. Sky gets away with a lot more when she's with me than she does around her mother. We both know that, and I'm well aware of her tendency to exploit me to the hilt whenever she wants something, but it's all aboveboard, hangs in the air so that we both know exactly how far she'll go and how far I'll let her. Only we never speak about it. Of course, I recall how I used to suck up to my own mom to get whatever I wanted. My mother surrendered to my wheedling for the same reasons I give into Sky: a combination of weakness in our characters and an unconscious desire to keep a close relationship. As the bread-winner, my dad felt he was left out of the connection my mom and I had. He felt he was being used. And for a while he was shamelessly—the old Oedipal shuffle.

Sky says she'd like to be excused from religion class. In the same breath she speaks about God, Jesus, and Abraham Lincoln. Like a lot of people, Sky has to be corrected about confusing the Bible and American politics. Suddenly the secular gaps in her life are beginning to manifest themselves. They're a frightening reminder to a confused, wishy-washy

atheist like me that there's a pretty big void out there if you don't structure a little corner of it for yourself to fit into. Maybe Dale and I should
have taken our girls to church, but I've always operated one foot in, one
foot out. I believe in a lot of things. I believe in people. I believe in the
healing qualities of love and water. I believe in biding my time until the
right moment and then going for it.

During my own school days, each of us was given a tiny, precious
Gideon's Bible by a solemn, grey-suited man who arrived in our class
like God's bureaucratic lackey. I brought my Bible home, wrote my
name inside the cover, and took to reading it—almost religiously—every
single night for a year. In red ink I underlined passages that seemed profound. It was my first bout with discipline and might or might not have
influenced me to become a writer and a long-distance swimmer. The
Bible's dramatic, lurid stories were gorgeous and scared the shit out of
me. It was a hell of a good read and made me feel part of something a
lot bigger than myself. At the time I probably even glowed with self-
righteousness. That was in the early 1960s when I was about the same
age Sky is now. I think I still held my mom's hand in public, but then
maybe I thought I was too cool and didn't. Perhaps I should ask Mom.
Maybe I should get on the phone right now, ask her how she's doing,
and thank her for everything.

It was the time of the early Beatles, John F. Kennedy's assassination,
the eve of the sexual revolution, before feminism had made its impact,
before the Vietnam War opened the doors to widespread cynicism and
corruption, before Tricky Dick and disco led to yuppies, preppies, rampant divorce, family counselling, doable day-care, political correctness,
channel surfing, and the Information Highway.

We used to stand in class to sing "God Save the Queen" and "O
Canada" and recite the Lord's Prayer. Most mothers were still at home,
and fathers took up the yoke of a mortgage and went to work for the
sake of the family. If there was even a television in the house, it only had
a few channels. To help explain things and keep us on the straight and
narrow, we had "God Save the Queen," "O Canada," and the Lord's
Prayer.

I was born in 1953, the year of Elizabeth II's coronation, and later
remember all the public images, the big paintings and photographs of

her when she looked bright, pretty, and optimistic. Today the shrunken old doll is distant, appalled, and disenchanted as she and her monarchy stand around with their pants at their ankles, pointing fingers at one another for all the hunting cameras.

What incredible mantras for children to follow—looking up at a photograph of the queen and singing in unison: "God save our gracious queen. Long live our noble queen. God save the queen…" Or, heads bowed together, doing the collective mumble of the Lord's Prayer: "Our Father who art in heaven hallowed be Thy name, Thy kingdom come, Thy will be done on earth as it is in heaven. Give us this day our daily bread and forgive us our trespasses as we forgive those who trespass against us. Lead us not into temptation, but deliver us from evil, for Thine is the kingdom, the power, and the glory, forever and ever, amen." Of course, a lot of us used to giggle, fart, or repeat favourite words in falsetto voices. Eventually, though, intoning the Lord's Prayer in every classroom across the land got too complicated thanks to the subversive revolt of rock and roll, the flood of other cultures, and the rise of so many splinter religions.

I once sang "O Canada" in the Mayfair Theatre, an Ottawa repertory cinema, with 150 souls. One young anarchist stood on his head a couple of rows down while everyone else stood in front of their seats looking forward in patriot love, strong and free and hopeful. But given our nation's faulty self-esteem, wonky dollar, English-French schizophrenia, and eternal inferiority toward America, "O Canada" sometimes seems more like a lament on people's lips, as in "Oh, no, Canada."

The last time I prayed among people was at my poor sister's funeral, a month before we came to Australia. A funeral in falling snow is too sad for words. I can't recall the last time I prayed alone. As for me and God, well, that still has to be worked out. Saved for a rainy day when the chips are down or I have no flesh-and-blood humans I can turn to.

Anyway, who in their right mind would go lightly into parenthood in an era so suspicious of God, a time of broken families, interpersonal McCarthyism, sex-role confusion, and environmental destruction?

All I can say about such dark moments of introspection is: Thank God for housework. Sometimes its simple metaphysics comforts me, helps me get past other nagging questions such as: What is the meaning of life? What would life have been like if I hadn't stayed home to be a househusband? What would Dale and I be like if we never had kids?

When I get back from hanging a good load on the clothesline, the sky opens up with fierce sunlight and I know the ocean is down there working the beach. Up here, now that the rain has stopped, the trees are filled with squabbling parrots and neurotic magpies. I'm in an Alice in Wonderland of butterflies. With this combination of thrashing wind and sunshine, my laundry will be dry in an hour. And for some ungodly reason a rogue line from a now-ancient Leonard Cohen poem comes to mind: "I lean illegally from locomotive windows."

8
Into the Drink with Lord Byron

A lot of people like to believe Byron Bay was named after Lord Byron, the Romantic poet, libertine, and open-water swimmer who died in 1824 at the age of thirty-six. All the Byronic swimmers, surfers, writers, travellers, artists, and romantics who converge on this most easterly point of Australia are looking for inspiration, searching for ways to free themselves enough to find out what makes them happy in a cranked-up world in too much of a hurry. Many who suffer from Byronism with its titanic assertion of the sensual freedom of the individual eventually seek their own version of a Paradise Lost in places like Bali, Goa, Maui, or Byron Bay. But, alas, Byron Bay was named by Captain Cook on his mapping voyage in the South Seas. When Cook saw this lonely, pristine cape, he dutifully named it after his boss, Admiral "Foulweather Jack" Byron, who was only one of the poet's watered-down forebears.

Lord Byron's masterpiece, *Don Juan*, is one of the longest poems in the English language and moves like a river. It opens with the line "I want a hero," then has the great flawed lover, Don Juan, improvisationally satirize many of the institutions, activities, and values of Western civilization as he travels. Byron's sexual appetites and flamboyant style of writing and living are better known than his aquatic genius. In Charles Sprawson's quirky *Haunts of the Black Masseur: The Swimmer as Hero*, I learned that the great Romantic was born with a contracted Achilles tendon. He surmounted the liability of a clubfoot by swimming. Water gave Byron complete freedom of movement, so he devoted most of his life to swimming whenever and wherever he could. "I delight in the sea and come out with a buoyancy of spirits I never feel on any other occasion," he wrote. "If I believed in the transmigration of souls, I should think I had been a merman in some former state of existence."

Byron seemed to cope with depression, writer's block, wanderlust, and romantic entanglements by swimming in lakes, rivers, and especially the sea. Aside from relieving stress, each swim fed his nostalgia for the classical waters of ancient Rome and Greece. Not the kind of swimmer who settled for a chlorinated pool, Byron swam the Dee and Don Rivers in Scotland, the Tagus estuary at Lisbon, the chilly sea off Genoa, the languid ponds of lush Italian and French villas, and the subterranean black meres of monks' abbeys. Just for the hell of it, he swam three miles down the Thames from Lambeth under the Westminster and Blackfriars Bridges. In Venice, Byron accepted a challenge with other rabid swimmers and started from the Lido and then did the entire length of the Grand Canal, stroking casually into his palace stairs after three hours and forty-five minutes in the drink. And he won. Byron is still associated with nocturnal dips in the Mediterranean—solo, ecstatic jaunts among the lagoons, coves, and cliff sides of Greek islands.

In 1810 Byron made his famous Hellespont swim in the narrow strait between Europe and Asia near Troy, with the hills of Gallipoli to the north. Here treacherous waters flow down from the Black Sea, sweeping any swimmer miles downstream and out into the open water of the Aegean. In *Hero and Leander*, an ancient myth retold by Christopher Marlowe, young Leander swims the Hellespont nightly to visit Hero, a priestess of the goddess Venus. One night in a storm he drowns making the attempt. Although Leander swam for love and Byron did so for glory, the poet managed to graft the ancient myth onto his own personal legend.

At the beginning of World War I, even a hundred years after Byron's death assisting the Greeks in their war of independence from the Turks, his inspired crossing of the Hellespont lived on through the ghosts of other swimmers, gods, kings, poets, and lovers. Byron had imparted swimming with a religious passion that offered freedom and heroism. In an age of clothed bodies the image of a swimmer in the water was a revelation.

In Gallipoli during World War I many Allied soldiers died at the hands of the Turks close to where Byron's Hellespont swim had reinvented the classical golden age. Gallipoli belongs to the Australians. Peter Weir's film of the same name chronicled the battle and gave actor Mel Gibson his golden passport to Hollywood. According to Sprawson, Gallipoli was a swimmers' battle; many of the soldiers swam to shore behind boats, engaged in a campaign to protect Attica from the Turks and invade the Ottoman Empire. Pinned down for months, the troops found a source of pleasure in the sea. Amid the carnage there were lulls on the beaches that recalled sojourns at seaside resorts. Photographs reveal Australian soldiers riding horses and swimming naked at the beaches near Gallipoli. Because of his reputation as an Olympic swimmer, the New Zealander Bernard Cyril Freyberg swam two miles along the shore in the duff at midnight to distract the Turks with flares he ignited on various shores. At the beginning of World War I, while it was still promoted as a romantic conflict, Byron's sensual heroics in life, art, and the water inspired a generation of smitten poet warriors who were slaughtered for upholding their ideals.

Like sex and travel, swimming raised Byron's spirits and satisfied the "craving void" he felt so often in the blaze of his short life. A wanderlust tinged with literary melancholy motivated the poet to write and swim, thus propelling the swimmer as romantic hero. Wherever Byron swam, it became sacred. Along the shores of the Gulf of La Spezia in Italy where the poet Shelley drowned, there was a cremation. As the flames engulfed his friend's body, Byron sought relief from his sorrow by diving into the sea and swimming two miles to his yacht offshore and back again to the funeral pyre. On the edge of these waters a plinth is dedicated to "Lord Byron, Noted English Swimmer and Poet."

Lord Byron never surfed or swam on the north coast of New South Wales, but the great Romantic should have been the namesake of Byron Bay. No matter; he would have loved this utopia. Each time I take solace from water I think of Byron because, as it was with him, swimming is my religion, physiotherapy, and psychotherapy. When I surf or swim, I'm back in the womb, plunging into my own mystery of water.

Whenever I'm not surfing, I swim at one of a dozen exquisite nearby beaches. These are better than world-class because most of them are only used by locals. The majority are remote, empty, and stunning in their beauty and variety. And they're as natural as in the days the Aborigines had them to themselves a mere two hundred years ago.

One of my favourite swims is the mile-and-a-half stretch from Wategos Beach to Main Beach at Byron Bay. I joined a group of enthusiastic water people known as the Stingray Ocean Swimmers, SOS, who swim year-round. The "club" has fifty people who call themselves non-members. This little joke was the result of a good-natured dig against a rival swimming organization called the Winter Whales, which has a selective membership, and from what I've seen, its members eat more than swim.

A handful of us in the SOS are sea devils who swim the fastest. We do it for the fleeting glory and despite the waves, the king tides, cyclones, jellyfish, and sharks. Our swim begins sharp at 8:00 a.m. each Saturday and Sunday. Briskly we walk from Main Beach along the tide line, confessing bizarre shark dreams to one another and speaking about love, money, cramps, mortgages, and other pre-aqueous chitchat.

Australians are famous for their sarcastic humour, colourful buggering of the English language, and happy-go-lucky outlook. They prefer Canadians to Americans and Brits, and they're easy to please if you refrain from showing them up. I've become friendly with one of the more irreverent members of Dale's motley Byron Bay High School English department. Phil is our most fearless swimmer. Perhaps his balls-out bravado stems from a recently collapsed marriage. He's practically the sole caretaker of two full-on boys who live with him in a bachelor abode that would likely improve with the right woman. Because Phil has a short neck, he's been nicknamed Turtle, or Turt, although he's also known as Sharky and Old Ironing Board Arse to his closet aquatic mates. Phil is extremely popular; everyone seems to like him. He revels in promoting a hard-drinking, party-animal facade that camouflages a more gentle, sensitive nature. The wandering outlaw of his own dark mind, Phil once proudly let Dale and me borrow a book of king and country, toil-on-the-soil poetry written by his grandfather. And like Lord Byron, myself, and most other serious swimmers, Phil uses water to hold his life together.

When I tell him I'll have to miss tomorrow's swim because of Sky's soccer game, he glances conspiratorially at a swimmer named Bob and whinges, "Mate, Oy reckon you gotta get your priorities straightened out. You gotta lay down the law at home." After we get to the beach at The Pass, we hike along a lush footpath that winds around the cliff tops and continues down toward Wategos Beach. The view as we stroll the narrow upper path is astonishing: miles of open sea, the cloud-wreathed peak of Cook's Mount Warning in the distance, the breaking surf peeling off in perfect tubes.

Ecstatic and a little scared, we assemble at the beach to begin in casual heats, slowest to fastest. An early wave of swimmers wearing goggles, fins, and snorkels duck-walks into the water and carefully folds under the crumpling shorebreak. They're followed by other groups every minute or so. Almost naked in skimpy Speedos and goggles, the last half dozen of us have to wait twelve minutes for everyone else to get a good head start. Bob's wife, who has just left him to take up with his mate, another swimmer, runs out and does a lovely, effortless dive under the waves. These three are always a little edgy, and I feel badly for Bob, who stands uneasily beside his new enemy. The consolation of being one of the fastest open-water swimmers doesn't seem enough to cheer up Bob.

Just before we leave, a woman who usually swims with us rushes up and says another swimmer was talking to a fisherman who said he caught two sharks this morning and *he* wouldn't swim across Byron Bay even if someone paid him. Phil laughs as the rest of us nervously look out across the water. "Bugga the fishermen and bugga the bloody shaks," Phil growls.

During the last couple of minutes before our heroic entry into the water, Phil always performs the same little ritual. He walks into the sea and carefully rinses his prescription goggles. Then he holds the lenses up to his eyes and squints across the open water as though the ocean weren't really fraught with peril but filled with treasure. Today when he walks back to join us he badmouths poor old Mother Teresa and Lady Di, then hops onto other members of the Royal Family and proceeds to soil each one in turn.

From our very first swim Phil took care of me. He brought me down to explore the local reefs, identifying everything good and bad in the water, desensitizing me to all its annoying horrors. Phil also introduced me to a few other open-water tricks such as how to swim with the muscle of the southerly swell that sweeps around Wategos and The Pass, how to negotiate the current in the calm gutters of big, churning waves. Mostly he taught me how to think: *Bugga the shaks, bugga the fear.*

Whenever you swim open water in the ocean, you always end up truly alone. Lying prone with your body and head half submerged in water, all you have is the sound of your own breathing, your own heartbeat, and the private confessional of your own fear.

As we wait to begin our long swim across the open bay, I consider my other fellow swimmers. Ian is an author and a Member of Parliament for the Green Party who was once famously photographed clutching the black prow of an American destroyer as he attempted to stop it from entering Sydney Harbour. Chris is probably the best all-round swimmer, and the oldest. Late middle-aged, he is also a wealthy doctor and president of our little nonclub. His wife, Robyn, who is an aspiring writer and nonswimmer, has a clipboard with all the start times, handicaps, and other vital statistics.

Together we gallop across the sand and start with a quick spear into the eight-foot shorebreak. Ducking under steep, rolling smashers, we swim along the ocean floor, our hands touching the wavy blond sand combed by ceaseless waves. Gradually our cluster elongates and breaks apart, and we each settle into our own long, introspective journeys.

Arm over arm, I realize how lucky I've been over the years, swimming and surfing in oceans around the world. But I've nearly exhausted the lakes and rivers back in Ontario and Quebec. And likewise the pools, swimming six miles a week with the Nepean Masters Swim Club. Winning gold and silver medals in the eight-hundred and fifteen-hundred-metre freestyles at the Provincials and Canadian Nationals is nothing compared to the freedom and exhilaration I'm experiencing now.

Below Cape Byron Lighthouse I swim in a deep trough between swells parallel to the shoreline, aiming for the outcropping of The Pass looming ahead, swimming out far enough so I don't get washed onto the rocks and thrown up like a slaughtered steer. Arm over arm, I keep an eye out for and am amazed by the breaking surf dotted with Neanderthal surfers. A pod of dolphins joins us, undulating steadily through the water around me. Arm over arm, I surge among tail-thrusting dolphins, thinking how much I really love this new life in Australia. Just outside the mad-dog surfers, I'm washed down the steep face of a wave with a pair of airborne dolphins, then suddenly we're buoyed on a mountain of water, still swimming toward the last section that will take me across the open bay, eyeing the tall Norfolk pines of Byron Bay at the end.

In open water, without many other swimmers and no dolphins, I must decide whether to take the inside line, following the natural contours of the bay. Psychologically it's seductive, but it can take longer because of the rip and breaking surf. Or I can swim out and find the straight-arrow line to the trees across the bay. Cursing Lord Byron and our obvious confusion about heroism, I decide to take the dramatic outside line, which means I'll get a better view of the outer reefs, though I'll be much more accessible to the hungry food chain working below.

I manage to settle into a long, comfortable rhythm, passing through a tennis court's worth of silvery fish, trusting their bigger cousins aren't smorgasbording somewhere nearby. Below, manta rays swoop beyond reach, and lumbering sea turtles slowly tilt to the bottom gloom of the reef. I dive and try to stroke the shelled back of a turtle, then realize I'm too deep and gaze upward, hoping I have enough air for the return trip. Arm over arm, arm over arm, I swim. On each breath, just above the waterline, I pivot my head and scan the ocean bottom with one eye while the other takes in the beach, the sweet, reassuring line of trees, the open sky. The end is still far off, and between breaths I continue my vigilant watch of the ocean floor twenty feet beneath me. I don't miss a single fish or shell, dearly hoping I won't encounter a great white the size of a limo, thinking there is a lot to be said for indoor pools, knowing all to well the dangers present here, my mind filled with the graphic details of recent human fatalities due to sharks. Arm over arm, I glide toward the tall pines, breathing now on my opposite side to site the black bulk of Julian Rocks, dwelling once more on shark logic. It's said that larger sharks prefer deeper water, and if schooling fish start acting erratically, you should leave the sea immediately. The same wise ones tell you not to panic when faced with a shark. Easy advice. Still, who really has the ability or nerve to eye-poke or jaw-punch a man-eater? Swimming in sharky waters, I believe, is a lot like life in general. But shark thoughts soon give way to speculations about myself in respect to the other swimmers: *Am I way ahead? Way behind? Way off-course?* Without interrupting my pace I lift my head to peek over the swell I'm on to see a lone swimmer. It's Bob, fifty yards to my left, taking a cozier inside route. I turn and spot another mate, probably Phil, twenty-five yards to my right, a little ahead of me but closer to the sharks of Julian Rocks. I drop my face back in the water and pick up the stroke, swimming hard with Lord Byron toward the pines and the red marker buoy I can't even see yet but know is bobbing somewhere ahead. As we swim, I worry, not about sharks or the unforgiving quarter-mile drawbridge of the shorebreak we'll soon bodysurf to the finish, but about my return to the structured rhythms of our life in Ottawa. How will I match this level of swimming, sustain this erotic, obsessive affinity with the sea? Will I ever be able to communicate the attractions of my other life in water?

9

General Advice on How to Avoid Shark Attack

You can't.

Even metaphorically speaking, sharks happen. No one is exempt. Sometimes it feels as if I have a whole litany of stories about sharks and laundry. Like most people, I've experienced shark attacks of one kind or another. That's why striving for an authentic life is so important. By authentic, I don't mean proper, conventional, or politically correct. I mean you should seek out and embrace the poetry in everyday life, because you never know what's around the next corner. Give little things the grandeur they deserve. Live it up while you've got the chance. For example, here at Stoneyhurst Manor we have no clothes dryer. Very few of our friends have dryers, even with all the tropical rain, the humidity of summer, and the impending winter of drizzle and fog. But there is romance in doing laundry here, especially hanging it up.

As I pull a load from the washing machine and throw it into an old wicker basket that could have come right out of our Brueghel painting, I can gaze straight over the ocean below. The open-air laundry room also overlooks our swimming pool and is at the end of the verandah overgrown with flowering bougainvillea, fruit trees, frangipani, and hibiscus that engulf the railing. Down wide steps I take my heavy basket of wet clothes and round the sunlit corner to the big drying rack attached to the side of the house. This is the same kind of tenement rack I fought with outside our high-rise window when we lived in Hong Kong, except this one I can stroll underneath to hang up the clothes. Already most of our duds have spots of rust from the clothesline. Corrosion thanks to the salt mists attacks zippers, rivets, anything with even a hint of metal. As everyone knows, like sharks, rust never sleeps.

This is the slow, meandering, sensual life I thought didn't exist anymore in the modern world, a calm, halcyon existence I believed I'd never have again. I run shirtless around here all the time in cutoffs and bare feet, a shell pendant on a leather thong around my neck. Because I'm not the same fearless nature boy I was in my youth, I yelp loudly whenever I'm hanging the laundry, imagining snakes and spiders in the long grass. Aggressive magpies swoop to spear centipedes and millipedes the size of fingers, their beaks tearing out yummy meat. The hill beyond the drying rack has a massive stand of trees sculpted by the sea wind, and beyond that are a series of disappearing hills that fade into the horizon of the hinterland.

I always feel like a million bucks when I'm hanging the wash. My beautiful, long-haired mother was only eighteen when I was born in 1953. In the brutal Ottawa winters of the 1950s and early 1960s she hung her laundry on days that could be twenty or even thirty below zero with wind-chill factors that would stun any Aussie. In the middle of winter every piece had to be clothes-pinned by hand to the line, strung out, then hauled back in frozen at the end of the day. Later my mom purchased aluminum pant and sock stretchers so that when the stiff wash was returned to the house the pants were stood against a wall or sometimes by themselves in the centre of a room, and presto, they were supposed to be dry and not need ironing.

For more than a decade I've done all our housework, except iron clothes, because I'm no Ironing John. Well, that's not quite accurate. I guess I've been badgered into ironing a hell of a lot more than I said I would. There's always a freaked-out daughter or wife who moans, "I'm late. I need this ironed right away. Oh, please, just this once..."

While humming along with smooth Perry Como or perky Doris Day, my mom used to iron carefully every shirt, pair of pants, dress, sock, piece of underwear, dishcloth, sheet, and pillowcase in the house. In 1959, when I was only six and Mom was twenty-four, I sensed even at that age a hint of loneliness tinged with longing in her, the same ache I've observed in myself more and more as I get older. It's a sadness Sky notices in me occasionally, then asks with deep concern, "Dad, are you angry with me?" I have to reassure her with a hug and pretend everything is peachy. I don't even have to close my eyes to see my mom and little sister, Jan, in our narrow yellow van Gogh kitchen as we listen to Doris Day singing the heart-wrenching words: "Will I be happy? Will I be sad? Here's what she said to me—*Que sera, sera,* whatever will be, will be, the future's not ours to see. *Que sera, sera.*"

Until the late 1960s Mom didn't have a clothes dryer. With raw hands she used a rough wooden scrub board and Sunlight soap and wrestled with a rattly old wringer washing machine. After the clothes were lugged around a big metal rinsing tub, she pulled the heavy, wet laundry from the washer and fed each piece into the rollers to squeeze out the excess water. Once, our neighbours' kid, Brian, let a finger get too close to the rollers. All of a sudden the machine gobbled his other fingers, his hand, and finally sharked the whole arm. Even forty years ago the sharks were out there looking for us. Over the years they've struck from time to time, the last being when my sister and nephew were taken in a house fire just a month before we came to live in this paradise.

But really, it's pointless to worry about shark attacks, especially while writing in this grand old house. Now the worst thing that can possibly happen to me is I might get knocked over by the butterflies flitting around the verandah. A heavenly light that emanates from the sunlit pool reflects off the tin ceiling of the old verandah and shimmers over the screen of my computer. Amazing. In this pastoral landscape I bask in the glow of light from the French Riviera. I'm smack dab in the middle of an Impressionist painting—man writing at laptop gazing out to sea, like a soft-edged, luminous Bonnard.

The other day, after I made lunch for Dale and the kids, I refereed my girls partway to their bus stop until we stopped to take a photograph of the tree-arched lane at the bottom of the road. I told my girls they should always remember the view because, after today, it would be gone forever. The lane reminds me of the French countryside in the Loire Valley or magic places in the south of England. Henderson Lane now has two signs: NO THROUGH ROAD and LAND SALE. But it should have a third: PARADISE LOST. We received a notice in the little mailbox at the top of our property where our green tree frog lives. It was a letter from Hammat Contractors Ltd. and said: "Dear Resident, we wish to advise you that we will be commencing work for Lennox Meadows Estate at Henderson Lane. The expected duration of the work is approximately sixteen weeks. We regret any inconvenience this may cause. Yours faithfully."

Hammat is going to build forty units in the valley that lies between this house and my view of Seven Mile Beach. Thankfully our property has a couple of shaggy acres of eucalyptus and the two rows of mammoth pines. Even now as a lepidopterist's dream of multicoloured butterflies float past my view, the surf rolls in, and the cicadas continue their mysterious, subliminal resonance, I can hear a small army of men assembling a half mile away. The remaining trees of the lane I photographed the other morning are going to be cut down. Our exchangees must have known this would be a good time to leave their house to Canadian tenants.

I hear the whining blades of whipper-snippers hacking at the ground cover. Other workers who follow are chain-sawing the big trees that will be fed into a voracious machine. This sleepy country lane was an enchantment to walk, especially early in the morning or just before dusk when renegade hares suddenly leaped by, snakes and lizards pulled back into the Disney gloom, and kookaburras, sea eagles, and parrots swooped in the trees whose branches formed a natural arbour below the great southern sky. The hillside now has forty FOR SALE signs, making the hill look like forty miniature drive-in movie theatres. People who buy these plots will have no sea view, no arboured lane to drive beneath. But each new property owner will have an intimate, unencumbered glimpse of their neighbours. It will be a tight little suburbia in the swamp, tucked into a boggy valley with uniform lawns and flapping clotheslines.

Rod, the elfin, weathered milkman who pulls up in his truck at the close of each day, claims this glorious meadow was once a sheep dip, a place where poison was applied to the mangy coats of sheep to protect them from disease. "Ground's too spongy," he says, sniffing. "Floods in the rains. And it's hotter than a breezeless hell in summer." Rod is a chatty, fifty-something guy who never fails to talk to me and my neighbour Steve on the dead end of Stoneyhurst. At exactly 5:00 p.m. he finishes his run and lingers to shoot the shit with us beside his truck. Although we all live on the ocean, Steve and Rod never go in the water, which I find curious. They've both mentioned issues with sharks and intimated that I must be daft to swim and surf each day in the open water. But then I've discovered that many people here love the proximity of the sea and the solace it provides, even though they never actually set foot in water. Rod looks out over Lennox Head and the sea below as though they're part of his private domain. His age and local status give him that right because he's lived and worked on dairy farms in these hills since he was a small boy. At one time after most of the area was already levelled by greedy woodcutters, there were more than three thousand dairy farms. Now there are fewer than a dozen.

Byron Bay used to be a bustling whaling town, but the trade was closed down in the early 1960s. Its grim abattoir dumped body parts into the bay and attracted marauding sharks that even to this day are blamed for fatal attacks. Now a mecca for alternative lifestyles, Byron exudes the aura of a counterculture hideout. Its lighthouse is famous on this rugged rainforest coastline. Byron's untouched natural beauty and perfect weather—thirty degrees in the summer and twenty degrees in the winter—and tropical current that allows swimming in the ocean year-round means too many people want to live here. But there are no jobs.

Like many people, Rod has survived by engaging in an odd assortment of careers. At the moment, instead of working on a dairy farm, he delivers milk seven days a week to put his two boys through high school and university. But he always has a twisted smile and is ready to gab no matter what else is happening in his hard life. The sound of his truck rattling along Stoneyhurst always brings my two girls running out of the house, because they like to give Rod the milk money. And even if they can't talk me into buying them a treat, Rod will often give them chocolate milk or a flavoured ice block. Yesterday his disgust at the tree-eating machine was barely contained. A slight working-class bitterness is sometimes just below the surface of his friendly banter. Before he left, Rod shook his head and swept his spindly arm across the horizon. "It'll all get bloody developed," he said with the finality of the voice of doom.

Instead of the sound of ocean waves, rustling leaves, and birdsong, I'm listening to a bone-crunching tree-eating machine. Our newfound paradise is being invaded and quite literally consumed. But my laundry is all hung out on the line. I ate the rest of a Greek salad from last night along with a nice butt end of French bread and washed everything down with a cold glass of guava nectar. I'm reading *The Lorax* on the verandah before I return to write, while the machine and its meaty crew of pot-bellied tree killers eat their lunch, no doubt under the ample shade of the gum trees they haven't gobbled yet.

The Lorax by Dr. Seuss is one of my kids' all-time favourite books. Published in 1971 at the apex of the antipollution drive that swept our planet, it tells the story of the Once-ler who lives in the far end of town where the Grickle-grass grows, lurking up in his Lerkim where he makes his own clothes out of miff-muffered moof. On special dank midnights in August the Lorax is lifted away to the days when the grass was still green and the pond was still wet and the clouds were still clean and the land was filled with the bright-coloured tufts of the Truffula Trees, mile after mile in the fresh morning breeze, with brown Bar-ba-loots frisking about as they played in the shade and ate Truffula Fruits.

All that ended when the Once-ler began cutting Truffula Trees and their soft tufts were knitted into Thneeds. The Lorax, a shortish, oldish, brownish little man, said, "I speak for the trees, for the trees have no tongues. What's that thing you've made out of my Truffula tuft?" The Once-ler then said, "This thing is a Thneed. A Thneed's a Fine-Something-That-All-People-Need..." In no time at all a factory was built and, oh, how the business did grow despite the Bar-ba-loots who played in the shade of the Truffula Trees that were all hacked down so there wasn't enough Truffula Fruit to go around and they all got crummies because they had no food in their tummies and had to leave to find food.

Even though the Once-ler was sad, he said, "But business is business! And business must grow regardless of crummies in tummies, you know."

And he began to bigger his factory. And biggered his roads. And biggered his loads. And biggered his money, which everyone needs.

When the Lorax returned, he sneezed and he snuffled. He snarggled. He sniffed. "Once-ler, you're making such smogulous smoke, your machines make Gluppity-Glupp and Schloppity-Schlop, which is glumping the pond where the humming fish hum."

But finally after the last Truffula Tree was cut the Once-ler said the word left by the Lorax seemed perfectly clear: *unless, unless someone cares a whole awful lot, nothing will ever get better*. And he tossed out the last Truffula seed, hoping the damage could be reversed.

Byron Bay is one of the most environmentally conscious places in Australia. It has vehemently banned fast-food chains and high-rises. Against the grain of progress, deluded Once-lers, Thneed needers, hungry tree-eating machines, developers, big corporations, galloping tourism, and greedy locals, the good people of this area are striving to preserve clean water, the remaining vestiges of rainforest, and the natural coastline.

Even though the tree-eating machine has started up again, I'm not going to let it or the idea of another shark attack get to me. Over the years because I've been at home looking after the kids, trying to write, and doing all the cooking, cleaning, and laundry, I also usually deal with the kids' teachers. Yesterday morning I had to speak with the principal about a meeting with Quinn's teacher.

Robyn, the principal, is a nice, soft-spoken middle-aged woman who swims with me and the other fearless chicken-shits of the Byron Bay Stingray Ocean Swimmers. Yesterday I reminded her that on my first swim with the club Phil took me out to the reef and sent me down to check out a six-foot shovelnose shark. Among the ruins of the old jetty and its sunken Liberty ship, the *Tasmania* (sunk in 1940 by a cyclone), he got me a little too close to a school of reef sharks. He told me the reefs were filled with sharks, dolphins, whales, sea turtles, manta rays, and thousands of shimmering fish.

I won't lie to you. Every time I surf or swim in the ocean sharks are on my mind. There's nothing better than being in the ocean, but there's nothing worse than the thought of getting taken by a two-thousand-pound predator with razor teeth, especially when you're a quarter mile out on a reef. And the more you're in the water, the more likely you'll have some kind of shark encounter. But given the choice between paddling alone to surf over a reef in the heaving Pacific and possibly meeting a shark, or taking on the phantom ennui of winter in a suburban town house, well, there really is no choice.

Only a few years before we arrived here, newlyweds by the name of Ford went in a dive boat to the reef past Julian Rocks a couple of miles straight out from Byron. According to one of the swimmers in my club, everyone in the boat pulled on their tanks, fitted their masks and mouthpieces, and dropped backward into the water. With great expectations they began their slow descent to the magical reef. Unfortunately a fifteen-foot great white made a beeline for the new bride. When the terrified groom swam between his bride and the huge shark, he was cut in half. The dive crew and other divers hustled the bride back up to the surface so they could clamber aboard the boat. Of course, the woman was completely hysterical. A week later her husband's head was found down the coast. The shark was caught by fishermen and dragged out bleeding to sea a few miles until it escaped, but not before it spat out a human torso. A few days later a helicopter pilot saw the shark drifting upside down.

Some years earlier a nineteen-year-old kid also named Ford was out surfing at Tallows Beach in a place ironically dubbed Cozy Corner, tucked beneath the headland of the Point Byron Lighthouse. A shark torpedoed up from the bottom and tried to take off his leg. Paddling for shore, the poor kid bled to death. For a while after the newlywed couple's tragedy, the cruel joke going around town was: "What did one shark say to the other shark? Have you tried a Ford lately?" At the moment none of the dive-boat crews will take out divers called Ford.

Last Sunday morning as we walked from Main Beach toward The Pass to begin our open-water swim, Robyn confessed she was having trouble sleeping Saturday nights before our long Sunday-morning swims. Sometimes when I'm in the ocean, unless I make a conscious effort, I think a lot about sharks. From time to time I even ruminated about them when I swam in the lakes and rivers in Canada. Most people believe there's something ominous in the water, and that scares the hell out of them.

At the meeting with Quinn's teacher, Jenny, and Robyn, I noticed

Robyn's neck and arms were still subtly pearled with tiny lacerations from the stingers of the school of jellyfish we'd swum through last Sunday. She wore them like a badge of heroism. In private she once admitted, "With fifty swimmers in the water the odds are fifty to one a shark won't take me. It's the victory of making it and beating the odds." Then, with a conspiratorial laugh, she added, "Rick, we must be out of our minds." Not exactly reassuring, I thought. At the same interview I felt the impressive tattooed swirls on my inner thigh all the way to my hip and across the front of my stomach—my own badge of courage. I didn't ask Robyn what scared her the most—the sharks, her teachers, her students, or their scrutinizing parents. My guess was that she swam in open water so she could face all the other fears in her life.

In 1988 while we were on our second trip around the world and living in Surfer's Paradise, two hours up the Queensland coast from Byron, I was out hanging my wash on the line as usual. Sky was two years old then, and we were in the doldrums of toilet training. I'd let her run around naked or in her undies, whip them off at the slightest hint from Sky, and then hold her over a toilet or a patch of grass behind a tree. As I put out the wash, I observed Sky make her way toward the swimming pool. My mouth was full of clothes-pins, and wet clothes were draped over my arms and shoulders. Sky bent down and crawled around the perimeter of the inviting pool. On our trip around the world that year I had just begun serious open-water swimming and had done many long solo swims in the Mediterranean and the Pacific with sharks.

Sky asked me if she could go into the water with her pink plastic ring from Seaworld. "As long as you stay in the shallow end," I mumbled, watching her slip the ring over her head. Sky leaped into the shallow end of the pool and floated inside her ring. With one foot and both arms she twirled herself as though she were going down a drain. She was a born fish, a true daughter of mine. Sky spun and spun, tossing her head back in ecstasy.

The line was sagging with the weight of our motley laundry, and I was running out of clothes-pins. To save pins I was masterfully attaching our underwear by looping it through the line. As Sky kicked with her legs, she slowly moved toward the deep end. I had a heavy pair of wet jeans, a fussy pair of eyelet curtains, and a thick pair of socks left to deal with, and only a short stretch of line. What I didn't notice was Sky leaning forward, then back. In an instant she slipped like a stone through her ring.

After I proudly attached the last sock with the last pin, I turned and spotted the empty Seaworld ring. The water in the pool wasn't even rippling. Heart-dead, I raced across the lawn and dived into the water. At the bottom of the pool I found Sky. She was smiling and holding her breath. I snatched her up and headed for the surface. When I pulled her out, she was still smiling.

Looking up into the lonely blue antipodean sky above our apartment building, I held her close, kissing her face and head all over. The clothes on the line were flapping nicely in a gentle sea breeze. The empty Seaworld ring nudged the side of the turquoise pool, and Sky said, "I love you, Daddy."

The year we lived in Hong Kong was shadowed by three fatal shark attacks and, toward the end, it was darkened by something much worse. We had a profoundly small Phillips washing machine in our apartment. It took forever to run through its cycle, even though the loads were the size of small tight-fisted pillows. When the machine spun, it shook and shimmied, romping out of its corner in the kitchen and hammering its way precariously close to the room where I was attempting to write the great Canadian novel. The astonishing floor-to-ceiling view outside our windows consisted of a vast expanse of ocean, the mountains, and the skyline of Hong Kong. Each morning a family arrived below our windows to fish. Because we were on the second floor and our building was on the edge of a cliff, my kids used to toss things out our windows, hitting the water. The warm South China Sea was green like pickle brine. Even with the windows closed, our apartment was always filled with the pungent salt smell of the sea and the sound of waves working against the rocks.

Dale was teaching at the Delia School of Canada while I taught creative writing a couple of evenings a week to expats who were mostly neglected pilots' wives. A writer friend named Margaret Dyment had mailed me her own precious copy of John Gardner's *The Art of Fiction* so I could teach myself to be a teacher. At the end of the first class one shy lady came up to me and asked, "Have you ever actually taught before?"

Quinn had turned two years old on the Cathay Pacific flight to Hong Kong. We lived in Discovery Bay on Lantau Island, thirty minutes away by ferry from the mighty engine of Hong Kong. During the day, Quinn and I were free to visit monasteries, primitive fishing villages, and Buddhist temples in the mountains. Most days we took the visually stunning ferry ride into Hong Kong, passing hundreds of boats and ships: junks, freighters, yachts, nuclear submarines, sampans, aircraft carriers, and ocean liners from around the world. For these sublime half-hour ferry rides over to Hong Kong I had a six-pack of miniature Robert Munsch children's books I used to fend off Quinn whenever she got unruly. Generally the Chinese of Hong Kong are famous for their disdain of Westerners, a kind of uncomfortable reverse racism. They refer to Westerners as *gweilos*, white ghosts. But they love children, and because I was always with Quinn, who usually rode on my shoulders, giving my tallness a surprising flourish with this adorable red-headed woodpecker smiling down at all the Chinese, I had total immunity from their displeasure.

The secondhand clothes dryer I bought and manhandled into a corner of our small apartment soon died, and we couldn't afford another one. So I was forced to use the dreaded clothesline outside our kitchen window. Most high-rises in Hong Kong had one of these frustrating contraptions with a rusty pulley system that worked a series of six short lines that could only accommodate half your laundry. They were hellishly back-breaking to load and unload because you had to lean the upper half of your contorted body out the window. First you had to reach out and peg your laundry, hauling on the pulley to run the clothes along the first line. The problem was that all the spit, dye, rain, bird shit, bean curd, snake soup, and dripping laundry from all the floors above found their way onto your laundry. The forty-degree heat and hundred-percent humidity in Hong Kong was so intense that clothes never felt dry. Overnight, green mould would velvet a leather belt, a shoe, or a purse left under the bed. In cool weather I hung our clothes inside the apartment on a rack and dried them beside the heater. In a few hours they were dry, stiff as the frozen pants my mom had taken off the line in our backyard in the 1950s.

The first shark attack happened at Silverstrand Beach, only a few blocks down from the expensive house on Clearwater Bay that our family friends, June and Don from Ottawa, had let us use when we first arrived in Hong Kong. Every morning for many years, for the sheer joy of a long, steady open-water swim, an elderly Chinese woman swam across the mouth of the bay until bad luck and her yin and yang collided with a killer shark. One hot morning, only a few months later, two brothers were fishing waist-deep in the water when one decided to go for a quick swim to cool off. He had his leg removed by a hungry shark and died in front of his uneaten, lucky brother. By the time the third person was taken, a tenacious, press-happy shark hunter from Australia was flown in to try to kill the shark. He believed a single shark was the culprit, enacting some warped kind of territorial imperative, a kind of shark logic. Each day the hunter's cocky photo appeared in all the papers, complete with a shark-tooth pendant around his neck. And so Hong Kong was caught up in the fierce grip of a real-life *Jaws* frenzy that set everyone on edge. Beaches were closed. Dragon-boat practices were cancelled. No one but fishermen, hard-core local swimmers, and foolish summer-starved Canadians ventured into the water.

Bilingual signs sporting ominous black fins were posted at all beaches: GENERAL ADVICE ON HOW TO AVOID SHARK ATTACKS. The signs warned: "Swimming is considered temporarily unsafe because there is a report of shark in Hong Kong waters. Do not swim when shark warning signal is hoisted. If possible, do not swim at dawn, at dusk, or at night. Do not swim alone. Do not swim if you are bleeding or have any open wounds. Stay in shallow water, as the larger sharks prefer deeper water. If schooling fish start to behave erratically or start to congregate in unusually large numbers, leave the water. If a shark is sighted in the area, leave the water as quickly and calmly as possible."

A day before the final shark attack Sky and I took a small ferry that chugged around Lantau, ending up at the fishing village of Mui Wo (Silvermine Bay). We took a double-decker bus to Cheung Sha Beach, a remote, two-mile beach whose mountains of waterfalls and blossoming flowers poured down to the sea. Sky was about seven, so we hiked a mile along the deserted beach, collecting shells and studying the low

Michelangelo sky of enormous thunderclouds that threatened to break above us. Off in the distance was China and the Pearl River delta. The gods had conspired to offer us fairly clean water and good surf. Perhaps I was a monstrous parent, but for an hour Sky and I tempted the shark god and the purpling thunderclouds of a nasty storm, putting all our faith in Neptune and our good karma as we speared in, turned, and bodysurfed waves back into the beach, screaming our heads off.

Even now while sitting amid my butterfly-filled view of the sea, I can't let myself think about that. It's much better to reflect on the first four years with Sky in Ottawa's Glebe when I hauled our dirty clothes to the laundromat because we were too poor to own a washer and dryer. I really enjoyed the half-dozen laundromats I haunted for years downtown before we became affluent and got ransomed by a suburban house with a painfully slow, accumulating equity.

Each laundromat had its own distinct location, ambience, shaggy notice boards, comfortable chairs, reading material, good machines and bad. Instead of doing the laundry every day as I do now, it was performed in a two- to three-hour jaunt once a week. After I got my four washers going, I could read a damp, soiled magazine while Sky foraged around the laundromat looking for something to do that was fairly honourable. In summer it was like Saigon, but I could often sit outside with my feet up and pleasantly read a good novel if I didn't have Sky in tow. In the winter, though, it would be so hot and claustrophobic with a storm howling outside that all the windows of the laundromat steamed up as though we were in a dryer ourselves.

In these laundromats I watched young couples experiment with domesticity, do their laundry together, chat as they folded their things into his and her backpacks, then stroll out hand in hand to play house. University kids crammed for exams or threw together essays as their entire shrinking wardrobe of grey laundry churned inside stuffed, red-hot dryers. Single moms who dragged along their gnarly offspring would sometimes look for respites between their half-dozen loads by lighting up cigarettes and trying not to give into the enormous unfairness of their lives. Men recently tossed out of their family homes muttered to themselves and painstakingly folded shirts, pants, and old socks. And the people who worked in the bowels of downtown laundromats—faces greasy from the steam and chemicals of dry cleaning, sick and tired of reluctantly giving out the same information and change for their noisy machines—seemed always to be taking out bunches of jangly keys to open fiery or cold dryers, or reaching up to their armpits into the mouths of washing machines filled with submerged clothes, as though they were thrusting their limbs into sharks to retrieve their own lives.

Just before we left the Glebe a new laundromat/restaurant called Wringers opened up. It was a hip place where you could sit at a bar, eat zucchini strips or an expensive wedge of mocha flan, sip a fancy drink, or pump back a few beers while watching TV. You could read slick magazines like *GQ, The New Yorker, Cosmopolitan, Rolling Stone,* or *Maclean's* in the company of other cool, urban sophisticates who acted as though they only incidentally had to deal with sharks and dirty laundry. Without the heat, discomfort, and sordid clientele of the shabbier laundromats, you could sit at a polished table or on a high bar stool and tastefully watch your laundry go round and round in your very own dryer. An outing at Wringers was a lot more expensive and maybe less interesting than the tenement-style laundromats, but as I Santa-Claused four bags of heavy laundry shamelessly back through the trendy streets of the Glebe toward our apartment, and Sky was rushing along to keep up with her dad, singing a tune she'd heard at the trendy laundromat, I thought that this wasn't a bad way to deal with dirty clothes.

In Lennox Head now, straddling my surfboard on the end of the reef above a deep-sea ledge I know sharks love to patrol, I go through the usual mental gymnastics. Is it really possible sharks can detect a single drop of blood from a couple of miles away? That their vision is seven times that of human beings? Or, in the tropics, you're about two hundred times more likely to take your own life than be taken by a shark? I used to think about sharks constantly. Now I enter the moment and realize where I am and what a gift it is to be in the ocean. What I really find myself in is a trance of such deep denial that I don't even give the *s* word a chance to grip my mind.

Australian waterman Mark Richards, four-time world surfing champion, once said he wouldn't surf Lennox Head anymore because of the sharks. Sometimes when I surf I ask anyone around who cares to listen, "Hey, has anyone seen one of Mark Richards's sharks?" Of course, the obvious argument for any surfer is that you stand a much better chance of getting killed, maimed, or chewed up while driving your car to go surfing, steering on your meagre side of a symbolic white line, a yard from other cars hurtling along at breakneck speed the other way. In fact, you're more likely to be struck by lightning, or die getting a piece of hot dog lodged in your throat so that you buy it while gagging for breath, cross-eyed and red-faced, then falling over dead into a pile of your own dirty laundry.

It can happen to anyone, anytime, anywhere. It's yer karma, man.

Deep in the heart of suburbia for five years I did a hell of a lot of laundry at our town house in Barrhaven. I had to do two big loads per day, or else I got so behind our life became apocalyptic. In colour-coordinated plastic baskets I carried the clothes down and put them into our big washing machine, then took them out and loaded the equally large dryer. I tossed in a small sheet of Bounce, turned the dial to thirty minutes, and headed off to write or do other housework. Just before they were dry, I whipped the clothes out gingerly and hung them right away to avoid ironing. They were usually a little damp, so I merrily draped everything all over the house, slum-landlord style, to save drying and ironing time and a little money, which drove Dale bonkers when she returned from work to find our house looking like a Bedouin tent after a massacre.

Unfortunately, because our laundry room in Barrhaven is behind a door in the basement's crowded furnace room, there are no windows, no swimming pools, no frozen yards, no open skies, no ocean or tropical birdsong, no poignant dramas of the human condition or sad refrains by Doris Day. And absolutely no possibility of a real shark attack.

I'm back in our Aussie house. In the distance enormous cotton clouds drift against the incoming surf. A lonely freighter and the white sail of a yacht disappear over the horizon. As usual the cows' heads are bowed and the magnificent horses stand silhouetted on the ridge. Casually I walk outside to check my laundry and breathe in a reassuring whiff of the sea. I brush a few of the really wet items with my hand and pull off some of the dryish ones, carrying them up and draping them over the verandah railing to dry in the sunlight. The pool is a jewel of shimmering, ravishing water.

Some days I sit on my surfboard and actually peer into the water to see if there are sharks. Like a fool, I look for them, half expecting one to arrive just for me. If people knew the vibe I was inadvertently giving out to draw sharks, I'd have every surfbreak to myself. Occasionally I see a school of fish moving beneath my board, an elongating mass as far as the eye can see, flashing silver in the light. And there are usually a dozen or so dolphins cruising around—dark, rippling shadows eating their way through these fish. Of course, the biggest myth of all is: if there are dolphins nearby, you're safe. From a great height in the sky kamikaze seabirds drop into the water, drilling for these schooling fish in a veritable Roman orgy with me as the uninvited guest. At these times I know there must be a lot of men in grey suits grinning below, waiting for sloppy seconds, gazing up at my feet and legs hanging turtlelike from my board. This food chain operates full-tilt while I sit in the middle trying out all the other shark clichés such as that their attacks are quite rare. My karma is fairly good. It couldn't happen to me; I'm a Canadian from the centre of the continent. Have I had such a complete enough life so far that I could be eaten by a shark now? And I'm always haunted by the bizarre memory of a funeral I attended in the late 1970s for my best friend Brent's father when, for some insane reason, I announced to everyone, "I'd be happy to die surfing a quarter mile out on a reef."

Sitting on my board on those days and squeezing my toes into fists, sensing the satisfying chiropractic toe-knuckle cracks, I realize: "My God, what a perfect signal for any marauding, even half-deaf shark." So, to be safe, I've asked all my Canadian and Australian friends to promise me one thing. If I ever get taken by a shark, please try to keep a straight face at the funeral. And help Dale and the girls with all the dirty laundry.

10
Hanging Ten

With my Byrning Spears surfboard tucked under one arm, I splash along the tide line in bare feet, staring at the morning glass. Little did I know when I quit surfing more than a decade ago to take up masters swimming, that one day, on the eve of a session of fairly hefty mid-life blues, I'd be delivered to a beach house on one of the tenth-ranked surf-breaks in the world.

As I continue lazily down Seven Mile Beach, I nod quick good-mornings to lonely old ladies in sun hats, and fishermen holding their rod tips in the air. Lovers kiss partially underwater, and retired couples amble in determined tandems as if they're outpacing time itself. From behind my sunglasses I offer silent good-mornings to the topless beauties stretched on their towels, some lying on one elbow and reading novels, their naked caramel backs sweeping down to bikinied bottoms, the other side of paradise.

A little farther on the beach is all but empty, the ocean an endless blue legend. As I sidestep the odd dead fish or pop a few bluebottle jellyfish, navigating around pearly seashells and starfish tangled in witchy sworls of seaweed left by the high tide, I feel alive to the core. Above, a sea eagle patiently circles the same spot in the ocean, getting ready to dive-bomb and take a fish. Behind rocks near a waving bank of seagrass, I stash my day pack, then unzip one of its side pockets to remove my Mr. Zogs Sex Wax. As I vigorously rub the sticky coconut wax back and forth across the deck of my surfboard for grip, it smells good enough to eat.

Out over the ocean, and parallel to shore, a straight line of five heroic pelicans flies low over the breaking waves, so elegant and noble in flight compared to their frumpy, put-out waddle onshore. But the waves are beckoning, so I rip open the Velcro and leash my ankle rope, yanking it to make sure it's tight and secure. *Lucky bastard*, I think, half expecting someone hot and bothered in uniform with a pen and clipboard in hand to struggle in shoes through the deep sand to haul me back to the tread-mill. Unperturbed, I eye a spot on the horizon where glassy swells break under a fluffy boudoir of clouds. This is it. I'm ready to rock and roll. Then, as though I'm spring-loaded, as though I've waited a lifetime for this, I run full gallop across the sand, timing it so that when the muscle of the swell oozes onto the beach, my board and I are airborne and we land on the full, high shoulder of the swell. On the outgoing surge of backwash I stroke out, paddling hard to avoid the dumping walls of the shorebreak, and then neatly slice through the gentle, rolling swells, picking my way through the breaking lines of surf to the outside sets just beyond the reef.

As I paddle out into the food chain, paced by a pod of dolphins who thread through the surf with me, I think that perhaps only a fool would venture out half-submerged on a thin fibreglass surfboard in the middle of the same ocean as *Carcharodon carcharias*, the underwater carnivore with the big fin and triangular teeth who can swim between forty and seventy knots.

Finally I sit up and straddle my board, taking in the coast and the impressive volcanic thrust of Lennox Head that seems to hook passing clouds near its summit. One day, I know, once I get a little more cocky and experienced, I'll have to surf over there at Lennox Point, infamous for building character and for character assassinations. But today in dazzling sunlight, floating alone on a benign turquoise sea, I feel rapture. I'm on top of the world and unbearably lucky.

Writer/surfer Matt Warshaw has written that surfers regularly find peace, beauty, solitude, and even God in the ocean. Now only a dozen other surfers are strung along the various breaks of Seven Mile Beach. Out on the horizon a mountainous set approaches, so I stretch over my board and paddle out to meet the first wave. I want to be in the right spot, where the wave rears back as the swell catches the reef bottom and breaks. I make it to a place where I can turn my board in a kind of aggressive submission and, as the wave sucks back, I paddle hard until I feel it take me. Quickly I stand, whooping for joy as I plunge, carving down the steep face of the wave. As the wave continues breaking right, I do a soul arch and groan with the deepest pleasure and amazement, cutting right, sweeping up and down until I find a nice high line where I crouch low, trimming the wave, my arms outstretched, letting time stand still, savouring the sacred moment of aquatic eternity for as long as possible inside the enormous curl, listening to the gurgle of water in my three fins, looking down along the steep curve of wall I'm riding, holding this poetry of fluid grace longer and longer until finally the wave begins to close out, runs out of juice, and I lean hard, slicing up and over the lip so that my board and I are airborne and we end up deep in the water, almost touching the hairy reef below. Right away I clamber back onto my board for another surf and paddle through incoming waves, my head down: safe, almost guilt-free, pure, unadulterated sex. Nothing like it.

When I was eighteen and living in Vancouver, I got the surfing bug after I saw and internalized the myth of *The Endless Summer*, Bruce Brown's classic 1960s documentary about the joy of two young surfers who search for the perfect wave while surfing around the world. In May 1972, after my first year at Simon Fraser University, when I pulled off a D plus average and a cautionary note that warned me I was officially on academic probation, I decided I had to go to Hawaii and surf. Or die. That whole summer of surfing in Hawaii changed my life and forever imprinted the metaphor of surfing as the ultimate pleasure. Every other summer had been spent at Norway Bay, fifty miles up the Ottawa River, where I first learned to love water, living like a wild Indian, as my parents and friends used to say, swimming, fishing, water-skiing, living for the water. In the summer of 1968 we moved from Ottawa to Vancouver for four years. There, in the California of Canada, I discovered real beaches, the ocean, nude swimming at Wreck Beach, Stanley Park, and diving off my best friend Bob McKnight's sailboat into the night sea of the vast outer harbour. I explored the pulp-log, driftwood-strewn beaches of Spanish Banks and Jericho and swam the romantic cliff-side coves of West Bay and Sandy Cove in West Vancouver. Not unlike the invisible narrator who reflects on eternal summer in Albert Camus's writings, I reclined with immortal friends, in my case Bri Rothwell, Dave Donaldson, Mark Baron, and Randy Trerise at Ambleside Beach, a ten-minute drive in my old Volkswagen from Handsworth High School in North Vancouver. Watching ocean liners and freighters slide under the great arch of Lions Gate Bridge, we drank beer and dried in the hot sun after cold swims in the sea, the smell of cocoa butter wafting off bikini-clad breasts and the sumptuous triangles of beautiful girls, dreaming of love, romance, and sex, with the music of Led Zeppelin, the Doors, Jimi Hendrix, the Beatles, the Stones, Steppenwolf, and The Who an avalanche heaven-sent to feed the hunger of my late-teenage soul.

Many people may never know what it's like to surf the big waves of an outer reef, but anyone who feels the need for nine holes of golf, a long swim, an outdoor skate, a shopping spree, a steady run, a day's fishing, or even one lone cigarette at the end of a trying day will know a little about what surfing can heal and transcend.

After surfing I feel young, strong, and confident—stoked to the max, as the Californian surfers used to chant. Since we arrived in Australia, I've been surfing, I'm almost ashamed to admit, sometimes twice a day. I'll even confess that I might prefer a good surf to anything else. Maybe I have the luxury of thinking that way because I've been married so long to a blond-haired Aphrodite I sleep with every night. But really, surfing is that seductive.

Without a doubt I'm one of the least elegant surfers on the north coast of New South Wales. But there are few surfers who love the waves, the freedom and the exhilaration of being out in the ocean the way I do. Perhaps, as a Canadian, I'm grateful for anything that sustains summer. The first few weeks I surfed here, before I was tutored by Bernie and Daffy and got hold of the proper equipment, I went out on a ratty, borrowed surfboard, a oversize T-shirt with Canada geese all over the front, a skimpy Speedo, and a bathing cap to protect my scalp of thinning hair from the brutal sun. Call me Ishmael, call me Queequeg, call me an idiot. A skinny Neptune, I paddled into the surf again for the first time in ten years. Even though I'd been a competitive masters swimmer since I quit surfing and figured I could handle myself in any water, I'd forgotten how insane it was to get into the lineup. In a changing tide the waves kept building, kept coming. I paddled out over the shallows, catching my hands on God knows what vile creatures on the reef bottom. I'd also forgotten that lying on your stomach with your back hyperextended, your neck straining up to look forward, paddling with your arms wide apart, the long muscles in your back tearing, you worry about damage. For a quarter mile, too, you dwell on shark logic and whether or not you're really up to a contest with the power of the ocean. As I paddled up and down the troughs, the waves got bigger and the effort to get through, under, over, or hammered by waves began to wear me out.

No local surfer would have been caught dead looking the way I did those first weeks in my Canadian surfer's get-up. Because the current had swept me north and out, my arduous paddle was substantially increased and I had to hump laboriously parallel to the shore to get back over to the cluster of waiting surfers. By the time I managed to flail my way to the outside so I could join them, I was so utterly wasted I lay on my board, panting.

The old Japanese proverb I have as an epigraph above my desk holds true for everyday life and writing as well as surfing: "Fall seven times, stand up eight."

On any given day of surfing there is the usual tribe of outlaws, loners, mystics, nice guys, and a lot more females than in the old days when I first tried the sport in Hawaii. Some wear Girls Rule surf vests and surf with as much edge and fluid artistry as the best of them. I belong with the well-behaved, older surfers on mellow longboards who meditatively straddle their equipment alone, taking in the scenery, trying to smell the roses, while the macho young thugs on short, high-performance thrusters shred waves and give us old farts the stink-eye for any real or imagined wave infractions. A lot of surfers these days are between the ages of thirty and seventy. I often wondered what these older surfers do, because they don't seem to have real jobs. They couldn't all be retired or on personal sabbaticals. They couldn't all be Canadian writers sneaking off for a quick surf. However, many older locals rearrange their relationships, their work schedules, their very existences around tide charts, weather reports, and cyclonic forecasts so that at any given moment of the day they can hit the water if the surf is pumping, because surfing has become the priority in their lives.

In many circles surfing is a dirty word. Like ski bums, beach bums, and skateboarders, surfers are associated with unruly adolescent behaviour by brain-deads who spout monosyllables. But surf-style beach culture has grown from a fringe subgroup of the 1950s and cottage industry of the 1960s to mainstream big business and has spawned billion-dollar industries that promote the modern extreme sports of skateboarding, snowboarding, windsurfing, bodyboarding, wakeboarding, bungee jumping, and tow-in surfing on twenty- to fifty-foot waves. Surfers have always expressed themselves by what they do and wear. Surfing is a sport for enthusiasts who want to *do it* rather than *watch it*. Attitude is all. For me surfing, the oldest of the extreme sports, is still the sweetest and least complicated. It lets the surfer be at one with the ocean, penetrating the heart of nature's purest energy.

Surfing is outrageous, unreal, mind-blowing, dangerous, and addictive, but it's also, elegant, sexual, relaxing, and peaceful. Above all, it's subversive. The missionaries in Hawaii, where the ancient sport of kings began, considered surfing too hedonistic and a distraction from the pious duties of Christianity. Surfing was born many centuries ago in the South Pacific. Before the missionaries arrived, the sport was an obsession for the ancient Hawaiians, a national pastime that had social and religious significance. It encompassed ritual activities that began with the selection of a sacred koa tree from which a board was carved, and it progressed to legendary surfing contests in which royal chiefs would vie for honours. The Ali'i, or hereditary chiefly class, were celebrated as the best wave and board riders. In 1831 a British missionary, Ellis, observed that when there was a sudden run of good waves, daily tasks of farming, fishing, and tapa-making were left undone while an entire community—men, women, and children—enjoyed themselves in the rising surf and rushing water.

Captain Cook was the first European to observe surfing, and he recorded impassioned, even poetic observations in his journals about his unusual fascination with the freedom of surfers. He described surfing as "the most supreme pleasure" and compared its effects to those of listening to music. Here was a guy, the consummate seaman, who had sailed the Seven Seas to map most of the unknown regions of the world, yet the poor guy couldn't even swim, let alone enjoy the physical and spiritual allure of riding waves.

Unfortunately Cook's visit spelled doom for most of the South Seas in the form of traders, missionaries, alcohol, disease, consumer goods, and wonky ideologies that followed in his wake. Like so many other integral activities woven into the religious and cultural fabric of Hawaiian civilization, surfing began to die out.

Ironically the sport may have been resurrected from under the blanket of missionary zeal by Jack London—American sailor, adventurer, socialist, gold prospector, alcoholic, and writer of the enduring, snow-flurried novels *White Fang* and *Call of the Wild*. Stressed to the max by their own mid-life blues, Jack London and his wife, Charmian, sailed out of San Francisco bound for the South Seas on their yacht, *The Snark*. In Honolulu Harbour they left their boat to camp on Waikiki Beach. At the turn of the century Waikiki was a long, pristine, empty beach, with the volcanic green-clad shoulder of Diamond Head jutting into the water in much the same way Lennox Head spears out into the Coral Sea here. London was brutally smitten by the surf bug and spent most of his time in the water surfing. He wrote an enthusiastic account in which he described surfing as "A Royal Sport for the Natural Kings of Earth." Surprisingly it appeared in October 1907 in *A Woman's Home Companion*, a national women's magazine. Then, in 1911, the article became an important chapter of his widely read travel book, *The Cruise of the Snark*. Words and photographs about the mystique of surfing in the islands spread to London's California, and surfing was jump-started into a craze that still captures the imaginations of even nonsurfers.

A year after London's piece was published the Outrigger Canoe Club was established in Waikiki to preserve surfing on boards and wave-riding in Hawaiian outrigger canoes. In 1911 the Hui Nalu (Surf Club) was officially organized to promote surfing among pure Hawaiians. The Paoa-Kahanamokus were a family of Hawaiian watermen who were members of Hui Nalu and lived in Waikiki. Among the five sons was Duke Kahanamoku, who later became one of the world's fastest swimmers and the grandfather of modern surfing. Duke wasn't from Hawaiian royalty, though his sterling character surpassed mere royalty. He was named after his father, who was called Duke in July 1869 when the duke of Edinburgh made a visit to the Hawaiian Islands. With the growing popularity of water sports in Waikiki, Duke and his brothers were employed as beach boys. They developed new boards and manoeuvres in surfing. In 1912 Duke went to California to demonstrate surfing and won a gold medal in the hundred-metre freestyle. His world record held until 1924 when Johnny Weissmuller nudged him out. "It took Tarzan to beat me," he used to say good-naturedly.

While the Allies in Europe, despite repeated bloody attacks and staggering loss of life, didn't gain more than a few miles at any point on the Western Front in World War I, Duke was in Australia showing the locals how to surf. The New South Wales Swimming Association had invited Duke to Sydney where he beat his own world record. In December 1914 the "Bronzed Islander" arrived at Freshwater Beach with a surfboard he had hand-carved out of local sugar pine. Most Australians thought riding waves on a board was a South Seas myth. But the beach soon filled with hundreds of skeptical spectators. Duke carried his heavy surfboard on one shoulder down the beach as if it were a coffin, ambled into the surf, and paddled through the breakers with a few locals swimming in his wake. Once he was beyond the outside sets he sat on his board and waited for the decisive moment, then easily paddled into a wave and stood, cutting diagonally across the breaker, riding the wave the entire length of the bay all the way into shore where he simply got to his feet and paddled back out to the amazement of the crowd on the beach. He proceeded to razzle-dazzle the assembled with everything from headstands on his board to tandem surfing with Isabel Letham, an eager local girl. And because of that one mythic day, surfing went on to become Australia's national pastime.

After the Great War, boards shrank and surfing spread from the Hawaiian Islands to California and Australia until World War II. Then, with the advent of fibreglass used for fighter planes, short, lighter boards were developed that revolutionized surfing around the world. In the late

1950s and early 1960s a tidal wave from Southern California beach culture and surfing movies like *Gidget, Beach Blanket Bingo, Ride the Wild Surf,* and *How to Stuff a Wild Bikini* rolled in with the beat and rhythm of Hawaiian steel guitar and groups such as Jan and Dean and the Beach Boys. Once the sport of Hawaiian kings, surfing became the anti-establishment pastime of lone gypsy drifters and soul-searchers until big business got hold of it and today the surfing metaphor is used to hype almost anything.

Here, in these Australian coastal towns and cities, surfing is so ingrained in the minds and activities of people that it can create a cultural vacuum that baffles nonsurfers. In Byron Bay surfing is even more all-consuming than hockey is in Canada or baseball is in America. The only activities I can think of that are as attractive, seductive, and potentially dangerous to one's health and relationships as surfing are maybe hard-core drinking and drugs. But for one glorious year I'm happy to let surfing swallow me whole.

Bob Dowling, my good neighbour down the street, generously let me borrow indefinitely his eight-foot-two Maddog. In the dark I walked home along Stoneyhurst from Bob's in a stunned euphoria of gratitude, looking across to the hinterland and down at the night sea, imagining what I would do on my new board.

Although Malibu surfboards can be more than twelve feet long, Bob's board is a mini-mal, a hybrid somewhere between a regular Malibu and a shortboard. Bob's mini-mal floats me better and makes for easier paddling, and I can catch almost any size of wave. My narrow six-foot Byrning Spears board, although very fast and light, makes me feel as if I'm screaming down a wave balanced on a pencil compared to the long, wide, forgiving Malibu.

When I start surfing again, I immediately got a few other hot accessories: Billabong board shorts instead of my up-the-butt-crack Speedos; an Ocean Earth surf cap instead of my masters swim cap to prevent the sun's rays from drilling deep into my scalp. The new cap also protects my ears and forehead and shields my eyes from the sun when I scan the horizon for waves. There's no denying that surf caps look goofy, and they're just starting to catch on here, especially with older, infirm surfers like me who don't have enough hair to protect the tops of their heads.

I have my new Creatures of Leisure leash around my ankle, and my short-sleeve Ultimate Rip Curl spring wetsuit that keeps my skinny torso warm and toasty and protects me from the sun. More important, it protects my ribs from getting bruised and my nipples from being ripped off by the wax on my surfboard. For the surface of my board I have Mr. Zogs Quick Humps Sex Wax ("guaranteed to be the best for your stick"). Quick Humps disappointingly smells like toothpaste or powdery baseball card bubble gum. I prefer the original Mr. Zogs Sex Wax because it smells like coconut, and every time I use it I get nostalgic for my old surfing days in Hawaii. The two local surf shops in Lennox, All Above Board and Beach Life Surf Centre, also sell Five Daughters extra sticky surf wax. A long time ago, as a young turk, I bought into all this Sex Wax stuff but now, as a father of two daughters, it only makes me more aware of what I'm up against: half the planet with their dicks like guns ready to take aim at my two girls.

And now that I appear to be buying into the whole adolescent macho game I've even acquired my first classic Mambo sports shirt. Among other things on the tag when I purchased this expensive Hawaiian surfer shirt was a peculiar credo:

This smart lifestyle garment is part of the Mambo range for the summer. This season we have devoted our energies to celebrating the entrepreneurial spirit of the great Australian Leisure Master whose philosophical guidance has inspired our vision and enthusiasm to create our own niche within the youth exploitation industry. Warning: we do not recommend you adopt the following principles of "freestyle" business management. However, we can point you toward good legal representation should you try.

- The Australian Leisure Master lives comfortably with no visible means of support.
- He has an office address registered to a Cinzano umbrella beside a half-empty pool in a two-star international hotel.
- He owns a clapped-out Charger but drives a late model two-door coupe registered to the twenty-three-year-old wife of a seventy-three-year-old bistro chain owner.
- He is most often seen in the company of deregistered solicitors, senior officials, jockeys, and English backpackers.

- He is registered in up to eight different Social Security offices at a time, under eight different names and occupations (movie producer, personal trainer, etc.).
- He has a tan in winter.
- He has never paid retail for anything.
- He is always available to help police with their inquiries.

So now I hit the surf in style. Even though it's raining and I'm shivering, as usual the anticipation is almost unbearable. The billowing weight of enormous storm clouds are a good sign, because the surf will continue to pick up with the wind from the storm out at sea pushing in a big swell. Fearlessly I wade over the smooth reef bottom, nimbly sidestepping holes, sea urchins, and razor-shelled rocks. Because it's an extremely low tide, halfway out to the break there is a vast sandbar, and suddenly I'm up and walking on water like a silly Jesus with a surfboard under his arm. Ahead, I still have to face the drawbridge; I can hear the thundering, brutal unforgiving sound of a half-mile wall of crumpling waves.

I'm hyped and pumped and ready to have a go, looking for the perfect wave. I study the relentless layers of eight- to ten-footers pounding the reef in front of me, standing on sand at the edge of a sandbar that waves in recent weeks have deposited over this part of the reef. *Incredible*, I think. *What an incredible life this is standing on a reef before the awesome power of the sea.* I don't want to be anywhere else. Without hesitation I punch through the first line of waves beyond the sandbar and paddle furiously to get outside, but am caught inside and take the full impact of a mountain of water. It sucks me up and wallops me down, drills me to the bottom, holds me under its turbulence long enough for me to realize I'm way out of my depth. No air. Blackness. My body mauled over the sandbar, poked and battered by the surfboard attached to my ankle. I know waves come in sets and that eventually there will be a momentary lull, but I've already taken too much water, my nose is filled with sand, and my eardrums have nearly exploded from the pressure of salt water and sand. With an instant head cold and a sinus headache and still underwater, I blandly think, *You've really done it this time.*

But I surface, and to avoid another beating on the sandbar, paddle like hell up the face of the next big wave, over the lip and down, looking ahead into the heaving water still coming. I continue to paddle until I finally power up and over the last wave in the set. Then, like a miracle, there is a lull in the sets. Enormous, gentle swells roll in, lifting me and passing harmlessly under me so I can watch their humped leviathan backs move toward shore, breaking in farther on the reef in a thunderous roar until there is only silence.

The storm has passed. The rain has stopped. Clouds part, sunshine beams on the earth and sea, and I straddle my board in wonder, alone in the rippling swells with God.

11
We of the Never Never

If I'd died and was lounging in a comfortable chair high in the heavens, or trying to cool my backside in a hellishly hot place, or disembodied and lost in time and space, I'd look back on my life and remember all the kids' parks where I'd whiled away so many happy hours with my girls. Playgrounds, no matter how dull and unimaginative their locales or play structures, are places of enchantment, the paradise of childhood dreams that even adults can sometimes plug into. Lord knows, I've dragged myself to the shimmering oasis of many playgrounds.

The other day I went up to the girls' bus stop early so I could have an unencumbered read en plein air and a swing at the little park above the hill that seems to overlook the entire country. In my hand was *On Water*, a lyrical meditation on water by Thomas Farber that I was rereading. I wasn't too afraid about my girls running across malicious vipers anymore on their way up and down Henderson Lane now that our charming roof of trees had been removed to widen our road for the new housing development. But now that trucks the size of houses wheeled around from North Creek Road and thundered down Henderson Lane, I was worried that some sun-parched, sweaty driver hunched over his steering wheel might not be paying enough attention to my kids going to and from their school bus.

As luck would have it, for the first time, I came face-to-face with the old guy who lives in the lee of the hill. His small house is nestled in an unhealthy grove of banana trees and a wispy thatch of sugarcane at the foot of Stoneyhurst and Henderson Lane. He was standing shirtless with a sagging chest and a tremendous hairy gut that hung over khaki army shorts—the picture of short-assed, stoic dilapidation and dignity. His surprisingly youthful-looking hair was swept back from a misshapen, leathery face. Since the tree eaters widened the road, his once-secluded house has been totally exposed right on the edge of the new thoroughfare. For a long time I was itching to meet this old guy after a couple of neighbours mentioned he was an old-fashioned Aussie—all man. They said he was an ex-army bloke, an embittered battler, a total recluse since the loss of his wife ten years ago. Apparently there was a falling-out with his daughters so that only the occasional grandchild now visits him. My girls claim that whenever they walk by the house he always watches them from his windows. And it's true. I've seen him checking us out from behind dark curtains. They think he's the local Boo Radley straight out of *To Kill a Mockingbird*, and the crooked, jungle-enshrouded house with the funny little purple Ford Holden caved in the now-truncated driveway sure fits the bill.

That day the old guy stood bewildered, rubbing his eyes and eating gritty dust, his house and property dwarfed by the convoy of trucks that passed by the front steps of his verandah. I'd just finished hanging another laundry, and earlier I'd taken out the old yellow surfboard my friend Daffy, the horticulturist/lawn cutter, had been kind enough to lend me. So I was feeling pretty chipper and mellow. I had nothing better to do than check out my hunch about this odd character. Although I felt slightly intrusive, I decided to walk up to him and start gabbing.

"I can't believe they cut down all the trees," I said, trying to show him how sympathetic I was to the memory of old Henderson Lane.

He stepped farther into the sunlight on the road and squinted. "They're a good mob, though. Utter professionals," he added, indicating the widened road and treeless landscape already pockmarked with excavations for the housing development.

Massive dump trucks rumbled back and forth, and a slow-moving water truck was sprinkling its way up his road to try to come to terms with the billowing clouds of dust that had coated everything. Instead of being pissed off about the trucks, he told me that during the war he'd been in the tank corps, and so I guessed all the dust and shuddering vibration from the big trucks had probably brought on a wave of nostalgia. He claimed the trucks sounded like tanks did when soldiers used to put oil drums on their mufflers as silencers to fool the Japanese. What came as a total surprise was that this so-called Aussie hermit was a bit of a chatterbox. His berserk eyebrows hooded the pain of his tired, shrewd eyes. When I told him a little about why we were in Australia, he said he didn't mind flogging his gums with me now that he knew I was Canadian and not American. He had seen my two girls and thought they were "a real nice pair of quinces, especially the friendly carrot-topped little tank."

"How long have you lived around here?" I asked a little nosily.

"Well," he said, not taking offence, "Oy came here after the war when it was still a relative paradise. Planted bananas and sugarcane. Ran a few cattle and sheep."

Apparently he'd trained in the western plains, claimed he'd gotten some shrapnel in his arms, legs, and face and leaned forward so I could verify the smooth scars in the wrinkled hide of his elephant flesh. He seemed pretty tickled to chat about the war, told me he had dreamed about being a paratrooper, but after the first time they pushed his arse out of a plane, swore he'd never go up again.

"They're going to throw up a lot more dog boxes like the ones on the hill," he said, pointing at the suburb rimming the hill above us. When the steel plate of a truck boomed and echoed after its massive load was dumped, we both gazed at the meadow below us that really did look as if a military operation were in progress. "Oy patrolled the top end of Australia near Broome looking for the Japs. Worked a bit across the water with islanders, Indonesians, pearl divers. In the main they were good, decent blacks," he said, nodding with approval. "Pommy white hunters used to shoot tigers. They'd be left bloated three feet high.

Smelled like the devil's abattoir. Inside the house Oy got a heap of medals that'd drape like an apron down my chest. The Japs would have poured in and overrun us if *we* hadn't stopped 'em. When they saw the bloody rising dust from our tanks, they decided they better bugger off back to their sardine island. Oy can't believe that after all we went through in the war, these whingein' scum we have now in the government in Canberra sold one of our biggest koala sanctuaries to the little bastards."

As I manly tried to explain my role as househusband and writer, and he imagined some of the awkward implications, his eyebrows twitched and he puffed up his sagging chest to pull in his impressive gut. Although it was probably a little beyond his comprehension, he attempted to grind and cantilever his way around the idea of any man voluntarily staying at home to look after kids. Still, I'm sure the poor old bugger missed his own girls whom he wasn't on speaking terms with now.

Then he finally launched into the saga of his domestic troubles. "One time when Oy came back from slavin' away in the cane fields in Queensland, Oy found out my woyf'd given all the bloody money Oy'd sent home to her father. Oy was so mad Oy tossed the whole mob over the fence to straighten them out."

Another convoy of trucks rumbled by, and he waved as though he were the foreman, and they waved back and tooted their horns, which seemed to please him greatly. Out of nowhere he winked and said, "Oy loik a woman who has spirit. Don't dampen a kid's imagination and sense of adventure," he murmured wistfully. "Oy still travel all the time, have a shelf full of maps you wouldn't believe. Oy travel in my mind." He peered at me then asked suspiciously, "What kind of books did you say you wrote, mate?"

When I described my collection of stories about French painters, and the novel about a young woman coming to terms with the suicide of her father, and the book I was struggling with on surfing and househus-banding, he listened intently without looking me in the eye. We both stood our ground as the water truck passed by again, this time gloriously soaking us with refreshing water. "Ah, the blissful piss of eyengels," he said happily, eyes closed. Licking his moist lips, he glanced around and leaned forward. "You know, mate, Oy always wanted to be a professional writer. Kept all kinds of notebooks. The place is full of first editions. At night when Oy can't sleep Oy always open up a book, or Oy'll write till Oy can't write no more. Ah, yeah, Oy reckon Oy should have been a writer." Suddenly he seemed embarrassed and put out by all the talk and added solemnly, "Don't get involved with anything you have to feed, that rusts, or has to be trucked."

Then nodding with absolute finality as though he'd given away far too much, he turned, walked into his house, and closed the door.

At that moment there were no more trucks, and even the dust had cleared a little. I wondered what kind of long, hard life the poor old bloke had really endured, how far he had travelled from the safe paradise of childhood to this life alone in a crumbling house crowded out by too much civilization.

Shaking my head, I sauntered up the steep, dusty road to the kids' park on the crest of the hill, wondering how tough I'd be when I was old, my girls were gone, and I had nothing but time and twisted memories. I was too hyper and reflective to read, so I placed *On Water* on the play structure, turned, sat in the biggest swing, and walked backward, staring at the breathtaking view. Then I let myself go, swinging forward, and back, pumping to get satisfying height and deep, long swings. A couple of times I straightened my arms so that my body arched back all the way in total abandon, seemingly out of control, eyes shut, lost momentarily in the bliss of childhood.

Swinging back and forth, I drank in the idyllic valley with its soft lines of mountains, patches of windblown rainforest, and clusters of farmhouses beneath the heat haze of a subtropical autumn. The long grass had recently been cut, so I was reasonably sure I wouldn't be bush-whacked by too many snakes. Ever since we arrived in Australia, this park has been deserted, the play structure empty and neglected, worn-out rather than well-worn, probably because most of the local kids had out-grown it and no new families had moved in. In its heyday it must have been filled with shrill laughter and happiness, but now a listless wind blew in the empty park that still seemed haunted by the ghosts of children and their wards. While swinging and casually keeping an eye out for the school bus to round the corner above the sea, I took in the empty silence and the big blue sky, thinking about a line from *On Water*—"deep water, bluer than longing." Then I began ruminating about some of the parks

I'd haunted and the women I'd met.

My old alma mater was the Tot Lot on the corner of Fifth Avenue and O'Connor in Ottawa's Glebe. Inside the mesh of its fence, beneath the shade of its spreading trees, I sat beached with mothers, caregivers, and occasionally another cranky dad along the edge of the sand. For the most part I remember getting a nice tan in bare feet with happy ladies while Sky learned to walk, to stop biting other kids, and to climb up the ladder of the slide safely, turn, and whoosh into the sanctuary of my waiting arms. She also mastered how to avoid getting hit in the chops by a rogue swing, how to share, and how to play well with others. And she discovered how to sing unselfconsciously for the simple joy of being alive while sitting in the boughs of the mountain ash I used to do wood carvings under. In the Tot Lot, Sky found out how to be herself, and I got a second chance to taste childhood.

Over the years I've been with hundreds of women, from the suburbs of Ottawa to the beaches of Hawaii, Australia, New Zealand, the Greek islands, the south of France, and Hong Kong. I won't deny women with children are attractive. In low-slung blouses, halter tops, T-shirts, jeans, shorts, or loose dresses blowing in the wind, they sit around the lip of a sandbox or push swings and strollers. They are happy, beautiful, and relaxed. Some men like wild, untamed women who drive pickup trucks, or tough, managerial women with calculating eyes who dress in smart, tailored suits with black stockings. But I have learned to appreciate the natural beauty of ordinary women who are in love with their kids.

I met Barb in the Tot Lot one spring morning. She was sitting on a wooden bridge our kids imagined spanned a Grand Canyon of crocodiles and other vile demons. For a week I'd noticed her because I'd spent hours there every day, teaching Sky about life in a sandbox and how complicated things could get. The Glebe is full of old churches and big trees. It's a trendy part of the city filled with charming parks, specialty shops, bookstores, and restaurants. Water from the Rideau Canal flows almost all around its borders. Raising Sky there in the early years before we ended up shipwrecked in the vacuum of suburbia was a gift. There were lots of kids and all kinds of things for them to do, and the neighbourhood was unusually stimulating for adults. For a laid-back outcast of the islands, a househusband drifting around with his daughter, the

Glebe couldn't have been a better place to assuage a restless nature—at least temporarily.

If you spend a lot of time with a preschooler, you sometimes need a kid-friendly prison in which to let your children graze. The Tot Lot had a fence around it, a self-locking gate, and a large, shady mountain ash that was perfect for climbing. In one corner was a *Lord of the Flies* tower with a steep, unforgiving slide and a great view of the known and unknown worlds. There were plenty of swings, clean sand, rocking horses, a couple of small badland hills, and enough bushes to pee behind. From time to time the fire station across the street exploded with siren-wailing trucks. Nearby was the canal, old Victorian houses, and the Fifth Avenue wading pool. For a few years the Tot Lot and its charming surroundings became my entire universe. I might yack with affluent yuppies; renters with barely enough for next month's rent; housewives; university professors; Swedish, French, Filipina and British nannies; and an oddball assortment of nervous men with their kids. Just outside the Tot Lot fence I'd observe drunks and junkies talking to themselves, an architect cradling his latest idea in his briefcase, a pair of lesbians working out a quandary in their relationship, and any number of unmarried, unencumbered health nuts rollerblading or jogging.

Barb sat with her lovely tanned face raised to the sun. With perfect white teeth, brown hair flowing back, and eyes closed, she was lost in the swoon of young motherhood. In her lap was her first son, Stuart, squinting at me and Sky in the fierce light. For the next eleven years Sky and Stuart, who are the same age, would become close friends. And Barb and her husband, Pete, would become *our* best friends. Both of our families would have more children. An unrepentant sun worshipper like myself, Barb is also somewhat of a manic depressive. Over many years she has become a lifelong friend and confidante. When I'm back home in Ottawa, we see each other nearly every weekend and call almost every other day. Barb had her kids right away; I waited a decade. I'm ten years older and an atheist who has travelled the world, while Barb has pined at home, living her life through her kids, Pete, her family and friends, and a deep, abiding faith in God.

Being a man looking after kids was tricky; women are suspicious, given their maternal instinct to protect their offspring and themselves.

With today's swamp of sexual politics, it's a wonder when men and women have easy friendships. I either make friends with women, or I'm brutally snubbed. Barb offered honest friendship. She also helped me out with practicalities: how to prepare a nutritious meal when you had no money, no food in the house, and you were sick to death of cooking; how to get through an eight- or eighteen-hour day inside with a small child when it was thirty below zero outside; how to laugh like a maniac at life's foibles instead of throwing a long piece of rope over a beam to hang yourself.

For adult and child the Tot Lot was like a small stage, a theatre of possibilities. All equations of happiness, sadness, love, hate, cruelty, adventure, supreme acts of generosity, kindness, bravery, and fun were held within the confines of its chain-link fence. Often all of this humanity would unfold in any given hour of play.

Way back then, in the mid-1980s, I was just starting to be a house-husband. I'd fill up my backpack with diapers, bottles, Wet Ones, snacks, and sunscreen, the last just having become mandatory equipment for any outing. With her helmet on, I'd set Sky into the bike seat of my Nishiki twelve-speed and we'd Jack-Kerouac around the parks of Ottawa. I'd pedal over to visit my sister, Jan, and my niece, Taylor. Or we'd show up at a jazz festival, a craft show, yard sales, bookstores, or outdoor cafés. Frequently, as I rode my bike, taking in the sights, Sky would fall asleep on the back so that I'd have to wobble along with one hand and reach with my other to hold her upright so her neck wouldn't snap. Travelling to Windsor Park off Bank Street below Sunnyside was like taking a trip to an English country village. I'd go via the Rideau River and down Cameron Street along the river, so we could check out the elegant swans and ducks among the reeds and breathe in the rank odours of the fast-moving river with its pikey seaweed smell that always made me long for the ocean.

But we always ended up at the Tot Lot. Tanned like a Hawaiian surfer, I'd arrive with an intensity and the big, sunny grin of someone who was doing exactly what he was meant to do. In sunglasses and a baseball cap turned backward, I'd swing one leg over the crossbar of my Nishiki and lean the bike against the fence. Then I'd unbuckle Sky, remove her helmet, lift her out of the seat, lower her to the ground, and watch her explode into the Tot Lot to find friends. And trouble. I'd see Barb sunning herself on the bridge, flashing me a Hollywood smile. Under her halo, saintly Deirdre would be breast-feeding one of her cherubs. Soft-spoken Marianne would be quietly reading in the shade to protect her lovely porcelain skin. And young Pete might be there with his boyish grin that begged for mischief. And suddenly looking after kids turned into something like a beach party. We'd throw a Frisbee, toss a football, turn cartwheels, climb trees, do chin-ups, mimic our children's most ridiculous requests, swing and gab or whoosh down the slide to pacify a terrified child and amuse an aged one. I might yack with other women, or sit on the grassy knoll for some stimulating conversation while gazing down at the swarm of kids playing in the sand.

One of the rumours going around was that in warm weather I lived at the Tot Lot and never went home. In fact, each day of my life began and finished with the place. If I ended up alone with Sky, she'd shout, "Daddy, Daddy, I want another push." She'd beg me until I'd get up and do her bidding, propelling her higher and higher until something would drop inside my stomach and I had to stop because the thought of what might happen to her if she let go or the swing snapped would be too much for me to take, even in my imagination. For hours we'd play store, using little stones to buy items—bigger stones—from Sky. Or if the sunlight was too ferocious, or when it was too cold or whenever it rained, we'd eat snacks, hunched inside the tiny red house.

Some days everyone would bring exotic containers of hummus, babaghanoush, tabouli, samosas, or hot tamale tofu chili. My specialty was homemade chocolate-chip cookies that everyone inhaled until they felt as if their chests were in vises. Deirdre brought cabbage-size muffins and atomic brownies. Because Marianne lived in an apartment beside the Tot Lot, she might surprise us with steaming burritos or cheese-and-jalapeño nachos. And a brick-size piece of Barb's carrot cake took five years off your life, but was worth the price. You could get into the most intellectual debates about the meaning of life, theology, politics, or the hot curry inside a kid's diaper. I had conversations with another writer who looked after his children at odd times because he owned a socialist book-store that employed volunteers. He once outlined a radical theory about refrigerators being totally redundant in our decadent society.

With some mothers I might discuss the paradox of history, whether or not there was a higher mathematics, solid geometry, or another untapped dimension in philosophy. With overripe lactating women I pondered the many fascinating dilemmas of soothers, bottles, and childcare. Should you or shouldn't you give your kid a gentle smack on the bottom to make a point? And how do you deal with the guilt that resulted if you did hit your child?

In the frazzled recesses of our minds we all wondered whether there would be life after babies, toddlers, and preschoolers. Parents with older kids already knew that answer. The kind, diplomatic ones bitterly kept it to themselves. The sickos always relished dropping little time bombs like: "Enjoy them while they're small. 'Cause you sure won't like 'em when they get older." And we solemnly promised ourselves never to get so darkly jaded about our own children when they aged.

Back then it always seemed to be sunny. All of our kids were preschoolers. Physically they were hell on our bodies because we were constantly bending with sore backs to snatch them up before they keeled over. We rushed to stop them from attacking other children, or saved them from staggering into traffic. Because we were perpetually attached to tots we looked like lumpy, harried marsupials, embracing our offspring to pacify, show affection, and make ourselves feel needed and loved. For years being in such close proximity to our children's bodies defined us as human beings. It was an overpowering love like no other.

Sky was very enthusiastic in the Tot Lot. One part-time, divorced, stay-at-home dad complained to another parent that Sky was so active she reminded him of the Antichrist. This was a man who had parented three children with three different mothers. Barb's second son, Charlie, used to crawl on one knee around the perimeter of the Tot Lot fence, trying to figure out how to escape. Whenever someone forgot to lock the gate, he would one-knee it out the gate as fast as he could, and later when one of us glanced across the street, we'd spot him crouched on his travelling knee, staring back at us as if it were Groundhog Day. Once, Stuart, Barb's other son, tossed a baseball bat and was unlucky enough to bean a poor sparrow on the head. Everyone at the Tot Lot was mortified until Sky bit another kid, the frailest, gift-wrapped little girl managed to fall sideways off the slide halfway down, a freckle-faced chub threw up his complicated snack, and a normally comatose child took a violent tantrum when he declined to leave the park to go home.

When we all decided to have more kids, none of us could afford to buy houses in the Glebe, so Tom and Deirdre moved to a nice little home in the mountains in Old Chelsea, Barb and Pete relocated to a hundred-year-old place in Sandy Hill, Marianne left for India, and Dale and I moved deep into the new suburb of Barrhaven.

Another wonderful park was in Hong Kong, only a five-minute walk from our apartment there. Quinn and I lived most of our year in Hong Kong in that place. On the edge of a cliff above an old ferry dock and just across the water from Peng Chau, it also overlooked the seedy, ancient village of Nim She Wan that caved in on itself behind a crescent beach. If I squinted out one eye to avoid the garbage-strewn beach and oily water, the view made me think I was gazing at a fishing village on a Greek island. From the park I could marvel at the long vistas of the Lantau mountains wreathed in mist, and the cleaner emerald sea along the coast. Here I spoke with mothers from around the world and listened to harrowing stories about wayward pilots and their randy, less-than-honourable wives. The women of macho U.K. soccer players said they were in Hong Kong for the short haul to make enough cash to return to Britain where, hopefully, their husbands would get real jobs.

One poor white South African dentist had recently fled to Hong Kong, leaving her good-for-nothing husband who was a successful writer of young adult novels. She was a bitter single parent now, worked all day inside people's open mouths, and let a shy part-time Filipina amah look after her two adopted black African children. The dentist seemed peeved that I got to float all over the bloody territory with Quinn as if we were on a carefree furlough which, in fact, we were. But that was our own business and not hers. She hated my good luck. And because I was a man and a writer to boot, there was no way I could ever be redeemed in her sad eyes. I worked hard to keep my girls and her girls entertained in the park. I tried my best to use the sandbox knowledge I'd gleaned over the years, but eventually her two girls started being mean to my daughters because of their mother's unrestrained resentment toward me. Even though the good dentist had the security of her salary while I only had the deep satisfaction of my naked liberty, squirrelled-away memories, and the $13.13 from my last royalty cheque, she was determined to stick it to me and poison our girls' time in the playground.

Over on the Hong Kong side, though, among the long, eerie shadows of high-rises, Quinn and I often roamed under the shady trees of the Hong Kong Zoo. We also had the Botanical Gardens, open-air street markets, and the massive walk-through butterfly and bird sanctuaries. Just for Quinn and me, Hong Kong Park had five separate theme playgrounds, each one appealing to a different whim and mood. Quinn would toddle from one level of the park up or down to the next, and I'd casually follow, looking into the bowels of Hong Kong, marvelling at the canyons of high-rises that showcased some of the most spectacular architecture on the planet. Using a timeless method, all the new high-rises under construction were encased in wispy green netting and complicated bamboo scaffolding. All manner of oceangoing vessels churned in the busy harbour, and planes continually approached and left the airport. A gleaming Rolls-Royce would pass by a black Porsche or a mustard BMW, then a double-decker bus whose upper level was open and filled with hysterical tourists would bear down on a half-naked man shouldering a bleeding side of beef as he wobbled along on his ancient bicycle. While enjoying the complexity of this M. C. Escher view I could talk with fascinating adults from a host of countries, or stand alone at the edge of the park on the precipice of this wondrous city of six million people and dream about the Hong Kong novel I was researching.

Originally in Hong Kong I was writing the Great Canadian Novel, but I got sidetracked and began to pen the Great Hong Kong Novel. It would take in everything from the present moment pretakeover in 1997 all the way back to the two battalions of half-trained young Canadians who were shipped there in November 1941. My research got so stuck on these poor innocent guys that I lost a taste for the rest of Hong Kong's history. Without the proper weapons, motor transport, or supplies, these boys were carelessly commanded by Ottawa to go and defend this distant colony. They arrived and lived it up, partying with expat women, and shamelessly enjoyed what was left of the high times of dying prewar colonial Hong Kong. Less than three weeks later two divisions of crack Japanese troops swarmed down from the south of China, fresh from an adrenaline-pumping killing spree. The bombing and shelling of

Kowloon forced all the British forces to retreat in panic, crossing over to Hong Kong Island at Blake Pier, the same place where I'd waited hundreds of times with Sky and Quinn to take our sublime ferry back over to our home on Lantau Island.

You have to be directly in charge of small children to realize how vulnerable and helpless women with kids have always felt in the face of men and the violent political agendas of history. Assembled within the thirty square miles of Hong Kong Island, the British forces waited in terror while the Japanese amassed on the Kowloon waterfront, getting ready for the coup de grace. As the Japanese gunners started shelling across the harbour and dive bombers screamed overhead, the besieged colony was given the final official word by Winston Churchill: "There must be no thought of surrender. Every day that you are able to maintain your resistance you and your men can win the lasting honour which we are sure will be your due."

When the Japanese army hit the island and swarmed through the streets and countryside, they killed almost a third of the Winnipeg Grenadiers and Halifax Rifles who were all in their late teens or early twenties. The Canadians were hunted down in every building, street, ravine, and lonely cliff-side beach. The Japanese even stormed into a hospital and butchered them in their hospital beds along with their nurses. Some were roped together and bayonetted. After the surrender, mere weeks after the big-eyed, gawky Canadians arrived, the Japanese let their troops go wild in the colony, raping, looting, beating up, and killing whomever they pleased. The Canadians who weren't slaughtered were herded into evil camps for the rest of the war. Hundreds were shipped to Japan to work as slave labour in punishing steel companies until many died of malnutrition and disease. Everyone has seen the before and after photos: cocky, smooth-faced young guys standing with cigarettes hanging out of the corners of their mouths, looking down with bright, hopeful smiles from the sides of the ship that took them from Victoria, British Columbia, on what they romantically expected would be the glorious adventure of a lifetime. But the pictures after their nightmare reveal acutely disenchanted, emaciated, unnaturally aged men who, after the war, were sent home to be plugged back into a country that had sent them as cannon fodder to protect Hong Kong for the

British Empire.

I stood at the rail of Hong Kong Park, gazing into the furious life of this modern city, reflecting on history as Quinn toddled precariously from swing to teeter-totter to slide. I thought about the young Canadian guys half my age living in tin shacks with no air-conditioning in the forty-degree summers and no heat in the drizzle of freezing winters, with only a cup of maggoty rice each day.

Numerous heartbreaking accounts by Canadian Hong Kong POWs detail the brutal atrocities performed by the Japanese: beatings, tortures, beheadings, starvation, and blatant day-to-day cruelty. And there was the monstrous insensitivity of the Canadian government when the POWs finally returned home in shame because it was said they hadn't performed in the manner expected by the British Empire. It was a bitter pill to swallow, even fifty years later. In hellish camps these guys passed their days filled with hard labour and no hope. For four years these young Canadians rotted. There was no end to the grinding horror of each day, no seeming end to a world at war. And for many there was no happy ending when they returned to their homeland. Whenever Quinn and I visited the places where Canadians had been during the war, or when we stood at the beautiful war cemetery above Chai Wan on Hong Kong Island, I felt overwhelming guilt and pity and shame. The shame of knowing that for the most part my biggest worry was finding someone interesting to talk to while I killed time with my kids in a park. But I always got through such bouts of gut-wrenching shame and guilt and rushed over to scoop up Quinn and hug her close. Kissing the warm top of her sweet head and revelling in the heat and life in her body on those occasions, I experienced overwhelming gratitude for my simple good fortune.

走

Back in Australia, even before I realized they were in front of me, my girls had danced off their bus and dodged the dangerous trucks, then charged over to join me at the swing. They tossed their backpacks into the long, snaky grass and attacked me with hugs and kisses. At the same time they jammed their little butts into my lap and began quarrelling about who would get on the swing with me. I chased them away, and they squealed and clambered onto the play structure. "Daddy!" they pleaded. "Come up here with us and look at the view." I left my swing and climbed to be with them. They were right: from the top of the play structure you could see the whole world.

In a quiet interlude without trucks we started down the steep hill along Henderson Lane. As we walked past the little house with the lonely old guy behind the curtains—lost in his reveries of his war with the Japanese and the current war with his estranged family—I thought about a reunion some time ago that we had at the Tot Lot. Of course, it was a chilly, sunny fall day. There were no other people in the park except us—seven adults and nine kids. With its ghostly, overgrown trees and tiny play structures, our magical park seemed small and ordinary. Our kids wandered around a little lost, looking gigantic, even criminal inside the enclosed fence. They didn't know what to do with themselves, legs and arms too long, minds elsewhere. As adults, I think we probably felt trapped, too. Our lives were much too complicated now to be held for long by the fading memories of our good times in the Tot Lot. We had all lived and played out other scenes, had moved on to new, evolving stresses. But, of course, finally, we had a ball: we all managed to cross the scary bridge; we chased each other up and down the slide; squashed ourselves together inside the little red house, pretending to suck our thumbs. On the swings we all swung in unison with our kids pushing us. Like idiot orangutans, Pete and I climbed into the branches of the mountain ash and in strained falsettos sang Eddie Murphy's version of the Police's "Roxanne" at the top of our lungs. Then, while we royally feasted on the windy, grassy knoll, someone mentioned I should write about the Tot Lot someday. After we cleaned up, threw away our garbage, herded our rowdy kids out, and locked the gate, we left the Tot Lot. And I don't think any of us have ever been physically back since.

12
Ironing John

Nothing in life really surprises me anymore. As the old saying goes, you have to take life as it comes, be grateful for the good stuff and deal with the bad. You have no choice in the matter. A nice malleable bend in your worldview can help, too.

It's the middle of April, and the air outside reminds me of a sweet day in early September back in Ottawa. The weather here is changing. There are new birds, mornings are about fifteen degrees, and it only warms up to twenty-four during the day. By five o'clock it's nippy again. The whales have started their migration up from Antarctica, and the mullet are running, which no doubt makes the dolphins, seabirds, and great whites happy. Most of the blossoms are gone; some trees are even dropping their leaves. The humidity has disappeared, the mosquitoes have eased up, and pine needles blanket the ground in our yard. It's now dark before Rod arrives in his milk truck, and last night when I smelled burning smoke in a fireplace, I almost got nostalgic for Canada.

This morning, once more, I accompany my girls to their bus stop with my surfboard, kiss them goodbye, and walk around the top of North Creek Road and down the steep hill into seven miles of breaking surf that seems to swallow our little town.

Without even a hint of wind I paddle into the glassy waves, get outside the impact zone, and straddle my board alone. Each gargantuan swell arrives silently, then breaks farther inside. I merely sit drifting in the current, pondering what to do with so much.

Then I take the last wave in a nice set, drop into the curl, and cut high along the lip, shuffling my feet to the nose, crouching into my bony Anglo-Hawaiian stance, hanging my toes off the board, arms outstretched, riding my wave, hanging ten, for what seems an eternity, as though I can suspend time and joy and embrace this absolute freedom forever.

We all go through some pretty bizarre rituals to prove things to ourselves. There appears to be a collective fear of weakness among men. Looking after small children wasn't something that came to me easily. I think it's quite a stretch for most men. Some can pull it off; others try and get tangled in their aprons. A friend of mine attempted the househusband gig for a few years after quitting his advertising job. The plan was to write a novel while looking after his two small boys. He had the luxury of a live-in Swedish au pair. But his wife, who had a rather high-powered job, left him because she couldn't adjust to his new nonstatus as househusband/aspiring writer with no income.

Yesterday I finally surfed Boulders, which is a frightening place five minutes down the coast. I went with a guy named Andy whom I'd met at our American friends Dennis and Melissa's house. From high on the cliffs at Boulders you can look down at mountainous surf as it sweeps past the point and breaks right below your eyes, then moves on over the inside reefs all the way to a distant beach. You can see the primeval back side of Lennox Head's Aboriginal-coloured layers of volcanic rock. And you can gaze along the magnificent coastline, miles past Broken Head, and feel what it must have been like a couple of hundred years ago when the Aborigines had this coast to themselves. Out on the end of the point is a cross that marks the spot where a rogue wave once swept a fisherman to his death. It's a deadly spot if you don't know what you're doing. But when good swells push in, it can be exhilarating.

To get into the water, Andy and I had to work our way down among the boulders and jump in off a slippery ledge, then paddle like crazy to avoid being hammered back up against the cliff face. After an exhausting paddle up and down the breaking inside waves, we went out to meet the monsters on the outside reef. The swells seemed to roll in from the edge of the faraway horizon. We straddled our boards and let the giant swells tumble in and lift us, then moved on through Boulders. Andy and I took in all the glory, savouring the moment.

Then, when the right wave arrived, it sucked back off the reef bottom and we both dropped down the face and rode in front of an avalanche of thunderous foam, feeling like kings. Andy, a good surfer, slashed and cut the wave without any problems. I was happy just to survive the drop and enjoy a pair of dolphins who joined us on our wave, their black skin gleaming in the water. And when the last section of our wave finally broke, the top was ripped off by a fierce wind that showered our faces so hard we had to close our eyes to the stinging spray.

Andy is a male nurse who works shifts, takes care of his kids, makes a lot of the meals, and generally hangs about the house doing what used to be infamously known as "women's work." Even in rough-and-tumble Australia, men are spending more time in the home with their offspring. But a lot of Aussie women are still pining for the day when their men will pitch in with the caring of children, vacuuming, and cooking.

I paid for my macho surf session at Boulders with a wrenched neck. It's so fused that I have the affected demeanour of Count Dracula, but that hasn't stopped me from doing a little more surfing. Out on the waves I find myself brooding about the recently received news that our exchangees are breaking the contract and are definitely coming back early. We'll have to get out of Stoneyhurst Manor by the end of June instead of December. My second workshop isn't filling up with enough writers for me to get the extra money we need. Dale put her neck and back out shouldering the stress from worrying about our exchangees' return and our potential expulsion from the Garden of Eden. Then, just before the girls were off to school today, I ran out of the garage, stiffly ducking under the door that was partway down, mentally taking note to duck on my way back in. I raged at my two girls who were in the car fighting, Quinn in the back seat, Sky in the front, taking a fury of fists and insults from her younger sister, both of them screaming with the windows rolled up inside the insanely hot car. All I wanted to do was fire in a missing lunch, a pair of shoes, sunscreen, and a leaking bottle of grape juice but I couldn't with the windows shut. Giving up, I ran back in through the garage, forgetting to duck so that my forehead hit the bottom of the door and I dropped straight to the concrete floor with a groan.

My girls actually stopped fighting to watch their dad who had just been yelling at them crumple to the ground. I was dazed and confused. Down for the count.

Needless to say I don't handle anger well. My own dad dealt with the bickering between Jan and me with something he rarely used called the Flying Hand. He always seemed to be bent over broken secondhand washing machines, lawn mowers, or toasters, venting his frustration on a machine that wouldn't work, kicking it, hurting his toe, and cursing, "Son of a bitch!" Like most 1950s men, my dad was responsible, hard-working, and maybe a little isolated. After a tough day's work at the office, there he was alone, dripping in sweat over a caved-in lawn mower, looking around for some relief from his mortgage, his ungrateful wife and two kids, and his lumpy, uncut suburban lawn rife with weeds.

While lying there peacefully on the cool concrete floor of the garage, I suddenly had an urge to call my dad all the way from Australia to Florida where he and my mom now basked every winter. I wanted to ask him for a little forgiveness. I wanted to tell him how much I loved him and how much I really appreciated all he did for us because now, finally, at forty-something bloody years of age, I could relate to his way of dealing with the world.

My father, a good manager for Beneficial Finance, was often kind and sensitive to the needs of his hardup clients. Most of his evenings he had the uncomfortable job of phoning clients to extract money from them, leaning on them, in some cases actually repossessing their belongings. From time to time we acquired the meagre household possessions of his unhappy customers who didn't pay back their loans. We got old fishing tackle boxes filled with rusty lures, beat-up guitars, skin magazines, tired clothing, orphaned chairs—a garage sale's worth of someone's bankrupt life.

For more than a decade my dad was in the Lions Club. He volunteered his free time to help in the community and to be with other men, running a snack bar for a hockey arena and breaking up fistfights with juvenile punks wielding switchblades. Dad let my sister, Jan, and I sell and eat too much crap at the snack bar. We got free skating, and I can still smell the ice, greasy french fries, and damp concrete. We listened to piped-in music, say, Mitch Miller singing "Roll out those lazy crazy, hazy days of summer," while going around the rink for a half hour one way, then reversing and skating in the other direction. Jan, Dad, and I used to bring Christmas hampers to poor families in Ottawa. We'd arrive at a family's house with canned goods and a frozen turkey, and they would actually give Jan and me candy canes, cookies, or even a wrapped gift.

My dad was famous for playing catch with my sister and me and our friends. In winter we often played hockey on a bumpy, uneven home-made rink he watered alone in subzero weather. On the road my dad liked to play football with us. We were always on opposite teams, and so competitive. I'd object to one of his decisions and confront him. We'd toss the ball back and forth until it hit one of us in the chops. If I fired it hard into *his* face, he'd chase me around our yard until I ran under a slumping clothesline that garroted him, dropping him to the dirt. Down for the count.

There was a lot of conflict with my dad. We were caught up in the age-old Oedipal thing with my mom. He worked like a dog from seven to six and came home to find a lazy, good-for-nothing son lounging around with his bride. I was a smart-aleck who complained constantly and disagreed with everything he said. My mother and I appeared to have a secret pact against my poor dad. Sometimes everyone seemed a little happier when he was out of the house. No wonder the breadwinners of the 1950s and 1960s could be such a cranky, frustrated lot. They had no real status in their own homes.

Around 1973, while I was attending Carleton University, I joined a radical men's consciousness-raising group. Twenty years before Robert Bly's landmark book *Iron John* spearheaded the weepy, drum-beating, weekend warriors of the men's movement, our group was ahead of its time. We were a dozen males, pioneers of the Confused White Men of Ottawa, whose members floated in and out of self-esteem, in and out of our weekly meetings. Even back then we were wild men looking to recover our lost fathers and our inner hunters. I was the youngest, certainly the most hopeful supporter of true love, being engaged and so in love as to announce it to the world too loudly and much too often. There were a couple of wise professors from the psychology and journalism departments, a few far-out grad students, a gay fellow with a ponytail, a quiet bisexual, and a guy in an open marriage who found it a lot easier to bonk other women than forgive his roaming wife. One guy was so violently bitter against women that he called his ex-wife and the sacred institution of marriage every vile name he could think of.

Each week our consciousness-raising group would meet at the home of one of these men, usually downtown in an old Victorian house. Having been raised in suburbia in a squeaky-clean, modern, blandly designed box, these dark, ghost-filled houses with stained-glass windows, oak mantels, droopy rock-and-stick filled macramé hangings, sweet smell of marijuana, sagging verandahs, and shaggy foliage-filled yards with slithering stray cats seemed revolutionary and romantic. In candlelight one evening with incense burning we sat on multicoloured pillows on the hardwood floor, earnestly sipping herbal tea sugared with honey from chunky clay pots, and worked at eating pineapple-size muffins. The misogynist began a long, vicious monologue on female genitalia that was a direct attack on my lovestruck, boyish optimism and upcoming marriage. He had nothing good to say about anything below a woman's navel, referring to it as the lice box of earth, the foul honey pot of joy, and the black hole of no return.

What I gleaned from my cynical mentors was this: feminism had kicked us in the balls and we had already dropped to one knee. What I learned from the good women in my Psychology of Women class was that there would be a new balance of power, a new harmony. Men had been repressing women from the Dawn of, well, Man. We had been in power that long and had taken too many liberties. We had abused our privilege as cowards, pimps, jailers, and brutal mates who wouldn't know how to treat a real woman properly even if it was written down for us in a contract.

Quite simply the relationships between men and women were deteriorating badly in the early 1970s. So many traditional bonds were unravelling. Men jumped into bed with their secretaries, or women married their bosses. Men and women left their families to hit the open road.

Gays came out of their closets. Women were working again more than they had during World War II. The Sexual Revolution, the pill, abortions on demand, and rock and roll all helped to loosen the conservative grip, and everyone, it seemed, was free to go hog-wild.

Alvin Toffler's book *Future Shock* promised four-day work weeks by the end of the decade. We'd have more time for self-actualization and peak experiences. More time to find ourselves. In the 1970s you could float, travel, drop out, go back to school, or back to the land and still maintain your place in line. The comfy middle class was experiencing a peaceful, easy feeling, and the motto of the day was "take it easy," echoed by the phrases "go for it" and "no problem" as the Me Generation took off down a myriad of open roads.

I got married in 1975, despite the bad vibes I picked up at the meetings with my men's consciousness-raising group. Some of my so-called mentors were pretty screwed up, and I was as rudderless as they came. Graduating with a degree in psychology, I didn't know who the hell I was or where the hell I was going. The only certainty in my life was that I was married to a beautiful girl who loved me as much as I loved her.

At that moment I decided I'd never get tied down by a nine-to-five job or a mortgage. Back then I also thought I'd never want children. I saw my salvation in terms of travel and surfing. And so a year after we got married, instead of going to work or war, Dale and I took off for a year to surf the perimeter of North America in a renovated Dodge van with a fake mahogany-panelled ceiling and an orange shag carpet stapled to the walls.

After today's surf, my neck is even stiffer and I know I have to find relief. I've heard that Melissa's husband, Dennis, was a rather unorthodox chiropractor in New Zealand before they moved here a few years ago. Officially he doesn't practise anymore, but does adjust a few select friends. Dennis is yet another househusband.

Melissa and Dennis are Americans. Dale and I met Melissa grocery-shopping in Ballina after she overheard our Canadian accents. The couple have been up to our place for dinner and we've visited them often because their two girls, Kaitlyn and Lyla, like to play with our daughters. Today I decide to drop by solo and suss out Dennis's chiropractor table. Dennis is an elusive beach sage who doesn't work and stays at home to look after his little girls. I've also heard he's something of a mystery man who may or may not have a trust fund and is probably on the lam from a shady past.

Melissa is a pretty, hardworking artist who supports a family of four by selling her celebrated etchings of dark, whimsical, sexy women. She tells me she wants to trade one of her etchings for a wooden tiki I carved. The etching I have in mind is a long horizontal piece called *Seahorses and Birds Underwater*, which shows a mermaid holding a smiling dolphin that takes her through a fantastical underwater seascape.

I always love going to Melissa and Dennis's little beach house built by a sea captain. For the past few years as a househusband Dennis has been renovating their South Seas hideaway. Their home is his work of art, his Sistine Chapel. He's transformed it with a Santa Fe–style adobe front courtyard and transparent awning that lets in the sunlight and reveals the stars, and covered the walls with hanging flower pots. With geckos, sun gods, mermaids, fish, starfish, and shell motifs cut into the adobe, and Balinese silk banners, tropical foliage, and a cow's skull with shards of paua shells glued all over it, their place has more ambience than most good restaurants.

In their driveway Melissa slouches against her prized 1962 pink Holden. She comes up, hugs me, and says, "Hey, Ricky, what's happenin'?" in that sweet, seductive American accent she hasn't lost in a decade of being in New Zealand and Australia. In my peripheral vision I notice Dennis skulking about the property, eyeing me a bit. Although Dennis can do wicked Jack Nicholson impersonations, he's basically shy and maybe even a little jealous of a man who's a writer sniffing around his artist wife.

Inside the house the walls and shelves are filled with paintings, books, sculptures, and beach-style curios. There are lots of cute photos and frilly things that belong to the girls. Because of its great artistic and domestic vibe, Dennis and Melissa's place is a communal focal point for the beach houses in Lennox. Often parents and their kids wander in and out of this couple's home—and their lives. Next door Dave and Rae

Cook usually drop over to say hello and share plates of interesting food. Dave is a science teacher at the high school and also the chief of the volunteer fire department. Rae is a potter with an infectious smile. Their young son and daughter are heavily sponsored by Billabong. Everyone in their family surfs.

"You should let Denny take a look at your neck, Ricky," Melissa suggests.

I stare across the room at the ominous padded chiropractic table, with a towel laid out for Dennis to execute one of his unorthodox adjustments, nervously listening to Melissa tell me how Dennis used to be a good chiropractor. With trepidation I imagine him doing a samurai knee drop that will cripple me for life and turn me into a human question mark.

There's something about Dennis, and everyone else at the bottom of the world in this lost seaside town. He's hiding some murky secrets, like all of us. And now he's renovating this little house and hanging out with his kids in lieu of a real job, letting time take care of things. His cruisey aloofness and laid-back refusal to be nailed down by the nine-to-five clock reminds me of myself. And while I can admire him for his maverick stand, I know exactly how uneasy he must feel under the scrutiny of people who judge him; it's the way friends and foes alike have passed sentence on me over the years.

Every time I'm here Melissa gravitates to her studio because she's a one-woman cottage industry. She's a focused artist who knows where she's going, even when her white cockatiel, Bill, flies berserk around the studio and alights on print-making equipment, art books, and her creations, which celebrate the playful darkness of feminine sexuality with hints of delicate colour, hearts, sea motifs, and other surprises.

Now Dennis walks by the door of the studio and eyes me warily, then tosses me an apple as a warning, a gesture of friendship, or an indication of territoriality. "Maybe I'll catch ya a little later down at the lake," he says, and disappears again.

Melissa can read my mind. She rolls her eyes and smirks. "Don't ask me to explain Dennis. Dennis is Dennis, and that's about all I can tell ya."

Ultimately I decline the offer of a chiropractic adjustment that Melissa says she can easily arrange, but after I leave, I decide to take my stiff neck to the lake for a cathartic dip. And besides, I want to check out Dennis—the Mayor of Lake Ainsworth—on his own turf.

Dennis has gone in the Toyota van to pick up his girls at school and bring them for a swim at Lake Ainsworth, which is at the end of their street, parallel to Seven Mile Beach and on the other side of a narrow road between the lake and the sea. It's a popular billabong for local families who want to seek refuge from the crashing surf and have a calm swim in its medicinal waters. Lake Ainsworth is famous for the health-giving tea trees on its banks that leech into the small lake and give it an iodine colour so that you feel as though you're not swimming in water but in blood. It's heavy and warm and perfect for open-water swimming. And there are definitely no sharks.

What fascinates me about Dennis is that, like me, he's been a kept man for years. Our wives bring home the bacon while we take care of home and hearth. Now that the men's movement has already gathered steam and is more or less spent, males have slipped the yoke of power off their shoulders and everything seems up for grabs.

Today all we know is that women don't want us to be macho and we can't be wimps. Our space is shrinking. It's a bit of a tightrope over sharky waters. As a group, men between the ages of thirty and sixty are somewhat of a worldwide joke. We're standing with our pants at our ankles, trying to get as much dignity as we can from being men. Trapped by more and more sedentary jobs in front of computer screens, more childcare, and more domestic work around our homes, we have less chance of becoming the heroes we always imagined ourselves to be one day. As women get tougher, take on more jobs, and move up the ladders of power, they're stepping on our fingers and watching us freefall.

When I arrive at the lake, I spot Dennis's green van backed to the water's edge. He's reclining in the rear with the doors wide. As if he were a splendid swami on oversize coloured pillows, he's reading a scrounged copy of *Vanity Fair*. A billowing batik canopy stretches out to shade his domain, and he cocks a vigilant eye above his magazine to make sure Lyla and Kaitlyn are safely swimming just offshore. I swim a few times across the lake to train for the upcoming Byron Bay Open-Water Swim Classic, but I almost feel I should bow when I stand under the canopy before this holy man of leisure.

Lying in the back of his van, Dennis is the quintessential househusband, languishing by the lake with his wards happily playing in the water. I pull on my goggles, gaze beyond the tea trees on the far side, and dive in to swim across the red lake. Seeing Dennis so carefree, watching over his girls in all this divine natural beauty, reminds me of how I've lived the past ten years. I'm looking at myself. Aside from all the free time and the total communion with my girls, I've also existed without a paycheque or any clear-cut status or any recognition from my long-lost mates. As Dennis basks in his glory by the bloody waters of his own billabong, I realize I've finally met Ironing John.

13
The Point

For me writing, like surfing, is a series of linked recoveries with an unknown plan. The other day, while watching Sky's soccer game, I noticed one of the other fathers was wearing a T-shirt that said HOT TUNA and showed a man at home surfing on an ironing board. I could have used a shirt with that exact image a few years back while I was househusbanding my sorry ass around suburbia. Back then I couldn't imagine that a few years in the future I'd be in Australia again, happier than I've ever been in my entire life.

From up at my window, and down in the surf, I've seen whales swimming from Antarctica to have their babies in Queensland. My first whale up close, though, is a revelation. Sitting on my board in a lull, waiting for the next set of waves, I turn and spot this great leviathan surge out of the water. Reaching for the sky, it topples over in slow motion like a collapsing high-rise, heaving up a mountain of spray. Forty tons, seventeen yards long, twelve feet high. Alone, I hoot and yell as though I've just seen a manifestation of God.

Then I notice my friend Daffy paddling out with his four-year-old son, Dylan, in a life jacket, crouched on the front of his longboard. Quinn plays with Dylan's older sister, Zoe, and Daffy's wife, Tanya, has visited us at our house to share local gossip, spill out her life story, and unload a little marital woe. A lot of locals have been dropping by to see us at Stoneyhurst. They all want to check out the Canadians, shed a little angst, and satisfy their thirst for the wide world.

Daffy is about the same age I am and has a long blond ponytail and a kind, handsome, weathered Hobbit face the sun gives even to young people who spend too much time in the outdoors. His accent is so thick, and his language so crammed with cornball Aussie back-country wisdom and mixed metaphors, that I can't really say I know what he's saying most of the time. But I understand what he's trying to get across: he's always having a go at the ropeheads, goths, ferals, hippies, crystal gazers, and other ne'er-do-wells among the great unwashed of Byron Bay. Because Tanya is going back to school to pursue a potentially frivolous art degree, and Daffy has to spend a lot more time with the kids, and because I'm the meddling Canadian househusband writer who has probably contributed to the uncomfortable new edge in his domestic life, he's a little pissed off with me but also curious to discover what makes me tick. He works for himself and has a flexible schedule that revolves around whether or not a good swell is pushing in. Out on the reef he'll paddle up and say, "How ya goin', Rick, ya filthy bloody bludger?" because he's never seen me working, and I'm always surfing. Daffy traded a comfortable, landlocked career as a hotel manager for the hard, uncertain work as a freelance horticulturist. Everyone in town knows Daffy. He drives around in an old jeep, pulling a tool trailer with lawn mowers and his famous ancient longboard strapped on top so that whenever he fancies he can paddle out for a surf. Daffy is one of the top pre-1968 Malibu longboard riders on the east coast of Australia, a rare breed from the old school who doesn't believe in ripping and slashing waves. He's a soul-surfer who takes a long, elegant line all the way to the end of the wave's energy. Daffy believes surfboard ankle leashes shouldn't be used. He claims there is an unencumbered purity to surfing an old, classic longboard without a leash—as natural as swimming naked.

I like to watch him surf because he has a distinctive, rangy style on his wide longboard, which he manoeuvres as if he were a lithe cat. Crouched on both knees, he swiftly paddles out in the old-fashioned Hawaiian way, stretches over his board, lines up a wave, and does his drop. He trims his wave, horizontal to the beach, surfing until it runs out of juice, then cuts up and shoots over the lip, grappling his board to paddle out for another. A waterman of the highest order, he can work miles of the open bay from the Point to the north end of town without an ankle leash, without missing a wave or ever losing his board.

What I really enjoy is observing him ride tandem with Dylan. He knee-paddles out with his son on the front of his board, takes the biggest wave of a set, and drops down the face, with little Dylan crouched on the flat, wide nose. Then his son stands, and they're both up, the two of them riding the board without a worry in the world.

On mellow days in the surf, I float with other surfers on the water, happy to be lying on my board, taking in the warm sunlight and gentle, glassy swells. There are always some young kids playing hooky from school, Daffy, a few other quiet regulars, and a couple of agro mongrels I've learned to steer clear of. Then a beautiful girl with dolphin-smooth breasts and a tremendous ass usually paddles out to join us. All eyes follow her as she takes whatever wave she wants, standing and shaking the water off her lovely curves, taking the wave so that her body disappears and all we can see is her head with its long, flowing hair as she moves fast along the breaking wave.

Daffy always breaks into his warm Hobbit smile as though he personally owns all the girls, the staggering view of the undulating coastline, and the entire Pacific Ocean. Frequently he says, "Rick, we'll have to get you to paddle over for a bit of a surf at the Point." Daffy brings up surfing the Point as a friendly offer and taunt, an ominous invitation to an unavoidable rite of passage.

On the surface Lennox Head is a quiet, friendly, conservative, family-oriented town of twenty-five-hundred souls. Lost in time, it's a Norman Rockwell beach town with two butchers, two surf shops, two gas stations, two fish-and-chip shops, two general stores, two video stores, a couple of small wooden churches, a CWA Hall, Chinese, Mexican, and health-food restaurants, a pizza shop, several funky clothing stores, a hardware store, a bank, a post office, a low-rise office building, and a sports field.

There is an open-air elementary school our kids attend, a voluntary fire brigade, a community centre with squash and tennis courts, a pub by the sea, a bottle shop, a bakery, and a bed-and-breakfast called Wave Hill House, above the roundabout. The sleepy little town is fronted by a seven-mile beach and nestled between the muscular, volcanic thrust of Lennox Headland and the rainforest of Broken Head. People with money live on the beach or on the rim of hills above town.

Because of an unpredictable cyclone season, king tides, and municipal bylaws, there are no restaurants or any buildings on the seashore, no high-rises whatsoever, no buildings crowding the coast. The beach here is empty and sacred, as natural as it was at the beginning of time. Rather than the sordid glitz of a California beach town, Lennox Head has the poky neglect, the slight stodginess, of an English seaside town. The beach, like the whole empty country, still feels as if it belongs to the Aborigines. Although friendly and warm, the people here mostly keep to themselves. Australians are funny, sarcastic, and quick to have a joke at your expense. Although they can dish it out, they aren't amused when you reciprocate. Their whole character is shaped from the years of splendid isolation they've enjoyed. Lennox Head seems to be left to meander in time, unhampered by the late twentieth century and the world's rat race. Most people have escaped from other parts of Australia or the world to live here, away from the complications of their former lives. I'm always on the verge of thinking: *Maybe I shouldn't be writing a book about this paradise. If the rest of the world knew about this place, it would be overrun by assholes the same way as Provence, Tuscany, the Greek islands, and Hawaii have been discovered through the overenthusiastic books of visiting writers.*

Surfers are romantics. On my first day at the Point I stand alone and nervously peer at the breaking waves, scared and excited by the fear. In wave terms the surf is around eight feet, but with the massive swell it seems as big as our two-story town house back home. It's a grinding, hairy, gnarly day. The famous maxim has it that waves aren't measured in feet but in increments of fear. To get into the water you have to watch the swells on the horizon and judge when it's safe to leap from the shore-line rocks and paddle as if your life depended on it, hoping you make it out before you're clobbered and thrown onto the razor rocks of the reef.

As I walk downhill through the tall grass to the water, I see a familiar Malibu longboard being punished on the rocks in the wave surge. Daffy is floundering in the deep soup of the churning surf, trying to swim back and collect his distressed board.

After he hauls his thirty-pound board from the water and finds the nose delaminated and chewed up, he shrugs and says, "Let's get wet, Rick." I swallow so hard I'm sure Daffy can hear me. Instead of looking him in the eye, I bend to grab my own eight-foot-two Maddog as he begins to stroll toward the horizon. This means we'll jump in off a dangerous ledge of rocks where even on a good day it's enough to set your voice high-pitched permanently. Grimly I follow Daffy along a well-trod, muddy footpath to the end of Lennox Point, while the colossal swells roll in from South America or Antarctica and break over the outer reef.

There's no sunshine to perk me up, and a hard rain drills into my shivering body, even through my Ripcurl spring wetsuit. I try to consider all the good reasons I should be back at my desk writing my book, doing the dishes and laundry, making the next meal, or standing without a blindfold in front of a firing squad. But instead we work our way down among the sharp, slippery rocks, deafened by the thundering surf. Then Daffy says nonchalantly, "Rick, back up. Look." My heart sinks when I see the wave version of the Canadian Rockies on the horizon, and we scramble back up among the rocks, our feet getting slashed, the wind blowing our big Malibu surfboards like banners, our hearts pounding. Just after I glance down to find a fairly stable rock for my bleeding feet to grip, the first wave of the set breaks and an Olympic swimming pool's worth of water rushes up to my face, which is bonily chinning itself up to God. I hold my board for dear life above my head like one of Moses' tablets, hoping I won't be hauled back, raked over the rocks, and shredded on the reef. And then, as the water starts to retreat, sucked back all the way to South America or Antarctica, Daffy yells, "Let's go, mate!" He jumps onto his board and paddles hard and fast. With no other options I leap onto my board and, on the forgiving shoulder of the outflowing backwash, inches over the shaggy reef bottom, paddle for all I'm worth.

I have to make it up the steep face and over the top of the first vasectomy-inducing wave, knowing if I don't get outside I'll be thrown onto the rocks and crucified. So I begin paddling even harder to avoid being caught inside the terrible legions of monster waves roaring in.

As I plunge into the fifteen-foot swells, eyeing the shifting peaks of A-frame water cathedrals breaking farther ahead, I have the biggest shit-eating grin of all time on my face. Daffy looks back over his shoulder to make sure I'm all right and following him out. In the thunder of mountainous surf I laugh like a maniac, thinking this is what my uncertain life as a crazed househusband has finally evolved into. I've reached some kind of personal destiny as I paddle to the outside of the glorious liquid canyons of Lennox Point in the Coral Sea, sniffing the sweet, salty brine, gazing into the vast depths of the ocean, then up at the dark-green-fringed volcanic immensity of Lennox Head jutting heavenward. Lock-jawed, I survey magnificent waves rolling in and sucking back as surfers take death-defying drops off curling two-story billows, and I wonder how I can possibly convince anyone that life can be so damn good, even for an aging househusband who may or may not have succeeded but who has thoroughly enjoyed pursuing the natural freedom of the search.

14
Snake in the Garden

I found out the hard way why a lot of surfers are beginning to wear helmets.

Out over the ocean the wind is blowing a gale, but up here the sun is shining, and when I gaze across the valley, all seems tranquil and harmonious. Because of the way I trimmed the treetops below, I can't see the new subdivision being gouged into the valley, only the breathtaking view down to the sea. Although I love them more than anything on earth, I'm still tightly wound up by my girls. Quinn isn't what you'd call a morning person. The only way to deal with her is to be patient and understanding. Sky rises every morning and tries to taunt Quinn into an argument, which is real easy. We're all trying not to yell and we're all striving to coexist. But as soon as Dale drives off to work, the girls start on each other, with me caught in the middle. I've been accused of being too slack with them and inconsistent. In other words, I'm wrapped around their pretty little fingers. But in this life, if one has to be wrapped around someone's fingers, why not those of two adorable little girls?

Unfortunately Quinn seems to be going through a particularly unreasonable phase. For example, if you pour her cereal in the wrong bowl, or give her the wrong colour shirt, or tell her to clean her room or brush her teeth, she often has a temper tantrum. This morning she has a particularly nasty fight with Sky when my older daughter offers to put Quinn's hair into pigtails. Quinn doesn't like the result and the two go at it. Finally I tell Sky to go ahead on her own to the bus stop because, as punishment, Quinn will have to walk with me to school. Quinn collapses, howling her lungs out, red-eyed and accusatory, and Sky whimpers, "What about the snakes?"

I collect my surf gear, make a snack, and clean up the kitchen, hoping Quinn will come around. Finally she creeps out of her room impeccably dressed and ready for school. "Daddy, can I please have some breakfast?" So I make her toast and peanut butter, spread the special way, pour milk into her favourite cup, and administer her vitamins.

She almost loses it again when I tell her to wear proper shoes and put on a jacket. I'm still angry with her, wondering how much a parent should or can take from such a sweet little girl. As we stroll up the lawn and down the road, the most glorious birds swoop by and palms sway in the fresh air. I carry my surfboard under one arm, and Quinn refuses to hold my other hand, so I guess our hostility works both ways. Then Quinn says, "Sorry, Dad, I don't want to be sent to frosty parents."

I stop walking, put my surfboard on the grass, and stare at the pavement. "Hey, Quintana, I'm going to draw a line." I drag a small lump of clay so that it scores a line on the road. Then I stand on one side and say, "That side of the line is your uncooperative behaviour this morning. This side is the rest of the day and the new, cooperative Quinn."

She seems pleased as hell and hops over to my side of the line, relieved to be rid of the bad old Quinn. I pick up my board, Quinn grabs my other hand, and we continue down the road until we get to the hill overlooking the valley of cows. As soon as we round the bend, we see the entire bay breaking with gigantic waves. Quinn releases my hand and runs along the fence until she comes to the first of the butterfly cocoons. I join her and squat to inspect the exquisite, mercurial sacks filled with butterflies that will soon blossom and fly away. Quinn glances down at the roundabout and spots best friend Lahni Brown with her big sister and asks me if she can walk the rest of the way to school with

Lahni. I say sure. Quinn yells for them to wait up, kisses me goodbye, and races off.

As I continue down the steep hill with the valley to my left, walking straight into the sea view, I realize I let her go because it will be easier for me to start hitchhiking to Byron from the upper roundabout. Quinn *has* apologized, and we've also made some constructive arrangements for her future behaviour. I think I've been a responsible parent, but once again, Quinn has managed to get the better of me.

In Australia there are few stoplights or stop signs because most intersections have roundabouts that allow traffic to keep moving. I stand at the roundabout above Lennox Head on the coastal highway that leads to Byron Bay, twenty minutes away, a surfer Jack Kerouac without a care in the world, dreaming of visionary possibilities and pointing my forefinger at the pavement, just ahead along the road, which is the way you thumb a ride in Australia.

A fair bit of time passes before any vehicles whiz by. As I hold my surfboard and gaze at the sky, I think about how I would have never learned so much about this place if I weren't a surfer, sniffing the wind, checking out the swells, looking out to sea every chance I get to suss out the waves, tides, and weather conditions. Because of my obsession with surfing and how much time, energy, and intimate knowledge of place it requires, in one year I'll probably know as much about this heavenly corner of Australia as anyone.

I don't notice the car stop until I hear a horn toot. Turning, I rush to catch up with a shit-kicked Holden with a killer surfboard strapped to the roof. A gnarly girl tosses out a couple of bungee cords and tells me to strap my board on. As I secure it, I notice a small, curly blond kid in a leopard-skin car seat who isn't buckled in. After I jump into the passenger seat with my day pack, I glance at the dashboard, which has a bumper sticker that says PURE FILTH, and a pile of tapes, several by a band called Psychotic Youth. "Ya goin' for a bit of a surf at Byron?" asks the girl beside me, who looks as though she's broken her nose. She's almost attractive, with a shell around her neck, long blond surfer-chick hair, and crooked white teeth. I tell her I'm going to hook up with a friend who lives in Byron and that we plan to surf Wategos. "Ah, yeah, you're Can-eye-dian," she says.

While I unload the abbreviated reason for my stay in Oz, I scan the incredible pile of junk on the dash: loose paper money and change, a couple of tired-looking toothbrushes, rusty scissors, leftover food, feathers, hash pipes, a pelt of fur, and bones. I'm sitting ankle-deep in magazines, Diet Coke cans, photos, clothing, and paperback novels, hurtling along at ninety miles an hour in a twenty-year-old crate on the narrow, hilly, winding road to Byron. Psychotic Youth is cranked up, and the little cherub in the back watches me talk with the eyes of an old soul.

When I turn to smile at the cute little guy, I notice that the back seat is even messier than the front. After roaming all over the back seat, the kid stands behind me, breathing down my neck the same way Jan and I used to behind Mom and Dad before seat belts became mandatory. Now I know why my dad invented the Flying Hand to give him a little personal space.

For the past year, the girl with the broken nose tells me, she's been living off and on in Nimbin, an infamous feral town up behind Byron in the hinterland. I tell her I took my kids there one weekend. Through rolling countryside of stone-walled houses and shaggy rainforest, Dale, the kids, and I passed giant columns of rocks that gave the eerie landscape the quality of a Chinese watercolour of Guilin. Nimbin, though, is a perfect example of the downside of paradise. It's a one-horse town full of junkies who wander the streets selling dope to make enough money to buy harder drugs. For a projected article I interviewed a needle-exchange worker. By 9:00 a.m. the addicts were already shooting up and buying and selling dope. The needle-exchange worker toured the sidewalks and public washrooms, which were designated unofficial safehouses for drug addicts. She politely refused to answer questions about the heroin issue, and even police officers wouldn't comment. A few heroin users opened up. One burnt-out guy about my age, a user for many years, told me most addicts needed a hell of a lot of money to stay on top of their habits. A person using $300 worth of heroin a day needed to sell five to six grams to create the turnover to support his own habit. A lot of the deals were done with out-of-towners. One lady who worked for the Nimbin Older Women's Forum serving soup on Friday mornings claimed heroin addicts suffered extremely low self-esteem. This was often the result of sexual, emotional, or physical abuse. "We shouldn't judge them too harshly," she said. "My own particular drug is nicotine, and there's a safehouse for alcohol users just down the road," she added, pointing to the local hotel.

"So whaddya think of Nimbin?" the girl driving me to Byron asks.

I don't want to tell her what I really think—that I once saw a teenage girl there like her slouched against a car just like hers. The girl was checking out the action coming and going to the washroom to shoot up. She bumped and gyrated with attitude and seemed to know everyone on the sidewalk. In a half-assed manner, and without even looking inside, she reached into the car to offer a milk bottle to a dirty-faced but grateful baby. Three junkies sat against the café wall, bleary-eyed and on the verge of vomiting.

"Didja get to visit the Nimbin Museum?" my driver asks.

"Yeah, it's a pretty interesting hippie hall of fame."

Outside the museum when I was there, a wasted man stood with a pit bull terrier that strutted around on a taut chain, its spiked collar choking it every time it lunged at someone. The dog's sadistic master eyed everyone to challenge him or his psycho canine, on any level, for any reason.

My family and I walked beyond the range of the dog's territory and into the creepiest museum I've ever been in. It was like shuffling through a dark cave on a bad trip to view a collage of hippie, drug, Aboriginal, and environmental cultures. There were enough contradictory spiritual aphorisms printed on the walls to start a handful of weird religions.

"Oy kin tell you weren't impressed with Nimbin," the girl says, smiling.

What I really want to tell her is that Nimbin is the kind of small town Charles Manson might like to settle down in if he ever gets out of prison.

What I do mention is that we enjoyed the hilltop village of Channon and its famous Sunday flea market, which is part joie de vivre circus, part Li'l Abner cartoon strip of country bumpkins with lumpy bodies in big boots and funny hats. Amid a New Age, hippie, American Indian, retro-renaissance, medieval stew, my family and I wandered around the craft and book stalls, exotic plants, food kiosks, garage-sale leftovers, jugglers, fire-baton-swinging ferals, aboriginal woodcarvers and musicians, drug dealers, Hare Krishna clones, and gawking tourists. Then we finished with a hike through the rainforest near the city of Lismore, once a famous river port in the nineteenth-century timber trade. We strolled through remnants of the Big Scrub, a forest of local red cedar, towering Morton Bay fig trees, all kinds of Aussie gum trees, and vines Tarzan would drool over. At one point on our hike we came upon hundreds of flying foxes perched upside down, like long-eared Siamese cats, on branches. We all gazed up, listening to them breathe. Then, for some reason, I rattled a long vine that ran up to the bats, and they all exploded, swooping away, their pterodactyl wings propelling them off the roof of the rainforest.

The girl driving me to Byron is on her way to Surfer's Paradise on the Gold Coast to surf and find work, so she can take off to meditate on a beach in Bali for a couple of months. Then she's going back to a small surfing town above Perth, twenty-five-hundred miles across the country.

"Does the father of your son help you out at all?" I ask incredulously, wondering what kind of life, what kind of chance, her kid really has.

"Ah, yeah, him. He sends money now and then so we can live."

The Lismore/Byron/Lennox area has the most single unemployed moms in Australia. I'm still bothered about the little cherub in the back seat who isn't buckled in. I see images of his mom ploughing into another car or one of the rainforest giants along the Broken Head Reserve road, and her kid flying through the windshield.

But he's okay for now, standing behind me as if I were his long-lost dad. He's polite, cheerful, and one of the best behaved little boys I've encountered in months. Here I do everything I should with my children, and this surfer chick breaks all the rules and sails through life without a care.

A light rain begins to filter through rumbling clouds as I saunter along the driveway, my surfboard under one arm. Dick and Deb are waiting for me on the verandah of their magnificent villa above Tallows Beach. Deb has taken my writing workshop, and I've surfed a few times with her husband, Dick. In my workshop Deb has been a gentle sweetie. At home she's even nicer. They're here for a year from Boulder, Colorado, working out the demons of their mid-life crisis, wondering how to proceed.

Deb is a psychotherapist who's also writing a book about healing through imagery. Wise, caring, and quietly perceptive—it's no wonder her practice burnt her out a little. Dick is an engineering contractor who owned a company with a couple of other partners. He managed to quit his job and duck out with his share of the company, which left him a tidy nest egg and more than enough to bring his whole family Down Under for a personal sabbatical. They bought a brand-new four-wheel-drive Jeep, a new motorcycle (complete with his and her leather gear), state-of-the-art laptops, wetsuits, and new surfboards after renting a sumptuous villa with a magnificent swimming pool. Owned by a local restaurateur, their villa wouldn't look out of place in Beverly Hills. Inside, its vast interior has expensive ceramic tiles and tropical wood flooring. With views down to the sea, it's elegantly furnished and filled with artwork. Their whole luxurious Mediterranean package is the flip side of Nimbin.

Lately, whenever Bernie is away on the offshore rigs, I've been getting into the habit of hanging out with Dick and Deb, and surfing with Dick. They always put out a fantastic feed when I arrive, and treat me like royalty because they're naturally hospitable, homesick, and a little bored with too much time on their hands. Dick and Deb seem curiously attracted by the fact that I'm soulfully driven by the love of my wife and kids, writing, surfing, and woodcarving. And not money.

Now we sit in the rain on their verandah gazing at that fabulous pool, sniffing frangipani and wild jasmine in huge Tuscan pots. Dick and I procrastinate about surfing because of the weather and because it's so pleasant to sit with Deb and eat and yack and bitch about how hard life is in paradise. We always compare notes about how to deal with our youngest daughters who bully their older siblings and hold the entire family to emotional ransom. Dick gets me another nonalcoholic beer, and Deb splashes a little more wine into their glasses and mentions something about confronting the illusions of youth we've all worked so hard to maintain. As rain tapers off, we talk about buying children's clothes, removing red soil from socks and pants, and forcing our offspring to love paradise, yet do their homework. When I tell them about the outlaw surfer chick from Nimbin who's doing everything against the grain, Deb relates all kinds of psychological and sociological explanations to balance the scales and make us sound like model parents. While we sit and relax, trying to articulate our place in the big scheme of things, watching the antipodean sky return, a pair of big black magpies alight in front of us, lean back, and let go with a warble of affirmation.

In a lull in the foul weather Dick and I pile our gear into his Jeep so we can go and check out the surf. If there's ever been a couple of fresh-faced novice surfers, it's us, but we have a fine time in the water. When Deb first introduced me to her husband, I pegged him as the straitlaced, clean-cut boy next door. He seemed uptight and a little lost without his job. But he has wild ideas about what he wants to pursue in the next few years of his new working life. He doesn't want to go back to the tread-mill of his old company. He'd like to open a gourmet cookie shop in Denver, but the idea of sitting by a cash register selling cookies, or mix-ing the big beater bowls of soft mix, quickly starts to sound like a doughy dead end. While in Tasmania Deb and Dick visited a vast pine-tree labyrinth an old man had spent eight years growing and trimming and now charged people to get lost and found in. Dick thinks about actually putting some of the money he got out of his company toward growing his own pine labyrinth when he returns home. His latest idea is to start a consulting company for men and women who want to do a mid-life crisis the creative way—with a so-called professional who will hold them by the hand and take them through the financial, emotional, and practical aspects of taking six months or a year off to find themselves and work out the sometimes nasty particulars such a crisis entails. It's an interesting plan, except that good and bad surprises are half the fun in life. Besides, right now they're living it up in their big villa, and Dick is trying to learn how to surf.

As we drive into Wategos, another bad-weather front is brewing, purpling the sky above the Cape Byron Lighthouse. The tide is coming in. Huge swells break without any surfers. The big smokers Bernie and I love to surf are closing out, but it's still holding up inside. A pod of dolphins frolics, ripping up and down the waves. In the distance Mount Warning is swathed in angry clouds. Without the sun the sea loses its warm turquoise appeal and takes on an evil iron patina that unfortu-nately makes it good and scary for sharks.

We saddle up and walk along the beach, past exposed barnacled rocks. As usual our enthusiasm is infectious; both of us are grinning like a couple of delinquent school kids. A stunning woman in an electric-orange thong bikini who's been jogging the beach decides to warm down with a few exotic calisthenics. Bending over in front of us, she puts one foot so far behind her head that Dick and I both get a headache.

Aside from the epic vistas, one of the many great things about Wategos is that you can shamble along the beach to the far end of the point if the tide is low enough and then jump in and paddle out to the waves. The beach here is scattered with more half-naked women. Some of these tanned goddesses bodysurf, diving in to catch waves, then standing to lift their faces to the sky as water runs down their sleek breasts. Out on the reef a few surfers paddle so fast diagonally across the bay to get a closer look at these topless beauties that other surfers could surf in their wakes.

We wade in, then paddle out through the muscle of swells, trying to dodge the biggest ones until we get outside. My first wave is a monster. I drop down the face and ride it fast, then crouch low while it closes out. And because I'm on an eight-foot mini-mal, I can work my way onto its nose to get more juice out of the energy curve of the wave.

In a half hour Dick catches more waves than he has in his whole career as a surfer. But the weather is deteriorating. The wind picks up, but we paddle out, anyway, and grab a wave on the outside that gives us such a rush when we drop down its face that I hear Dick let loose a bloodcurdling "Yeeehaaa!" before we're both drilled.

The poor weather is now a storm. I should be happy with all the rides I've already taken, but I yell above the howling wind, "Hey, Dick, I'm going out for one more!" He's had enough. Splayed on his board, he nods, then feebly begins the long paddle in through churning swells. Surfers and skiers will tell you it's always the last wave or the last run down the hill that does you in. With the gods severely frowning at me, I turn and paddle into the heaving surf, hoping to see dolphins, but apparently they've decided it's too rough even for them. The waves increase in size; the sea is really blown out now, the swells wrapping around the point at Little Wategos, rolling into Wategos, breaking all over the place, the wind typhooning. Neurotically I try to get into a good takeoff position but end up winded near an older woman on her board. "Isn't this just lovely, mate?" she asks, smiling with her wrinkled

Aussie face, gazing into the angry Michelangelo sky that hangs bloated above our heads. And I have to agree. I feel blessed by this gift. She must have picked up my vibe because she says, "Oy've surfed here for years and Oy still get stoked, even on a blown-out day like this."

Her sun-ravaged face looks as though it's recently been in a bad fire. I'm not surprised when she tells me she's lived here for twenty years. The woman informs me she and her husband have done a lot of things to survive on this coast: he's been a salesman and a teacher; she's worked in fish-and-chip shops, a lawyer's office, and the government. But now they're developers. "*Developer* is a dirty word around Byron," she says. "No one wants this area to change. No one wants the high-rises, the Japanese tourists, the highways, and the airports." She shakes her head. "But ya know, between the Greenies, the Aborigines, the politicians, and the developers, nothing ever gets done around here, anyway."

When the next set arrives and the first wave sucks back, the woman and I sprint-paddle into it together. But right after our drop we collide and the tip of her board whacks me on the back of the head. She winces and watches me pull off my cap and check for leaks or tears in my scalp. There's a bit of blood and a small rip in the flesh, and she nearly chokes with apologies. "Ah, don't worry about it. I'm having the time of my life," I say, grinning, though I do reconsider the uncomfortable notion about a shark's ability to smell a drop of blood from a mile away.

My head has a big lump covered in blood, and my leg has taken one of the fins of the woman's board so that it's bruised and swollen, too. But I feel so alive and happy to be out in that wild water that I nearly break into song.

To avoid an unwanted rendezvous with a blood-sniffing great white, I paddle hard into a steep inside section to catch my last wave of the day. I'm gliding along with the whole Pacific behind me when I suddenly realize I've made a terrible miscalculation. Now I'm too far inside, too far down the beach, and headed into the rocks. I panic and leap off my board to avoid the murderous shorebreak in front of me, thinking my borrowed surfboard will end up shattered on the rocks with me attached to its leash. Like a broken lawn chair, I wash in from the jaws of a six-foot break that's drawbridging in every ten seconds. I'm a fool, but during a brief lull I attempt to shoot out, then get trapped in the rip that takes me even farther along the rocky coastline. Paddling harder until I can touch bottom and hop between sharp rocks, I scuttle in as an annihilating wave hammers down, stranding me on a sandspit. Thunder rumbles in the roiling clouds, and wind slices the tops off the breaking surf, tugging and shaking my board and me so much I'm sure I won't be able to hold on. While I cut up my feet working back through the rocks to Dick on the main beach, the storm slams down around my ears. The lashing rain whips the life out of me, and at this point I take everything quite personally as I try to protect the fragile glass skin of my surfboard. Finally, as I struggle over to Dick, who has scrambled to the rocks to meet me, I see how worried he is. But when he notices the maniacal grin on my face, he just says, "Rick, I think we better call it a day."

By the time Dick and Deb and their two kids dump me off at my house, I feel like one of Robert Hughes's abused convicts after enduring a hundred lashes. Before they leave the couple presents me with a small poster of the North American Native chief White Cloud that Dick saw me admire in a Byron shop.

My kids are out back by the pool, not swimming, because they know they aren't allowed to without adult supervision. What they are doing, though, is much worse. In the pouring rain they're washing red mud off their legs, feet, and clothes. They're also filling up muddy red running shoes in the pool so that an evil, elongated cloud spreads on the turquoise water. Even though my girls are happy and proud of their initiative and cooperation, my heart sinks when I realize how much work it will take to restore the clarity of the pool. The garage is flooded with water and rain is still pouring down. I have to make dinner and clean the house before Dale arrives. I have to hang up laundry that's still crammed tight and wrinkled inside the washing machine. I'll have to pull it apart and drape it on a makeshift clothesline in the cold, damp garage, then rinse the salt water from my wetsuit and hang it up to dry. Later I'll have to spend the entire evening helping Quinn assemble her Native American project, and also assist Sky with the deadly details of her essay on Paraguay.

Our pool is flooding, and I stand in the rain backwashing it with the electric pump to bring the water level down, shivering because I'm still chilled to the bone from surfing. I curse the fact that I have to work so hard to maintain the pool, even though the girls don't use it much anymore except to wash their muddy shoes. Muttering in the dark beneath palm trees in a sublime deluge, I listen to the thunderous surf and breathe in the great soul of this coast, knowing one day soon I'll be back home shovelling snow in suburbia, dreaming of a moment like this.

As I finish backwashing the pool, I hear Rod's milk truck sputter to a stop at the dead end of Stoneyhurst, then run out front to get a couple of cartons of flavoured milk for my girls. We don't talk much in the dark because it's raining like hell and he's in a hurry to finish his route and go home. All he does is smirk and toss off, "Enjoyin' winta so fa, mate?"

I tell the girls they can sip flavoured milk with straws while they soak in a hot bath, but only if they promise not to fight. Even though I'll have to wait for a hot bath later when the heater kicks in again, I'm happy to have a little time to myself while the girls bathe. I bring the rolled-up poster to my desk, sit, and look out into blackness. Because of the storm, the swell is running high. It's so big that even with the windows closed the air reverberates with the noise of a thousand jet engines. Waves roll into the shoreline for miles up and down the coast. The churning ocean is like an enormous waterfall out of control, and for a moment I fear our house might be uprooted and washed down to the sea.

Carefully I unroll the poster Dick gave me. Beneath Chief White Cloud's eagle-feather headdress, his strong, sad face stares at me with great dignity and reproach. The caption above him reads: "Our belief is that the Great Spirit has created all things, not just mankind, but all animals, all plants, all rocks, all on earth and among the stars, with true soul. For us all, life is holy. But you do not understand our prayers when we address the sun, moon, and winds. You have judged us without understanding. Only because our prayers are different. But we are able to live in harmony with all of nature. All of nature is within us and we are part of all nature."

I weight each corner of the poster with books so that Chief White Cloud and I can stare at each other. I'm doing most of the work on Quinn's Native American project, mainly because it's something that intrigues me. These days it's nearly impossible to avoid the swamp of political correctness about Natives, so all you can really do is go with your heart and gut. Here in Byron there's an excessive romanticism about North America's indigenous people. They seem to like our Natives a lot more than their own Aborigines. But then I'm guilty of the same thing. Back home I probably wouldn't watch Natives carve totem poles, dance, or play music. But down here, like other phony tourists, I can't get enough of everything Aborigines do.

For Quinn's project I checked out a library book called *Native American Portraits: 1862–1918* by Nancy Hathaway. In it there's a haunting photograph of Sitting Bull wearing a cotton shirt and a buckskin jacket with a fur collar. "No Indian that ever lived loved the white man," he once said. "And no white man that ever lived loved the Indian." The photograph was taken by George W. Scott in the 1880s. Sitting Bull's eyes penetrate you, me, all of us, forever glassy-eyed with profound sadness and bitterness. On the brim of his hat is a magnificent butterfly, just above his wrinkled brow. He has the hard face of a brooding man that no apology could change. On another page is a photograph of Geronimo on his horse. He's wearing a bandanna around his head. Tight-lipped and grim-faced, he's riding off to a tragic moment in history with the white man's words hounding him to his death: "Geronimo: the most fiendish, cruel, and bloodthirsty of the Apaches now defying the United States and Mexico." The book is a catalogue of lost souls forever frozen in time, reminders of how, on an epic scale, things can go permanently wrong.

Tomorrow there will be twenty-eight flat cardboard Native American projects hanging on the walls of Quinn's grade two class. Twenty-seven adorable Australian kids and one even more adorable Canadian kid will be wearing papier-mâché headdresses, passing wampum and peace pipes around the classroom. Still, I can't let Quinn waltz into class with a project titled: "No Indian That Ever Lived Loved the White Man." Revising history and educating the young is a good start and a difficult proposition. In another book, *Speaking of Indians*, Ella Deloria, a Dakota writer who became a scholar and produced books about her society and grammar and a Sioux dictionary, wrote something in 1944 that pretty well sums it up: "All that which lies hidden in the remote past is interesting, to be sure, but not so important as the present and the future. The vital concern is not where people came from physically, but where they are going spiritually."

Now I'm even a little less critical about some of the scruffy characters who descend from Nimbin and the gloomy hinterland around Byron Bay with appropriated Native American garb—First Nations tattoos, hairdos, beads, leather pouches, fur vests, moccasins, jewellery, pendants—as if in some confused way they want to welcome back the sacred spirit of a defeated people from another one of history's fuck-ups. Beating drums, calling the wolves, sleeping in teepees, smoking peace pipes, living close to the earth so far away from the clean white rooms you and I fight to uphold.

I hear too much water splashing in the bathroom, and realize my girls are bickering, even screaming. I rush down the hall and push open the door of the foggy room. "Stop fighting!" I shout. "I want you to clean up in here, go to your rooms, and get dressed. Then start your homework while I make dinner." My free time is up. Soon Dale will be home and the evening roller coaster of hellish, sweet rituals will commence yet again.

I need one more quick breather. So I go out and stand under the verandah light, savouring the cold, fresh scent and the roar of surf and primeval rain hammering on the tin roof. I stare at the lush, dripping foliage of our wild front garden until I spy something peculiar in the light more than twenty yards away. Slowly I walk down to the far end to the part of the house we were told not to use. There, draped over the rafters under the overhang of the verandah roof, is a snake skin. Its owner was obviously coiled around the rafter and slowly, over a period of hours, shed the skin. The serpent was eight feet long, likely a diamond python or, what they call here, a carpet snake. Gently I pull the skin down; the end near the head is still moist. I hold it near the light and carefully tug it, and suddenly it's another foot longer, stretched so I can see the delicate tracings of eyes and even the nostrils, the mouth and the contours of a jaw line, perfectly reproduced. I sniff and come away with a smell like old meat, then shudder. At that point I decide to hide the snake skin in the garage away from the terrified eyes of Dale and the girls—all nine feet of the transparent, quicksilver spirit.

15
Good News from the Secret Annex

There is nothing in the world like a long sea view to lift the soul, even when the vista is half obscured in mist. I'm still grateful for the quiet splendour of this isolation while I gently tap away at the keys of my laptop during long, uninterrupted days of monsoon rain. Every morning the ocean is engulfed in a damp British Isles fog, and now only the white manes of blown-out surf are visible. Dark birds wheel through the swollen sky, horses and cows graze forlornly in the rain, and I can't resist disturbing the fragile balance of nature. A gorgeous butterfly is caught in one of the trampoline-size spiderwebs that inhales and exhales in the wind across my ocean view. From time to time the butterfly gathers its strength to flap itself free. A black spider the size of a rodent lurks in the shadows beside the verandah, either waiting for the butterfly to die of exhaustion, or enjoying the show before it dives into a smorgasbord ecstasy of colour. Even though I've been pushing *Charlotte's Web* on the girls at night, hoping to desensitize them to our dastardly, cohabitating friends, I'm still on the side of butterflies. So out the door I go, down the stairs of the verandah, and into the backyard to get the pool scooper. Then, with its long reach, I probe the distant web, pluck silky strands a couple of times and, suddenly, the butterfly is free.

One of Sky's new school friends is a Jehovah's Witness. Her mom sidled up next to me at a recent school dance, and when I mentioned surfing, she suggested we go out together. She had tracked us down, because we're still fairly new to town and, apparently, needed enlightenment and soul-saving. When we found out she was a local queen bee for the Jehovah's Witnesses, we tried to inform Sky as diplomatically as we could that we didn't want to get involved with the JW as a family here in Lennox, or anywhere else.

The next day two impossibly clean-cut lads arrived in the rain at our door, seemingly out of nowhere, to deliver a pamphlet called *Why Is Life So Full of Problems?* I glanced over at Dale, who looked at me as if to say, "Problems, you wanna talk about problems?" Most people must open their doors and see those words and get a sudden stab of recognition, because everyone's life is full of problems. Along with graphic images, the pamphlet listed grim statistics about crime, our besieged environment, poverty, hunger, and war, supplemented by a few words about family breakdown, unwed mothers, homelessness, drug and alcohol abuse, rampant immorality, and other signs of "civilization gone rotten." According to the JW, these problem-filled times are the "last days" and soon God will intervene. The world's other religions have failed, but true religion—the JW—obeys Christ's command to preach the Good News of God's Kingdom worldwide in 230 lands, no less.

The earthly paradise on the pamphlet is amazing. An Oriental mother and daughter pat a dangerous black bear near a huge blueberry bush. A little blond boy feeds a deer. A Middle Eastern mom and dad hold their four-year-old daughter up to stroke a ferocious lion, while a black couple saunter up a hill with big smiles because their baskets are full of fruit. And at a sustenance-giving tree in the foreground an evangelical man in a plaid shirt gives a pigtailed girl an apple, while a woman in a sari eats an apple as another lady dressed like a 1950s mom bends forward with her basket full of the fruit. Above this a cagey squirrel and an inquisitive police dog gaze on in absolute serenity and wonder. The air in JW paradise is clean, the mountaintops are rimmed with snow, and a river meanders through a perfect valley with forests, abundant fields, and waterfront properties that must be worth at least a half million dollars each. The only *problem* with this wonderful image is that it sidesteps reality.

God knows, the world has always been falling apart. These days families *are* in trouble. And after all the years that have passed since Sigmund Freud took a stab at plumbing the human psyche, and all of his followers added their two cents, we seem even more screwed up than ever before.

Thinking about how to save people, wishing there really was such a thing as the good old days, or the great days to come or, more realistically, good days now and again, I stare down at my glorious valley that's so unlike the fantasy depicted in the JW pamphlet. Lennox Head, cut off from the rest of the mean-spirited, overcrowded, ugly, complex world, is pretty decent and blessed with so much.

Sky continued to play with her JW friend until one day her friend's mother brought Sky home. Since it was Sunday, I was concerned the kid's mom would step into our house and unleash the full fury of missionary zeal. And I was right. She breezed in with an armload of religious publications. She could obviously spot a heathen in trouble a mile away. Dale and I stood speechless as she unloaded her spiel. Unfortunately Dale took the bait, and soon they were in a heated discussion about God and finding a real home in an unhappy world of nonbelievers. While they talked in the kitchen, I began cleaning the counter and cupboards, sweeping up murdered ants. Maybe a little too histrionically, I compressed an egg carton, cereal boxes, and tin cans. I emptied the dishwasher, then scraped dirty plates and filled the dishwasher, hoping Dale would get the hint to ease this woman's fire and brimstone out of our house. But Dale is kindhearted and an enthusiastic conversationalist who is naturally curious about how the world works.

I shook out carpets and stickhandled a broom around the house, and soon it was almost seven o'clock and the kids hadn't eaten. I was ready to scream, but the kitchen—in fact, most of the house—was now immaculate. Finally, when the Jehovah's Witness woman left, I blasted Dale for letting her get her hooks into us. Of course, Dale and the girls thought I was wrong about this woman and her daughter and the motivation for their sudden earnest friendship. Reheated pizza was hurriedly swallowed and washed down with flat Coke. The girls couldn't understand why I had been so rude. Even Dale was convinced I was a boor for castigating the kind, poor woman who was only trying to be a good neighbour.

Less than a half hour later, while Dale and the girls were still bad-mouthing me, the side door to our house opened and the JW woman stepped in with an enormous stuffed white bear with a red heart in its paws. She also had a letter for Sky from her daughter and three videotapes that helped to further her religious doctrine. As gently as I could, I reached over and put my hand on her arm. "Sky can be friends with your daughter as long as they keep religion out of it." By this time, Dale was on my side and spoke up. "Sky's best friend in Canada, Narmeen, is Muslim, and they never let religion get in the way of their friendship." The lady smiled knowingly. "The Muslims are in need of saving them-selves. Oh, yes, I was once unsure of myself," she said darkly, "skeptical, like you, before I found the true—" In unison Dale and I said we weren't interested. She stepped forward and pressed the videos on us once more. Her eyes refocused on Dale, because she had made a little headway an hour earlier when Dale actually brought up her religious beliefs. But she didn't look at me because she knew I knew she'd never get to me. I would leave this earth a doomed soul, who would no doubt suffer eternal damna-tion or something equally uncomfortable, such as another suburban winter back home.

By the time the JW woman left, our confused kids had been emotion-ally shark-attacked. It was like finding out Jesus, Santa Claus, the Easter Bunny, and the Tooth Fairy were actually used-car salesmen. Sky ran into her room and slammed the door. Quinn was under her bedcovers whimpering. Dale was lying in our bed staring at Melissa's etching of the mermaid holding a dolphin swimming through its fantastic underwater seascape. Out in the clean kitchen I stood alone, gazing at the ridiculously oversize, uncuddled, white teddy bear with the red heart in its paws.

The next day I was invited to Quinn's classroom to see twenty-eight life-size faces of teddy bears that had been clothes-pinned on a long string near the ceiling. There was one bear drawing for each angel in the classroom. Some really did look like the inquisitive faces of teddy bears; others had the appearance of frisky werewolves. Certain childlike ones uncannily resembled the haunted faces of children. Seeing twenty-eight adorable silhouettes peer back at me with such imploring honesty inspired me to reassess my own cynicism about the goodness of humanity. Jenny Close's grade one classroom always reeks of innocence and hope and makes me realize children are the best cure we have against all the bad things in the world.

I think I know why a lot of writers drink. They distill everything through their heads, hearts, and guts and foolishly attempt to turn it into words. Sometimes I'll do almost anything rather than sit my ass down to write. Sometimes I eat, do odd jobs around the house, study myself in the mirror, pace the rooms, hold my dick, or stare out the window. Even when the juice is flowing and I can't wait to get back to my desk, the neurotic anticipation that I might be writing either great literature or dog shit leaves me so agitated I need release. Luckily I have Dale and the girls, housework and swimming. I quit drinking the first weekend of 1973 and haven't had a drop since, but I understand why a lot of writers get caught up in the habit. With my obsessive personality, if I'd kept drinking, I wouldn't be alive today.

Winters are pretty tame here compared to back home, but even in paradise I've succumbed to the chill of the winter blues. The black mood. Sore throats, sucking on cough drops. Because Australian houses aren't heated, everything, each piece of clothing and furniture, every towel, utensil, book, and computer key, is cool to the touch. Our beds are profoundly damp and cold. The air inside our lonely house is frigid, and all the smart-arsed Aussies are always chanting, "You're Canadian, mate. You should be used to this weather." Yes, I say, but we have insulation and central heating. Here the only way to get warm is to go to bed under a ton of blankets, take a hot bath or shower, drink something warm, or find a little shelter in the sun out of the wind.

Writing at my desk in front of this sea view, sipping a glass of mango nectar with two ice cubes as if it were expensive Scotch, I figure I've never been happier in my life. To get warm, I swept the floors, washed the bathtub and toilets, and had a hot shower. Because of all the sun and salt water, my hair appears deceptively thick, though it's actually murderously thin. I'm wrapped in a blanket at my desk, trying not to stare into the closed-off part of the house with the fireplace. A few books are open on my desk: *Light Years* by James Salter, *On Water* by Thomas Farber, and *Anne Frank: The Diary of a Young Girl.* The house is absolutely still. Sky is sleeping bundled in blankets on the verandah. She came home early from school with a bad cold and the shivers—pale as a ghost. I made her hot chocolate, set her up in a lawn chair in a cozy corner of the verandah protected from the wind, and let her sleep in the warm sunlight. Just before she nodded off, I brought her a hot-water bottle, and she looked up at me with such gratitude and ferocious love that I hugged her and closed my eyes, remembering the early years when our bodies and minds were fused day and night until I seemed to disappear into her entirely. Now this lanky kid is already showing signs of independence and becoming a young woman. Modest now because she's so humble, sweet, caring, enthusiastic, blossoming into a natural beauty. A few weeks earlier when she was running along the beach in a blue bikini, I noticed her perfect body and carefree smile tormenting boys and young men.

All this commotion about the Jehovah's Witness, God's unhappy kingdom, and civilization gone rotten has spooked us. At night Sky and I have been dipping into Anne Frank because my daughter has to read the diary for school. Each night we talk about Anne as though she were living at Stoneyhurst Manor with us. In the dusty library of this house we found a yellowed paperback copy of the diary. The black-and-white photo of Anne on the cover is so creased with lines that her brave, pretty face appears shattered. Most of the pages are folded over from so many young girls who have read the book alone at night in bed. In a sleeve inside the back cover there's a library card filled with the handwritten names of more than twenty little girls, like cult members, with names such as Katy, Rebecca, Vicky, Susan, Kathleen, Nadia, Debbie, Karen, Sasha, even Anne, and now Sky.

I'd forgotten how troubling Anne's book is, and not just because of the horrors of the Holocaust. Among other things, her diary tells of the secret isolation of girls and their universal uncertainties about living, parental conflicts, love, heartache and longings. Hers is one of the most engaging voices you'll ever read, and the diary is one of the biggest-selling nonfiction books in the West. On her way to the secret annex where she spent the rest of the war in hiding, Anne wrote: "So we walked in the pouring rain, Daddy, Mummy, and I each with a school satchel and shopping bag filled to the brim with all kinds of things thrown together.... We got sympathetic looks from people on their way to work. You could see by their faces how sorry they were they couldn't offer us a lift; the gaudy yellow star spoke for itself." After Sky and I read the line, "I hid myself within myself," she made a very astute comment: "Dad, Anne Frank kind of reminds me of Aunty Jan."

It was true. Like Anne, my sister, Jan, had been born happy. She used to love people and had a trusting nature. She wanted everyone else to be happy, too. Before the holocaust of drinking got its hooks into my little sister, she had an innocent tenderness. Anne's words—"Leave me in peace, let me sleep one night at least without my pillow being wet with tears, my eyes burning and my head throbbing. Let me get away from it all, preferably away from the world"—could have been Jan's words later in life. Unlike her psycho brother, Jan never took chances. She always played it safe, never got a driver's licence, and never travelled. Jan rarely left her house, yet she died ten feet inside the front door of her home. She died a month before Dale and I escaped to Australia, and I'm still harbouring an enormous guilt about not being able to save her the way big brothers are supposed to. We lived the first twenty years of our life together. We were best friends, buddies. She worshipped me: a rapt audience of one. Even though I was sixteen months older and nearly a foot taller, she used to introduce me to all her cute friends as an affectionate tease when we were teenagers: "This is my little baby brother, Rick." She was much smarter and better behaved. An absolutely loyal friend, she was pretty with long dark hair and white porcelain skin. Jan was never attached to material things, but she loved dogs, cats, and horses, as well as wild things like birds, squirrels, and raccoons that lived behind the big sundeck of her isolated house in the Gatineau Hills. Perhaps she discovered that animals were a lot less complicated and more dependable than people. Eventually she learned to treat plants and animals better than people, because at some point, a very long time ago, she succumbed to a weakness for drinking.

It's always tempting to freeze childhood and remember it as a lost paradise of innocence and purity. There's nothing in the world like the idea of a magic childhood: my little sister and I held close in a cocoon of love, security, and enchantment. We used to play with our teddy bears, a wolf, a dog, and a duck: Big Ted and Little Ted, Wolfie and Donald. After supper we'd sit for hours in each other's room and play, then go to bed happy. As we got older, I'd come into her room, sit on the edge of the bed, and seriously discuss our hopes and dreams, the volatile intrigues of school and our girlfriends and boyfriends.

The year after John F. Kennedy was shot, we got two Beatle albums, *Twist and Shout* and *Long Tall Sally*. We'd play the albums over and over on a little square record player. Lifting the arm with the needle and placing it on the disc, we waited until the salt-and-pepper noise of the needle began scratching the vinyl: "Well, she was just seventeen, and you know what I mean, And the way she looked was way beyond compare..." Like a huge, breaking wave, the Beatles swept up our whole generation. Beatlemania was so profound and complete it became a new religion for many of us growing up in the 1960s. At corner stores Jan and I purchased Beatle cards and compared and traded them for our favourite Beatle—baby-faced Paul, pensive John, floppy-eared George, and cross-eyed Ringo Starr. I can still smell that sweet powdery pink bubble gum we got inside the cards. We chewed big globs of it until our jaws ached. Every few months a new number-one Beatle song arrived to cheer us up. For about eight years the albums kept coming while we travelled from the safety of childhood into the dangerous realm of teenagers.

In the endless summers at our cottage in Norway Bay under the big pine trees, we set our record player on the picnic table and listened to the Beatles with our friends. This was the big spawn of the baby boomers. The early 1960s was a time of remarkable energy despite the anxiety of the Bomb, the Pill, and the Sexual Revolution. As kids, we danced, held hands, swooned, and kissed under the spell of Beatles magic. We all knew the titles, the love-tugging sentiments and words by heart from listening to those Capitol records hundreds of times: "She Loves You," "I Should Have Known Better," "I Want to Hold Your Hand," "This Boy," "Please Please Me," "Love Me Do," "Eight Days a Week." For most of us hide-and-seek was the favourite game: the excitement of being pursued in the dark, evading detection, the smell of pine needles against your face while lying on the ground, the seaweed-fish smell of the flowing river, the exhilaration of hiding with someone else, even kissing them while everyone else was looking for you. Lying in damp leaves under an upturned boat with your heart pounding, or behind someone else's cottage, and then running for home before you were touched was sublime. But for some reason hide-and-seek terrified Jan: being alone in the dark, being pursued, being caught. At a certain age she refused to play anymore. Jan never played on a team, never won any medals, trophies, ribbons, or prizes. She refused to compete or play games, yet everyone was drawn to her vulnerability.

Twenty-four years ago, after a half decade of drinking like a maniac, I quit forever. One night in 1971 while driving drunk I went through the windshield of my first car, an orange 1960 Volkswagen. At a party I'd consumed countless bottles of beer and glasses of vodka and orange juice. Five minutes after I dropped off two pretty girls from the party I careened around a corner in the famous black rain of North Vancouver and slammed into a telephone pole, so drunk I didn't even remember hitting the pole. I took forty-five stitches in my face, got two black eyes, and had glass embedded in my forehead, eyelids, and chin. My knee went through the radio, and the steering wheel broke across my chest. My green-striped rugby shirt, jean jacket, and cowboy boots were soaked in blood. After surgery a friend drove me home and I staggered into my mother and father's bedroom like a stitched-up Frankenstein monster at 2:00 a.m., still plastered. I can still see them cowering in their bed, staring in horror at their massacred son. In the morning while my parents sat me down for a serious talk, Jan, who was only sixteen, crept into the kitchen. When she saw me, she broke into painful sobs, rushed over, and hugged me so hard I thought nothing bad could ever happen to either one of us again.

I was eighteen, still cocky, invincible, and tough in my deluded innocence. I never got behind the wheel of a car after drinking again, but I drank even harder for another year and a half. As the saying goes, I drank enough for a lifetime. It was August 1972, and I had just returned from a glorious summer surfing and living with my girlfriend, Jerry, in Hawaii for two months. Our family was moving back to Ottawa after four years of living on the side of Grouse Mountain in North Vancouver. I had an old girlfriend, Sandra, to hook up with again. Jan had old flames waiting. We flew home ahead of my mom and dad who drove from Vancouver back to Ottawa with our family dog and a cabin cruiser on a trailer, doing the trip together, travelling alone without kids in what was called a second honeymoon and might now be termed a creative mid-life crisis. Unfortunately for our neighbours at the cottage, this meant Jan and I lived at the bay in August, completely unsupervised. We were reunited with the kids we'd grown up with, except now we were all raging teenagers, drinking, smoking, and falling in love with someone new every day. While Jan and I drank in the sweet passions and pleasures of our youth and tried to relive the memories of our idyllic childhood summers at the bay, our cottage became the focal point of everything.

Most evenings we'd drive up to Holmes Country Store and buy eight twenty-four-bottle cases of beer. We backed Brent's Dodge Demon up to the cottage and bucket-brigaded the two-fours from the car trunk to the fridge and a bathtub filled with ice. We were all good-looking, immortal, and tanned. All day we swam and water-skied behind Jamie's boat. We washed our hair in the river and combed it until it dried in the sunlight. Then, later, with our sun-bleached hair fluffed, we put on our favourite cutoffs and T-shirts and converged on the cottage. Each night with our hormones raging we sat around in the living room of my mom and dad's old cottage, waiting for the booze to kick in and listening to the throbbing music of Jethro Tull, America, Alice Cooper, the James Gang, the Rolling Stones, The Who, and Yes pumping out of atomic speakers. Everything would escalate. These earthshaking parties usually spilled out the front door, and neighbours would arrive to intervene in lovers' spats or break up drunken football games on the dented roofs, trunks, and hoods of parked cars. Sometimes we'd end up drinking down the road at River View Inn, cranking up the jukebox, dancing, necking, and often fighting with the local country folk. And on the hottest August nights, in the river while skinny-dipping in moonlight, we'd fall in love.

Late in the morning after each party we shovelled up vomit, collected bottles, emptied ashtrays, and repaired broken windows and punched holes in the walls, then swept out the entire cottage. Long afternoons were spent on the beach, or we'd swim out to lie comatose on the raft, dreaming of the next night's drunk. None of us listened to the warning. It was as though we were living in the sweet desperation of wartime, drinking and taking lovers as though there were no tomorrows.

Out of the heightened fever of this legendary summer of 1972 Jan and I took divergent paths. Even though she'd finished high school in Vancouver with straight A's, in Ottawa she started a job and got married almost right away. I drifted into an open-ended arts degree at university and moved through a dreamlike fog of summer nostalgia, poor study habits, sports cars, and girlfriends. And then one evening I disgraced myself at a 1972–73 New Year's Eve party where I consumed a mickey of vodka and a dozen beers and got into a fight. I destroyed a table horsing around with a barbell set and lost the friendship of Jamie. That night when Jan and I stepped out the door of that party, we fell drunk into the snow, one on each side of the front porch. It was a pathetic end to the glorious year of 1972. The very next Saturday at the cottage on a snow-mobiling weekend with the lads I had an epiphany. I lifted my bottle of beer and said, "You know, this stuff really isn't good for you. I'm going to quit." My friends scoffed.

But I did. I read more novels, lifted weights, ate health food, and swam at the university. I took up writing and got serious about life. I met Dale and hit the road in my blue 1969 MGB.

Meanwhile Jan was married to a guy who loved to drink as much as she did. Like most deluded drinkers, he claimed he could hold his liquor. Jan had a miscarriage and continued drinking while her marriage unravelled and her self-esteem plummeted. She quit her job and began a new one with the Canadian government. She also started seeing the man who many years later would become her second husband.

When I was a teenager, my parents and sister dragged me to the library. Although I finally became a reader, a writer, a book reviewer, and a university English literature lecturer, I hated books back then. Every two weeks they'd haul out a dozen volumes each, bring them home, and buzz through them like termites—hundreds and hundreds of books while I lived a restless existence of perpetual motion, a hyperactive kid with no sense of direction and no brakes.

Jan passed a lot of time in her room reading. At some point she became an unhealthy serious reader and discovered the double-edged sword of solitude. She was consumed by what we now call "issues about her self-esteem and weight." Her weight fluctuated most of her life. We both got acne. Mine was so severe that for a half decade it nearly drove me to suicide. For both of us the drinking that began in earnest around 1970 acted as an emotional crutch, easing the pain of our adolescent paranoia and fears: Jan's weight and insecurity, my acne and manic restlessness.

Jan always loved horses. She drew portraits of them, and the walls of her room were covered with the photographs of horses. Her biggest fantasy was to have a horse of her own and go riding every day. She read all the horse books and saw all the maudlin horse movies: *My Friend Flicka*, *Thunderhead*, *Black Beauty*. We even watched hours of *Mister Ed* bad-mouthing his owner, Wilbur. On TV Jan and I also watched *The Man from U.N.C.L.E.*, *Lost in Space*, *Bugs Bunny*, *I Spy*, *The Invaders*, and all the cowboy movies on Saturday afternoon as well as the swashbuckling flicks and war films. We had nicknames for our favourite TV characters and sometimes, for a treat, we ate meals on tiny TV tables that wobbled and spilled our fish and chips and chocolate milk. After spending twenty years in front of a TV set with someone, you bond. Our love and companionship was so intense, it was like a marriage of souls.

Most of my relatives have lived long, happy lives. Unfortunately drinkers and their unholy obsessions lurk in both my family and Dale's. One grandfather died a canine death on the streets of Montreal. Another relation, at the end of her life, beat the bottle but succumbed to a heart attack alone in a Daytona Beach hotel. A restless uncle was a romantic Jack Kerouac type who drank and smashed up carloads of beautiful women. My wise, forward-thinking mother used to hold him up as an example of what I'd become if I kept drinking. The uncle eventually went to jail for a decade—entered it fighting and then, rehabilitated, walked out middle-aged and humbled forever. He married a wonderful teacher who loved the good man he'd become and always was. They had a son, and the uncle moved on serenely without booze. Distant aunts, uncles, and cousins were taken away or consumed one way or another by alcohol.

For five years I drank to get drunk and feed my restlessness. Jan drank from about 1970 until a year before she died in the house fire in

November 1996. Somewhere along the line she lost the ability to live life sober. For twenty-five years she lived in a shark-infested pool.

Alcohol had my sister in its evil grip so badly that it gradually built a wall between us. Jan gave into alcohol after any emotional crisis she couldn't handle, and when she was on a binge, she'd drink and drink and not eat. She'd be on a roller coaster of I love yous and I hate yous. We all tried to get her institutionalized but were told that if she wouldn't cooperate, she couldn't be held against her will. Like most alcoholics, she denied the very existence of her problem. Jan was scared to death of doctors and hospitals and any confinement other than her own self-imposed exile. In some ways she was the haunted spectre of what I might have easily become if I hadn't quit drinking. If I hadn't met Dale. If I hadn't had my own kids, swimming, and that huge component in life—mysterious luck.

A few hellish days after my sister died in the house fire with my four-year-old nephew, my mother and father flew up from Florida where they live six months of the year. They returned to do one of the things you weren't supposed to do in life—attend the funeral service of their youngest child. I was asked to give a eulogy. In front of two hundred unhappy strangers, family, friends who had grown up with Jan at the cottage, and members of the community of Chelsea, I spoke about how much I cherished the memory of our twenty years of life together with my mother and father, who were the best parents any kids could have had. Then I launched into an incident that had happened when Jan and I were about five and three.

One morning we got up early and went downstairs to find the paint my mother and father were using to redecorate some rooms upstairs. I poured a gallon of white paint into my little red wagon along with a gallon of red and mixed them until I concocted an electric-pink. Like a possessed Cat in the Hat, I got us started with brushes, rollers, and bare hands and feet until we painted swathes on the floor and walls, the washing machine, the record player, the stairway, an old fridge, a guitar, books and everything else in our manic path. Of course, it was my fault; back then Jan would never do anything wrong to upset anyone. Because I had said it was all right, she had trusted me completely. For one shimmering, tension-breaking moment all two hundred people at the funeral laughed as I described how this pink haunted our lives for years, and how my poor father broke a hairbrush on my bony ass for instigating this unspeakable artistic frenzy. As I told the gathering about how close I'd been to my little sister those first twenty years and how much I loved her, how we listened to the Beatles on our little record player, my throat suddenly constricted. Most of the people in the church had no idea how reclusive and troubled my sister had been the past twenty years.

Where do you go when you're caught in the grip of death? Jan was here, now she was gone. She exists only in the minds, the hearts, and the memories of a brother, a mother, a father, two husbands, her surviving children, and her friends. And now I think about her every time I glance out this window in Australia and see those lonely horses on the cliff above the ocean, tails waving in the onshore breeze, the magnificent sky a perfect backdrop to eternity. Jan was a sentimental romantic, who could also switch on a caustic intellect, a recluse's encyclopedic peephole knowledge of the world. Sober, she could talk on the telephone enthusiastically and with great warmth, but face-to-face she couldn't sit still. One minute she'd be up pouring a drink of water, or booze, and unreasonably scolding the children around her, or she'd be alone on the verandah dragging desperately on a cigarette because she couldn't cope. Being confronted by her cherished brother, a reformed alcoholic, only made her feel threatened, guilty, ashamed, and judged.

For many years she wrote sad, beautiful poetry that I encouraged her to develop: "From here, where are the stars/upon the ground so low/infinity is complete/our heads forever bowed." A long time ago she had played guitar, written songs, and performed them with her best friend, Janine, in Vancouver. One of her favourite songs was Janis Ian's "At Seventeen," a bittersweet tune of adolescence. "I learned the truth at seventeen that love was meant for beauty queens..."

The nature of Jan's unhappiness is still a disturbing mystery. I scare myself to death when I think about the genes lurking inside Sky, who is so much like me, and Quinn who has Jan's stubbornness and brains. How can I channel these girls of mine safely through the evil waters so they can also enjoy what is wild and free, yet survive their own summer of 1972?

Were Jan's black depressions the result of drinking, or did she drink to survive the blues? Often she seemed to have no self-esteem, as though she were a ghost lost in her own life. She retreated more and more into her house in the Gatineau Hills, and finally into herself. She cared for and loved her three children and her husband, but no one could save her. The grip of her depression and fear was so ferocious it nearly killed her several times.

The four horses have moved up the hill, near the top of the ridge, still eating with their heads bent low, their shadows twenty feet long in the sunlight slanting down into the soft lines of the hinterland. A white horse, a black horse, and two lovely roans—my sister's horses grazing in a paradise she never found.

Sitting here with the sea eternally rolling in, I try to come to terms with Jan's death and this diary of Anne Frank's I've been reading at night with Sky. I think about how vulnerable my little girls are, how precious they are to me. I imagine Anne walking with her family through the pouring rain to their new accommodation where they lived for the remainder of the war in sealed attic rooms in what Anne liked to call her beautiful secret annex. "I'm sitting cozily in the main office," she wrote, "looking outside through a slit in the curtain. It is dusk but still just light enough to write to you. It is a very queer sight as I watch people walking by...who besides me will ever read these letters...? It is lovely weather and in spite of everything we make the most we can of it by lying on a camp bed in the attic where the sun shines through an open window...."

This is my own secret annex from the world, looking out over the sea as time moves ever onward. I'll never forget this view, this place, this frame of mind: horses cavorting on the ridge, surf breaking in the distance, birds making raucous music, burning leaves wafting their smell in my direction. But how can I speak of such joy when Jan and Anne were locked away in their own secret annexes, waiting for the Nazis, or sharks, to break down their doors?

Nearby Steve is riding his lawn mower. He's cutting his grass, no doubt dodging the big snakes. I decide to walk over in bare feet to bring him two buckets of pinecones for his fireplace. When we first arrived in

Lennox and told Steve about Jan and the house fire, he could tell her death had followed us all the way to the bottom of the world. Now he turns off his mower and wipes sweat off his forehead with the back of his hand, his face breaking into one of his warm, intuitive smiles. "What's new, mate?" he asks. I tell him I've been reading Anne Frank with Sky for her English class and feel compelled to work the doomed girl into my book. Steve reveals that on a backpacking odyssey through Europe when he was a young bloke he actually visited the Anne Frank House in Amsterdam. He says it made him feel angry about what she had to go through. As he talks, I can visualize the still waters of a canal, darkened rooms. I sniff the musty, narrow hallways haunted by the soaring spirit of a young girl.

Right now I don't feel guilty about Jan or Anne or anybody while I'm living such a blessed life here. I've lived through my own nightmares, and I'll suffer again in the future. I'm like Jan and Anne, I guess, pouring out my heart on paper. Except I'm writing from the point of view of a man who has almost absolute freedom. This is the kind of freedom Jan was missing and lost. The kind Anne was trying to defend and celebrate.

In the late afternoon when the wind drops, my American friend, Frank "Kiko" Michael, picks me up in his old van cluttered with construction tools. Kiko has taken off work early to surf with me. Sky is watching TV, and Quinn has gone to Lahni's after school. Kiko and I drive into Lennox to the dead end of Dress Circle Parade where we park above the ocean. As we strip and get into our wetsuits and then wax our boards, the heavens open up. Radiant sunlight illuminates the entire ocean. Whales breach. Miraculously we have the place to ourselves.

The break we head out to near the boat channel is actually named Frank's Spot, after Kiko who has surfed here with his mates, the Three Amigos, for many years. For every wave Kiko achieves, I get severely rag-dolled over the falls. But I paddle back out for more. Kiko glides effortlessly into big waves I can't handle. But I'm happy to watch and learn. Between the thrashings, as we drift, it's peaceful and mellow. We don't talk much because we don't know each other that well. Kiko seems to have a lot on his mind but isn't ready to spill any of it just yet. During a lull in the waves, he describes surfing in Hawaii, California, and Mexico. There's no wind, and we can hear the waves breaking as they move farther onto the inside reef. It's a sacred privilege just to be out there on our boards in the middle of the ocean.

Finally, when the tide drops too low, Kiko tells me he's taking the next wave in. I nod and watch him masterfully descend the face of a steep wave, his hawklike countenance regal, riding with his arms and hands, even his fingers, outstretched to balance, human poetry in motion, until he disappears in a train of white water.

Alone, I watch a sea eagle swoop to snatch a fish out of the water. It flies so close I can see its rusty, shimmering brown feathers, its pure white head, its furious eyes searching the air until it catches an updraft and soars away, gripping the fish in its talons, the fish still swimming fifty yards in the sky.

I paddle into my own last wave, riding in front of the curl with ease, sliding along and then dropping into another glassy inside curl that breaks and takes me in fast over the reef. Fascinated, I look down at the colours of the sea bottom rushing below me until I realize with a sinking feeling that I'm surfing in barely a foot of water. Suddenly I run out of liquid altogether and hang up on the reef, snapping a fin on my surfboard and slashing my feet.

Bleeding, and with a sheared-off fin in one hand and my surfboard tucked under my other arm, I carefully walk over the sharp reef until I reach a shallow sandbar. Everything considered, it all seems like some kind of validation, and I arrive at the van with a silly grin on my face. Kiko just says, "Don't worry about it, amigo. I can glass in a new fin for you. No prob."

Everyone wants quick answers or shortcuts to give their lives meaning and stability. Jan was a fantastic sister to grow up with. She loved me intensely, perhaps set me up on a pedestal she had to topple now and again. If only Jan could have found the door to my secret annex. But in the secluded house of Jan's night, even her big brother couldn't save her.

16
Romantic Egoists

I can still smell the cocoa butter Jerry and I used to rub on each other's body as we fried in the Hawaiian sun—young, invulnerable, and free. Not yet twenty, I was seduced by the ocean and the beach while living in Vancouver for four years. In the spring of 1972 I took the next step and headed for Hawaii to learn how to surf—three weeks alone near the beach in a room at the old Edgewater Hotel with a lot of beer, Ernest Hemingway, and Scott Fitzgerald and the music of Neil Young's "Everybody Knows This Is Nowhere" and "Who's Next?" and the Rolling Stones' "Exile on Main Street." I spent most of the day swimming and surfing the mythic breaks of Waikiki from Ala Moana to Diamond Head. It became my private paradise.

On my second day I fell brutally in love with Jerry, an American girl from Nebraska. She was a couple of years older than I was and worked as a nanny in a mansion in Kahala on the other side of Diamond Head. We met in the dark one night on the beach in front of the Reef Hotel. It was love at first sight, sweet and all-consuming, and for the next three weeks we passed as much time as we could together. I returned to Vancouver on my charter flight and then flew right back to Hawaii, living with Jerry in the mansion she worked in because the family was on a transcontinental trip and said she could have me as a houseguest while they were away. They left us the keys to a Jaguar XKE, a 1969 Camaro convertible, a cabin cruiser, and enough booze to start the Roaring Twenties all over again. The melancholy, elegant mother of the children Jerry baby-sat was one of those tragic domestic alcoholics. Her husband was up to his eyeballs in sordid love affairs and crooked business deals with the Mafia, all of which his poor wife tried to survive with a lot of help from the bottle. Although their small children seemed on their way to ruin, Jerry was a breath of wholesome Nebraskan air in that tainted household. For three glorious weeks we had the empty mansion to ourselves. The master bedroom had a king-size bed and a sunken marble bathtub. In a backyard shaded with palm trees swaying in the trade winds, there was a swimming pool surrounded by a tall hedge filled with blossoms. I was a nineteen-year-old kid, an insatiable dreamer. Hawaii, a beautiful girl, an empty mansion near the beach— I thought I'd parachuted into heaven. Every day I explored a different beach, swam the crystal waters, surfed my ass off, and became a bit of an alcoholic.

I always wanted to write stories that would make people feel the way certain songs did, those that spoke of such unbearable longing that you wanted to get up and do something crazy. Driving with my lovely blond American girlfriend in the Camaro convertible along the highway, checking out the ocean for surf, we listened to the rhythmic, opening beat of Argent's "Hold Your Head Up."

Whenever I hear the lyrics of that song, I still get a rush: "And if it's bad, don't let it get you down, you can take it. And if it hurts, don't let them see you cry. You can take it. Hold your head up..." I always think about driving that coastal road with Jerry, coming back from surfing Mokapuu, squinting into the evening sun, and gazing out to sea with enough longing and desire to fuel the Camaro.

At the beginning of *Moby Dick*, Herman Melville's famous metaphysical novel about the ocean, he ponders water-gazing:

Circumambulate the city of a dreamy Sabbath afternoon. What do you see? Posted like silent sentinels all around the town, stand thousands upon thousands of mortal men fixed in ocean reveries. Some leaning against the piles; some seated upon the pier-heads; some looking over the bulwarks of ships from China; some high aloft in the rigging, as if striving to get a still better seaward peep. But these are all landsmen; of week days past pent up in lath and plaster—tied to counters, nailed to benches, clinched to desks. How then is this? Are the green fields gone? What do they here?

Right now I'm looking out at the ocean in Australia and I remember everything. So many holy grails. Eventually, for most romantics, it's a tough road. So many romantic egoists, insatiable dreamers, and outcasts spiritually dissatisfied with ordinary life overreach for more than life has to offer. And in those terms they become a little doomed.

The bells of the ice-cream truck have just tinkled, so I run out with money to buy a tub of honey/macadamia nut ice cream for my girls. The ice-cream man often sports a Hawaiian shirt. He's grown a goatee and wears funky sunglasses. Sometimes he arrives angry and bitter. Other days he'll be buoyant and philosophical. Today he gets an edge when I say, "With all the rain it must be tough to sell ice cream."

Grimacing, he replies, "Look, mate, I'm lucky to have a bloody job up here."

Often I see him parked in his truck in the lot above Lennox Point, gazing at the horizon of swells.

It's said we're living in an age of narcissism that evolved out of a need to find meaning. More and more we seem to look into ourselves to discover what—the costs of being too self-absorbed? Some people can't help searching for what they may never find. That's the way it's always been. Even prim and proper Captain Cook was profoundly smitten, literally sailing into the unknown to find new worlds. In 1775 he wrote in his journal: "The truth is, I was willing to prolong the passage in searching for what I was not sure to find."

Since we arrived in Australia, I've spent most mornings in the ocean and a lot of afternoons in libraries tracking down the important books I've read over the past twenty-five years. They add up to a kind of jumbled thesis about romantic egoists, hubris, and Paradise Lost. If you look up hubris, you might find an ambiguous noun that means "exaggerated self-confidence often resulting in retribution." It was a shortcoming or defect in the Greek tragic hero that caused him to ignore the warnings of the gods and to transgress their laws—a flaw of mad vanity or mega-lomania, a passion for grandiose things, an attempt to transcend human possibilities. The hero with hubris takes more from life than life has to offer. He overreaches.

Living above the ocean with a lot of time on my hands—languor even—I dwell on my own personal gallery of hopeless romantics like Lord Byron, Paul Gauguin, D. H. Lawrence, Bruce Chatwin, Jack Kerouac, Robert Louis Stevenson, Virginia Woolf, Ernest Hemingway, Scott Fitzgerald, Lawrence Durrell, and Henry Miller. When Hemingway was young and decided to become a writer, he said he would make a career out of alienation. Reading Hemingway's *A Farewell to Arms* my first year at Simon Fraser University in Vancouver launched me into a passionate desire to become a writer. It didn't matter that I couldn't spell or put two sentences together, or that I had only read one real novel. I was seduced by Hemingway's tragic notion of corrupted innocence, and the way Hemingway found intensity in everything he did, looking for that purity of line in living and writing about fear, love, and war. I came across a few pages of swimming in the last section of *The Sun Also Rises*. The main character, Jake Barnes, stoically takes his lost illusions into the ocean during solitary, epic swims that made me realize I'd been swimming over the years not just for the pure joy of it, but as a means toward salvation and self-therapy. I read all of Hemingway's short stories, his novels, his memoir of Paris, *A Moveable Feast*, and the legendary Carlos Baker biography. From my vantage point as an inexperienced young man, writing and travelling like Hemingway seemed the perfect way to escape and find myself.

Before my first trip around the world in the mid-1970s, I'd been lucky enough to work as a shipper/receiver in Shirley Leishman's bookstore in Ottawa. Every book that came into the shop had to pass through my hands. One afternoon I came upon *Henry Miller on Writing* and spent the rest of the day reading it on the sly. I was taken aback by his religious fervour for writing. Miller was joyful, exuberant, irreverent, upbeat, and rough around the edges compared to many other famous glum writers of literature. Early on he decided to write about himself, his friends, his experiences, what he knew and remembered and saw with his own eyes. He wasn't interested in "literature." He was a professional enthusiast, an imaginative prose writer who wrote about life's epiphanies. With a healthy dose of joie de vivre, Miller penned autobiographical books about what it meant to be a man journeying through life.

From time to time I jotted down a few Miller passages: "Art teaches nothing, except the significance of life" and "If we have not found heaven within, it is a certainty we will not find it without" and "Writing, like life itself, is a voyage of discovery." *Henry Miller on Writing* traces the author's escape from a boring job and conventional life in Brooklyn to an amazing, uncertain journey that took him to Greenwich Village, Paris, Greece, and Big Sur. For a couple of days in a biblical rain I read the notorious *Tropic of Cancer* while living with our friends Bob and Linda in their little yellow house in North Vancouver: "I have no money, no resources, no hopes. I am the happiest man alive..." While Dale and I were first island-hopping in the Greek islands in the 1970s, I read Miller's Greek travel memoir, *The Colossus of Maroussi*, which is a spiritual travel book and a classic of mid-life crisis. He swam naked in the Mediterranean and hiked around the islands like Robinson Crusoe: "For hours at a stretch I would lie in the sun doing nothing, thinking nothing. To keep the mind empty is a feat, a very healthful feat too. To be silent the whole day long, see no newspaper, hear no radio, listen to no gossip, be thoroughly and completely lazy, thoroughly and completely indifferent to the fate of the world, is the finest medicine a man can give himself."

For Miller in those pretelevision days it was a lot easier to be detached and unplugged. In this stressed-out age of information overload we could use a little of Miller's old-fashioned, laid-back wisdom. At one point I uncovered another book, *Durrell and Miller: A Private Correspondence.* Durrell was a twenty-three-year-old aspiring writer who wrote a fan letter to forty-three-year-old Miller in response to the controversial publication of *Tropic of Cancer.* It led to a lively, intimate, twenty-five-year correspondence between two of the most celebrated writers of their time. Durrell eventually wrote *The Alexandria Quartet,* one of the great literary bestsellers in mid-century that has since gone out of favour along with

Miller and Durrell's chauvinistic brand of literature. But in the late 1950s and early 1960s, they were icons. Durrell wrote to Miller: "Soon I must get down to this blasted fourth volume. A complimentary copy of *Mountolive* is on its way to you. You'll probably find it stinks if you like Kerouac; I have only seen one [Kerouac] sent me by Anaïs. Found it unreadable; no, I admire it in a way, as I admire *Catcher in the Rye*…. But ouf, the emptiness really of this generation of self-pitying cry babies. We have our own group in England. And how can you not see that God or Zen is simply a catchword, as Freud was in our time…the egoism cult is very bad for young men. They think if they splash about in the bath it's interesting because it's THEM." Both writers are oppressed by the younger generation and apprehensive about the self-absorbed new world that would go on without them.

Nothing seems to change. My generation, the boomers, are hostile toward and terrified of the generations following us who will eventually turn us into babbling dinosaurs. My favourite book by Durrell is *Prospero's Cell*, a slim travel memoir about Durrell and his first wife, Nancy, and their almost perfect, short year in an old house on Corfu. While travelling in the Greek islands, Dale and I visited Durrell's house and swam in his lagoon. He and Nancy had an idyllic life until the approach of World War II drove them from their paradise, which seems a lovely metaphor for life itself—idyllic youth gives way to the melancholy backward glance of old age. "Each morning when I am back on the warm rocks," Durrell writes, "lying with my face less than a foot above the dark Ionian…we lie under the red brick shrine to Saint Arsenius, dropping cherries into the pool—clear down two fathoms to the sandy floor where they loom like drops of blood. N. has been going in for them like an otter and bringing them up in her lips. The shrine is our private bathing pool; four puffs of cypress, deep clean-cut diving ledges above two fathoms of blue water, and a floor of clean pebbles." And finally after history and the war caught up with them, he rhapsodizes in the epilogue:

> The day war was declared we stood on the balcony of the white house in a green rain falling straight down out of heaven on to the glassy floor of the lagoon; we were destroying papers and books, packing clothes,

emptying cupboards, both absorbed in the inner heart of the dark crystal, and as yet not conscious of separation. In April of 1941, as I lay on the pitch-dark deck of a caique nosing past Matapan toward Crete, I found myself thinking back to that green rain upon a white balcony, in the shadow of Albania; thinking of it with a regret so luxurious and so deep that it did not stir the emotions at all. Seen through the transforming lens of memory the past seemed so enchanted that even thought would be unworthy of it. We never speak of it, having escaped: the house in ruins, the little black cutter smashed. I think only that the shrine with the three black cypresses and the tiny rock-pool where we bathed must still be left. Visited by the lowland summer mists the trembling landscape must still lie throughout the long afternoons, glowing and altering like a Chinese water-colour where the light of the sky leaks in. But can all these hastily written pages ever recreate more than a fraction of it?

Miller visited Durrell on Corfu a few months before the war broke out and wrote *The Colossus of Maroussi*: "I had entered a new realm as a free man—everything had conjoined to make the experience unique and fructifying. Christ, I was happy.... It was almost high noon when the boat pulled in at Corfu. Durrell was waiting at the dock.... Before sitting down to lunch we had a swim in front of the house. I hadn't been in the water for almost twenty years. Durrell and Nancy, his wife, were like a couple of dolphins; they practically lived in the water. We took a siesta after lunch and then we rowed to another little cove about a mile away where there was a tiny white shrine. Here we baptized ourselves anew in the raw."

Miller was also forced out of Greece early in 1940 because of the war. He returned to New York and then took a wild cross-country trip that culminated in another famous book, *The Air-Conditioned Nightmare*, his irreverent, blistering critique of America. When the war ended, Miller discovered Big Sur, California, where he lived until 1957. While there, he wrote his memoir *Big Sur and the Oranges of Hieronymus Bosch*—meditations, essays, and portraits of life in Big Sur. It chronicles the fifteen years he lived in a kind of Dreamtime in a place above the ocean similar to our setup atop the Coral Sea. The book has a front cover that shows a mist-laden Big Sur that resembles the far north coast of New South Wales. In a torrent of words Miller describes the peace and contentment, the forest, sunshine, and fog, the blazing immensity of the Pacific and the steady roar of breakers.

In the 1950s Big Sur had the same spirituality and magic Byron Bay possesses today. Miller's grateful soul responded to the atmosphere and landscape of that part of California the same way mine has replied to Byron Bay. A stunningly beautiful, underdeveloped coastline similar to those of the Mediterranean and Scotland, Big Sur had its own wild community of painters, writers, musicians, dancers, mystics, geniuses, cranks, Beats, and the original flower children who would become Whole Earth hippies. Living in his house above the Pacific, Miller wrote, read books, and went for long walks and swims. He battled with ants in his kitchen cupboards and snakes in his rafters, intensely loved, nurtured, and survived his kids, and pretty much lived the way I do here: "I am constantly reminded that I am living in a virtual paradise...it may indeed be the highest wisdom to elect to be a nobody in a relative paradise such as this rather than a celebrity in a world which has lost all sense of values." One of the first things Miller discovers, though, is that paradise contains flaws, and that wherever living is cheap and nature is inviting, a means of supporting oneself is difficult. But Miller was able to stay because he could generate an income by writing. He also became something of a crazed househusband.

It strikes me as hilarious that a writer who had an unjust reputation as one of the most infamous literary pornographers and misogynists—"the oversexed monster who wrote *Tropic of Cancer, Sexus, Quiet Days in Clichy*"—attempted to become one of the first househusbands as he describes in *Big Sur*: "To walk six miles with a bucketful of diapers is no joke.... To devote a whole morning to a three-year-old boy full of piss and vinegar is a job for someone with six hands and three pairs of legs." But for a time he was so enamoured by the sacred pleasures of being a househusband that he stopped writing as I did and let himself be swallowed by his newfound domestic joy: "No one is awake yet. I tiptoe about, get the fire started, make breakfast, and between times spend long minutes standing over the baby's crib. She looks just like an angel when asleep. Soon she will be cooing and chirping and gurgling.... I want to hold her in my arms a while, talk to her in her bird and dog language.... It's too lovely a day to waste time writing books which will only be condemned. No, I'll do something I really enjoy. I'll make a watercolour or two."

When nap time came, he lay down with his children, hoping to replenish his powers for the second half of the day. Usually he was more exhausted after his nap, and I fully understand what he meant by "the hours that lay ahead moved like lead."

For a man of the early 1950s, Miller was ahead of his time when it came to his sentiments about men, women, and children:

> That's the hardest thing to ask a man to do—take care of tots from three to five years of age, bouncing with energy, and shut up with them in one room, especially during the rains. In the winter when the rains came we were marooned. I fed them, changed their clothes, washed them, told them stories. I didn't do any writing. I couldn't. By noon every day I was exhausted. I'd say, "Let's take a nap." We'd get into bed, the three of us, and then they'd begin scrambling, screaming, fighting with each other.... As much as I loved them I couldn't handle the situation. It was something I'll never forget. That experience increased my respect for women, I guess. I realized what a tremendous job women have, married women, cooking meals, doing the laundry, cleaning the house, taking care of children, and all that. This is something no man can understand or cope with no matter how hard his work may be.

When his daughter, Val, was nearly three, Miller walked beside a stream, pointing out birds and trees and telling her stories. He'd pick her up and carry her on his shoulders the same way I used to transport Sky and Quinn when we sang "The Man Who Broke the Bank at Monte Carlo." Miller writes in *Big Sur*: "I'll never forget the first song I taught her. It was 'Yankee Doodle Dandy.' What joy, walking and whistling with this kid on my back. Anyone who hasn't had children doesn't know what life is. Yes, they were a great blessing."

In the same book the supposedly scurrilous author observes: "Lucky the father who is merely a writer, who can drop his work and return to childhood at will! Lucky the father who is pestered from morn till sundown by two healthy, insatiable youngsters. Lucky the father who learns to see again through the eyes of his children, even though he become the biggest fool that ever was."

A funny, womanizing American novelist, expatriate, doting father, neurotic fool, true, bohemian, and would-be sage, Miller got away with more hubris than any artist of the twentieth century. He was a late bloomer who didn't start writing or "living" until he was thirty-three. But, by the time of his death in 1980, Miller had spent fifty years shamelessly proclaiming that life was enjoyable and that happiness had little to do with money. He wrote for the fun of it, and that was all he wanted to communicate to others. His raunchy books reek of life. Well into his eighties, he was still riding his bicycle, playing Ping-Pong, and falling in love with attractive women more than half his age.

In the mid-1920s there were no creative-writing workshops for Miller, so he took off to find the world and forged his own way to interpret it. He went searching for those evasive things we all look for. Miller had rejected the traditional male roles of worker, provider, and head of the family. After reading Miller, a lot of middle-aged men left their wives and families in pursuit of an imagined real self. Although Miller's literary reputation peaked in the 1960s when many people aspired to live the way he did in Big Sur, the next decades weren't so kind. A massive reevaluation of male writers and their reputations took place after feminism kicked in, and Miller was quickly thrust into the doghouse. Nevertheless his books are still in print and sell all over the world. He was an original. He had a tremendous influence on other writers and artists as well as on his insatiable readers.

I remember one amusing photo of an ancient Miller in front of a window painted with blood-red paint and the words in black letters: NIRVANA NEEDED. Unlike Gauguin, Hemingway, Fitzgerald, Kerouac, and company, who had all succumbed to the wrath of hubris and died rather young from alcoholism, loneliness, or suicide, Miller managed to get away with a hell of a lot with his crooked smile. Dominating life, he lived to the ripe old age of eighty-nine, writing, painting, and spewing out his own brand of joyous optimism. Miller wrote books that exuded infectious freedom, and he paid no attention to his critics, his reputation, or the conglomerates and their accountants who controlled publishing. He was one of the few romantic dreamers who discovered the secret to day-to-day happiness.

Even though our time in this house is running out, I greedily cut down more treetops to open up the view I love so much. Unfortunately the long muscles in my back have spasmed and I can't surf. While swimming the mile and a half alone from The Pass to Main Beach at Byron, I had to pull out and painfully breaststroke in over the reef because my back and neck had seized up. I don't know if it was the initial sore back that did me in, or my neck got worse because as I swam I thought about being all alone in so much open water with sharks.

This morning I plan to spend the day with a romantic egoist who lives in a Spanish villa he built himself, overlooking the magnificent breaking waves of Boulders Beach. Kiko is an American house builder and aspiring writer/artist who has more real stoke than any surfer I've met. As a surfer, he's lived and internalized the *mana* from California, Mexico, and Hawaii. He's been married about as long as I have, and his wife, May, and their three kids get along well with Dale and our girls. Even though May and Kiko have lived in Australia for years, they're still American. Back in the early 1970s they got married on a bluff overlooking the surf in Santa Cruz in a wedding out of *A Midsummer Night's Dream*.

May is a stay-at-home mom and a queen bee for the cool crowd in Lennox. At first when she tried to get Kiko and me together, intuitively knowing we should, he was standoffish because his wife had also graphically laid out my whole househusband program. And he sure didn't want any part of *that*. We all met at a huge party May threw for Kiko's return from a two-month mid-life crisis in California, Hawaii, Mexico, and Bali. He'd bought a lot of jewellery he hoped to sell with May's help so he could get out of the house-building business.

The next Sunday when May invited us for a Mexican brunch I ended up talking at the table with Dale, May, Melissa, and other women while all the kids pestered us. Kiko avoided me, no doubt pegging me as a New Age flake in an apron surrounded by women and squalling kids. Men don't seem to socialize much with their wives during the day in Australia. But Kiko eventually walked over and, out of begrudging courtesy, mumbled, "Howzit goin'?"

"Aside from our house being a fuckin' snake pit of weeping, yelling, and unfulfilled longing—great!" I replied.

Something clicked in Kiko's brain, and his face blossomed into a moustachioed Cheshire grin. "Well, amigo, we should go for a surf sometime." Then he spirited me away from the Mexican brunch, literally and symbolically, after more than a decade, bringing me back over to the men's camp.

As it turned out, Kiko and I proved suitably demented and intense enough in the water to cement an immediate brotherhood. Straddling our boards on the reef one morning, staring out to sea in a lull between sets, I confessed a desire to escape the househusband business and he admitted he didn't want to build houses anymore. Kiko had just taken out a scary loan to build a new house on spec because his last client was taking him to court. He wanted to open up a little bagel shop and make furniture that was art. "Hell, I want the lifestyle you have, Rick," he told me.

I explained it had taken years for the writing and teaching to evolve out of the househusband trip, that this was the first year my two girls were both in school, and that I was just getting back on my feet and hadn't published a book in a decade.

The sun was shining, and we had the waves to ourselves as we drifted toward the boat channel. When I told Kiko about my lingering obsession with Gauguin and my first book about famous painters, he insisted I drop by his place and see a magazine article about a modern-day Gauguin.

A day later I'm in front of his house above Boulders Beach. Kiko answers the door and we stand there like a couple of twisted old men. Over the phone earlier I mentioned my back and neck problems to him, and he told me he'd also put out his back laying the foundation for the new house he was erecting. Now we buoy each other with black humour. "It's the human question mark," I say, pointing at him.

"Amigo, you're looking pretty crooked yourself," he retorts, leading me with a weary shuffle into his book-lined study.

His villa is impressive. The floors are covered in cool, earthy tiles and the adobe walls are painted in warm, bright tones. The decor is an eclectic blend of Mediterranean, California, old Hawaii, and Mexico.

Like a lot of people, Kiko is a hopeless romantic, but he seems to be going through a much more serious mid-life crisis than most of us. He's a short, youthful, middle-aged Peter Pan with long, sun-bleached hair from working outside as a builder and surfing most of his life. Originally from New Jersey, he woke up one frigid, ball-shrinking morning a long time ago, decided he had a gutful of cold winters, and headed to the tropics for good.

As I stand in his study with its million-dollar ocean view, I scan the art monographs, novels, and books, magazines, and photographs about surf culture, my mouth salivating. When Kiko talks about the stoke and spirituality of surfing, the *mana* inherited from the islands, the tribe, and the golden breed, I believe him. He's a soul-surfer of the highest order and knows I've published a couple of serious books, carve wooden tikis, and am an accomplished swimmer, all of which help to make up for my shameful deficiencies as a surfer. Kiko also knows I'm researching my new book and am fishing around to connect it with other levels beyond househusbanding.

"I got this when I was back in the States," he says, handing me a paperback of Cormac McCarthy's novel *All the Pretty Horses*.

I haven't read it yet but I'm certain I'll like a modern western classic about young men moving on horseback toward an impossible dream of the past.

"Go ahead," he urges. "Borrow whatever you want."

As I check out the shelves and make a little pile for myself, he tells me that when his kids leave home he wants to simplify his life, move out, paint, and do the Gauguin thing on an island. I remind him that his kids, like mine, won't be leaving the nest for another fifteen years. I also refresh his memory about what happened to Gauguin in the South Seas—no man is an island and all that. But Kiko is restless and needs a change in his life, something dramatic like building a catamaran and sailing off to Polynesia. As I look at his handmade miniature surfboards and wooden fins, I understand why he thinks he might need to forge his creative soul on paper or canvas.

To cheer Dale and me up about our exchangees who will soon be on our doorstep to turf us out of Stoneyhurst Manor, I pick out *Lost Continent*, Bill Bryson's hilarious account of travelling across America: "I come from Des Moines. Somebody had to." Kiko offers me another book called *Morning Glass*, a memoir by the famous 1960s pro surfer/waterman Mike Doyle who now lives in Mexico, still surfing and painting in late middle age. While reading the dust jacket, I discover a missing link to my househusband book. Doyle makes no apologies about explaining his whole life in terms of his passion for water. Kiko then shows me his special stock: two immaculate piles of *The Surfer's Journal*. Over the years I read *Surfer* magazine until it seemed so juvenile, poorly written, and choked with silly ads that I stopped even opening it. But *The Surfer's Journal* is a sumptuous literary surfing magazine for older surfers. It has world-class photographs of waves and almost no ads, is filled with thought-provoking articles on surfing history and life, and contains a seemingly never-ending array of colourful, aging personalities who have been consumed by the natural sport of kings.

"Take a few home to read," Kiko insists. "They'll blow your mind." Already my brain is processing the potent *mana* he's turned me on to in his book sanctuary. Then he hands me an issue of *Vanity Fair*. "Ever hear of Peter Beard?"

I shake my head.

"He's the modern-day Gauguin I was telling you about out in the surf."

Kiko gives me the magazine and leaves the room while I skim the article and glance at the eccentric American photographer's outrageous images. On the inside cover is a shirtless picture of Beard as a middle-aged Greek god. On his shoulders is a beautiful naked young woman. The caption reads KENYA'S PETER PAN. Another less glamorous photograph reveals Beard in obvious pain after being gored by a rampaging elephant. The artist is a playboy, recluse, adventurer, trust-fund derelict, and saviour of the African wilderness. A glamorous drug addict once described as half Tarzan, half Lord Byron, he lives in Kenya on a forty-five-acre property that adjoins the land once owned by Isak Dinesen, who wrote *Out of Africa*. Beard says: "I don't mind the word dilettante. A dilettante means someone who does what he loves."

Apparently the photographer has been doing the Gauguin shtick for more than forty years, living in a cluster of permanent tents on a ranch called Hog Farm. Beard sits up at night by lamplight toiling on his curious art form—a combination of photography and collage. He calls these oversize diaries scrapbook collages—volumes packed with layers of photographs, rodent skulls, candy-bar wrappers, mysterious newspaper headlines (WOMAN SAVED FROM SLIME), bones, rocks, line drawings, quotations, fish skeletons, a dung beetle foot, and dribbles of Beard's own blood. They form a personal and historical archive of his strange and fascinating Gauguin-esque life that has seen him cross paths with rich and famous people like Jackie Onassis, Candice Bergen, the Kennedys, the Rockefellers, Francis Bacon, and Mick Jagger. (Beard once won $2,000 when Onassis bet him he couldn't stay underwater for four minutes.)

On a certain level Beard is just another celebrity nomad like Bruce Chatwin, someone who is fascinating to speculate about but ultimately impossible to abide by. An early self-portrait of Beard taken at Africa's Lake Rudolph in 1965 shows the unbearably handsome photographer lying on a beach. The lower half of his body is inside the mouth of an enormous crocodile while Beard casually writes in his journal, his womanly back tanned and smooth, his blond hair streaked by sunlight. A swath of blood, Beard's no doubt, is splashed across the bottom of the beach with a caption that reads: I'LL WRITE WHEREVER I CAN.

Kiko returns with a swollen diary that looks like one of Beard's collage affairs. He took it with him on his recent soul-searching trip and stuffed it full of quotes, epiphanies, drawings, pictures, diary entries, wood, flowers, and shells. Kiko is like a proud kid showing me his school project. Obviously he was inspired by the Beard article before he took off for his South Seas walkabout. Suddenly I realize my book about a crazed surfing househusband has become a lot like Kiko's and Beard's collage diaries— an unruly heap of journals, rough drafts, shells, wood, curios, clippings, quotes, and retrieved memories that I've assembled in Australia.

I once read that most twentieth-century art is the art of collage. Who knows? Beard's submarine-sandwich photo-diary collages might well be the best way to contain all the shit that comes at us. Just before I leave Kiko's house with my newfound *mana* and precious booty of magazines and books, he smiles and says, "You'll have to come for a surf at the Point with the Three Amigos."

When I return to Stoneyhurst, the sun is out. A very light breeze rustles the palms. Butterflies dart across my awesome view. I pick up the old field binoculars and survey the valley, then scope the hillside of grazing horses. Next I scan the horizon out to sea and am suddenly rewarded with the silver geyser of a spouting whale. It's a bloody Melvillian miracle.

Strange to think that the first few months here we couldn't sleep at night because we were so lonely, scared, and hot. Now we seem to know everyone and we sleep in long pants, long shirts, and socks and pile on the blankets to keep warm. Dale and I and the kids have been gone from our life in suburbia only six months, yet it feels like years. We don't even think much about our former lives. We miss our collie, Ruby, more than anything. As long as our families and friends are healthy, we feel content to be cut off from the real world. We'd be happy to stay here forever.

At my desk I can't resist dipping into the excerpts from Madonna's private diaries that are also in the issue of *Vanity Fair* with the article on Peter Beard. For me the two pieces are a fascinating window on the slippery slopes of hubris. Madonna's private diaries deal with her life during the making of the film *Evita*. For almost two years she lived vicariously through Evita Perón. Madonna had written a letter to the director Alan Parker, listing all the reasons she was the only one who could portray the Argentine demigoddess, insisting she understood the woman's passion and pain. There are a number of still photos from the movie. One shows Madonna's pouty, contemplative face, revealing an ambitious, determined young woman who from the bottom of her heart, through all the hype, the self-doubt, and hubris, wants the world to love her, despite her arrogant, in-your-face disposition. Fans outside her Buenos Aires hotel room chanted "Eva Madonna," and graffiti was painted on the walls, proclaiming, EVITA LIVES. GET OUT MADONNA.

In her diary the superstar chanteuse records:

Last night I dreamed of Evita. I was not outside watching her. I was her. I felt her sadness and her restlessness. I felt hungry and unsatisfied and in a hurry. Just as I had earlier in the helicopter, suspended over the earth on the way to meet President Menem. As I gazed down on all of Buenos Aires, my mind started drifting. I tried to imagine how I would react and what I would do if, like Evita, I knew I had cancer and I was dying. I could finally understand the feverish pace at which Evita lived during her last few years. She wanted her life to matter. She didn't have time for the bureaucracies of government. She needed results. The idea of death is not so horrible if one can leave behind a legacy, and Eva did not want to be remembered as a girl from the sticks, or a B actress, or the wife of the president. She wanted to be remembered for her goodness. The desire of someone who has lived her life completely misunderstood.

Reading Madonna's words prompts me to think of Jean Louis Lebris de Kerouac, better known as Ti Jean, Sal Paradise, lonesome traveller, desolation angel, dharma bum, memory baby, or just plain Jack. I've been dipping into Kerouac's fiction and reading some of his letters. He was the king of doomed romantics and bulleted through life in his youth, then became a stay-at-home hermit with a broken soul, dead at forty-seven. In the late 1940s Kerouac smelled a rat in American consumerism and conformity and decided to hit the road on his mobile search for *it*. Long before the dawn of the Computer Age, he had a premonition of things to come in the eerie quiescence of postwar suburbia: "You take a walk some night on a suburban street and pass house after house on both sides of the street each with a lamplight of the living room shining golden, and inside the blue square of a television, each living family riveting its attention on probably one show; nobody talking; silence in the yards...it appears like everybody in the world is soon going to be thinking the same way, electrified to the Master Switch."

Written in the late 1940s and early 1950s but not published until 1957, Kerouac's second novel, *On the Road*, took him from the innocence of literary obscurity to an unhappy success that more or less hounded him for the rest of his life. In a letter he scribbled on the run, dated August 23, 1948, he said: "I have another novel in mind, *On the Road*, which I keep thinking about: two guys hitchhiking to California in search of something they don't really find, and losing themselves on the road, coming all the way back hopeful of something else."

On the Road became the Bible of the Beat Generation and made Kerouac a reluctant cult rebel. With psychotic energy and passion it extols the virtues of jazz, sex, drugs, booze, travel, and a mystic attachment to nature and God. "Somewhere along the line the pearl would be handed to me," Sal Paradise says in the novel that is an autobiographical hymn to restlessness and is credited with launching the back-to-nature rucksack revolution of the 1960s. All of us lost romantics converging on Byron Bay in search of *it* or the pearl owe something to the wanderings and divine yearnings of Kerouac.

Accused of being a deadbeat dad, the King of the Beats is held responsible by many for the troubled life of his only child, Jan, who was raised by her mother. Kerouac only met his daughter twice: in 1961 at a paternity hearing and again in 1967 after paying the minimum $50 a month in child support. During this last encounter, when Kerouac heard Jan was on her way to Mexico with her boyfriend to write a novel, all he said was: "Yeah, go to Mexico and write a book. You can use my name." By denying his paternity, Kerouac might have inadvertently helped his daughter become a junkie and then later a prostitute and an alcoholic. But with his alcoholism and disposition, he knew he couldn't even help himself. Without literary assistance from her father, Jan somehow managed to write two autobiographical road novels as Jan Kerouac, then died of kidney failure a couple of years younger than her dad.

Racked by guilt and other shortcomings real and imaginary, Jack slid into slow suicide due to alcohol-related causes induced by the spiritual discouragement of an enormous, unfulfilled romantic longing that had troubled him his entire life. Maybe if he hadn't ducked out on his daughter but embraced her, his life would have been different. He might have sidestepped the Void by replacing some of his all-consuming angst with the nurturing benefits of fatherhood. Accepting, guiding, and loving his daughter or any child might have been Kerouac's real road to salvation.

Jack started fresh-faced, passionate, and daring—the sweetest, most visionary young guy you could imagine. But he died in haunting loneliness that last year in 1969, a confused, bottom-feeding loser. Parked in an oceanfront house on the west coast of Florida with his wife and sick, overbearing mother, he felt the whole world was out to get him. So he suffered like a saint, staying at home and drinking with the shades drawn against the Florida sun, watching too much television, electrified by the Master Switch. For some reason he couldn't even take solace from all that water in the Gulf of Mexico on his doorstep. It might as well have been a desert as far as he was concerned.

During his short lifetime, Kerouac was adored by readers and misunderstood by tight-assed critics. After *Time* savaged *The Dharma Bums*, Henry Miller rallied to his defence and wrote to Kerouac's publisher: "From the moment I began reading the book I was intoxicated.... No man can write with that delicious freedom and abandonment who has not practiced severe discipline.... Kerouac could and probably will exert tremendous influence upon our contemporary writers young and old." In the early 1960s Kerouac was slated to write a documentary narration for a big film on another deadbeat dad, Paul Gauguin, but *Rebel in Paradise* never materialized. On his last television appearance, trapped by William F. Buckley's slimy, loaded question about politics, Jack answered woundedly: "Being a Catholic, I believe in order, tenderness, and piety."

Kerouac was a restless dreamer who wrote with a lyrical voice that gave the ordinary a heightened, sacred quality: "Meanwhile I have American Beauty red roses growing in my rock garden, corn growing, melons growing, grapes coming squeezed out of arbour joints (that's right), a chair in the sun every morning to read the *Diamond Sutra* in, two blue spruces out front, a Japanese tree of some kind, a big old barn big enough to make a movie studio in, an extra room with eaves in which I'll splash paint and paint divine paintings (my own way), a room to sleep in, with treeleaves swishing in the screen, and a room to write in..." After years of overreaching for a lot more than life had to offer, fuelled by depression and disenchantment, his drinking out of control, Kerouac spent his last evenings alone at his typewriter engaged in a sad, nightly confessional. In the introduction to *Lonesome Traveler*, he bravely wrote: "Final plans: hermitage in the woods, quiet writing of old age, mellow hopes of Paradise (which comes to everybody anyway)..."

Jack's friend, the novelist John Clellon Holmes, said the tragedy was that Kerouac worked so hard to project to the world his own vision of ecstasy, a sacrificial romanticism: "If he'd only known how the world worked, he never would have broken his heart over it." In August 1949, twenty years before he died, while travelling to find America with his soulmate Neal Cassady (immortalized as the ecstatic sexual outlaw Dean Moriarity in *On the Road*), Kerouac wrote: "Some people are made to wish they were other than what they are, only so they wish and wish and wish.... I don't want to give up. I promise I shall never give up, and that I'll die yelling and laughing."

Like a lot of romantics, Jack Kerouac lost his balance. He couldn't integrate the quiet security of home with the sublime reach of the open road. Although he never found the pearl, I'm sure he currently resides somewhere this side of the golden eternity.

17
House Inside the Waves

They're pretty big gnarly themes—corrupted innocence and the holy ocean of eternity, the promise of youth, lost illusions, the immensity of the open road, and Paradise Lost. Then there's the sweet melancholy of searching for the impossible, a thirst for travel, adventure, love, freedom, and enlightenment, the heroism of grand Odyssean quests, the whole gorgeous dark night of the romantic soul. If romantic posturing can't bring happiness, what's left? What is possible? The problem with hopeless romantics like Jack Kerouac, Paul Gauguin, Ernest Hemingway, Scott Fitzgerald, Lord Byron, Bruce Chatwin, and company is that their highs are a lot higher and their lows are a hell of a lot lower than those of your average dreamer who plays it safe and develops a survival instinct that keeps him grounded on the straight and narrow. But if that means playing it safe and missing those wild glimpses from the summit, I don't know...

Today the girls are staying at home because Sky was at her dance performance the night before until almost midnight. Early in the morning she was stricken with fatigue and smelled a chance for a day off. Dale agreed to let her lie low for part of the day, and when Quinn got wind of it, she developed all sorts of mysterious symptoms herself. To avoid a nasty insurrection I gave in and implemented Plan B. Because we're leaving Stoneyhurst Manor at the end of the month, I'm happy to let myself be taken into the seductive cocoon of my little girls so that we can savour a day together up at the house. I'll be honest. A fair bit of time with kids can be hellish. But over the years my girls have grounded and centred me, given me a reason always to strive to become a better person. They give back a lot more than they take. Anyone who goes through life without meaningful contact with kids is missing something profound.

Like millionaires on the French Riviera, the three of us sit in blazing sunshine on the cool verandah at the wicker table and chairs. Quinn's chicken butt is nestled in my lap, my chin resting on her head so I can smell her sweet, clean hair. Sky is sprawled beside me with her head on my shoulder. Looking out to sea and getting ready to eat our hot porridge, I say, "I want you guys to remember this always, okay?" They nod in unison, wrapped up cozily in their goofy housecoats.

For about five minutes time stands still and everything is harmonious until Sky breaks into tears. Five minutes without the weeping and gnashing of teeth might actually be our Aussie record. Mumbling through spoonfuls of porridge, Sky weepily confesses she hates playing soccer on an all-boy squad. Back home she was the star on her girls' competitive club, but here there are no girls' teams. Sky is the token girl on a macho scrum of little shits. They're always urging her not to take the ball up the field but to pass it to one of the other players, a boy. Then Quinn starts up. "In practice," she whimpers, "all they do is put me in goal and try to hit me with the ball." It's true. The boys ignore Quinn on and off the field as though she's invisible. The upshot is that because her coach isn't the most sensitive individual, we're allowing Quinn to leave the team and sign up for a dance class with the promise that she'll play soccer again back in Canada. We've encouraged Sky to tough it out, though, because in spite of everything, she's still playing well and her team is leading the league. And we talked to her coach, who is alert to the undercurrents of player dynamics, given that his laid-back, ponytailed son isn't exactly the star of the team. In my cynical prekid days I never dreamed I'd be the sort of parent who'd get off on supporting their kids in sports. Occasionally bellowing from the sidelines like a maniac until my voice is raw, buoying the team with my cheers, I marvel at the fact that Sky and Quinn are much better athletes than I was at their ages.

To keep our minds off uncomfortable things, I decide to allow the girls to help me make some killer chocolate-chip cookies and great homemade golden carrot soup. I call Steve next door to see if he has any extra butter and find out he's quite ill with a bad cold in a house full of sick kids. So we whip up a batch of my cookies without too much drama. Then, out on the verandah table, my girls slice and dice carrots, leeks, potatoes, onion, garlic, and one very hot little red chili pepper from Denise's garden. Later we pour hot soup into bowls on a tray and add a heaping plate of cookies. I put a dollop of sour cream and lots of ground pepper and coriander leaves on top of each bowl, then we trundle over to Steve's. Arriving at his front courtyard, I lift the latch and we push through the gate. The water in his swimming pool is rippled by a wind blowing off the sea. When we spot Steve and his sick kids through the patio windows, I'm reminded of a leper colony. Steve makes the sign for slitting his throat and croaks, "Oh, mate, thanks. You better just leave it at the door. You really don't want to catch what we've got." On the way back to our place I give my girls the standard lecture about how good it makes one feel to do something kind for someone else for no particular reason.

We while away the rest of the day making boomerangs and carving wood. The girls want to make their own tikis, so I rough in a couple for them and they begin shaping and sanding their little pieces for hours on the verandah.

Over the years I've dabbled in carving wood and stone, everything from small wooden jewellery to abstract sculptures the size of televisions. Originally I was inspired by the primitive carvings and sculptures Paul Gauguin did when he lived in the South Seas. I took up woodcarving to take the edge off my neurotic tendencies and wanderlust and to feed my creative desires. Compared to the cerebral box canyons of writer's block, working with wood is a soothing physical joy, and it's communal and portable enough to do at the beach, in parks, and on the front porch while supervising volatile kids.

On our second trip around the world in 1988, I started carving walking sticks out of olive wood on the French Riviera and then used oak in the Greek islands. While we were travelling in New Zealand, I created sculptures and wooden jewellery vaguely inspired by local Maori artists. On the west coast of South Island I thought I died and went to heaven as I trudged with Sky under one arm along beaches through surreal mazes of exotic driftwood. I filled my pockets as I waded through seemingly millions of small pieces of nature-sculpted hardwood that had been deposited by the surf or transported down swift rivers from snowcapped mountains.

Just off Auckland harbour on Waiheke Island I hooked up with a crazed German hippie sculptor whose beautiful wife took a shine to Sky and me at a nude beach. For a couple of days I brought Sky to this beach and innocently cavorted with naked women and their kids. On the second day one woman saw me carving a small piece of local wood and invited me to meet her boyfriend at their place on the cliff above the beach. He carved unusual abstract wooden pendants that he sold for a lot of money in galleries. They lived in a funky hand-crafted wooden house built on an old truck. Aging hippies, they had run away from Europe to New Zealand to live in a counterculture bubble out of time in the land of milk and honey.

Later on during that trip we lived in Hawaii for three months. Between surfing, swimming, and chasing Sky all over the beaches on the islands, I perfected the art of carving my own style of tiki pendants. I created my tikis out of koa, a rare hardwood of the acacia family that the ancient Hawaiians used to make their surfboards from. My tikis are miniature sculptures of elongated faces. These tiki pendants hang by leather thongs and are worn as amulets, charms, talismans, or jewellery. I've probably carved fifty and sold about thirty. Their primitive, sensual forms are inspired by our travels around the world and particularly the South Seas where we've visited art galleries and museums with strange, primitive sculptures and carved weapons and utensils created by ancients and moderns. Because no private individual could ever possess any of the museum pieces I kept seeing, I decided to create my own.

Each sculpted tiki is different and possesses within it hidden power or *mana* that emanates from the place where it was discovered. And this *mana* accumulates over time and is supposed to ensure safety and good fortune. I use found pieces of roots and driftwood and begin by carving away unusable material and work toward a new, radical shape that's suggested by the original piece. To live up to the inherent beauty of the wood, I work carefully, down from gouges, rasps, and knives to small Japanese chisels and finely graded Italian needle files. I sand each piece with 100- to 220-grit sandpaper, then hand-rub and buff the finish with two or three coats of tung oil, also known as China wood oil. The best tikis have a finish that resembles the ripples in sunlit water, or gleam like the coat of a well-groomed animal. This whole process is a time-consuming, passionate endeavour and offensive to all machines. To do anything less would rob the wood of its potential to live again in a new shape.

In Australia I've been going nuts with all the exotic hardwoods, especially bloodwood. Kiko has a garage full of Australian and American wood he's been saving to do art with one day. Whenever I visit his place, he offers me small pieces. Dale says that every time I go out the door I come home with more wood. Our verandah is littered with chunks, blocks, roots, branches, and contorted slivers. Since we came to Australia, I've carved walking sticks, jewellery, sculptures, and a couple of interesting boomerangs.

I received my first boomerang that same Christmas Jan and I got the Beatles albums *Twist and Shout* and *Long Tall Sally*. A week ago an Aborigine in Byron who was going to teach Dale how to carve and play the didgeridoo asked me where I'd gotten the bloodwood tiki I was wearing around my neck. After I told him I carved it myself, his attitude changed completely, and even though I'm basically a white tourist, he knew I was a bit of a blood brother. So we talked about boomerangs. Because they were nomads, he told me, early Aborigines designed and made their weapons, tools, and utensils for maximum effectiveness and portability. Everything they owned had to be carried long distances. If one piece could do a number of jobs, it saved them the hassle of having too many possessions. Carved from the iron root of mulga or bloodwood and used as a weapon and for hunting, the boomerang was also employed as an eating utensil and as a tool for making fire and scraping and smoothing other implements. And, I suspect, for fun. On moonlit nights on the beach in Byron I listen to Aborigines bang pairs of boomerangs together as musical instruments to accompany the blood- and bone-driven rhythm of didgeridoos.

The day after playing hooky with my girls I decide I need a little adventure and more wood. I walk my daughters to their school bus stop, then continue down to the roundabout above Lennox and stick out my finger. The plan is to hitchhike to Broken Head Forest Reserve where I've heard the rainforest grows right down to wild, deserted beaches. I want to look for wood, and one of the secluded stretches of sand, King's Beach, is a nudist hangout I've been meaning to visit.

I get lucky on my first ride. A truck stops just up the road and I run to hop in. The driver is Ian, the friendly old guy who manages Wave Hill House, the architecturally stunning bed-and-breakfast perched on North Creek Road. He's wearing a Rusty surfing cap and an old surf T-shirt tucked over his gut. Ian and his wife, Alison, were named community sponsors for our teacher exchange. Initially we spoke on the phone and they were welcoming. Ian put me onto a few secondhand cars. The couple gave us a grand tour of Wave Hill House, then we didn't hear from them again. Semiretired, Ian has his hand in a number of interesting projects around town. He knows everyone, and everything. As I give him the polite version of the tricky roller-coaster ride we've been on with our Aussie exchangees and our current need to find a new place to live, he flashes me his mischievous used-car salesman smile. He's obviously heard all about it—the whole town is aware of how the Canadian/Aussie exchange has blown up into something of an ugly scandal. But aside from dealing with our unhappy exchangees who have failed to make their Ottawa exchange work, and apart from waiting to get the go-ahead from the New South Wales Teachers' Association so we can rent a new place, our Australian teacher exchange has been a bloody triumph from our point of view.

"Oy've got a plyce down on the beach in Lennox you and your woife can tyke a look at," Ian tells me.

"Are you kidding?" I say. "We'll come by tonight." Then I explain that I'm on my way to Broken Head to explore the isolated beaches for wood.

"Oy'll drive you to the paking lot," he insists. Then, with an odd, filthy grin, he adds, "You'll really love King's Beach, mate."

Just this side of Byron Bay we drive under a darkened natural arbour of enormous trees and end up inside the Broken Head Reserve. I wave good-bye to Ian and walk down a trail to the beach. Enveloped in deafening birdsong, I also hear and smell the crashing surf of the ocean. Then I come upon a private view of rugged beauty that is astounding. Huge, phallic outcroppings of volcanic rock anchor each end of the bay, and waves roll in, dumping tons of water on the sandy beach.

All of a sudden it hits me why Ian sarcastically said I'd really love King's Beach: up and down the shore, under trees, in rocky grottos, and on the sand naked men bask in the sunlight—centaurs, minotaurs, satyrs waiting and watching with their potent shlongs hanging like lethal weapons. Some are doing unbearably flexible stretches on the sand, their dicks and butt cracks no doubt sticking in the sand. Others smoke meditatively beneath the shelter of gnarled trees or against rock outcrops. One middle-aged man with a straw hat looks up hungrily as I stroll by— obviously I'm now on the menu. As I hurry along and feel all those hungry eyes examining me, I understand how vulnerable and *visible* women must feel most of the time around men. So I stride the entire length of the beach until I reach the tide pools and arrive at a kind of trail I hope will lead me to another cove, hopefully one filled with naked women, or at least somewhere I can sit and be anonymous.

Scrambling up the cliff along a track that would piss off a goat, I cling to the cracks and fissures of a rock face, grasping at the skinny stalks of small trees. Finally I pull myself to the top and gaze at the seascape below. Unfortunately the footpath has disappeared, so my first mistake is to try to go through the rainforest to find a road or a new way to a more southerly beach. But the farther in I thrash, the more dense the undergrowth becomes. Then I have an idea—my second mistake— and decide to descend a deep ravine to the sound of waves below. Here the undergrowth is filled with creepers that have thousands of barbs, spikes, and thorns. Soon my arms and legs are lacerated and bleeding as I hurtle through the undergrowth. Covered in blood, thorned branches stuck in my hair, I puff from exhaustion as I crouch lower and lower so my backpack doesn't get caught in vines and creepers. Defeated, I backtrack, and a half hour later I pick my way back down the same vertical cliff face I climbed earlier.

In private I quickly change into my bathing suit so I won't give the boys a free show. When I return to King's Beach coated in sweat and blood, I place my stuff under a huge branch, then run over the sand and spear into the drawbridging shorebreak. I let the rip take me out and I swim around beyond the impact zone, careful to keep clear of the odd fellow swimming near me.

Like something out of Herman Melville, there are perhaps twenty naked loners moodily sitting on their towels or in their rock grottos staring out to sea. One sinewy, bearded man who looks like D. H. Lawrence paces the beach like a sentry, his dick slapping the middle of his thigh, no doubt driving some of the other boys crazy under the trees. There is a feeling of intense loneliness and a furtive silence I've never experienced before in nature with so many people. Most of them are alone, oiled up and tanned chocolate with no tan lines, each man sunning himself in total isolation. Love isn't in the air, but there is a certain carnal lust, the same kind of frightful concentration I've observed in strip joints where men gaze intensely at the stage, consumed in silence by the gyrations of female dancers. From out of the gloom one hopeful man arrives with a Frisbee in his hand. Another steps back into his underwear, pants, shirt, and hat and then begins the long, slow climb back up to the parking lot and his other life. A man who easily weighs three hundred pounds and carries a flabby wheel of blubber from his chin to the lip of his crotch lumbers down to bask like a hippo in the clear tide pool well inside the shorebreak. Along the wilder end of the beach another man gallops into the surf and gambols alone in the waves while others watch from shore.

I begin to eat my lunch, sitting on my homely scrap of towel under a tree. When I finish, I climb the stairs from the beach and notice many of the car licence plates are out-of-state, as though most of the men here come to disrobe and feel safe in the remote sanctuary of King's Beach. In the lot I see a bloke step out of his Queensland truck. He looks like any other tradesman from around here. Getting undressed, he could be one of the dads of my daughters' friends, and I think how tough it must be to be gay in such a cruel, judgemental, straight world.

Ambling over the trail the opposite direction from King's Beach, I peer through Tarzan vines to Broken Head, Suffolk Park, and all the way along Tallows Beach to the Lighthouse on the cliffs at Byron. I decide to go down to the beach at Broken Head and ground myself a little again. Trudging in the warm sand and watching with envy as surfers zigzag up and down perfect three-foot diamond waves, I pass clusters of young women stretched out in bikini thongs reading novels beside upturned surfboards. In blissful abandon they lie on the sand, their nippled breasts proudly taking in the sun. Farther along the beach I spot a guy reading a novel called *The Alchemist* by Paulo Coelho and ask, "Enjoying the book?"

"It's supposed to be about finding your destiny," he says. "But it's a little over the top, mate."

I remember a line on the cover of the book: "A fable about following your dreams." I've heard other people describe *The Alchemist* as a self-help book disguised as a novel, but here in Byron, at the moment, it has the status of the Bible.

Peter turns out to be an aspiring writer from an inland town called Wagga Wagga. A young teacher out of work, he's reading *The Alchemist*, Bruce Chatwin's *The Songlines*, and other deep books his estranged girl-friend, the Feminist, put him onto. Now he's living with a new partner, one less intellectually demanding but easier to live with. When I tell him I'm a writer, he says he was trained to be a teacher but really wants to be a writer.

"Well, you should probably do both," I suggest. "It's a long life."

For a year, Peter explains, he lived in Ketchum, Idaho. "I used to walk by the house where Ernest Hemingway killed himself," he informs me as if that might impress me as a writerly credential.

But I know that house, know Hemingway inside and out. In the last year of my psychology degree I wrote a long, involved paper on Hemingway. For a while I even modelled my writing and to a certain extent my restless travels on him. In the opening pages of my first novel, *Cartoon Woods*, the main character commits suicide the same way Hemingway did. In 1961 in that house in Ketchum, Hemingway placed a shotgun in his mouth and blew away his head, his depression, his waning manhood, his old age, his declining literary powers, his flagging sex drive, and the impossible persona and legend he could no longer live up to.

Beside Peter's brand-new surfboard is a leather-bound journal, a designer pen, and *The Alchemist*, splayed open no doubt at some revela-tory chapter. Tanned, relaxed, clad in designer sunglasses, and full of intelligent confidence, Peter exudes the magazine image of what a writer should look like. A little self-consciously I sketch in some of the highlights of my modest househusband/writer program to Peter. He's interested in knowing how I juggle writing, travel, and looking after children. I tell him that at the moment I'm carving a lot more than writing and that over the years energy and inspiration have come in waves, and in various disguises. When I ask if he thinks he's ever going to have kids, he says that was one of the issues with his ex-girlfriend, the Feminist. "I'm too irresponsible to have kids."

I smile. "I was scared shitless of kids. We were married for a decade before we had our first. And when I ended up staying at home to look after them, it was one of the best moves I ever made. It saved my life." That catches Peter by surprise and makes him think he has a few options. "What kind of stuff are you writing?" I ask.

"Stuff about an out-of-work teacher from Wagga Wagga who craves the ocean and is still in love with his feminist girlfriend."

Now that's deep.

We both laugh and stare out at the waves. Then, like a mirage before our eyes, a beautiful girl returns from the surf. With her back turned to us, she casually peels off her wetsuit in the warm sun. In panties she towels herself off, then slips on a denim skirt, whips off the soggy panties, and hooks up her bikini top. Peter and I both watch her walk away with a seductive wiggle down the beach, leaving her purse, wetsuit, surfboard, and novel beside the towel. Neither one of us cheapens the moment with a verbal response.

A little later I hitch home with a guy who pulls out of the road from King's Beach. Classical music crescendoes inside his car, which is air-conditioned like Greenland. Driving with the steel-eyed focus and teeth-bared concentration of a pilot on a mission, he reminds me of a young Rock Hudson and has the kind of nose that should be on a gold coin. Only in his late twenties, he's a high-powered chef from Brisbane who's come down to visit his mom and dad. He slipped away from his folks for a quick dip at King's Beach, and when he spotted me hitching, after no doubt seeing me promenade my sorry ass along his beach earlier, probably thought he could save me from more humiliation. Sarcastic, deep-voiced, and funny as hell, he makes a few cynical cracks about staying with his mother and father at the family abode in Ballina. But I can tell he obviously loves them. He plans to open his own restaurant, learn how to fly, travel the world. He seems to know exactly where he wants to go in life and isn't the sad, romantic gay stereotype you associate with Rock Hudson—arm around a starlet, handsome, vacant, gentle eyes smiling tragically at the camera.

No one knows how strenuously I defended my heterosexual honour at King's Beach. I certainly don't want to confess my ordeal to Ian. Late that afternoon he fails to notice that my arms and legs are slashed when Dale and I meet him and his wife Alison in town at their place on Raynor Lane. Both of their children have moved out and are living on university campuses. Besides managing Wave Hill House, Ian says they own two properties in Lennox—this place and the house directly behind on the main street of the town. He's aware that our budget is a couple of hundred dollars a week and we need a furnished place. Right away.

Raynor Lane runs parallel to the beach and the main road. The old two-story house isn't exactly on the beach, but an empty block of land directly in front allows for a breathtaking view right down to the water. I can tell Dale is as excited about this beach house as I am. Already, for both of us, Stoneyhurst Manor is history. Under the carport is an outdoor shower head Ian explains he installed for rinsing off after being in the ocean. Just inside the side door of the house is a washer and dryer and another indoor shower. A little farther into the house we walk through the living room past a big wooden desk enclosed by bookcases. In the back of the main floor we enter a sumptuous master bedroom with a king-size bed and en-suite bathroom. Dale tries to keep a lid on her enthusiasm as we follow Ian and Alison upstairs. Here there is a bedroom for each of our girls, as well as a kitchen and a dining room with sea views. Ian slides open the patio door and we step onto a spacious sundeck overlooking Seven Mile Beach. The air is wild, the churning ocean so close, just at the foot of the property across the lane. Enormous surf rolls in, and we can barely hear ourselves speak. It's as though the house itself is inside the waves. Almost tearfully Dale glances at me, clutching my arm. Then she whispers, "Oh, my God, Ricky, I just love it."

Ian tells us he and Alison raised their kids in this old house back when Lennox was a one-horse town surrounded by bush farms and not a hell of a lot else. "Without exaggeration," he says, studying the heaving ocean, "Oy reckon a place on the beach on Raynor Lane is one of the choicest spots in Australia."

Standing on the deck, Dale and I smell and feel the salt blowing off the ocean. We're both nearly giddy with vertigo. Wind buffets the palm trees, scraping the skin of the house. I squeeze Dale's hand as we both look at Ian like a couple of kids and blurt, "We'll take it!"

18
The Three Amigos

Because we lived for a year in Hong Kong and are now in the process of a messy exchange of houses in Australia, we were glued to the television the other night watching the Hong Kong switchover. Mournful Prince Charles, more tight-assed than ever, gave the farewell speech relinquishing British control of the colony. After ninety-nine years, power was returning to the Chinese in Beijing. Governor Chris Patten, who for nearly a decade took so much abuse while hammering out a workable constitution and suffering the hellish politics that led to this historic moment, was emotionally restrained in his final speech. Chinese troops marched into the city to uphold the new order of the Communist government. All the hardworking, partying foreign expats were wondering how this new regime would impose itself on their inflated colonial lifestyles. With deep ambivalence the Hong Kong Chinese themselves were warming up to the realities of the handover that could mean disaster or become the so-called ascendancy of the Asian century.

They even hauled out old David Frost onstage, who appeared tickled pink to have his opinion solicited at his ripe old age. To a cluster of Australian journalists he cleverly remarked in his over-the-top English accent something to the effect: "The lucky Australians who live in the lucky country Down Under live in a veritable Eden, holding Asia and the rest of the world back from their peach of a country."

Two hundred years earlier on a fabulous voyage to discover the great southern continent, Captain James Cook sailed along this eastern coast of Australia right by the view from my desk at Stoneyhurst Manor. In 1770 while gazing across the deck of the *Endeavour*, the botanist on the voyage, Joseph Banks, meditatively reflected each day as he drew illustrations of flora and fauna specimens and wrote in his diary. When he saw a group of Aborigines walking along Seven Mile Beach, he was so intrigued he wrote: "Not one was once observed to stop and look toward the ship; they pursued their way in all appearances entirely unmoved by the neighbourhood of so remarkable an object as a ship must necessarily be to people who have never seen one."

After an unhappy couple of hundred years with white people, it's no damn surprise the Aborigines didn't bother to glance up. Now it seems the whole New Age world has arrived to appropriate the ancient wisdom of this unassimilated race.

While living in a house on the New South Wales coast in 1922, D. H. Lawrence saw this remote country as "an open door, framing blueness. You just walk out of the world and into Australia." Lennox Point, where I love and hate to surf, was formed twenty million years ago in the Cenozoic Era from rivers of lava that flowed out of Cook's Mount Warning. The first rays of sun to touch the Australian mainland each morning fall on the summit of 3,825-foot-high Warning.

One of the first Europeans to settle this area was the namesake of Lake Ainsworth. James Ainsworth arrived in 1842, the same year the settlers who escaped the Irish potato famine purchased farmland where our house in suburban Ottawa now stands in vinyl-siding heaven. More than 155 years ago serious life trajectories were decided, sometimes by the flip of a coin: heads, Lennox Head, Australia; tails, Barrhaven, Canada. The whites' title to the land in Australia and back home in those days was "a preemptive right" of the first European settlers. In an environmental genocide worthy of Dr. Seuss's *The Lorax*, the giant red cedar cutters arrived and whacked virtually every tree in this section of the Big Scrub. According to the 1922 reminiscences of Ainsworth's son, John, the area in 1847 was inhabited by more than five hundred Aborigines. Their nomadic hunting grounds extended from Broken Head west to the Big Scrub. They followed the seasons to the coast to hunt, gather food, and fish. Each spring in September they migrated to the beach for salmon fishing and assembled on North Creek during the oyster season. Ainsworth wrote: "In catching fish they used what they called a tow-row—that is a finely meshed net attached to a stick bent in the shape of a bow about eight feet across between the two ends. This gave a bag effect to the net and with a tow-row in each hand the blacks could surround the fish schools in shallow waters and catch them by the hundreds. The cordage of these nets, which were very strong and beautifully woven, was made from the inside fibre of the stinging tree and from the bark of the currajong."

The whole coastline from Lennox down to Bundjalung National Park and up to Byron Bay and the Gold Coast is rife with the physical traces of the ancient Aboriginal tribes who once inhabited this paradise before the white invasion. The hardworking, intolerant white people who arrived here simply moved in and forced the Aborigines out. The Nyangbal tribe had a well-established *wandaral* or bora ring (initiation site) in the heart of Lennox Head that gives evidence of their ancestors' spiritual activities and ownership. It's still situated near the Megan Crescent cricket field one street west of Dennis and Melissa's funky Santa Fe house on Stewart Street. The bora ring is now fenced and maintained by the National Parks and Wildlife Service of New South Wales. Although the site is open to visitors from around the world, it's no longer available for Aboriginal initiations.

In Australia as in many parts of the planet the arguments about indigenous people and immigrants continue to rage. Some tourist brochures here still promote images of half-naked Aborigines with spears gazing up at jet airliners. In a textbook Dale uses in her English class at Byron Bay High School, I discovered an Aboriginal poem by Kath Walker called "No More Boomerang": "Work like a nigger for a white man's meal/Now all civilized/Got television now/Now we got atom bomb." Race is one of the central issues of our time. If the truth be known, I think most of the people in Lennox and Byron are frightened by Aborigines. Because of many Aborigines' decline from tribal dignity to urbanized dereliction, there is a lingering, collective guilt on the part of the whites. It may be likened to a family with a faltering individual in its midst. For everyone concerned, what is the moral, healthy way to proceed?

One of the basic problems between the whites and the Aborigines is their mutual inability to perceive what is sacred to the other. Think of Uluru—Ayers Rock—and the Sydney Opera House, one a tremendous turdlike mound, the other a gargantuan Moby Dick of a building. Big, sacred entities thousands of miles apart that draw money, spirituality, and tourists, both suffer from overexposure and set up an interesting focus for the black/white chasm. Although multiculturalism is healthy in Sydney, it is the tourist images that stick: an Aborigine standing in the sunset near Uluru; a group of desperately bland, trendy white people wining and dining at Ayers Rock. The warped images illustrate the distance between the races. What a refreshing image it would be to have a group of Aborigines at a candlelit dinner in front of the Sydney Opera House.

Like any other place, the lost continent of Australia is an accelerating, difficult swirl of subcultures hollering out their needs and desires. While dipping into Robert Hughes's *Culture of Complaint*, I ran into this: "The future in a globalized economy will lie with people who can think and act with informed grace across ethnic, cultural, linguistic lines. And the first step in becoming such a person lies in acknowledging that we are not one big world family, or ever likely to be: that the differences between races, nations, cultures and their histories are at least as profound and durable as their similarities; that these differences are not divagations from a European norm, but structures eminently worth knowing about for their own sake. In the world that is coming, if you can't navigate difference, you've had it."

What I love about living in Byron and Lennox is the grand illusion of paradise, the primitive and exotic, a sea of dreams colliding with the global apocalypse of cybersurfers that is already upon us. Even with the romantic notion that high technology will solve the world's problems, it's not really surprising that in such a climate of rampant materialism and consumerism there are probably more dissatisfied people than ever. That's why travellers and tourists are drawn to Byron's down-to-earth cultural cosmos of alternative lifestyles, surfers, artists, and other romantic dreamers. It's the place big-city people want to escape to. People still crave the simple, authentic essence of what the Aborigines knew for thousands of years as they took pleasure in bodysurfing waves, carving wood, tossing boomerangs, or lying around naked on the warm sand with meat sizzling on the barbie.

To ease the anxiety of the big-house swap, Dale and I throw a Farewell to Stoneyhurst Manor, Lost Generation Dress-Up Party. Thirty-five friends file through our doorway each outrageously garbed as a character from a book, a movie, a painting, or rock and roll. I moon about in a red-and-white sailor's shirt and pleated khakis, the moody Jake Barnes from Hemingway's *The Sun Also Rises*. Dale is the love-lost Daisy Buchanan from *The Great Gatsby*. Dennis arrives skivvied in black, a slippery, demented, at-times suave Salvador Dalí who communicates in perfect pidgin with Kiko who is a drop-dead Paul Gauguin just back from Tahiti, paintbrush in hand, palette still dripping with colours. Rae Cook comes as an untamed Janis Joplin with her very blond surfer husband, Dave, who is a spooky-looking Jimi Hendrix. There is a shady, cigar-smoking Fidel Castro; a randy, tartan-kilted Braveheart; and a virginal Princess Leia. Steve and Sherry arrive as the regal Julius Caesar and his scheming Cleopatra.

We're a shameless, thirty- to fifty-year-old mid-life crisis crowd that enjoys listening and dancing to the cranked-up music of the Beach Boys, the Rolling Stones, Crowded House, the Eagles, Little River Band, Cold Chisel, and Midnight Oil. One by one I'm embraced by tantalizing sluts, Santa's helper, lop-eared pirates, a dopily bearded shark, Dolly Parton's front bumpers, an impressively armed Bonnie and Clyde, a pair of funereal Mortitia Addamses, and a naughtily miniskirted schoolgirl. Aussies always show up at parties with their own grog-filled eskies—coolers—that they squirrel away in private corners so they can forage back and forth. Some guzzle tequila, rum, wine, or beer. Others smoke dope in the snaky shadows of the verandah, dreamily taking in the sea breeze. With a Mexican shawl over his shoulders, Bernie slinks in shifty-eyed.

At first I mistake him for Anthony Perkins's dangerous mother from *Psycho*, but he's attempted some stodgy Mexican rendition of *Whistler's Mother*. Feeling a little restless, Melissa sheds her dress, lets down her hair, and emerges transformed into a sexy, buckskinned cowgirl. Dick strolls in late to the raging party in a surfing wetsuit. He has an overly large wooden tiki hanging on a leather thong around his neck and wears a surfing cap whose goofy brim is flipped up. When Dick asks a crowd of people who gather to guess who he is, he squares his jaw, thumps his chest, and shouts, "I'm Rick!"

A couple of days later Bernie and I are driving to Flat Rock. He's headed back out to the oil rig on the Timor Sea and says he really needs a surf before he goes. With his busy schedule of upcoming trips, he's already aware our surfing days are numbered. Except for telling me a few sad details about broken marriages, Bernie never really talks about anything personal. But after only a short time our friendship has become quietly intense. He seems happy to have a mildly psychotic surfing companion to help him sustain his lost youth. And he's willing to drive us up and down this coast, searching for the perfect wave, or even lousy waves, as long as we get wet and have a good time. To pay my way I usually whip up a batch of my chocolate-chip cookies that have now become an important ritual of our surfing.

Immense waves tumble on the outside reef at Flat Rock, and there are also fast inside beach breaks. Each mile-long swell wraps itself around a point that is basically a nasty ledge of rock that juts from the bay and reflects the outline of the continent. The far side of the ledge is considered by many to be one of the sharkiest spots on this coast. With our hectic house swap going on and my shaky karma, I'm excited but a little wary about testing waves in an area known to attract monsters of the deep.

We reach the secluded parking lot and see that the waves are going to be big. What's more, we have the place to ourselves. So we strip, pull on our wetsuits, wax our boards, and hurry in between the steep dunes and down to the vast golden beach. My heart pinches. It's everything a beach ought to be—visually stunning, sunny, warm, and redolent with solitude and sensual pleasure. Even though it's still only spring in Lennox, it feels closer to high summer. Like a kid, I can't wait to surf. The outside waves seem too daunting, although everyone claims they're not as powerful or dangerous as those at Lennox Point. I watch a swell slowly arrive, and when it catches the reef, it jacks up to twice its original height. As the lip feathers and the wave breaks, Bernie grins and says, "Looks like we struck it rich again, mate."

In deep sand we stroll to the water and are dwarfed before the massive wall of the drawbridging shorebreak. As we leash up, I notice the sky is almost the same blue as the sea. Without wind the waves are glassy and suddenly skewered with dolphins leaping in quicksilver arcs. "Hey, Bernie, look at all the dolphins!" I cry out, as excitable as an annoying kid brother. He's seen dolphins his whole life but still responds to them as though they're potent magic. I point, feeling cocky now. "Bernie, let's paddle out to that big outside wave over there."

Scanning the horizon with eyes used to the empty ocean that surrounds lonely oil rigs, Bernie rolls his eyes with feigned disgust. "Let's get into it then, you filthy bastard."

We wait for the right lull in the shorebreak, then spear in with our boards on the backwash. Paddling like crazy until I'm casually stroking up and down through the smooth swells, I follow Bernie, who seems to know where it's easiest to manoeuvre. The waves are a hell of a lot bigger now. We stroke up the face of a wave and down the backside of the elevator drop, then paddle hard to climb the next one before it breaks. The rush is magnificent. Just to be allowed to work the massive wave trains that tumble in from the horizon is a privilege. We get so tired of paddling that we rest our chins on the decks of our boards for a moment, then continue.

Finally, when we reach the outside, we stretch over our boards, panting, totally spent but relaxed. I feel the usual mental and physical euphoria kick in about the same time I spot a long grey body and a big fin surface. It's at least nine bloody feet long. My guts turn to jelly. "Holy shit, Bernie!" I yell, and he looks over at me in panic. We stare into the eerie beauty of the deep water, expecting the jaws of death until we both realize it's just another pod of dolphins arriving. Terror gives way to relief, then awe as we watch them gleam through the water beneath our boards, so close we can almost touch their skin.

Steep outside waves relentlessly roll in, and we stroke into as many as we want to surf. We suicide-drop down clean faces, gliding until our waves began to close, then shoot up and over the backside and paddle out hard for more. Each time I take a drop I let out an "Aouuhh!" of joy. Bernie always seems to get as much of a kick out of my enthusiasm for surfing as he does with the surfing itself. In a lull between waves we straddle our boards and drift together, totally free in a world where freedom is so rare. The sun warms the back of my wetsuit and my mouth, nostrils, ears, and body have been reamed out by so much salt water that everything feels swollen and profoundly clean.

Splashing me with a handful of water, Bernie says, "Mate, have a look at that."

I paddle around to face the shoreline and take in a vision to reassure the souls of a couple of fathers with young daughters. In the distance a carefree young girl rides a horse along hard-packed sand. The embodiment of an innocent dream, she gallops toward the far end of the beach, her long hair flowing behind her. In silence Bernie and I gaze at her until she slows to a trot and lets the horse walk into the water. Gently she goads her mount farther and farther into the perilous water until the horse swims her through the lagoon.

One of the last things we do at our old house is talk half of the eight families who live on their two-acre kingdoms into assembling at the dead end of Stoneyhurst. This is a street once notorious for its lack of solidarity, but Dale has managed to get our neighbours together for the First Annual Stoneyhurst Lawn Mower Race. Absurd as it might sound, I've cleaned up my old nemesis, the ancient, pop-riveted Briggs and Stratton Blue Thunder lawn mower whose throttle is held open with nylon stockings. In the past few months I've actually bonded with this rattly stoker-stencher and almost enjoy the brutal five hours it takes to shear our big mother of a property. Of course, this is an all-male race; Dale, Sherry, Beth, and Sunny stand on the sidelines. Steve proudly sits at the controls of his snake-slashing ride-on mower. Rob perches on his ride-on, and Bob has his machine revved and ready to go. Along both sides of Stoneyhurst our kids stand around, a little concerned about silly middle-aged adults racing lawn mowers. A coolish, damp breeze wafts off the sea, the sun hangs above the hinterland, and parrots squawk derisively in the trees. When Dale whistles, the engines roar, dogs bark, and in bare feet I bolt ahead of the pack, pushing my mower, running and screaming as if I've just won a million dollars.

All fun aside, we knew it would be a messy house swap. After two months of faxing back and forth between the school boards in Canada and Australia, trying to work things out so we could get the money to stay and finish our exchange, we received a nasty eviction notice from our exchangees. They hope that if they force us out of their house, Dale might get spooked enough to break her exchange contract and leave the country. But we haven't come all the way around the world with our kids to be turfed out of Oz by our unhappy exchangees five months early.

On Friday morning Melissa arrives in her Toyota van like an angel in the sunshine. She helps me move two loads of our belongings out of Stoneyhurst Manor and deliver them to our house inside the waves on Raynor Lane. Melissa also lends a hand to clean up Stoneyhurst so that we leave it spiffier than when we moved in. One of the north coast's most successful artists, Melissa is a smart, healthy romantic with both feet on the ground. She knows what's what and has a great built-in shit detector. I liked her the first time we met. She adores Dale, and our kids get along famously. "Don't worry, Ricky. Am gonna tell ya flat out," she says in her laconic American drawl. "Yer gonna be even happier livin' down on the beach."

Still, when Melissa carries away the last small box and I step out alone on the verandah for the final time, I'm heartbroken. When I look out, my horses are grazing dreamily above the ocean. In the near future this land will probably be taken over by housing that will radically change the feel of this country town by the sea. In the valley below, the builders of the new subdivision are still gouging away in a cloud of rising dust. For a long time I've been whingeing to everyone about how much I'll miss writing and living at Stoneyhurst Manor. There can never be another house with the same magic. Here my writer's block vanished because I found my muse again. Already I lament the loss of its Shangri-La seclusion, its butterflies and liquid squabble of magpies, its turpentine smell of eucalyptus gum trees, its noisy flocks of rainbow lorikeets and pink gallahs in the blossoms of melaleuca trees. I'll never again moodily pace the verandah and take in the long, glorious vista to the sea. This last morning when I glance out it's extraordinarily blue, and so flat that for miles I can actually see the dark outline of the reef. For seven months I've been lucky to live here like a king. Even though I already feel the proximity of nine-to-five suburban Canada looming with its endlessly dull winter and predictable routines, we still have another few months at our house inside the waves. So I move back in, lock the patio door, and walk through the darkened house and out the door to join Melissa in the van.

The next evening we're in our new kitchen enjoying the ocean just across the back lane. There's something powerfully calming about having all that sea at your doorstep. Friends have dropped by to bring us food and small housewarming gifts. Everyone is oohing and ahhing at our new beach house when we're clobbered with an angry phone call. Our exchangee accuses us of not leaving the key to the part of the house we weren't supposed to use—the section with the fireplace, sauna, and master bedroom. I politely tell her the key is on a hook above the counter, left of the stove. She says they refuse to pay the $350 we insist they owe us for unpaid bills in Ottawa accrued because they've abandoned our homestead in suburbia early. Half an hour later she's on the phone again. "We're missing two expensive squash rackets," she snarls.

In a bland Canadian Muppet voice, I retort, "We don't play squash." Then I tell her where she might find them, but not where she can put them when she does. That prompts her to make a number of other shrill accusations, but I maintain a level voice and remind her we're not malicious thieves. We're good people. Unfortunately when I mention how much we loved and cared for their house and how we treated it as though it were our own, she explodes and claims we left the house in a mess. Towels and sheets Melissa and I meticulously folded haven't been shelved properly in the linen closet. Sections of the bookcase are no longer in alphabetical order. Worse, we rearranged some furniture—for example, the old oak desk placed in an alcove of the dormer window facing the sea.

"If you've rearranged things in our house, we'll just put them back where they were, or we might thank you for discovering a new way to appreciate our house," I say.

These words only inspire her to unload another vicious tongue lashing, which she punctuates by slamming the phone down in my ear. My stomach is a knot of razor blades. Slowly I drag my ass upstairs and lie on the floor in front of Dale and our friends. Like a thousand-year-old man, I listen to various theories concerning the bad style our exchangees have shown. Then I moan, "I really don't think they're finished messing with us."

Although we're living in a more comfortable house in an even more beautiful location, we don't really get to enjoy it during the next few days. I drank a big bottle of Pepto-Bismol and get a little twitchy when someone comes to the door. Now that we aren't secluded a lot more people arrive unannounced.

A day later I'm in the Beach Life Surf Shop where I spot our male exchangee pacing outside. As if reenacting a Wild West shoot-out, he's obviously expecting I'll step into the street. Perhaps he needs a confrontation to ease the accumulated hurt and frustration of their failed teacher exchange. Unfortunately I'm going to be the target of the fury he stored up during those months he spent in our suburban town house, waiting for winter to end. All I can really think about, though, is how each month on the Gold Coast hundreds of thousands of Australians in heavy parkas pay good money to wander inside a building that simulates a winter wonderland. Many Aussies who visit the Northern Hemisphere are as enthusiastic about the mystique of winter as I am about summer. Still, I tell my friend behind the cash register of the surf shop to keep an eye on me in case I need her as a witness to an assault. Then I stride over to our exchangee and, before he can say anything, reach out my hand and say, "I hope there's no hard feelings about the exchange."

Of course, he doesn't take my hand. Instead he trembles with rage as though every orifice in his body has been plugged for an eternity, then screams, "Get facked!" He wants to hit me, and I'm ready to defend myself if he even breathes on me. Finally he growls, "There's a black torch missing."

"Torch?" I murmur. Then I remember. "You mean the flashlight? We kept it under the bed with a candle and matches for all the times the power went out."

"What about the fackin' trays? Who said you could cut down the bloody fackin' trays?"

"Last December you told us that if you'd gotten around to trimming a few of the treetops, there'd be a great view. Well, I got around to it."

The fun isn't over. Two days later I'm at my new desk writing when a rusted white ute pulls up and the female exchangee steps out as if she's bloody royalty. She inserts an envelope into the jaws of our mailbox at the end of the driveway, then speeds off in the ute.

The letter is three pages long and written in pseudo-legalese, ghostwritten by our exhangees' solicitor daughter. Without doubt it's one of the most amazing pieces of creative writing I've ever read. There's a list of atrocities we've supposedly performed on Stoneyhurst Manor. A trumped-up catalogue of ridiculous damages that includes: one missing Tupperware container—$15; gardening and weeding not done—$200; repainting garage door damaged by our girls' pink chalk miniature artworks—$20; the broken (already broken) toaster—$28; a missing picture-frame hook—$10. The total: $1,511. It's all fabricated and absurd, of course. And if we don't pay up, they say they'll be forced to take matters further and to initiate civil proceedings in the small-claims tribunal.

Dale has taken this dispute rather badly. The idea of a messy courtroom drama in a foreign country has pretty well flattened her. In bed I read aloud more funny passages of Bill Bryson's *Lost Continent* and administer morning and nightly neck massages to exorcise the bad vibes from our exchangees. In our spare time we're dealing with this annoying couple but still managing to suck the life out of our Australian exchange. Luckily we're friends with half the town, which I'm sure rankles our reclusive exchangees.

Sky's soccer team won the grand finale at Lismore Stadium, taking home the big trophy and gold medals for each player. All season the team didn't lose a single game, and despite the misogynist tendencies of the club's boys, Sky earns respect. She's learned a lot about heart and desire and sticking it out, things that will no doubt come in handy in sports as well as in life. Already five foot six, she's doing her best to push me and Dale around, and has to be hounded toward every word, every number, every second of school, which she dislikes. Sky has no interest in school except as a place to unfold her mushrooming social life. Of course, she's a big hit here; she's the exotic Canadian who has to be bullied through the rest of her school days by her poor mom and dad. What goes around comes around.

Quintana has her seventh birthday party with lots of little friends. They eat the usual birthday food on our sunny deck above the beach. Quinn rips open an alarming number of gift-wrapped stuffies and more bloody Barbies. Sky supervises the girls while they have a scavenger hunt and play games on our private beach. Then Dale plugs them all into *101 Dalmatians* while we mop up.

Because of the ongoing stress from Stoneyhurst Manor and because we know our time here is limited, each morning we can't sleep, so we bolt up just before dawn. We've always dreamed of living right on the ocean, and this is our moment. Dale and I stroll down our short drive-way, cross the back lane, and barefoot it along the worn path to the spot where the grassy dunes become sand. There, framed between the foliage of rustling pandanus, we enjoy the entire sweep of Seven Mile Beach from Lennox Point to Broken Head. With only just the rolling surf and swollen sky blossoming with the fiery glow of the rising sun, we begin our lengthy morning walkabout.

I always show Dale the fort I helped our daughters make in a little protected hollow of the beach. The girls and I heaped driftwood on a couple of the weathered posts of the ancient tea-tree breakwater. Inside their fort Sky and Quinn have hidden precious shells, feathers, fish and bird skulls, and wild sponges.

Dale and I have been feeling a little vexed ever since we got the paperwork back and found out that to immigrate to Australia, just to fill out the official forms, we'd have to pay $1,500, which we'll never see again. There is a rigorous point system to get into this country. Points for age, education, skills, and current bank account. We'd get points for our university degrees and work skills, but our bank account is always shamefully overdrawn. No one ever seems to take into consideration the impressive balance of our soul account. And because we're well over thirty-five we'd lose too many eligibility points. They either want rich old farts or young, very skilled people with money. Before we left Canada we were warned not to jump ship while we were on the teacher exchange. Now we discover that it would cost us $3,000 for our dog, Ruby, to endure a three-month quarantine. We'd have to sell up in Canada, burn our bridges, and take our kids away from their friends and family. And Australia is so far away and expensive to get to that no one would ever visit us.

One Sunday morning Dale and I rise before dawn as usual and head outside. The first thing she says to me is: "I can't believe we're living here." We constantly taste the weather the way lighthouse keepers, fishermen, or sea captains do. At night with storm surf on a high tide it feels as though our house will be hauled out to sea. On a flat day at low tide the ocean looks as serene as a desert.

No matter where we go we can't escape progress and development. The people who own the land beside the empty property in front of our place are building a mammoth house on the beach. The other day piles of sand and gravel and an ugly cement mixer appeared beside our path to the water. All the charming low-rise beach cottages of the old Lennox waterfront are being pulled down and replaced by two-story hotel-like structures. Workmen told me that next week the foundation for the neighbour's house will be poured. So while we revel in our modest share of paradise, we're witnessing this monstrosity being erected right beside our beach. After living here for only eight months, we've already become insanely possessive about maintaining the traditional Lennox. I want it frozen for all time the way it was when we first arrived and got seduced by its spell. One can only imagine the trauma that ensued when the Aborigines had to relinquish most of this continent after the white invasion.

It's still quite cool, with a kingdom of white clouds jumbled at the horizon. There isn't a soul on the beach. As the sun pops above the horizon, literally the edge of the world, the planet's curve, the entire sky becomes the ceiling of the Sistine Chapel—glorious and God-inspired. Dale tells me about the mysterious clouds wreathing the summit of Mount Warning, and the mother whale with baby she watched from the top of Wategos with her outdoor-learning class. The young one breached, thrusting its tail upward. Hand in hand, we splash in the water toward the Point. Neither of us can take our eyes off the morning glass. To describe a wave the Italian novelist Italo Calvino once wrote: "To translate its every movement into words, one would have to invent a new vocabulary and perhaps also a new grammar and a new syntax, or else employ a system of notation like a musical score."

Above the tide pools we walk single file along a muddy trail in front of beach houses, then cut past Dress Circle Parade. I point out Kiko's break—Frank's Spot. The surf churns dangerously over the shallow reef where I cut my feet, lost a fin, and walked like Jesus. From this spot we look back along the whole bay cranking with surf. Salt mist drifts over the town and beaches for miles down the coast to Broken Head. Pods of dolphins shimmer through the glassy swells. "Ricky, why can't we stay here for good?" Dale asks, reminding me of the eighteen-year-old girl I fell in love with two decades earlier.

I smile ruefully. "You know, Bear, I don't even want to think about it, because we have to go back home." Even though I feel this beach town and the deep friendships we've made are our destiny, we both know we can't stay. It comes down to bureaucracy, geography, and dollars and cents. And for our kids it would be an emotional impossibility. Just then a line of pelicans flies low over the breaking waves. It's all too much, too painful to imagine surviving without. Since the early 1970s, Dale and I have spent every fourth year of our married life travelling and following waves on islands in the tropics. Yet somehow we always end up in the heart of a cold continent.

"Rick," Dale breathes dreamy-eyed as she glances at me and then out to the waves, "some day I want to do the light of breaking waves." For most of her life Dale has been known as an artist. She's done portraits in Vancouver's Stanley Park and in Waikiki's Kapiolani Park. Over the years she's painted oil and acrylic landscapes and subtle watercolours. A demanding teaching career and kids put serious artistic drives on hold. "When we get back home," she says, "I'm going to do big stained-glass paintings of breaking waves."

We continue all the way to Lennox Point, staring out at a handful of dawn patrollers taking vertical drops in the formidable waves. Squinting at the horizon, Dale says, "You're right, Bear. The waves are a lot scarier here." As though materializing out of a nineteenth-century novel, an old wooden bench comes into view above the Point. We sit together and marvel at the panorama of sea and sky. In the distance we glimpse a few other early-morning dreamers strolling our beach. A dog runs ahead of them. We can faintly hear it bark as it races along the water, turns, then lopes back to its owner. Dale lays her head on my shoulder.

Slowly we get up and walk back home along a trail made in the grass from years of surfers hotfooting it down to surf the Point. Dale and I are esconced in one of those almost painful, fleeting bubbles of perfect happiness. Nothing can improve this moment.

Then, up ahead, I spot Kiko, Neil, and Mihkel coming toward us with their surfboards tucked under their arms. Part Three Stooges, part Three Musketeers, the Three Amigos are heading for a late-dawn patrol session at the Point. Resplendent in wetsuits, sun-bleached hair, and love beads, the trio smirks with the relaxed, tough confidence men have in the company of other men who are temporarily free of their wives, kids, and mortgages.

Kiko is in the middle. "Hey, Ricky, howzit goin'?" he asks. I mutter hello, and Dale is reintroduced to Neil and Mihkel. For years these three have surfed longboards together. They exude a powerful bond and a cruisey lightness of being.

"Amigo, why aren't you surfing with us this morning?" Kiko asks, pained at the thought of me walking with my wife in the proximity of so many good waves.

"Yeah, Rick," Dale says a little uncertainly, "you should go for a surf."

I'm like a little kid who's been given permission to ride his first bike. "Jesus, this is great! I'm going to run back and get my wetsuit and board. You guys wait here for me, okay?"

The Three Amigos stand there laughing as I turn and race off, leaving Dale to walk back home. Alone.

19
THE WHOLE SOUTH SEAS KITCHEN

The days and weeks have been slipping away rather sweetly. A lot of the people around here who have forsaken material aspirations to disappear into a laid-back 1960s lifestyle have great health, low stress, and no apparent worries about future prospects. Sliding into the pleasant oblivion of a beach life so far removed from the tightly wound modern world, who can blame them? Most days, as with the Aborigines precontact, you can have the beach to yourself—seven miles of it. A famous poster showing endless layers of breaking waves cascading in at Lennox Point says it all: NORTH COAST PERFECTION.

On a certain level I've become troppo—just another middle-aged white guy gone native. I now spend as much time carving tikis as writing. My tikis reflect Maori, Polynesian, Balinese, Celtic, and Aboriginal art and the work of Paul Gauguin. Every time I begin I try something new. With a different nose, mouth, eyes, chin, forehead, sometimes a tiki's face takes on the elongated appearance of a sensual body. Other times they're merely abstract suggestions of captured forms. As a result, each sculptured tiki is unique and fun.

Beside our kitchen windows I sit for hours at an old table covered with pieces of gnarled wood and my miniature hand tools. My carving space has a great sea view and is flooded with sunlight and the sound of rumbling waves. Sometimes I carve out beyond the carport near the banksia tree. In front of the beach is also a good place. There I can check out the waves and get into the local vibes of my neighbours. Whenever I'm hot I go for a quick dive in the ocean or back upstairs to work in the shade for a while.

I can really appreciate why early North American First Nations and Inuit and Australian Aborigines took such pleasure and pride and felt the need to express themselves in bone, wood, or stone. When they weren't hunting and gathering and hustling their asses off to stay alive, they took the time to let themselves become possessed by a medium— the same way writers are driven to express themselves with words on paper and surfers are taken over by water and make art with waves. Now I understand the mystery of how the ancients' carved tools, weapons, and art objects took on the spiritual *mana* of each carver and the circumstances and the place where they were created.

So far I've carved a growing tribe of tikis with names like Elephant Man's Handsome Brother, Lennox Sea Horse, Shark God, West Wind, Byron Surf King, Manta Ray Man, Little Neptune, and King of the Waves. I'm calling this series Picasso Goes to the South Seas, and I've already sold a few for a hundred dollars each, the ones I can part with, that is. As a labour of love, I carved Dale a bloodwood tiki made up of a dozen interlocking heart motifs of various sizes and shapes. I traded another tiki for one of Melissa's Wright's astonishing horizontal etchings, *Seahorses and Birds Underwater*. In bed Dale and I never get tired of looking at the long-haired girl holding on to a dolphin who is taking her through a magical underwater Dreamworld. Melissa has asked me to give the opening speech for her latest art show, *Love and Other Intimacies*. And for each of my surf-dog friends I'm carving a tiki I'll present as farewell gifts.

After school today, on a low tide, Quinn takes me by the hand to the beach to check out small squiddling fish, crabs, anemones, spiky sea urchins, seashells, old coins, smooth pieces of broken glass, and other hidden treasures. Lost for two hours with the warm sunlight on our backs, we wade around exploring the shallow tide pools. At seven Quinn is loyal, affectionate, and happy. Currently she's probably my best friend. It's an almost unbearable joy to be with her because, in a way, the love you have for a small kid is a lot stronger than the love you'll ever feel for an adult. We strip for a quick bodysurf, Quinn squealing with delight as we're taken by the waves. Because Quinn is missing four or five teeth, every time she opens her mouth to smile she looks like a Montreal Canadiens hockey player from the 1950s. Out deeper on the reef we dive under the clean, dumping waves and listen to clicking shards of broken shells and coral.

Raynor Lane is fairly short and runs parallel to the beach—a dozen old wooden houses jumbled on the waterfront and another dozen strung along the other side of the lane. Living in a house inside the waves with dazzling sunshine and the incessant roar of surf, I sometimes find it tough to concentrate on writing. From my new writing desk I've got a view right down to the beach: a church of blue sky and ocean. Whenever I become restless, I get up, run across the back lane, stampede through the sea grass over the small dunes, sprint across the sand, and spear up and over the shorebreak into the waves. Really, it's become a sad race against time—how to savour every moment of this splendour to the fullest before we fly back to our other life in Canada.

All of the houses on this side of Raynor Lane have large sundecks with staggering ocean views. It's a little like living in a roomy lighthouse. But compared to Stoneyhurst Manor I have to work at my privacy and fight distractions. For example, this morning on the beach the tide has climbed high in a curving sensual line and a beautiful young woman is doing up the bikini top of another sleek tanned beauty. Besides having a seven-mile beach at my doorstep, I have to cope with the traffic of cars, neighbours, and the odd strolling tourist perambulating our back lane; it's the usual beach life with everyone living more or less in the open behind thin walls. Living at the beach, we've also become intimate with sand, sunlight, wind, salt, and rust. But we have no mosquitoes or ants, and so far no venomous snakes and poisonous spiders.

John, a retired neighbour down the lane, has resided here for decades. His legs, arms, and face look as though they barely survived a nuclear blast. I wince at his sun-damaged skin that doesn't look like flesh anymore, thinking about my mother's skin cancer and my own sun-buggered, acne- and car-accident-scarred skin and how much grief it will bring me and how rough it will look when I'm older. How dearly some of us will pay for the sin of our sun worship. "Anotha rippah die in parodoyce," John always says, lowering his newspaper and sweeping a scabrous arm across the ocean view. He's trained a cheeky flock of huge, strutting white seabirds who will now only feed in the open block of land in front of his house. Being retired, he's devoted himself to these freeloading birds. With the dry edge of his shirt he slyly swabs one of the innumerable running sores of skin cancer on his poor face. Knowing that I'm the *Can-eye-dian writer*, he unloads scandalous news bites about my country and the United States because every day from deep within the shade of his beach house he watches the news with a vengeance. To many Australians, America is the bane of their lives and the entire world. John dismisses the local politicians as bullshitters and says all the money is going out of Australia.

Another old neighbour has succumbed to the bitterness of old age and a warped nostalgia for a White Australia that is slowly disappearing. One day when I casually mention the problems England is having with unemployment, he lashes out, "It's all the bloody niggahs. The niggah lovers are pushing everyone around."

After the soulful release of a long surf this morning, I stash my board, rinse the salt out of my wetsuit, and hang it up to dry. To help maintain a friendly rapport with the wild young cannibals next door, I join them for a little Frisbee throwing in their empty yard. A half-dozen surfies with spiked hair, tattoos, and carefree fuck-you-attitudes, they rarely wear shirts or shoes—like me—and shamble about as though tomorrow will never come. I've surfed with them out on the reef, but young surfers are notorious for their stoic silence in the water. One bloke takes a few courses at university, another works part-time, and the others coast on and off the dole. At the moment their lives revolve around surfing and chasing a string of healthy girls who float in and out of their tumble-down house. Half-naked and crazed, I prance about with my lucky shells on a leather thong around my neck. For ten minutes I toss a Frisbee back and forth with the lads, fiendishly running and jumping to catch it behind my back to razzle-dazzle them. Finally I say, "Thanks a lot, you guys. I'll catch ya later," and hobble back to the sanctuary of our house for a power nap.

Our neighbours on the other side of the surfers are Tony and Lynn Serf. Lynn is the quiet, thoughtful secretary at our daughters' school. Somewhat of a legend, Tony is a board shaper for Town and Country Surfboards in Byron Bay. He has his own line of boards all bearing his name. Like a lot of South Africans, he left his country to find a home in the South Pacific. He lived in Hawaii long enough to embrace the spiritual power of Polynesian *mana*, surf the waves of legendary breaks, and become a master board shaper. Then he discovered Byron Bay. Lynn and Tony chose Lennox Head to raise their two boys who are now mostly grown and on the way to their own discoveries.

Early in the morning, I see Tony alone on his sundeck. Tall, dark, and rangy, he broods with a smoking cigarette, his eyes locked on the incoming surf. His age, smoking, and surfing lifestyle have given him a Marlboro-Man-as-surfer look. Long ago during his lifeguarding days in South Africa he saw former Nazis languishing on the beaches.

A little later I watch Tony casually knee-paddle out on his customized twelve-foot Hawaiian longboard. For a quarter hour I observe him on the outer reef, drifting meditatively on his board. It's a glassy morning with a powerful swell running ahead of a storm hundreds of miles out at sea. Dale and the girls have left for school and I've already done my wash and hung it on the line near the carport. The tide is right, and the wind blows lightly offshore. Except for Tony, it looks as if I might have the whole ocean to myself. But I don't want to paddle out and crowd him, so I stand in the shadows of our deck, waiting for him to make his move.

Clean, mile-long swells roll in from the horizon and break over the reef in front of Tony. Still, he straddles his board, rising on each swell, then disappearing into each deep trough. Being so tall and gangly and hunched over on his modified replica of an ancient Hawaiian longboard, Tony stands out among a hundred surfers. A big set now approaches. Tony casually stretches over his board and begins to stroke into the biggest wave of the set. In one fluid motion he springs up and takes his drop, then trims the peeling wave. After days of sea-gazing, he's obviously paddled out to the right spot and waited to catch the best-shaped wave in weeks, gliding high on its shoulder, riding it with the impressive ease and grace of a natural waterman. Standing perfectly relaxed like Duke Kahanamoku of Hawaii, he diagonally rides the wave's curl across most of the bay. As his watery mount closes out, he gracefully manoeuvres his longboard into a smooth, arching cutback to catch a steep section of another wave. Then, with the same upright elegance, he surfs in the opposite direction across most of the bay again, oblivious to the world.

More than twenty years ago when I first began writing stories about the South Seas, Timothy Findley inscribed a copy of his bestselling novel, *The Wars*, with a little friendly advice I've been turning over in my mind ever since: "For Rick, with thanks and good wishes. Just don't stay on those islands forever."

One of the first books I stumbled upon in our new house library was *The Confessions of a Beachcomber: Scenes and Incidents in the Career of an Unprofessional Beachcomber in Tropical Queensland*, a memoir published in 1908. E. J. (Ted) Banfield, its author, wrote four books in twenty-five years while living on Dunk Island, and died at seventy-one in June 1923. Born in the Beatles' Liverpool a little over a hundred years before "Can't Buy Me Love" was a hit, Banfield left England with his family and settled in Melbourne, Australia. His father and uncle began a couple of very successful newspapers. Later Banfield wrote for one of their papers in Sydney. In a bid to escape the rat race, he transferred to the coast of Queensland to write for *The Daily Bulletin* in Townsville. On a short trip back to England he met Bertha Golding and married her in 1886. Apparently nervous exhaustion and the stress of modern life put an end to his newspaper employment, so he left in 1897 for Dunk Island off the coast between Townsville and Cairns.

The Aborigines once called Dunk, Coonanglebah, but the small rainforested island in the Coral Sea was renamed by Captain Cook for Lord Montague Dunk, the Earl of Sandwich who was the stodgy namesake of the Sandwich Islands—mercifully redubbed Hawaii. Living on the beach on Dunk Island for twenty-five years and writing four books about the place, Banfield gave expression to a state of mind and the myth of the South Seas. Our idyllic South Pacific life at Stoneyhurst Manor and here in this house inside the waves might have some parallels with Banfield's residence on Dunk. When he arrived burnt-out on the island, he was forty-six, the same age I am now. We both suffered spiritual and physical impoverishment as well as writer's block. We both managed to escape the world to blend reality with romance and find a kind of paradise on earth. Banfield did it for a quarter century; my family and I will end up with twelve lucky months here.

In my mind there's a fine line between a beachcomber and an artist or writer—wandering aimless along a beach collecting, always searching, hoping to discover something you're not sure about. Art and beachcombing are romantic as hell, but many people construe them as a waste of time. Both are soul-enriching, but there's no real money to be made. Banfield notes in his book: "If you wish to increase a man's happiness, seek not to increase his possessions, but to decrease his desires."

In their house near the beach Ted and Bertha Banfield were free to swim, fish, explore the reefs, walk the beach, and grow their own vegetables and fruit. They befriended the local Aborigines and learned how those indigenous people had adapted to and thrived in their environment for thousands of years. Being a writer saved Banfield from succumbing to the usual hedonistic sloth of Polynesian paralysis. The articles he wrote for magazines overseas were later collected and published, eventually making him an Aussie legend. People all over the world read his books, which are classics of the beachcombing life. For the past hundred years a lot of people have desired what he found: a simple, fulfilling existence beside the sea with a hell of a lot of free time to smell the roses.

According to what I gleaned from one biography of Banfield, he was, like many of us, a little inclined to bouts of dark depression. But he had a mercurial ability to rise above it. And unlike a lot of people he also had a loyal, supportive wife and no real job worries and lived for his last twenty-five years in a tropical paradise. Having walked a thousand miles of beaches all over the world myself, I can't think of a better profession than that of beachcomber. Who knows? Heaven might be an endless stroll along an Australian beach. Although Banfield's books are thoroughly charming rambles of an energetic, likable man, I probably like the simple innocent freedom of his beachcombing works more than the actual process of reading them because, at times, his language is outdated and the jaunty, pedantic British tone of his wordy, dear-reader voice can be off-putting. But to be in the inspired mind of someone who discovered true happiness and obviously found his paradise on earth is something rare:

> When there are eight or ten islands and islets within an afternoon's sail, and miles of beach to police, variety lends her charms to the pursuit of the Beachcomber. Landing in one of the unfrequented coves, he knows not what the winds and the tides may have spread out for inspection and acceptance. Perhaps only an odd coconut from the Solomon Islands, its husks riddled by cobra and zoned with barnacles. The germ of life may yet be there. To plant the nut above high-water mark is an obvious duty. Perhaps there is a paddle, with rude tracery on the handle, from the New Hebrides, part of a Fijian canoe that has been bundled over the Barrier, a wooden spoon such as Kanakas use, or the dusky globe of an incandescent lamp that has glowed out its life in the state room of some ocean liner, or a broom of Japanese make, a coal basket, a tiger nautilus shell or a bottle cast away far out from land to determine the strength and direction of ocean currents.... One lucky beachcomber casually picked up a black-lip mother-of-pearl shell on an island some little distance away. It contained a blue pearl, the price of which gave him such a start in life that he is now an owner of ships.

Knowing Banfield, if he had ever found such a priceless pearl, he would have simply given it to Bertha. Cashing it in for money would have done nothing to increase their happiness.

Today Banfield's lost paradise has been found, developed, packaged, and sold to the world. One hot deal for the the newly dubbed Island of Peace and Plenty is the Romantic Interlude: five very special nights start from $550 per person twin share, $730 in a beachfront unit. And on Dunk today you'll find the Beachcomber Restaurant, EJ's Café, Banfield's Grave (Ted and Bertha together for eternity), and a museum. Imagine a quaint Robinson Crusoe life but with guaranteed comfort. Banfield's paradise now offers game-fishing trips, scuba diving, jet ski and catamaran rentals, and evening nature walks. The island is aggressively sold as a place that will help you forget everything that's unimportant and remember everything that is.

Slam.

Dunk.

Another even more famous white guy who went troppo in this neighbourhood was Robert Louis Stevenson. He finished out his short life on an island in Samoa in the middle of the Pacific. Samoa isn't exactly next door to Dunk Island, which is 960 miles north of Byron Bay, but if you draw lines to connect them, you get a long, skinny triangle and soon realize they're close, given the vast, lonely size of the South Pacific.

Originally my first book, *Tender Only to One*, was inspired by the final years of Paul Gauguin's life in the South Seas. Like Banfield, Stevenson, and I, Gauguin decided he had to find the most isolated romantic place on earth to be happy and do his art. Because I'd already been a surfer, I'd managed to surf and sample a fair bit of the primitive beauty of California, Hawaii, Tahiti, Fiji, Bali, Sri Lanka, New Zealand, and Australia. But as I began to write my little Gauguin book, it became a collection of linked stories about doomed romantic painters and the writer, Robert Louis Stevenson.

One of the books that has kept me island-travelling is Stevenson's *In the South Seas*, which is about a lot more than the search for the perfect island. The South Seas have always been a state of mind. I've taken many trips there, both real and imaginary. Although Hawaii isn't really in the South Seas, it defines the South Seas of the imagination. Over the years Dale and I have tried to assuage our obsession with beaches and islands on a half-dozen two-month sojourns in the Hawaiian Islands, and it was there, with my wife, that I learned about three of the more important things in life: how to love, surf, and write.

A little more than a hundred years ago Stevenson took a house on the beach at Waikiki. He was an incurable romantic who found true happiness living near the sea, listening to the sound of waves. The restless, beloved Scottish romancer, prodigious letter writer, world traveller, and famous author of enduring classics such as *Treasure Island*, *Dr. Jekyll and Mr. Hyde*, *Kidnapped*, and *A Child's Garden of Verses* made three South Seas voyages before giving into his grand exile in Samoa.

I've read most of Stevenson's stuff. All his biographers seem wildly enthusiastic. In most quarters Stevenson is considered an untarnished saint, though his literary reputation is much less solid. I can personally relate to an impossibly skinny guy who had a sense of suppressed energy, as though the mainspring of his imagination was overwound. The romantic adventures of his travels and writing enabled him to escape the drabness of everyday life. Like most people, he had a youthful imagination ignited by romance and adventure, but unlike most people, he demanded the same stimulation in his adult life. He was a man preoccupied with dualities, a man whose seductive, upbeat personality shines through everything he ever wrote, and even shimmers off the mountain of literature written about him.

Stevenson was born an only child in Edinburgh in 1850, the son of a famous father and grandfather who had built most of the legendary lighthouses on the Scottish coastline. He was a sickly boy deeply attached to his nanny, Cummie, who adored and nurtured him, drenching him in her wild Scottish imagination and a violently strict Presbyterianism that helped shape his thoughts on the duality of human nature. Stevenson's own romantic yearnings were fired by stories of the sea, lighthouses, islands, shipwrecks, pirates, and roving adventurers. Although he wasn't a surfer, because back then no one even thought about surfing outside Hawaii, his knowledge of waves, tides, currents, swells, rocks, sandbars, and headlands provided by his lighthouse-building father as they tramped the Scottish shorelines was used in writing his first popular book, *Treasure Island*.

As a result of being bedridden for much of his life, Stevenson was forced to live in his imagination, the perfect realm for a writer. *Treasure Island* was written before he even set foot on a tropical island. While Stevenson was visiting Australia in February 1890, a journalist writing an article on him for the *Sydney Morning Herald* asked which island was Treasure Island. Stevenson coyly smiled and said, "Treasure Island is not in the Pacific." Or any other real ocean on any map of the world, he might have added.

Everything Stevenson did was accelerated by the real threat of an early demise. In university, after he began to travel and hang out in the underbelly of Edinburgh, London, and then Paris, he struggled with anti-bourgeois sentiments. Although his father funded his subsidized bohemian lifestyle, they were at odds with each other because Stevenson decided to become a writer rather than a lighthouse engineer.

The Scottish author's ultimate act of rebellion was marrying an older, previously wedded woman, Mrs. Fanny Van de Grift Osbourne, who had a son, Lloyd, and also a pretty seventeen-year-old daughter, Isobel (Belle), in tow. Fanny's wanderlust helped to mobilize Stevenson. After his father died, he had no obligation to remain in Britain and was free to go where his health and heart required. Using the funds from his father's estate and money an American newspaper editor offered for a series of letters describing his experiences in the South Seas, he took off on a one-way voyage away from his beloved Scotland.

Sick in mind and spirit, he was looking for an earthly paradise. He and Fanny decided to give their mid-life crisis free rein. A flamboyant romantic in an age of romantics, he set sail in June 1888 with his extended family and his mother on the ninety-four-foot, two-masted schooner *Casco*. Gliding out of San Francisco's harbour into the open Pacific, they sailed on, rising and falling with the rolling swells, the wind rattling in the ropes and wooden riggings. As the muscle of the creaking vessel moved through the water with graceful strength, heaving the ailing writer's weak stomach into his mouth, the wind, salt, and sea lashed his flesh. Stevenson leaned even farther over the railing and gazed for the last time on the American continent; he didn't realize he'd spend the rest of his short life in the Pacific islands. But at that moment he was happy; he had that unbearable feeling of escape, sailing into the unknown.

For six months he roamed the South Seas, visiting the remote Marquesas, the Tuamotus, and Tahiti. Along the way he read James Cook's and Herman Melville's accounts of the Pacific and recorded in his journal the ancient legends, old Polynesian poetry, and strange stories about white misfits, dispossessed royalty, daring adventurers, rabid missionaries, pirates, and cannibals who ate "long-pig," or human flesh. Finally Stevenson's eccentric entourage anchored *Casco* in Honolulu's harbour. Right away Stevenson took a palm-shrouded, ramshackle cottage on the then-deserted beach of Waikiki four miles away. Shedding clothes and the cloak of Victorian respectability by walking the beach and sea-bathing, he went native and settled in. There, in his house inside the waves with the sound of roaring surf and trade winds blowing through the shuttered windows, he continued writing up the notes of his journal, which would eventually become *In the South Seas*, a classic of Pacific travel whose opening chapter offers this delicious premise: "The first experience can never be repeated. The first love, the first sunrise, the first South Sea island, are memories apart…"

Stevenson's obsession with the South Seas began, like mine, in Hawaii at Waikiki, the world's most famous or infamous beach, depending on your point of view. As young men, both Stevenson and I internalized the myth of the South Seas through the words of one of the first English novels. Published in 1719, Daniel Defoe's *Robinson Crusoe* tells the story of a young sailor shipwrecked on a desert island who desperately wants to escape back to civilization. Somehow Stevenson and I got it all ass-backward: at some point in our youth we both decided to escape the restraints and responsibilities of civilization and return to some kind of imagined paradise on a desert island.

Even a hundred years ago Stevenson felt Waikiki was so commercialized that he wrote about the "unjust but inevitable extinction of Polynesian culture by our shabby civilization." But he got on famously with the king of Hawaii, David Kalakaua (nicknamed the Merry Monarch), who had read and enthusiastically discussed *Treasure Island* and *Dr. Jekyll and Mr. Hyde*. Kalakaua's court on the grounds of his Uluniu estate near the current Hyatt Regency Hotel was the centre of music and culture, and his name appeared as the author of *Legends and Myths of Hawaii*, edited by R. M. Daggett. Stevenson was appalled and impressed by the huge, quick-witted king's capacity to put away several bottles of champagne and brandy at one of the most famous luaus in Hawaiian history, hosted by Kalakaua in honour of the Scottish writer. With everyone draped in the heavenly, scented aloha of flower leis, the great outdoor feast of chicken, pig, poi, raw fish, seaweed, roasted kukui nuts, and baked dog (a favourite dish of the king's) was immortalized by the photographs of Arthur Richardson.

In the wake of "Christ and commerce," Kalakaua tried, over the years, to restore the health and culture of his people, particularly their traditional storytelling and ancient hula. In vain he also attempted to protect the Hawaiian monarchy from a group of ruthless businessmen backed by American military forces. On the day Stevenson left the Hawaiian

Islands to find another paradise farther south in the Pacific, Kalakaua arrived with more champagne and a gift of a miniature schooner bearing the inscription: MAY THE WINDS AND WAVES BE FAVOURABLE. While the Royal Hawaiian Band played "Aloha Oe," Stevenson set sail once again, leaving behind a Hawaii that would never be the same.

My own, obviously continuing bout with Paradise Lost began in 1972 at the tender age of nineteen. I got it into my head that I had to live in Hawaii, or die. Like Stevenson, I had also discovered that a beach on a tropical island is one of the most natural and potent antidepressants. For most of that summer of 1972 I lived in Waikiki on the island of Oahu. To say that it was a life-altering revelation when I first stepped into the dazzling brilliance of Waikiki Beach and saw all that turquoise surf rolling in would be an understatement. Back then Waikiki still had faint remnants of its former Polynesian lifestyle that offered sanctuary and a healing space for the soul. The royal descendants of Kamehameha the Great, who had united the Hawaiian Islands, lived in Honolulu but retreated to modest wooden cottages in Waikiki to get away and swim, fish, or paddle the waves on surfboards and outrigger canoes. I lived in a charming run-down hotel called the Edgewater that was engulfed by lush foliage and ancient coconut palms that had been planted by Hawaiian royalty. In the humid air of my small room as I drank beer and gazed out the open wooden shutters, I listened to the blissful murmur of tropical birds and took in whiffs of salty sea air, plumeria (frangipani), and wild ginger—the essence of the islands. Without enough funds, without a shred of talent or the proper discipline, I decided then and there to become a world traveller and a writer like Stevenson.

Back then Waikiki was starting to become the air-conditioned nightmare of high-rises that now crowds that famous beach. It was still a laid-back seaside village with languorous, friendly Hawaiians who sold puka-shell necklaces, flowered leis, and fresh papaya, guavas, pineapples, and passion fruit. Already for decades planes and boats of hysterical tourists had been pouring in to defile the islands, but somehow the *mana*, the spiritual power of the aloha spirit, held sway. Among the crowds of *haoles*—white foreigners—I still remember seeing jeeps full of cocky, drunk, fresh-faced GIs roaring around on R&R before their murderous stints in the Vietnam War that was still raging. A quarter mile out on the coral reefs I surfed like a young god with local Hawaiians, and on all the beaches I observed some of the most beautiful women on the planet "undraped and bedecked in flowers, frisking in the vales of Eden." Without success I was seeking the answers to the eternal questions I'm still pondering: Where do we come from? What are we? Where are we going? As a hopeless romantic on my first visit to the islands, I even had the good fortune to fall brutally in love.

Being a landlocked child in Ottawa, I had read South Seas romances such as *Robinson Crusoe, The Coral Island, Peter Pan,* and *Treasure Island.* Every Saturday I rushed over to crowded St. Richard's Church to be mesmerized by enchanting movies like *Kidnapped, Mutiny on the Bounty, Swiss Family Robinson,* and the unforgettable 1949 version of *The Blue Lagoon.* A frustrated suburban kid living in the middle of the continent, I was totally seduced by a dream of islands.

Even though the South Seas has always been a state of mind, one-third of the globe is covered by the Pacific Ocean—seventy million square miles with a scattering of thirty thousand of the most glorious islands imaginable. In the golden age of eighteenth-century Pacific exploration, traveller's accounts from seafarers like Cook and George Vancouver sparked the imagination, and later, writers such as Melville and painters such as Gauguin, sent back words and images to America and Europe that offered the physical and spiritual bounty of these distant lands to dreamers. In poetry the English Romantics Lord Byron, Percy Shelley, and John Keats proclaimed the uplifting power and romance of water and beaches. Swimming and the beach were means to express rebelliousness, individualism, and pleasure. Restless travellers always on the move were constantly searching for more sublime destinations, fresh sensations both physical and spiritual. Once Britain and the Continent were exhausted, the South Seas became the new ultimate escape to freedom that was beyond civilization.

Nothing since Lord Byron had been martyred while fighting for the independence of Greece appealed more to the reading public in Europe than the idea of a romantic invalid like Stevenson exiled in a South Seas hideaway. After sailing among the Hawaiian Islands, Tahiti, the Marquesas, and all the way to Australia twice, Stevenson wanted to find someplace so far away it hadn't been desecrated by civilization yet. He finally settled and built a house called Vailima on the island of Upolu in Western Samoa, which was unspoiled and also had the most efficient steamer postal service in the Pacific. Stevenson lived the South Seas fantasy, wrote happily, and thrived with Fanny and their extended family. To the American writer Henry James he wrote: "I was never fond of towns, houses, society or (it seems) civilization...the sea, islands, islanders, the island life and climate make and keep me truly happier." Vailima, on the side of a hill overlooking the sea and surrounded by great trees and the endless music of birds, was similar to Stoneyhurst Manor. The Scot once commented: "I have never lived in such heaven."

And because of the mutual respect and admiration Stevenson earned from the kings and commoners in Samoa, he became a sacred legend the locals called Tusitala, the Teller of Tales. He wrote every day, got embroiled in the bitter island politics, and died at forty-four, a couple of years younger than I am now. His tomb atop Mount Vaea, overlooking the capital Apia and the bay, is a national shrine that bears lines from his immortal poem "Requiem": "Under the wide and starry sky/Dig the grave and let me lie.... Home is the sailor, home from the sea,/And the hunter home from the hill."

To shrug off a galloping melancholy associated with the towering high-rises of Waikiki and my immersion in Gauguin's dark personality while writing *Tender Only to One*, I got into Stevenson's invincible spirit of cheerfulness and left to find my own desert island. In a converted coffee shack on the volcanic slopes of Mauna Loa on the Kona coast of the Big Island of Hawaii, Dale and I lived like Adam and Eve. Our shack was just above Kealakakua Bay where James Cook was clubbed, stabbed to death, and dismembered in 1779 by the Hawaiians who had worshipped him as their reincarnated god. I surfed and swam the deep indigo waters off the forbidding Kona coast and collected koa wood to carve tikis. For breakfast we made papaya, banana, and mango shakes, and for lunch ate tofu, avocado, and bean sprout sandwiches.

To escape the hectic pace of Waikiki, Stevenson also visited the Kona coast. He went to the village of Hookena that had been described as the last Hawaiian community in the islands. On horseback the Scot made a trip along an old coastal trail from Hookena to Puuhonua O Honaunau, the City of Refuge, which is now a historical site. He was delighted to get away from the white society of Honolulu to wander among the ruins, temples, and grinning gods of ancient Polynesia. What impressed him most was the Great Wall, a massive rampart of lava blocks twelve feet high that enclosed an area of several acres which, in times of war, was used as a place of safety for women and children, and warriors defeated in battle. Once inside the enclosure, they were *kapu*, or sacred, and couldn't be touched. Here, among the monumental ruins of the ancient Hawaiian civilization, the Scottish writer found a place he thought was the authentic Polynesia.

For me Stevenson was such a breath of fresh air compared to the notorious, self-pitying Gauguin. After reading Stevenson's novels, stories, and some of the Vailima letters, I developed an unusually strong affection for the man and the writer who, despite family stress and responsibilities and constant illness that left him bedridden, maintained a constant zest for life. At the time I was writing my Gauguin book I was desperately trying to get published and worrying about the outcome of becoming a parent, and so the spirit of Stevenson's buoyant optimism helped save my life and my first book from total darkness.

When Dale and I left Kona to live on the island of Kauai in a little cabin, I read a book about the German Expressionist painter Emil Nolde, who travelled the South Seas in 1913, just after Gauguin and Stevenson both died there. Living in the mountains of Kauai, we had to burn firewood at night to keep warm, but during the day we drove down to swim and surf at some of the most remote beaches on Earth. Nolde remarked at the contrast between what he perceived to be the vital natural life of beach-loving natives and the artificial, diseased existence of civilization.

But Stevenson had already noted these leftover, flawed sentiments about the Myth of the Noble Savage when he wrote *In the South Seas*. Instead of penning just another romantic adventure, Stevenson committed himself to reveal issues about anthropology, ethnology, and late-Victorian imperialism. His journeys had given him a painful understanding of the cultural tragedy of the South Seas caught between its dying past and the callous greed of imperial powers. And he wanted to tell the world. He knew what was going to become of Polynesia. Given the terrible economic and social ravages and the grim record of continued nuclear testing in the South Pacific, *In the South Seas* still serves as an accurate and sincere warning that, unfortunately, wasn't heeded.

Almost twenty years ago, long before the mortgage and kids, while living with Dale in that idyllic coffee shack on the Kona coast of the Big Island, I wrote a short piece on Robert Louis Stevenson that I put near the end of *Tender Only to One*. Using my own words and some of Stevenson's, my voice through his voice, I make no apologies. Even after so many years of shadowing Stevenson in his books and his island travels, reading other writers' versions of the Stevenson legend, and now while living in Australia in our house inside the waves, this is still the closest I think I'll ever come to understanding the man:

My Dear Colvin:

Just a little word to let you know the rest of the household is asleep, leaving me alone with this cranky lantern. I have been out again riding on Jack. The fellow shows more courage and judgement than a seasoned soldier because our jungle at night is quite fearsome. In the forest, some nights the whole ground is strewn with phosphorescence, so that it seems a grating over a pale hell. I walked with Jack by the sea and looked at a steamer out in the harbour with its lights and tourists. When I rode back home on Jack in a hot black shower of rain, I think he felt the same way I did when we approached the lights of Vailima. A mixture of exultation and relief.

I want to tell you about a shack I visited when I was on one of the Hawaiian Islands. One day I intend to write it up as a book, but I must tell you something peculiar. I had gone out for a long walk with a silly wooden cutlass. I walked alone on a trail shaded by the kind of enormous trees we enjoy in parts of England. I passed an undulating taro patch and two white churches, one Protestant and one Catholic. Much later I came upon what appeared to be a deserted shack. When I opened the door, I saw the remains of a man curled on his bed with the Devil's own regiment of insects and rats feasting on his carcass. He produced a frightful odour. But I took a good peek about before I left. There were a few photographs, some rotten food, tobacco, books, and an empty keg of whisky. I must confess I was a wee bit of a thief, for I kept a photograph of him. Oddly enough the photograph looked like me, which as you can imagine disturbed me not a little.

When I asked around town, I was told the man deserted the ships two years ago. He had not been well for months. His death seems to me altogether typical of the South Seas myth. I have not mentioned this incident to Fanny, or anyone but you, because of the man's uncanny resemblance to myself. But the memory of his body on the cot in that shack produces a rather odd melancholy in me.

Lately I have been rereading parts of my grandfather's diaries with a new outlook. Everything appears to be happening simultaneously. For example, when I look at this photograph of my sad, lost sailor, somehow all the connections of time and space converge. I haven't been able to explain myself very well. A man's duty is to himself, but if he is intelligent he will realize he is much better off with a full day in the company of others. These moments by lamplight, the expeditions along the rivers, and my gallivanting through the jungle at night with Jack are precious, but Lord, no one should cut themselves off from the flow.

You are continually questioning my life here on this island and I can assure you that it is difficult and at times harrowing, but I would not trade it for another. I know what kind of weather you are having at home in Edinburgh.

Today we woke up to a warm rain shower at 5:30. After hot tea and bananas, I sat down to write until 10:45. Then I was out in the garden breaking my back with dear Fanny, swatting mosquitoes off each other. After our midday meal, I read and played music for two hours. Have I mentioned before that I have been rereading Flaubert's letters? I sometimes feel that it is indecent to read another person's letters, but what a thrill. Rather like my adventures. Later on I sat down to write and instead dwindled the afternoon away in the bath eating heavenly mango. I finished with a nap on the verandah. In the early evening there was a large formal dinner, cards, and then a cold pint of beer before bed.

At this moment I indulge myself with you. My dear Colvin, how one feels the reassurance of the word. How grateful I am that I can fill the ferocious gap between myself and the world with words. Adieu, dear sir, as I blow out the lamp.

Yours ever,
RLS

20
Aquatic Intermezzo

...roll on thou deep and dark ocean, roll...
—Lord Byron

Out in the ocean during a long lull I scan the open water for any dark, unfriendly shapes lurking about to challenge my karma. I always ruminate and sometimes sing or even talk to myself when I'm alone on the reef. The human brain averages twenty-five to thirty thoughts a minute. Alone in sharky surf I can double that. I was surfing the other day after a shark attack at Sharps Beach, just the other side of Lennox Point. A young guy duck-diving with his board under the waves went down and a six-foot shark torpedoed up to chomp his board, grazing his face and cutting his elbow so that he bled into the sea. Right after that every local surfer was more or less obliged to return to the water to conquer his fear.

At the moment I get so spooked by the concept of meeting a shark that when the dolphins appear I try to catch the next wave into shore. But I miss it and decide to drift on my board in the sets and lulls and duel with fate. Avoiding the basic notions of shark logic, or any logic, I remain there, repeating out loud the first few things to pop into my head: *The quick brown fox jumps over the lazy dog...down here in the*

Southern Seas is where I belong...look out, helter skelter.

Squinting in sunlight and attempting to make out the approaching set of waves, I hum-think a Beatles song I've recently listened to on one of my *Anthology* tapes. Those early drafts of the Beatles' recordings reveal how much fun they had with music and show the progression of their fluid creativity. While Derek Taylor—the Beatles' former press agent turned author—claims the Liverpool quartet was the twentieth century's greatest romance, John Lennon liked to deflect such notions of grandeur by saying they were merely a band that made it very big—more popular than Jesus Christ! Taylor goes on to say that the Beatles provided the soundtrack for the plottings of the baby boomers. In other words, the writers of teenage love songs were the emotional architects of my generation. Think of the boundary-pushing journey they took us on: "I Want to Hold Your Hand," "Strawberry Fields Forever," "Lucy in the Sky with Diamonds," "The Long and Winding Road," "Maybe I'm Amazed," "All Things Must Pass," and "Imagine." In some ways the Beatles' individual destinies became a blueprint of our fates. Recorded in 1968, "Helter Skelter" is a rough, impromptu jam session of a song that appeared on *The White Album*, then went on to infamy, poisoned by the evil Charles Manson. But for me Paul's urgent, passionate voice and lyrics move and gather momentum like sex and the sweeping rhythm of a surfer on a breaking wave: "Look out, helter skelter, da, da, da, da, da, da, da, da, da, helter skelter, da, da, da, da, da, da, da, da, da, helter skelter, da, da, da, da, da, da, da, da, da."

There's no wind now, and faraway swells rumple the horizon. Silently I twist and stroke into a wave, paddling with such authority, desire, and anticipation that I hate to think what life will be like back in Canada without all this.

Surfing with friends here has opened the door back into manhood. But unfortunately the sport has become an addiction. Australia must be the only country in the world where the entire population understands the passion for swimming and surfing. And Aussies display a decidedly hedonistic addiction for the sea and water sports. Living in a nation of beach lovers, I find myself moving from one wave to the next, sick with a desire to surf and be in the ocean. Like a drug addict or a man succumbing to a spectacular affair with a dangerously seductive woman, I'm tempted to say surfing's lure is as strong as sex. The magazine *Tracks* asked its readers which was better—surfing or sex. Sixty-two percent said surfing, but then fifty-one percent mentioned they thought about surfing during sex.

Paddling into the swells again, I turn, stroke hard, drop down the wave's face, and elegantly carve a high line, crouching lower to feel along the translucent glassy wall, then standing in a soul arch as the muscle of the surge washes me all the way to the beach where I transcend time and become a god.

One of the tricks in life is to find meaningful things to ground you in the here and now. Like work, a hobby, a sport, a relationship—be it with a friend, lover, spouse or, if you're real lucky, small kids. Even though the Beatles had a mountain of glory, fame, and money, those things didn't always ensure love, happiness, peace, or contentment. Today at my writing desk I look out through pouring rain to the ocean and see an Australian Geographic truck parked near the water. Two guys are changing into wetsuits. I run across the lane and discover they're attempting to catch a small seal that lost its way. One of them laconically says, "He should be lolling around somewhere south of Sydney, mate. Not all the way up here to buggery."

I'm impressed and intrigued. Sydney is a twelve-hour drive to the south. I tell them I have a wetsuit and want to help.

The other guy says, "Yeah, no worries. Bring along a pair of work gloves, though. Because when you grab him, he'll try to take a noyce piece of your hand."

In the house Quintana is still tucked into bed surrounded by stuffed animals—sick with a questionable cough and sniffles. As soon as she gets wind of the baby seal, though, she's up and dressed and holding her umbrella, as obedient and healthy as a crack soldier. I climb into my wetsuit, Quinn opens her umbrella, and we hurry through the warm drizzle down to the beach. About twenty yards offshore the seal weakly flips one flipper up and down as though waving at us, while seabirds swoop and circle, waiting for him to give up so they can have a fresh meal. The two Australian Geographic rescue guys quietly study the seal and instruct us to crouch in case he heads for the beach. The plan is to bolt out and scoop up the seal in a net as soon as he's far enough onto the sand. But he isn't going to be that cooperative. We follow as the seal drifts and swims along the entire Lennox beachfront. I carry the net and Quinn scampers ahead, directing people off the beach with her umbrella as the rescue guys' jeep rolls behind us, waiting for the seal to come in. But the seal moves farther up the beach in the rip, continuing to elude us. Meanwhile the writer and photographer who did the piece on me at Stoneyhurst Manor—CANADIAN WRITER SWAPS SNOW FOR SUNSHINE—arrive and wave at Quinn and me. By now the rain has stopped, the sun is blazing, and the sea shimmers with glassy waves. They both climb aboard the jeep with the two Geographic blokes while Quinn and I trudge ahead like militant environmentalists.

As the seal meanders up the east coast of Australia, a young surfer with two cameras around his neck joins the parade. He wants to photograph the seal, the jeep, and the expanding procession, hoping to get a career-making shot. When his girlfriend arrives, we pile into their car and drive another mile along the old beach road to wait for the seal to do a Robinson Crusoe landing. But the seal keeps floating in the current, absolutely uninterested in going ashore to be captured, taken to Seaworld, and flown south to the cold where he belongs. Miraculously, on his suicidal journey, the seal has travelled half the eastern coastline of the continent without being taken by a shark. Several times as we chase him for another mile he beaches himself but flippers back out through the shorebreak when we approach. In the end we all give up. No one is able to catch the seal and bring him home.

Needless to say, Quinn is a mess, and now, back in our house, I have a real invalid on my hands. Sky arrives from school and tosses her backpack onto the floor. When she hears our story and sees Quinn mooning about the baby seal, her big-sister response is: "You're such a psycho chicken. Get over it." That sends Quinn off the deep end and, as usual, I'm caught in the middle of a barroom brawl of accusations, weeping, and gnashing of teeth. So I herd them out of the house to toss a tennis ball back and forth to relieve the tension.

We cross the lane and say hello to the workers at the new two-story house whose construction is now well under way. I've been watching this huge mausoleum rise, listening to the sound of men at work: a parked cement mixer going round and round; workmen pedalling in on old beater bikes or roaring to work on motorcycles or rusty utes with screwed-up mufflers. Some days the workers' girlfriends meet them after work for a bottle of wine and a picnic of wild promises on our beach. From my writing desk I've seen the beach clawed back and levelled with heavy equipment. Recently fifty telephone poles were pile-driven into the earth and covered in cement to stabilize the structure. Bricklayers have come along to trowel up the walls, and now most of the windows have been set into the shell of the building that a retired man and his wife are erecting for their last years of glory. Eventually all the small, old-fashioned Raynor Lane cottages surrounded by frangipani trees will be replaced by these gargantuan, hermetically sealed ocean-liner buildings that face the sea.

Quinn chases butterflies among the piles of dirt at the job site, while Sky pats Harry, the good-natured pit bull who has more personality than a Las Vegas nightclub entertainer. A little girl races along with her yellow scooter, her right leg propelling her forward with rhythmic swipes and glides as she yells, "Don't let Harry get your tennis ball!" Apparently the dog has swallowed a number of balls. In fact, Harry's been taken to the vet so many times to have his stomach opened that his owner says if it happens again, the dog will be put down. When Quinn snatches up our tennis ball, Harry's hungry eyes follow the trajectory of the ball from the ground to the inside of my daughter's shirt. Then the pit bull licks his chops and drools as Sky scratches his oversize head.

The surging roar of the waves beckons, so I motion my girls down to the beach. The tide charges toward us in a rush and hiss as I follow the girls, who scamper ahead through the sensual line of foam, beachcombing for more wild sponges for our collection. These tawny-coloured sponges are embedded with sand, tiny seashells, and seaweed and come in all sizes, textures and bizarre shapes. Along one protected wall under our carport we have brimming baskets and pails full of sponges, seashells, skulls, skeletons, feathers, rocks, encrusted bottles, and pieces of drift-wood. Although we already have more luggage than the next Rolling Stones tour, we intend to haul most of this home to Canada to remind us of the sea. Even with their hands and pockets full of sponges, Quinn and Sky continue to bicker until I lob the tennis ball at Sky's butt. That makes them squeal and race toward the beach away from their dad, leaving a trail of sponges from which I can easily select the best.

Later, as I stand with my hands in a sink of warm water, gazing out at the ocean, I realize once again how much I enjoy doing the dishes in this house. Facing the waves, Dale meditatively sits on the deck with her feet on the rail, nursing a cup of tea, a paperback novel closed in her lap. Quinn and Sky put on a Beatles tape and we drink in the immediate, mood-enhancing vibe of "Eight Days a Week." Bobbing their heads to the music, they sit on stools, a pair of angels keeping me company until Sky asks, "Daddy, after you finish the dishes, can we have a tickle fight?"

The ocean gives you a double life. Skateboarding, snowboarding, and skiing aren't the same as surfing. The terrain varies, but the road and the mountain don't move. In surfing each wave is radically different and unpredictable, and water is elemental, the major constituent of all living things. "The wind speaks the message of the sun to the sea, and the sea transmits it on through waves. The wave is the messenger, water the medium," writes photographer Drew Campion in *The Book of Waves*.

I paddle out once again and the first wave is a gnarly beauty that rears back. When I take the drop too early, I tumble over the falls and get drilled into the reef, almost all the way to our house in Barrhaven so that I fully expect to wash up on our Canadian driveway. But I surface, roll onto my board, and sprint-paddle out for more waves.

In the past few months I've surfed every break along this coast, forsaking almost all else to spend time in the ocean. On a certain level I've embarked on a quest to find the meaning of *it*. Each break is unique in terms of waves, sharks, reefs, beauties in thong bikinis, headlands, rainforests, beaches, vistas—and proximity to God. From north to south, within an easy fifteen-minute drive, I can surf at Belongil Beach in Byron Bay, The Pass, Wategos, Little Wategos, Cozy Corner (site of a nasty shark fatality), Broken Head, Lennox, the Boat Channel, Frank's Spot, the Point, Sharps, Flatrock, Shelley's, Angels, North Wall, and South Wall

Ballina. All are radically different, with every possible surfing condition from raging cyclonic storm surf to perfect, silent, glassy mornings.

A little later, back in my house inside the waves, I look up from my laptop to make sure the Pacific really is rolling in across our back lane. Reassured by the smell of the sweet, salty brine that makes my teeth grit, I gaze at the palms that blow in the late-afternoon breeze, rattling against our sanctuary. Soon, in a cyclone of needy love, my girls will arrive with their bulging backpacks and hopeful, sunscreened faces. And after I make vegetarian burritos and rice pudding for dinner, I'll be off tonight to teach, entertain, and learn from ten aspiring writers in Byron Bay. Paradise.

Other than the fact we'll have to leave soon, nothing seems to bother us anymore. Even the latest bullying letter from our exchangees on the hill doesn't bug me too much, although it's a little stressful for Dale. Because we come and go and know everyone in town, the dispute is almost an abstract issue now. The new, very short letter begins sarcastically: "We refer to your last letter and are pleased that you seem to have made so many friends in the area." It goes on to list three more damaged items: a slat in an old rattan cane chair we piled pillows on to protect, a wooden support on an even more ancient but not antique bentwood rocker, Sky's name handwritten on the wall behind a coat rack. The letter ends with the absurd: "We will consider our options and contact you further, yours faithfully."

Defused and out of venom. We hope.

When I return from my writing workshop in Byron, I'm in high spirits. I love running workshops: getting the group to jell, encouraging each writer to get his or her deep thoughts and hearts on paper, finding the hidden connections among things. Tonight we workshopped a chapter of a novel, a memoir, a short story, a children's book, and a handful of poems. Now, like some restless nineteenth-century writer sitting by candlelight I listen to the brooding sea outside an open window, eager to write myself. Dale and the girls are tucked into their beds in fresh sheets I washed and hung on the line in the sea breeze. Summer has really kicked in, but I still have a tough time associating hot tropical days and humid nights with the relentless approach of Christmas. The ocean has heated up nicely and is getting even more turquoise. Today the tide was out so far we ran around like demons on the sandbars, bodysurfing waves on the outer reaches of one sandbar, then diving off another into our private lagoon. Underwater with my girls, I snorkelled along, checking out the fish on our spooky reef, lost in time until a sudden biblical storm cloud arrived from the south over Lennox Point and we galloped in over the shallows as rain hammered down, hounding us all the way back to the house.

It's pretty late now, but I don't want to sleep away the short time we have left here. So I get up, go out, and walk across the lane in the dark down along the trail that has been worn in the grass mostly by my feet in the past few months. Up on the grassy dune I face the black Pacific rumbling into our beach, half expecting Captain Cook to sail by with the ghosts of Lord Byron, Paul Gauguin, Robert Louis Stevenson, Ernest Hemingway, Scott Fitzgerald, Jack Kerouac, Henry Miller, the Beatles, and Bruce Chatwin in tow. The wind howls fiercely as I search for this imaginary boat of Romantic dreamers who spent most of their lives in the clouds and paid dearly for it.

Earlier today at an outdoor café in Lennox while reading a magazine article about Tom Garrett, lead singer of Midnight Oil, and Australian surfing icon Nat Young, I came upon a couple of lines I haven't been able to shake: "There's no such thing as adventure and romance. There's only trouble and desire." I stand near our pandanus tree, gazing out at the white phosphorescence of breaking surf and the spectral outline of Lennox Point, wondering why after a year of living at the beach I'm still filled with an adolescent desire and longing, why I'm still trying to fig-ure out how to break out of my own vanity and fear. Maybe the Big Mystery is that you never really find *it*, especially when you only look in one place.

Slowly I walk back into the house. Upstairs I peek inside each girl's bedroom to make sure my daughters are all right. Then I rummage in the fridge's freezer and, with a bowl of Byron Bay supreme butter pecan ice cream, return to my desk, sit, and continue writing. Who can possibly ask for anything more?

21
Gidget, Big Kahuna, No-Holds-Barred Luau

"Reeeef!"

In the predawn blackness of our bedroom I hear thunderous waves churn into the beach. Then I detect another faint whisper. "Reef." Finally there's a chorus of high-pitched voices. "Reeeeef! Come out and play!"

"They're here already, Rick," Dale says. "Tell them to be quiet or they'll wake the girls."

As soon as I pull back the curtain, I spot the Three Amigos—Kiko, Neil, and Mihkel, a trio of hopeful, middle-aged fools. Grinning and bleary-eyed in the dawn, they press their faces against the window and chant, "Cookies."

My coconut chocolate-chip cookies have become famous here, even with hard-core surfers. At first the Amigos were nervous and suspicious about my househusband program and the whole cookie thing. Then, early one morning, we came in from the surf at the Point and stripped off our wetsuits, our feet bleeding from the reef, the muscles of our upper bodies pumped, ripped, and bruised. While leaning against rusty old cars in the parking lot, I pulled out a plastic container of my cookies.

After their first hesitant taste, the boys were hooked and I was compelled to produce a steady supply for their addiction. Since then most of my Aussie surfing buddies have quietly taken me aside to procure the recipe.

Rick's Coconut Chocolate-Chip Cookies

In a large bowl cream a half cup of butter and a half cup each of white and brown sugar. Add one egg and a half a teaspoon of vanilla extract. Mix until smooth. In a separate bowl mix one cup of white flour, one-and-a-quarter cups of oatmeal, a scant quarter teaspoon of salt, and a half teaspoon each of baking powder and baking soda. Add three-quarters of a cup of sweetened grated coconut. Mix everything and add one cup of milk chocolate chips. Gently hand-roll golf-ball-size dollops of cookie mixture and plop onto an ungreased cookie sheet about an inch apart. Bake at 350 F. for eight to ten minutes, depending on the heat of your oven.

Note: Always use butter softened to room temperature and milk chocolate chips. You can use regular oatmeal or put oatmeal in a blender or food processor to powderize. If you powderize it, use only one cup rather than a cup and a quarter. Use a good-quality cookie sheet. Cookies should not be overbaked. Because they are softish, let them cool before you take a spatula and transfer them to a container. They should be soft as they cool down and then firm up so the final product will almost have the chocolate texture of a luscious brownie. Don't be surprised if it takes a few times to get the quality you want down pat. Don't be surprised if they come out a little different each time, especially with the slightest change of ingredients. Be warned that if you eat too many cookies they'll give you heartburn like a vise tightening your chest. You might feel as though you've been hit by a big rogue wave and you may even find it necessary to toddle off for a quick nap.

Because of my rabid passion for surfing and an overzealous comment I made about the curvaceous, tanned derriere of a tall Reef Girl in a thong bikini ad for Reef Surfwear in a surfing magazine, the Three Amigos have begun calling me Reef. The nickname solidified after a wonderful early-morning session at Flat Rock with Neil, another South African who's found sanctuary in Oz. After Neil experienced an abusive stint in the South African army, three years at Durban Art School, the usual number of soul-shrinking jobs, and a stint as a co-owner of a restaurant that went under in Adelaide, he and his wife, Christine, landed in Lennox. During a serious health crisis that laid him up in the hospital, Neil became even better friends with Kiko, who paid loyal vigils to his bedside. As a result, Neil has that overwhelming gratitude and hunger for life that hovers over someone who has cheated death. A mature, solid family man with two older boys, Neil also has a boyish streak and a devilish chipmunk grin and can be quite intense and silly in the head.

These days Neil has structured his work so he has Fridays off to surf. In South Africa he surfed Jeffery's Bay, one of the sharkiest places in the world. Out on our reef his annoying respect for deep, dark water means he sometimes dwells on what is almost certainly below the surface of the waves. Whenever Neil says, "Reef, look at all those fish. Hope nothing bigger's eating them," I launch into flights of literary reverie and think of a line from a Herman Melville poem, "The shark glides white through the phosphorous sea," or W. B. Yeats's beautiful sea with its murderous innocence. Neil is getting to the age where he usually pays for his surfing with a stiff neck, pulled back muscles, and banged-up knees. He claims Lennox Head is a town where old surfers come to settle and raise their families.

That morning after surfing at Flat Rock where Neil pulled off elegant high-on-the-shoulder "magazine shot" waves, two Reef Girls came out of the waves, their wetsuits gleaming. Neil was drying his suit and surfboard, fussing around in the trunk of his car, and lecturing me about not getting cookie crumbs on the seats or a single drop of salt water on the paint job of his precious vehicle. The two girls arrived at the car next to us and pulled down their wetsuits, exposing lovely tanned backs. And then, unbelievably, they turned around. Both had long, sun-bleached hair, pretty faces, white teeth, wondrous breasts, and no doubt towering intellects. Dolphins were plying the bay, and the surf was grinding into the beach. Neil was still organizing his toiletries and disentangling bungee cords for the roof rack when I casually tapped him on the shoulder. His pursed lips and dull eyes revealed he was more than a little put out by my interruption. But when he turned to see the squirrelly look in my eyes and then glanced at the astonishing pair of Reef Girls, naked from the waist up, he froze. Then, in his quiet, terribly civilized South African accent, he hoarsely whispered, "My God, Reef."

Like most restless surfers, Neil gets up at first light, sticks his head out a window, and scans the horizon for swells. He loads up his car and hits the beach parking lot in town. Solemnly he stands at the railing, checks out the waves, tastes the wind, estimates its direction and variations over the next few hours, then calculates everything with respect to the incoming or outgoing tide. After that he drives to the outskirts of town to check the wave conditions from the top of Lennox Point. Once in a while he'll drive farther afield to study the surf at Boulders, Sharps, or Flat Rock. In their sputtering, oil-belching vehicles, Kiko, Mihkel, and Neil usually rendezvous at my place on Raynor Lane because I'm right on the water and central. Depending on the tide and how long the wind stays off the surf and the amount of stink-eye we're willing to endure from our respective wives, we choose a spot and surf for a few hours of bliss.

Describing the act of surfing to a nonsurfer is like telling someone about your last session of sex. The atmosphere, circumstances, buildup, and quirky characters who participate in the event are as interesting as the lovemaking itself. And so it is with surfing. Aside from the waves we caught and the extraordinary Reef Girls we saw that morning at Flat Rock, we had the pleasure of surfing with a one-armed surfer named Terry. As Neil and I were paddling together in absolute glassy conditions with a gentle swell jacking up to good-size waves on the outer reef, we watched the one-armed surfer take his drop and execute a fine wave. When we caught up with Terry, he told us surfing legend Bob McTavish was a friend who personally shaped all his boards. "Ah, yeah, McTavish likes to tell everyone Oy paddle in circles," he joked, effortlessly thrusting with his one good, meaty arm as Neil and I humped our boards through the water, wheezing like old dogs.

Terry always straddles his board just outside the breaking waves and waits. Swells roll in, lift him, then roll on into the beach. But he waits patiently for the right wave, then windmills furiously with one arm and makes his drop, left or right, and never fails. Along with a true waterman's skill acquired over a long period, he's got guts and is always cheerful. In his presence a rowdy crowd will turn mellow, almost reflective. Terry's got the right grip on life. A better grip than most of the two-armed surfers I've met, myself included.

Often we see long-haired hippie Jeff in the surf, sharking the waters for waves. Because summer has arrived and the ocean has gotten warmer, a lot of surfers go without wetsuits. The atmosphere in the waves and on the beaches has become more like Hawaii or California again. Jeff is the quintessential local, aging surfer. Unencumbered by a wife, kids, or a nine-to-five job, he camps just down Raynor Lane in a tiny flat whose walls are covered with photos of scantily clad Reef Girls and posters of surfers on awesome waves. He works part-time installing hardwood floors, selling the odd surfboard, and teaching at a surf school in Byron. His old Volkswagen van is rigged for camping, working, surfing, and making out. The Three Amigos, some of my other surf-dog friends, and I might have become Jeff if we hadn't been saved from ourselves by our good women.

One day, after watching me carve tikis in front of our house, Jeff tried to offer me a few questionable-looking opals in exchange for one of my best tikis. As usual I was in dire need of cash, so I sold him a tiki for $100 to wear around his neck. Because he fancies himself a carver, I suspect he'll try to mass-produce my tikis for a quick profit. He's also carving and stockpiling didgeridoos he plans to sell for a killing in Sydney during the 2000 Olympics. Although Jeff is one of the finest surfers around, he can be territorial and quite aggressive out in the water. One day while we both dropped in on the same big wave and were nicely accelerating along the glassy wall together, he flailed his arms and screamed, "What the fuck are you doing, mate? Tying your shoelaces?"

The far north coast is rife with a scary number of surfers who have mortgaged their lives so they can live near the beach and surf. A lot of surfers, fishermen, junkies, retirees, windsurfers, skateboarders, single moms, and wannabe artists have ended up shipwrecked here. They're escapees from the urban rat races of Sydney and Melbourne or from constricting inland hick towns like Broken Hill, Towamba, Grafton, and Wagga Wagga. I've met people from Japan, Israel, Canada, the United States, France, and England who are living here indefinitely. They're all lured by the great weather, surfing, fishing, and a laid-back beach lifestyle. Dale has always known about and happily gone along with my gravitational pull toward the beach. But now she's a little concerned and has intimated that in only one year here I've begun my decline from a sensitive, considerate househusband toward a hard-core macho surfer jerk.

Now, after being serenaded by the Three Amigos, I pile my surf gear into Kiko's van and we motor off for a dawn patrol. Neil and Mihkel follow in Neil's car and we head to Wategos for a surf. The night before I made a batch of cookies for the boys, so we're all set. As we round the corner above Wategos, we see twenty-five layers of peeling waves breaking all over the place with only a handful of lucky surfers quietly taking their drops. Everything seems in slow motion, and I think of a nice line from James Hamilton-Patterson's book *Playing with Water*: "The sea turns over and over, a geological machine smoothly meshing its gears and grinding up time itself." Kiko looks at me and grins. "Shall we imbibe, Reef?"

When you get to a beach, everything seems possible. If hedonism is a belief that the most important part of human destiny is to have a good time, then that's exactly where the Three Amigos and I are headed. Like a quartet of Hollywood gunslingers or pilots, we stride along the scumbled sand, our surfboards tucked under our arms, checking out the waves and the babes. We walk as far as we can to the end of the point and jump in with our boards, surrendering to the warmth of the Pacific. Up and down through the silky swells we paddle until we're outside the reef. Then we discover why there aren't a lot of other surfers here. The sea is filled with jellyfish. Kiko and Neil catch the first big wave. I watch their heads trim below the lip of their wave as they disappear toward shore, leaving me alone with Mihkel and the jellyfish. Daintily we paddle along, dodging foot-long tentacles, which occasionally sting our wrists, forearms, and legs. I count a half-dozen dolphins flying through the waves and playing around us. Covered in swollen welts, I quickly stroke into a full wave and do my drop, glimpsing the Byron lighthouse set against the sky. Then, as I cut back and accelerate along another steep section, I gaze at Mount Warning and the soft line of mountains beneath ragged clouds—perhaps for the last time.

A little later, out in the water, Mihkel says, "Mate, it's incredible. Here we are an Estonian, a South African, an American, and a Canadian— the new Australians." Mihkel is an art instructor who slogged out a decade teaching at a grim little school a couple of hundred miles inland before he and his wife, Sue, earned their plum jobs on this coast. He has thick, long blond hair and piercing blue eyes the ladies swoon over. A gifted artist and absolute gentleman, he doesn't live to surf anymore. He surfs because being in the ocean still makes him happy and he enjoys the company of Kiko and Neil. For years the Three Amigos surfed with their longboards California-style and had most of the waves to themselves. Now the longboard revolution has made the traditional boards fashionable again, especially with aging baby boomers.

After a while the Three Amigos and I get tired of battling the jellyfish and head back to shore where we sprawl on the sand, scanning the horizon. Truant adults playing hooky from our lives, we talk about our wives and children, where we've been, and where we're going. The air fresh, the waves eternal, the summer seemingly endless.

To celebrate the end of our time in Australia, Dale and I mount something outrageously appropriate. Dale makes up blue palm-fringed invitations for fifty of our Aussie friends and their children to attend a wicked, no-holds-barred luau on the beach in front of our house: "RICK AND DALE'S FAREWELL. Gidget, Big Kahuna, No-Holds-Barred Luau. Saturday, December 13, on our beach, Raynor Lane. Fun beach activities and Luau. Party under the full moon!"

From Canada our friends Diane and David arrive with their two boys in time to help us prepare for the luau. Early in the morning Dale and Diane and all the kids collect hundreds of perfumed frangipani blossoms to make Hawaiian leis. David and I haul out an outdoor spit and begin preparing vast quantities of beef, chicken, pork, and fish. We lay out a steel screen mesh on the sand under a mountain of firewood so it will be easy to clean later.

From a big ghetto blaster old-time rock and roll booms. As people start arriving, the sun sinks toward the hinterland. David, who grew up in the early 1960s surfing and playing cricket in the south of England, organizes a rousing game of cricket for the kids on the beach at low tide. In the heat sixty men, women, teenagers, children, and babies slouch on chairs, prop themselves against dunes, or sprawl on the sand. Some make sandcastles, talk, or stare at the incoming waves. Others drink beer and wine or surf or swim. Up at the house David and I and the Three Amigos sheath a big table with long, wide banana leaves, cover them with tropical flowers and cut-up papayas, guavas, mangoes, and grapes, then load all the hot meat from the spit. Down at the beach a roaring fire is lit and the music is cranked up. Another table of salads, breads, dips, cheeses, desserts, and drinks is ready, and everyone waits for us to bring the ceremonial meat to the water. All of my surfing mates wear Hawaiian leis, fabulously loud surfer shirts, and filthy shit-eating grins. As the kahuna, I sport only an old pair of jean cutoffs, a hand-carved tiki, and a lei. In one hand I hold a walking stick with a whalebone vertebra jammed on top. Kiko, Mihkel, and David lift the feast of meat, fruit, and flowers, and slowly we march to the beach. Neil follows, rhythmically banging bongo drums and howling at the sky. As we descend from the dunes to the beach, backlit by the setting sun, everyone looks up as I lead the procession of surf dogs with our pagan luau.

From out of the waves Dennis emerges with a big fish he's speared on our reef. Quickly he puts on a tank top with SURF'S UP scrawled across the front and adds a flower lei and a Hawaiian straw hat. Kiko tosses Dennis the bongos, and he pounds away in a trance as though able to bring back all the good times from the past year, perhaps even recapture our lost youth.

After it gets dark and everyone has eaten enough; after we all do the limbo in front of the fire; after everyone who wants to bodysurf has done so; after the kids get bored and park themselves in front of the television back in our house; after friendships are solidified, promises made, kisses sealed; after the guitars are passionately strummed, the fire stoked, and every nostalgic song sung—the crowd thins. Then, sometime after midnight, only a handful of the lads are left, pleasantly drunk, so I drive them home, delivering each one safely to his door.

A few days later, out of thoughtfulness and goodwill, Kiko's wife, May, and her kids arrive with a big cactus in a terra-cotta pot. Dale, May, and the children decorate it with tiny white Christmas lights, set it on a box covered by a Mexican blanket, and nestle our wrapped gifts around its base.

On Christmas Eve I phone the Three Amigos, encouraging them to tell their kids to wake up early Christmas morning so they can get the festivities out of the way and sneak out for a surf with me before the wind comes up. By nine the next morning we're all out at Flat Rock with the dolphins. The heavy rain actually keeps the wind off the thundering swells, which get bigger and bigger with the tide. It's pumping—a gift— and I paddle out with the boys, hooting and catcalling with sheer joy. Each of us takes wave after wave, rights and lefts, then we stroke back out for more. Still the stunning swells tumble in, drawing back and breaking into waves a quarter mile long.

In a lull between sets, floating in the middle of the ocean, I gaze at the magnificent open sky. Sniffing the sweet salt air, savouring every last second of my time here, I say, quite seriously, "As soon as I get back home, my life will be over."

Mercifully none of the boys has a smart-ass retort. They're reflective, too, stoked from all the good waves. Then Neil propels himself into one of the biggest waves of the day. In a freeze-frame I see his cocky horse's-ass grin as he flashes a peace sign at me before he's sideswiped and annihilated by a freight train of water.

The rain whooshes down, the skyscraper swells surge in, and we all catch more waves. It's delightful—and a little dangerous and exhilarating. Finally, straddling our boards, waiting for another good set, I yell, "I wonder what all the good dads are doing this morning?"

And the Three Amigos scream back, "Who cares?"

I've never really been an ardent fan of T. S. Eliot, yet for some reason I think about his haunting *The Love Song of J. Alfred Prufrock* and the strange music of its poetry, and know, too, that "I have heard the mermaids singing, each to each."

I've climbed my share of gnarly summits, but a hopeless romantic has to expect to live mostly on the wrong side of the dream. I'm pretty sure our old life back home won't fit us quite as well. Thinking of the hundreds of photographs we took this year, seeing in my mind's eye the happy, smiling faces of Dale and my two girls and all our new friends, I know this year wasn't just a dream. It might have been too much of a good thing. I definitely fear going home, living away from this ocean. In the end, though, I do what every surfer must do. I turn and drink in the waves one last time.

EPILOGUE
No Time for Jet Lag

As with a long sea voyage, one of the great advantages of a thirty-hour flight is that it gives you plenty of time to get your head around a few things. Crossing the international date line, I'm already sucker-punched by jet lag and confused about night and day but wide awake in the middle of eternal blackness somewhere over the Pacific Ocean.

In a plane of sleeping strangers I'm the only one not dozing as I read under a solitary light that burns into the pages of Robert Hughes's *The Fatal Shore*. I also flip through John Pilger's *A Secret Country* and James Cowan's *Sacred Places in Australia*, as well as Paul Theroux's grumpy *The Happy Isles of Oceania*. I'm trying to bring a little coherence to so much material because I'm returning to Australia as a journalist to write about the Olympics in Sydney and produce a nostalgia piece on Lennox and Byron. I take notes and pretend that my apprehension concerns the two long pieces I have to write and not what I might find in Australia where I lived the happiest year of my life. The standard notion—you can't go home again—hangs close to my heart.

In the two and a half years since we returned to Canada from Lennox, the marriages of two of our favourite couples have broken up. Unfortunately one partner from each couple has fallen in love with the other so that our idyllic seaside town of twenty-five hundred is now caught up in an apocalypse of shifting loyalties, wild accusations, and unhappy children. To top it off, a late-night phone call from one of my surf-dog friends warned me about cyclones and some trouble involving tiger sharks, great whites, and helicopters.

Things couldn't look more untidy for this two-week quest I've thrown together cheaply at the last minute between finishing teaching at Carleton University and starting a new writing class the day of my return. With our whole town torn to pieces by interpersonal strife and the reappearance of my old nemesis—*Carcharodon carcharias*—the plans to savour a little sweet nostalgia, swim another Byron Bay Open-Water Swim Classic, and surf my ass off with my beloved mates, seems doomed from the start. But then perhaps when I attempt a little reconciliation in the marital war zones of my friends it will be a cinch to paddle out to the reef to take on old whitey.

Like most Commonwealth countries, Australia has had an appalling racist past, but it has also assimilated more than its share of cultures with relative ease. With the Sydney Olympics, Australia is dealing with growing issues raised by the relationship between its original indigenous inhabitants and the settlers who came from overseas. The reconciliation issue for race relations had become a national fixation and hangs in the air like smoke.

Whether they've been there or not, everyone seems to have an opinion about Australia. Some like to take potshots. Paul Theroux, in *The Happy Isles of Oceania*, calls Australia an underdeveloped country bewildered and at times terrified by its own emptiness. When Theroux asked white Australians what *walkabout* meant, they told him it was an Aborigine's furious fugue, a bout of madness, in which he shambled off the job or out of the shelter and headed into the Outback. And poor Theroux himself, who lives alone now in bookless Hawaii, after publishing more than thirty-six books in thirty-three years and alienating most of his family and friends, is suffering his own bout of madness. On his own sudden walkabout, after the collapse of a twenty-five-year marriage, he paddled aimlessly in the South Seas to write a book, travelling with a chip on his shoulder the size of Tasmania.

The Pacific Ocean is endless. I muse about the boomerang, which for the Australian Aborigine is a symbol of eternal return. A map I study indicates that one-third of the planet is covered by the Pacific. I'm dead tired and start to give in to fatigue. As I drown in the swirls of pink, blue, orange, black, yellow, and white dots and lines that make up a photographic image of wind patterns of the Pacific, I suddenly realize it looks exactly like some of the old Aboriginal paintings I've seen. The early Aborigines, whose cave paintings predate the pharaohs by twenty thousand years, evolved an art that could conceptualize what their world might look like from a satellite in space.

It's obvious. The ancient Aborigines had it all over us. They knew who they were, where they'd been, and where they were going. And why.

As I nod off, reflecting on the wisdom and dignity of the ancient Aborigines, my thoughts swirl like waves. I'm lost, standing onshore with my surfboard, looking out into eternity. But I'm not there to surf. I'm searching for a ship. My board is actually a small piece of that vessel, something I use to stay connected to my spiritual ancestors who were ancient mariners.

After our glorious walkabout in Oz, we stepped back into our Canadian town house. It was silent, odourless, bland, and small. The furnace wafted out dry, dead air. With glowing tans and bleached hair, we slumped amid our mountain of luggage and stared at one another in disbelief.

A few days later we got clobbered by the Storm of the Millennium. From January 5 to 9, 2.9 inches of freezing rain and 5.6 inches of snow and ice pellets fell on Ottawa, causing more than $100 million in damage. (The average monthly precipitation in Ottawa for January is 2.4 inches.) Twelve thousand army troops were brought in for the cleanup and to staff community centres that opened their doors as soup kitchens and places to sleep for the thousands of refugees who straggled in from storm-damaged, powerless homes. A state of emergency was declared in eastern Ontario, and Ottawa became a deadly, shining ice castle. Without electricity people froze to death or endured the killing effects of the cold and darkness. All schools and universities were closed for a week and many people lost water and hydro for more than two weeks and then the temperature plummeted to twenty below zero with a wind-chill factor of forty below.

Perhaps there was a certain Nordic poetry in making big snow sculptures of dolphins with Quinn in the backyard and gazing into the cold, crisp air as ice sparkled in the sunlight. In moonlight I watched a neighbour watering his skating rink, steam rising in the subzero night. After surfing and swimming at beautiful beaches every day for a year, I found myself with another perspective on water after the storm.

Of course, we all plugged back into our never-ending routines of family, friends, school, and work. But from the other side of the world Australia still fuelled us. I began swimming six miles a week with my swim club and won medals. I taught my own writing workshops and began lecturing at university. Dale mounted a gorgeous art show of huge stained-glass waves called *Mind Like Water*. While writing my book I published a half-dozen excerpts in magazines and travel anthologies. And then, without a wife and kids, or even a set of car keys in my pocket, I was on a flight alone back to Oz.

I always seem to arrive in Australia on the tail end of a vindictive cyclone. My jet lag is so ferocious I can barely speak to Melissa Wright, who picks me up at the airport. I'm numb and disoriented, definitely not the perky chatterbox she remembers. The first thing Melissa says to me as her eyes assess the canned-asparagus patina of my Canadian winter undertaker's skin is, "God, Ricky, ya gotta get a tan."

On the way to her house I listen as she tells me how moved she was by her daughters, Kaitlyn and Lyla, at the Anzac Memorial Day ceremony the previous week. It celebrates the 1915 heroics of the Aussies at Gallipoli in Turkey and the obvious lessons about the futility of war and the first break with British imperialism. An American artist who supports her family of four by selling her celebrated etchings, Melissa has only lived in Australia for seven years, yet Anzac Day for her and most Australians, no matter what their origins, is the one time they feel Australian together.

Mercifully, before I see anyone else I know, Melissa deposits me at their little beach house. Kaitlyn, ten, has generously given up her room for me. She and seven-year-old Lyla are good friends with my daughters and have left me adorable hand-painted cards to welcome me "home." The girls are still at school, and Dennis is out somewhere. Because it's raining in paradise at three in the afternoon, I tell Melissa I have to lie down for a quick nap.

I close the door to my little South Seas hideaway, flop onto the futon draped by a billowing silk mosquito net, and survey Kaity's little girl's room of mermaids, sea monsters, dolls, kid paintings, an enormous mobile of tropical fish, and a photograph of my daughters. Gripped by the fever of jet lag, I feel as if I'm submerged in one of Melissa's magical underwater etchings.

After sitting vertical in a plane for thirty hours, I'm horizontal in the dark, listening to the rain, sniffing the familiar salt-and-salad smell of the Coral Sea, my whole being overcome by the churning roar of the ocean. I think about my tiny nephew and my sister, Jan, who perished in the house fire. A house inside the waves would have given my sister perfect sanctuary. A house inside the waves would never burn.

Early the next morning I awake in the dark before anyone else and decide to check out the beach. Because Cape Byron is the most easterly tip of the continent, the sun rises here first. It's still dark as I barefoot it down the end of the road to one of the most stunning beaches in the world. It occurs to me that this empty strand with tumbling surf and Lennox Head's green volcanic snout poking into the heavens looks exactly like the early photographs of Hawaii's Waikiki Beach in 1888 when Robert Louis Stevenson lived near Diamond Head.

The sun is a welder's torch line of red fire on the horizon as I splash along the water's edge toward our old beach house. Because of the tail end of a North Queensland cyclone, the bay is breaking with dangerously high white surf. It's so blown out there isn't a single dawn patroller surfing. Already a lot of the beach has been eaten away by heavy seas. New reefs of rock and tree roots have been exposed where there was beach. The wind howls furiously and the sea crashes around me. And as I walk in the predawn I still haven't seen a single person.

Although the Aborigines never surfed boards like the ancient Polynesians of Hawaii did, Captain Cook wrote about Aborigines swimming and bodysurfing the way I did every day in front of our beach house: "Whenever the surf broke over them, they dived under it and to all appearances with infinite facility rose on the other side. At this wonderful scene we stood gazing for more than half an hour, during which time none of the swimmers attempted to come ashore."

When I arrive at the beach in front of our house on Raynor Lane, I stop to enjoy the moment I've been dreaming about for more than two years. Many of the original cottages have been replaced by huge concrete fortresses that face the sea. But our old house is still there shrouded in tangled vegetation—and memories. The lights are out and another car is parked in the driveway. I think about our friends in happier times before their marriages unravelled and their lives turned into temporary nightmares. Up on the sundeck Dale and a few of the other women would be drinking local coffee and eating croissants, glancing out at Neil, Mihkel, Kiko, and I surfing a quarter mile out on the reef. Looking up, I try to see everyone together again, but the deck is empty. Instead I peer into the window where I used to write. In the last few months when I knew I'd be flying back to winter in Canada, I wrote less and less. I'd surf early in the morning before it got blown out, write at my desk for a while, then run down to bodysurf the big waves until I was spent. Afterward I'd shamble in, throw myself onto the sand, dry in the sunlight, and start carving wooden tikis like a possessed Aborigine. When the kids came home from school, we'd go bodysurfing and then explore the tide pools till dusk.

As the sun comes up now, I stride through the soft beach grass to sit on the stone steps near the water. I've heard stories about how the early whites along this coast herded Aborigines to their deaths off headlands like Lennox. A couple of years ago I surfed mighty waves, took ferocious drops, and was surrounded by cruising dolphins that were so close I could smell fish on their breath. Gazing at the sacred reality of the Lennox headland, I'm struck by the notion that all the Aborigines' sacred places aren't man-made, whereas all the hallowed sites of white people are human fabrications.

The idea of plunging into the Pacific again leaves me a little queasy after swimming competitively for a couple of years in a chlorinated pool and the lakes and rivers around Ottawa. I've gone in here to surf and swim hundreds of times before. Although it's autumn on the north coast and the temperature drops dramatically at night, the water is still warm. It's time to let my shaky karma have a go with the wrath of the shark god. Whipping off my clothes and galloping into the water, I spear through the wall of the shorebreak and swim over the sandy bottom for as long as I have the nerve, hoping I won't meet nose-to-nose with one of my hungry friends. I take another breath and swim even farther until I float on my back and glimpse heaven. I'm the only person on this vast beach, swimming naked in the Coral Sea.

When I return to shore, I get back into my shorts and T-shirt and wander to the end of the beach. I stroll up North Creek Road and then down Henderson Lane and am startled when I spot the new housing development that looks as though it's been there since the beginning of time. I was told the proud old guy who lived in the wonky house at the foot of the hill passed away last year. It's still very early as I meander dreamily along Stoneyhurst, peeking through the tropical foliage at the houses, recalling the people who filled our lives a couple of years earlier. Stoneyhurst Manor appears exactly the same, except we're not living there anymore or ever would. At the dead end I reach Steve's place, then continue back into Lennox without seeing a soul.

I'm thirsty for some real adrenaline and want to surf, but the cyclone has made that impossible for a while. Instead I fantasize about working out a miraculous reconciliation between the bitter rival factions of my estranged friends. But that would involve healing more than twenty-five people.

Over the next two days I listen to my friends for hours, hearing many versions from different people. Some days I feel like Santa Claus as I hike to their houses with my backpack bursting with gifts my girls and Dale sent along for various friends. Early one morning I arrive at the rented house of a friend who once lived in a Spanish-style villa above the sea. She sits bewildered at a table with her three kids eating breakfast. Seeing them holding their life together is one of the most heartening sights I've ever seen. Everyone these days has been caught up in this kind of breakup with family or friends. I hand out the gifts of Canadian beaver caps and stuffed moose, chitchat a bit, then lean back and absorb an incendiary blast of pent-up rage and accusations about the unfairness of life, marriage, and separation.

Sharks make everything more difficult and unnerving in and out of the water. Because of recent shark encounters and the cyclone that's hauled back the beach and exposed a black reef of razor rocks, the Byron Swim Classic is cancelled a couple of days before the event. After flying from the other side of the world to swim in the meet, I'm pretty disappointed, but I'm also a great believer in having a Plan B. So I walk the mile-and-a-quarter beach from Byron to The Pass with forty-five members of my former Stingray Ocean Swim Club. Forty-two of them decide to stay at The Pass and do the shorter swim. Three of us walk over the ridge to Wategos Beach, and I let myself be talked into doing the long swim with only two other guys. There's no sun to perk me up, and glowering clouds hang above the angry sea. But I've fantasized about doing this swim for two and a half years. As we move toward the water, Bob looks out at the ocean and says, "The shaks ah bad, the werst evah, Rick."

Nevertheless, we dive through the shorebreak and begin swimming in the heaving sea along the rocky coastline, dodging surfers attempting the scary swells at The Pass. I stroke hard to avoid their razor fins, and when I lose sight of Bob and Chris, I have no option but to plunge on. Eventually I settle in and just swim, feeling the euphoria of a hero, arm over arm across the sharky reef and the open bay all the way to the tall Norfolk pines at Byron.

The next day when I head into Byron Bay again the storm has vanished, the sun shines, and it's suddenly summer. All the dreamy romantics, surfers, travellers, and freaks are there. At Linley's Bookstore I sadly discover the owner is on the verge of selling her shop so she can retire. But Linley hugs me emotionally and buys some copies of a travel anthology called *Literary Trips: Following in the Footsteps of Fame* that contains a piece I wrote about Bruce Chatwin in Australia. On the counter I spy a stack of *Waterlog: A Swimmer's Journey Through Britain* by Roger Deakin. Before I left Canada a friend put me onto the book but I didn't have time to read it. Linley suggests I hook up with Roger and do a reading together. At a Byron pub I end up in front of fifty people with Roger. I read about Chatwin's notion of restlessness and his idea that all those who have resisted civilization have a secret happiness. Roger reads from his maverick swimming book that critics have dubbed an aquatic *Songlines*. This lucky bit of synchronicity solidifies a great friendship between watermen.

Now that the cyclone has passed and is replaced by five-mile arching rainbows that bless the coast, we're back in business. The wind subsides and the swells clean up. They roll in from the other side of the world, break, and peel off perfectly. Paddling out with Kiko, Neil, and Dennis, I realize that getting on a surfboard after more than two years is almost a joke, even though I've been swimming competitively. Big swells unfold on the reef in layers of vertical walls that we have to spear under, over, or through. After charging the walls for twenty minutes, getting pounded, and swallowing far too much water, we have arms like noodles as we finally make it to the outside and straddle our boards. This is my epiphany. After thirty hours of flying and more than two years away from paradise, I'm sitting on my board in a state of utter bliss. Since I've already swum over the reef from Wategos to Byron in only a skimpy Speedo and a pair of goggles, I've shaken my fear of sharks and now luxuriate on an eight-foot Heart & Soul surfboard, surveying the rain-sodden, mossy green emerald of Lennox Point.

My best wave comes on a half-mile swell that stealthily lumbers in from a thousand miles, hits the reef, and sucks back. I paddle into it, take the steep vertical, and maintain my balance, gliding straight down the face to the bottom and letting the entire Pacific push me as I ride the glassy walls. When I paddle back out grinning like a maniac, Dennis is there. In his middle-aged, sweet American twang, he says, "Jeez, Rick, I wish I had a camera to take a shot of you doing your drop. It would have been the one you could take back with you."

But I don't need a photo. It's inside me.

Arriving almost unannounced like a ghost from the other side of the world, slipping into the envelope of time and space of this dream journey, was a good way to ease myself back into Oz. I'd be a liar to pretend my failure to mend the broken marriages of my friends wasn't a downer. In my heart Lennox Head and Byron Bay will always be more than Paradise Lost. And for all the rest there is always hope.

ACKNOWLEDGEMENTS

I owe thanks first to my wife, Dale, and my two daughters, Sky and Quinn, who enabled me to find myself as a husband and a father.

I must thank Mother Ocean, and on the other side of the great wave, my real mom, Eleanor, who always knew I'd be a writer. Thanks are also due to my dad, Tom, whose wicked humour I inherited and which has helped me survive life's marauding sharks.

Thank-yous go out to our many friends in the two small towns of Lennox Head and Byron Bay on the far north coast of New South Wales, Australia—a paradise I've tried to immortalize in this book. Experiences there, in and out of the water, perhaps saved my life and certainly reshaped it. Eternal gratitude must be given to my surf mates Bernie, Kiko, Neil, Mihkel, Dennis, Daffy, and Dick, as well as to Phil and the Byron Bay Stingray Ocean Swimmers and all the dolphins that protected and entertained me in the waves.

Special thanks to my intuitive friend and mentor, Tom Henighan, who helped with the title of this book.

Also deserving of my gratitude are the swimmers and coaches of the Nepean Masters Swim Club; all my creative-writing workshoppers past and present; and Larry McDonald and Bob Lovejoy, who made it possible for me to write and to teach what I love in the English department at Carleton University.

Thanks also to the editors of the *Ottawa Citizen* who published excerpts from this book when it was a work in progress: Lynn McAuley and Susan Allan for sending me back Down Under to write about Oz; Mike Gillespie for the creative editing and perfect chapter titles like "Into the Drink with Lord Byron"; and Charlie Gordon and Jenny Jackson for giving me books to review when the sharks were particularly unnerving.

My gratitude to Victoria Brooks, editor of the travel anthologies *Literary Trips: Following in the Footsteps of Fame*, who published two of this book's chapters as travel pieces.

Homage to the memory of my sister, Jan, my Norway Bay friend, Jamie, and my oldest surfing buddy, Ottawa filmmaker/surfer Frank Cole, who was murdered while crossing the Sahara Desert.

I must thank our generous friend Barb Beams who helped fly my family down to Australia. And, of course, I owe a lot to my tricolour collie, Ruby, who lay by my desk and gave such unconditional solace.

Thanks to all the nurturing women, life-affirming kids, and the lucky, sorry-assed, crazed househusbands of the world.

Finally I am incredibly grateful to my editor and publisher, Michael Carroll, who phoned me up from Vancouver for the manuscript and helped bring *House Inside the Waves* to life.

MORE NEW NONFICTION FROM BEACH HOLME PUBLISHING

LITTLE WHITE SQUAW

a white woman's story of abuse, addiction, and reconciliation

Eve Mills Nash and Kenneth J. Harvey

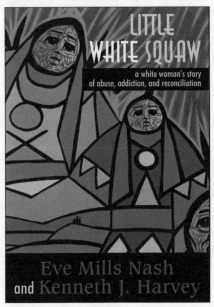

Little White Squaw is the story of a woman shaped by childhood sexual and emotional abuse, alcoholic family members, religious fanaticism, and the superstitions of a fortune-telling grandmother who "reads the cups."

Eve Mills Nash was born into a poor working-class family in rural Atlantic Canada. From an early age she felt a special kinship with Natives from a neighbouring community and set out to be accepted as one of "them." Her struggle to ease the pain of childhood traumas draws her to a fundamentalist religion where her desire to serve God is defaced by an angry preacher.

Turning her back on Christianity, Eve plunges into a world of alcohol, drugs, abusive men, and the occult. After several suicide attempts and three failed marriages, two to Natives, she finds hope through the recovery program and people of Alcoholics Anonymous.

Twelve-step meetings, Native elders, a blind healer, wilderness retreats, moose-hunting expeditions, and a return to the world of academia all become part of the healing process. But it is Eve's reconciliation with a loving Christian God that allows her to face the death of a granddaughter, two unexplained house fires, and her eldest daughter's addiction to cocaine, ultimately breaking the cycle of self-loathing.

MEMOIR • 440 PP • 0-88878-427-9 • $22.95

BEACH HOLME PUBLISHING WWW.BEACHHOLME.BC.CA